ALMIRA'S CURSE;

OR,

THE BLACK TOWER OF BRANSDORF.

A ROMANCE.

BY THE AUTHOR OF

"ELA, THE OUTCAST," "THE OLD HOUSE OF WEST STREET," "THE ROBBER'S FOUNDLING,"
"THE GIPSY BOY," &c.

> There's a spell upon my fate—
> My days, my nights are doomed to woe;
> And a curse lights on all who dwell around me.
> *Old Play.*

LONDON:

PUBLISHED BY EDWARD LLOYD, 12, SALISBURY-SQUARE, FLEET-STREET,
AND G. PURKESS, 60, DEAN STREET, SOHO.

ALMIRA'S
CURSE;
OR,
THE BLACK TOWER OF
BRANSDORF

CHAPTER I.

SAINT. SWITHIN'S NIGHT.—THE BLACK TOWER.—THE MYSTERY.—THE FOUNDLING.

GENERATIONS have been swept away by the remorseless scythe of Time ; ages have passed, and are forgotten, as though they had never been ; the bright sunshine and luxuriance of many hundred summers, and the howling storms of as many winters, have done their work in the vast theatre of nature, have passed away and gone ; new laws, new systems, new customs, new people,—verily, a new world, has succeeded since the strange, the exciting, and the awful events which form the subjects of the present tale occurred ; but Time, which has made such devastating havoc among all other things, has failed to destroy this startling record ; and often on a cheerless winter's night, when the fierce winds howl in the hollow gusts without ; when nipping frost binds every lake and rivulet, and the drifting snow buries every object in obscurity, the venerable gossips, with their wondering families, will assemble around the blazing fire, to recount the marvellous legend of THE BLACK TOWER OF BRANSDORF.

The attention of the curious traveller is directed to an old stone cross, which marks the spot on which it stood ; but not a vestige of the tower itself remains. Time has long since crumbled its once massive walls into dust, which has been dispersed on the winds of Heaven.

The Black Tower of Bransdorf surmounted a lofty eminence, dark and frowning, like a mighty prison, or the habitation of some evil genius, who, in its gloomy but spacious chambers, planned the misery and destruction of mankind. From time immemorial had it reared its hoary head, half buried in the misty clouds ; and all traces of the period of its creation were entirely lost. In fact, it might have been supposed to be coeval with the creation of the world ; so venerable was its whole appearance.

It was on the estate of Sir Aldobrand de Lancy, in the possession of whose family it had been for more than a century ; but, at the time of the commencement of this narrative, it had not been inhabited for many years ; and the inhabitants of the nighbourhood avoided it as much as possible, with a feeling of awe and dread ; for fearful were the stories related of it : and he would have been considered a fool-hardy individual—indeed a very madman, who ventured to approach it after nightfall.

Nor was this superstitious dread confined to the lowly rustic alone ; the wealthy ands noble did not care to venture within its precincts ; and Sir Aldobrand, whose castle wao situated not more than a quarter of a mile from it, had ordered its doors to be secured, s . that no one, who might even have had the courage to do so, should gain admittance to it Here, then, the Black Tower was left in its gloom to moulder into decay ; but it was only in places that the ravages of time had had the least effect upon it. The stubborn walls of the old hall, in particular, had remained unshaken, although many of the smaller rooms were gradually sinking to the earth.

A solemn silence reigned here, where once was heard the noisy laughter of conviviality. Echo had long slept in silence ; she awoke not to the tread of mortals ; her verberating tones no longer whispered round the arched roof.

The courts presented a prospect of chilling desolation ; huge fragments of the building, fallen from their towering heights, lay scattered on the broken pavement, which was nearly hidden by the thistle, hemlock, &c. On the tops of the battlements waved the long grass ; while the yellow flower and the ivy twined round their sides, except where, interrupted by a broken archway, which discovered interior apartments, overgrown with rank weeds, beneath which lurked the poisonous adder, and the long-lived toad.

At a short distance from the tower was a little hamlet, comprising only a few scattered straggling cottages, (it is now a flourishing market town); situated on the brow of a majestic hill, overlooking the country for miles around, was the noble castle of de Lancy. It was a splendid edifice, which still remains, although it is now fast falling into decay. Its grey turrets, aspiring towers, and encircling battlements, must impress the mind of the stranger with terrific images of feudal wars, when the lofty fabric re-echoed the arousing notes of the martial trumpet, or the harsh resounding cannon, threatening destruction to the castle and its inhabitants ; while the liberal hospitality that had reigned within, the native politeness of its noble owner, and the cheerful countenances of the domestics, insensibly led the mind to rejoice, and feel the blessings conferred by wealthy munificence towards those whom fortune had not not so brightly smiled upon.

It was St. Swithin's Eve, and a right down genuine St. Swithin's Eve it was. The day had been particularly close, sultry, and oppressive, and, as the afternoon advanced, the ponderous black clouds that overspread the horizon gave timely warning of the boisterous night that might be expected.

Night came on; all was dark and dreary; the old Black Tower was enveloped in tenfold gloom; the atmosphere, which in the day had been so oppressively hot, was now cold and turbid; not a glimmering star shot forth its feeble rays through the thick clouds which overed over the scene. The screech-owl, hid within her solitary dwelling, pierced with her horrid shrieks the ear of night. The winds moaned along the battlements, and the long windows rattled around the tower. The peasant sought his humble tenement for shelter, and his family gathered around him with terrified looks.

And now the wind abated, and as its last gusts died away in sullen echoes in the adjacent forest, the vivid lightening blazed athwart the sky, the thunder pealed forth its mighty artillery, and the bursting clouds sent forth their overwhelming showers upon the earth, swelling lakes and rivers, and threatening many of the humble dwellings of the peasantry with destruction.

Old Sampson Hewly, with his dame and the rest of the family, consisting of two stout young men, his sons, and the pretty Barbara, his only daughter, were seated round a blazing fire in the cottage parlour at the time the raging elements were enacting this tempestuous scene without, and the pale countenances of the females plainly showed the terrors their minds were undergoing. They huddled themselves together in the chimney corner, between Sampson and his sons, as close as they could get; and as the heavy rain beat furiously against the casement, and the lightening darted into the room, they frequently raised their hands and eyes towards Heaven, and breathed a silent prayer for protection.

Sampson was poor, but his honest old heart was the seat of every virtue. A stranger to vice, he had passed the morning of his days in useful labour, and he was now spending their evening in calmness, contemplation, and retirement, with no other employment but that of superintending the neighbouring peasantry who laboured on the domains of Sir Aldobrand de Lancy; whilst his sons followed an employment more suited to their youth and robust constitutions.

Most fiercely raged the tempest until it became perfectly terrific. There was scarcely an interval of a second between the roaring peals of thunder, and the lightening illumined the whole face of nature with its lurid and frightful glare.

Barbara and her mother trembled, but old Sampson and his sons remained perfectly calm; although it was only now and then they exchanged a word with one another.

"It is, indeed, a fearful night," said Sampson, in reply to some observations which one of the party had made; "the blessed saints protect all those poor creatures who are exposed to its terrors. We should be thankful we are so well provided for."

A loud clap of thunder interrupted him; and they all remained silent for several minutes after this.

"If the old walls of the Black Tower of Bransdorf stand such a tempest as this, father, I should say that they may bid defiance to time in future," at length remarked Hugo, the eldest son.

"Aye, boy," returned Sampson, "and many a rough tempest have they withstood already. Ah! it is just five years this very night since the Lad Editha de Lancy disappeared in so mysterious a manner from the Black Tower, in which her husband Sir Martin De Lancy had confined her from the third day after their marriage. Poor lady! it was an unfortunate union for her."

"Alas, it was," observed Dame Margery; "and she was so young, so beautiful, and so amiable too, and Sir Martin appeared to be fo fond of her, which he must have been, or he would never have risked the displeasure of his father by marrying her without his consent. Whatever could be his reasons for behaving to her with such cruelty so shortly afterwards?"

"Ah! dame," said her husband; "that is a mystery which I fear will never be unravelled; and it is not for such as us to possess any prying curiosity upon the subject."

"And is it not also strange that Sir Martin should have disappeared also so soon afterwards, and that nothing has been heard of him since?" said Barbara.

"It is," replied her father; "and I have often racked my brain in a vain attempt to penetrate the mystery. But I feared no good would come of their nuptials after the awful scene which took place at the altar. That scene, and the fearful curse uttered by the dying woman, can never be forgotten by those who witnessed it. It is believed that her troubled spirit now haunts the old Black Tower of Bransdorf, and——"

"The Holy Virgin protect us!" interrupted Margery, with the most terrified look; " don't—don't, Sampson."

"Nay, dame, what have we to fear? we never did her harm while she was living, and we need not therefore entertain any apprehensions of her spirit, if it be, indeed, permitted to revisit the earth."

" Hold, husband, for Heaven's sake. Ah! what was that?"

" What, dame, what?"

" Did you not hear a noise?"

"Aye," answered Sampson; " I must be deaf, indeed, I wot, if I did not. I heard the thunder."

" No, no," said Margery, glancing timidly towards the casement; "it—it was a very different sound to that, Sampson; it was between the pauses of the thunder, and it resembled—there! there!"

A wailing, dismal, hollow cry now, indeed, smote the ears of them all; and Hugo and his brother started to their feet, and looked around them; while Margery and her daughter clung together, and seemed afraid to move or speak.

All was still again; for even the thunder paused for a long interval.

" It was only the wind," said Sampson; " though to those who are superstitious there is enough, according to all legends, to excite their imagination; for it is said that, on the night of St. Swithin, all the evil spirits are abroad, howling in concert with the tempest, and exulting in the universal scene of horror and desolation."

" Oh, dreadful!" faltered out Barbara and her mother, at the same time devoutedly crossing themselves.

" Yes, as I was before saying," remarked Sampson, " there is a strange mystery connected with the fate of poor Lady Editha and Sir Martin. I am afraid there has been some foul play, which God grant may be brought to light. It is an undoubted fact, that some strange noises have been frequently heard to proceed from the Black Tower since it has been uninhabited, and I have often felt a strong desire to examine its deserted chambers."

" Gracious Heaven!" ejaculated Margery; "you cannot know what you are saying, Sampson."

" Indeed, but I do, though, dame; and one of these times, moreover, I am half inclined to believe that I shall be induced to follow the bent of my wishes."

" Do not think of such a thing, Sampson," said Margery; "for who knows the danger you may involve yourself in; besides, has not our present good master, Sir Aldobrand de Lancy, strictly prohibited any one from entering the tower?"

" True; and I would not readily disobey his injunctions; but still, I do not think that I shall be able to withstand my curiosity much longer; besides, Sir Aldobrand need never be any the wiser. I have frequently had most remarkable dreams respecting the Black Tower; and it was only last night that the form of poor Lady Editha appeared to me in my sleep, all clad in white, and in a solemn voice, which I think I hear now, implored me to visit that gloomy building. I cannot, for the life of me, help thinking that there is some fearful mystery attached to the Black Tower of Bransdorf, which I am destined to be the humble instrument of unravelling."

" Nay, Sampson," remarked his wife; "this is not like your usual good sense. You must surely be dreaming still."

" Indeed, dame, I am not," returned Sampson, " but see; thank God, for the sake of those who are shelterless, the storm is abating."

The storm, indeed, seemed to have pretty well exhausted its fury; the rain came but sluggishly down; the lightning ceased to flash; and the thunder rolled off in the distance, until it gradually died away. Sampson walked to the casement, and looked out upon the dreary scene beyond.

The cottage was such a short distance from the tower that they had a complete view of it; but now the darkness was so intense, that it was impossible to distinguish any object, however prominent.

Suddenly, however, an exclamation of surprise from Sampson attracted the attention of the others, and they advanced hastily towards him, to ascertain what had excited him in such a manner.

"See!" he ejaculated, pointing in the direction of the lofty eminence, on whose summit the Black Tower stood. "Do you not behold? What inexplicable and extraordinary mystery is this?"

The whole party stared with equal amazement; for they beheld a broad glare of light streaming from one of the lofty casements of the tower, and could almost imagine that they saw shadowy forms passing to and fro in the apartment from which the light proceeded. But a minute or two, however, and the light was gone, and all was wrapt in the same profound and intense gloom as before.

"What are we to judge from this?" said Sampson.

"That some persons have entered the tower, at any rate," said Hugo; "perhaps to shelter themselves from the storm."

"Or more likely it is those troubled spirits of which you have been speaking, Sampson," said the superstitious old woman, with a look of alarm. "Grace defend us! I wish the frightful old tower was razed to the ground, or that we did not reside so close to it.".

"I am lost in wonder and perplexity," said Sampson; "but I am more resolved than ever to endeavour to fathom this mystery."

"Oh, for goodness sake, do not think of such a thing!" ejaculated Margery. "The bare idea makes my very blood run cold."

They resumed their seats by the fire-side, and a dead silence of several minutes ensued; but suddenly it was broken by an appalling shriek that vibrated on the air, that seemed impossible to have proceeded from any human being. They all started to their feet, and gazed at each other with looks of terror and amazement; and Barbara and her mother were so frightened, that they immediately sunk on their knees, and buried their faces in each other's bosom, as if expecting that their eyes would encounter something awful.

"There could be no mistake in that, at any rate," remarked Hugo.

"No," said Arnold, his brother; "never before did I hear so awful a cry."

"It must have proceeded from some poor creature in distress," observed Sampson. "Come, come, we must not allow any foolish fears to overcome our sense of duty and of humanity, when an unhappy fellow being may stand in need of our aid."

"For the love of Heaven, what would you do, Sampson?" in trembling accents, demanded his wife.

"Do!" repeated the former; "what every honest and sincere Christian ought—endeavour to render assistance to those who may need it. Put a light in the lantern, and follow me, Hugo; Arnold will remain here to quiet the foolish fears of his mother and sister."

"Oh, for goodness sake, do not be rash, dear Sampson. Consider the danger in which you may place yourself; and this is St. Swithin's night, too!"

"Tush!" ejaculated her husband, impatiently; "such foolish scruples would ill become me. Hark! there it is again."

Another dismal shriek, but not so loud as the first, and which seemed to proceed from some more distant spot, was now heard while Sampson spoke, and the teeth of old Margery and her daughter chattered in their heads.

"There is not a moment to be lost," said Sampson; "even now the poor unfortunate may be beyond human succour. Come, Hugo; we are armed, and have nothing to fear—I would even face a whole legion of devils in the cause of humanity. Arouse yourself dame, and fear not; we shall soon return."

"Alas, alas! I fear not." returned Margery; "and, oh! what would become of us, should anything happen to you?"

Sampson made no reply to this, and the light having been placed in the lantern, they, issued forth from the cottage; Barbara and her mother watching them with anxious eyes until the glimmering light was entirely hidden from the sight in the obscurity of the darkness.

Sampson and his son pursued their way with cautious steps, in the direction from whence they imagined the sounds had issued, and frequently holding the lantern above their heads to accelerate their view, and in order to ascertain whether they could distinguish any object; but nothing met their gaze, and they began to fear that their praise-worthy efforts would not be crowned with any success.

The storm had now entirely ceased, and the atmosphere was less cloudy than before;

but the earth was wet and swampy, and Sampson and Hugo had frequently the greatest difficulty in proceeding.

As it appeared that there was no chance of their being able to discover any human being who might need their aid, they were half inclined to give up the task in despair, and to return home; when scarcely had that idea entered their minds, when once more a piercing shriek vibrated their ears, and they were now certain that it came from the direction of the old tower. They raised their eyes immediately towards that ancient building, and again beheld a broad light gleaming in one of the casements, and, at the same time, the dark shadows of what appeared to be two human forms flit hastily by.

They paused for a second or two, and were uncertain what do.

"This is a most extraordinary mystery," said Sampson, "and I am resolved to endeavour to fathom it. We will make our way to the tower, Huge."

"But may there not be danger?" Suggested Hugo. "Suppose that robbers should have taken up their abode in the tower, our lives would probably have to pay the forfeit of our temerity. I think, father, that you had better abandon that idea."

"No, no; I have made up my mind, and come what may, I will this night, if possible, penetrate the secret of the Black Tower. A powerful impulse urges me on, which I cannot resist; so, come, boy, let us proceed. We will watch beneath the walls of the tower to see whether any person emerges from it before we venture to enter it. See, the light has again disappeared."

They continued to advance until they had arrived at the eminence on which the tower stood; and with slow and cautious steps, shading the lantern, began to ascend it. The wind had now again risen, and whistled in fitful gusts around, murmuring in solemn echoes through the different apertures of the ancient and gloomy fabric.

Having arrived beneath the walls of the tower, they walked around it, and gazed up at the casements; but all was involved in impenetrable darkness, and not a sound, save the murmuring of the wind, disturbed the solemn silence which universally prevailed.

They perceived that one of the doors was blown from its hinges, so that there was nothing to obstruct their entrance; but, before they did so, they took the precaution to listen and to peep into the court on which the door opened; but not the least sound disturbed the quiet around and within the building, and nothing but their own shadow on the broken pavement met their gaze. Still Hugo would have persuaded his father not to venture any farther, as he knew not the danger with which it might be fraught; but the old man's curiosity was excited to an unconquerable degree, and he therefore refused to listen to his son's advice.

"We have proceeded thus far," he remarked, "and we should be cowards now to retreat. Keep close to me, Hugo, and fear not; for I feel certain we have no danger to apprehend."

Having entered the desolate court, they made another circuit of the building, and then entered by a broken archway, and shortly found themselves treading the ancient hall.

Profound was the silence that reigned around, interrupted only at intervals by the moaning of the wind, or the dreadful cry of the screech owl. The bat fluttered past them in the dim light emitted by the lantern, which only served to render the utter cheerlessness of the place more visible. The walls were dripping with noisome moisture; and, in several places, the once magnificent tapestry that had adorned them, hung in mildewed tatters, rotted by the damp, or devoured by the rats, who had taken up their abode in that once noble edifice. It seemed quite clear that this part of the building had not for some time known the tread of human foot before, and Sampson and his son became more and more involved in wonder and bewilderment at the light they had witnessed but a few minutes before in the casement, and the shadows which they were certain they had seen hurry past.

"That could be no delusion," said Hugo, in a whisper; "and I really cannot help thinking that we are running into very great danger by venturing to explore the old tower."

"Psha, Hugo!" replied the old man, testily; "I never thought you a coward before; "but, if you really apprehend danger, you can return home, and keep your mother and sister company till I come back; for my own part, I have ventured so far, and my curiosity is so much excited, that I am determined to proceed."

"Indeed, father," said the young man, "I am not such a coward as you seem to take me for; but prudence and caution, in such matters as these, are always necessary. As you are resolved to pursue your inquiry, of course I shall not think of leaving you to do so alone; however, I cannot see what good can result from it.''

"The shriek we heard, I am certain came from the tower," remarked Sampson; " it proceeded from a female, some wretched being, who, perhaps, has sought a shelter here from the storm, and it may not yet be too late to save her. Come, come; let us proceed.''

At that moment they heard a loud rumbling noise immediately beneath the spot on which they where standing, and which gradually died away in an indistinct murmur. Hugo looked at his father with some expression of amazement and hesitation, as he said, in a subdued tone of voice—

"That is a strange noise, and would seem to indicate that there are some persons moving in the subterranean apartments underneath this old hall. Recollect, father, what may be the consequences of our intrusion, and let us postpone our examination to some future occasion. We had better eontult Sir Aldobrand upon the subject, who, no doubt, will take immediate steps to solve the mystery."

"No, no," returned the old man; " my curiosity will not brook of any delay. The dream I had last night is strongly impressed upon my memory, and I cannot help thinking that I am destined to be the discoverer of some important secret."

"But the noise, father, the noise?"

"Oh, that was nothing more, I dare say, than the falling of the old ruins below. This delay is foolish; the sooner we get the business done, the sooner we shall return home ; and I dare be bound that your mother and poor Barbara will frighten themselves almost to death until we get back.''

Hugo saw it was useless to attempt to argue with, or to persuade his father, so he withheld his observations for the present, although it was not without many misgivings that he did so.

They moved towards the end of the hall, but they were obliged to do so with the utmost caution to prevent their feet from coming in contact with the numerous fragments of the ruins which were strewn over the pavement.

They passed beneath a low arched doorway, and began to ascend a spiral staircase, which they imagined would lead to that part of the tower from which they had seen the light.

All was perfectly silent; nothing was to be heard but the low, hollow sound of their own footfalls, and they were not long in arriving at the top of the staircase, and then found themselves in a spacious corridor, with apartments opening on each side, and which had suffered little or nothing from decay.

Sampson was about to proceed to the door opposite to him, which was partially open, when his attention was arrested by an exclamation of astonishment and horror from Hugo (who carried the lantern), and, turning round, he beheld him gazing, pale and trembling at something on the floor. He advanced towards him.

"What is the matter now, Hugo?" he demanded; " and what is it you are gazing at so earnestly, and with such terrified looks?"

"Look, look; do you not see?" answered Hugo, in a faultering voice, and pointing towards the floor; "blood, blood! fresh blood!"

Sampson now took the lantern from the hand of his son, and stooping down, he examined the spot which he had pointed out more minutely. It was true; marks of blood stained the floor, in a direct line from the spot on which they were standing to the opposite door.

"Some bloody and inhuman deed has been perpetrated here, and that this very night," said Hugo. " Let us instantly away, or our lives may most assured have to pay the forfeit of our daring."

"This discovery," returned Sampfon, " makes me more determined than ever. Murder has been committed, and that acounts for the dreadful shrieks we heard. We must endeavour to find the body of the unfortunate victim, and may thus be the means of bringing the foul assassin or assassins to justice. Come, come; Providence knows the integrity of our intentions, and will protect us from every danger. All is still, and it appears evident to me that the old tower is now entirely deserted, except by ourselves."

They moved slowly on, still tracing the blood as they proceeded, and throwing the door wide back upon its hinges, looked into the room. It was spacious and lofty, and there were still some remains of costly furniture in it, which was in a complete state of preervation.

Sampson and his son looked upon the floor; it was stained with blood in several places, as if a violent struggle had there ensued; and on one spot was the complete impression of a human hand. There was also a small trinket lying close by, which had evidently belonged to a female. Old Sampson and his son shuddered.

"It was probably here," said the farmer, "that the dreadful deed was committed. And see, Hugo, this must, from its position in the tower, have been the very apartment in the casement of which we saw a light."

"No doubt of it," replied Hugo; "but it is surely now useless to roceed, for it does not appear that we shall make any further discovery."

"We know not that," returned Sampson; "the body of the ill-fated murdered woman is probably lying in some part of the building, and it is necessary that we should try to find it, so that we may have an opportunity of discovering who she is. We have proceeded thus far without interruption, and I therefore feel satisfied that we have nothing to apprehend."

They now examined the suite of rooms beyond, but found no further traces of blood, and their further search in that part of the tower was abruptly terminated, for all the other doors were fast secured, and did not appear to have been disturbed since the tower had been abandoned. Sampson could not help expressing his disappointment, for the murder still remained involved in the same state of impenetrable mystery; and so it seemed likely to be.

They now returned to the apartment they had just quitted, and they were about to descend the staircase, in order to endeavour to explore the other part of the tower when their attention was arrested by a low, pitiful, wailing sound, which seemed to proceed from some part of the room. They both started, and turned back.

"Did you not hear that?" asked Hugo.

"I did," replied his father. "It was certainly the cry of a human being."

"It was; and proceeded from this room. To me it seemed like the cry of a child."

"There, again!"

The low cry of an infant was now once more distinctly heard, and they directed their eyes to the opposite end of the room, from whence it seemed to issue.

There was a low couch on that side of the apartment, and Sampson and his son were astonished to behold something moving beneath the covering. They both rushed towards it, and tearing the covering away, to the unutterable amazement beheld beneath it, the innocent form of a lovely female child, apparently not more than two years old; and who, frightened by the glaring of the light in the lantern, and the strange faces which gazed upon her, began to cry piteously.

"Sweet innocent!" ejaculated Sampson, as he took the weeping child in his arms, and endeavoured by caresses to quiet it; "art thou the offspring of the unfortunate being who has this night fallen beneath the knife of the inhuman assassin? Alas! alas! early, indeed, have thy sorrows began. But how was it that the wretch spared thine innocent life?"

The clothes of the child were of the richest quality, but were in many places stained with blood; probably the blood of its unfortunate parent. Sampson and his son shuddered, as this idea flashed upon their brains; and looked at the beauteous face of the infant (who had now become calm, and was innocently playing with the silvery hair of the old cottager) with the deepest compassion.

"Providence be thanked for sending me here to preserve thee, my poor child," said Sampson, fervently; "oh, how horrible would have been thy fate, hadst thou been left to perish! Hugo, did I not tell thee that I was certain I was destined to make some important discovery? This poor infant will I protect, until its relations, if it have any surviving, be discovered; and the guilty perpetrators of this night's bloody work shall be brought to justice."

"But what can have become of the body of the wretched being whom we suppose has been murdered?" asked Hugo.

"It is most likely concealed somewhere about the tower," replied Sampson; "but we have not the means of examining it further. Sir Aldobrand will be sure to cause a strict search to be made when he is informed of these remarkable particulars. Come, boy; we may be very well satisfied with this our one night's adventure, and had better now return home. Oh, dear! how astonished will your mother and sister be when they behold our little foundling."

The kind-hearted Sampson kissed the lips of the infant, and wrapped it carefully in his cloak, to shield it from the night air. He desired Hugo to lead the way with the lantern and they emerged from the tower in the same manner in which they had entered it.

A lovely calm had now succeeded the storm that had raged in the early part of the evening; the wind had subsided into a gentle and refreshing breeze; and the chaste moon. bursting from behind the ponderous clouds which had hitherto obscured her silvery face, imparted a brilliant hue of glory to the whole face of nature.

The infant had sunk to sleep, and Sampson, nestling it still closer to his bosom, with his son quickened his pace to arrive at home, where he was certain that old Margery and her daughter would be so anxiously and impatiently waiting to behold them again.

CHAPTER II.

THE BROTHERS.—THE BRIDAL.—ALMIRA'S CURSE.—THE DEATH AT THE ALTAR.

WE must now trace our narrative back several years prior to the events which have been recorded in the foregoing chapter. Sir Martin and Sir Aldobrand de Lancy were, as has been intimated, brothers; the former two years the senior. They had both received the honour of knighthood from their sovereign for their heroic deeds in arms, in which they had emulated their gallant father, Sir Hildebrand de Lancy, who had now retired, stricken with years and infirmities, from the care of acting life, and awaited his exit to a better world with the calm resignation and confidence of a Christian. Sir Aldobrand, although his brother's junior, had been married for a period of two years to an amiable lady, who died in giving birth to a son; and he took her loss so seriously to heart, that he quitted his native land, in the hope that in change of scene he should find some consolation to his deeply lacerated bosom.

In the meantime, Sir Martin became enamoured of the charms of the beauteous Editha, the only daughter of Sir Reginald de Balfour, by whom the passion of the lovers was sanctioned, and it only wanted the consent of Sir Hildebrand to complete their happiness.

A family feud had, however, formerly existed between Sir Hildebrand and the father of Editha, which the former could not forget; and he therefore not only peremptorily refused to give his consent to the nuptials, but, enraged at his son's determination to persist in making Editha his bride, he retired to one of his mansions in a distant part of the country, and left Sir Martin in quiet possession of De Lancy Castle.

It is necessary to describe the characters of the brothers more minutely, so that the circumstances of their future conduct may be better explained.

From their earliest days of childhood, Sir Martin and Sir Aldobrand had formed the strongest attachment for each other. This attachment ripened with their growing years. Their sports, their pleasures, and their afflictions, were the same; even the disposition of each, though originally different, received a tincture of similitude from the other.

The leading feature of Sir Martin's character was a fierceness that brooked neither control nor reproof. He was brave, but his valour degenerated into ferocity, and knew none of that gentle mixture which distinguishes the human from the brutal nature. Generous to his friends, but implacable to those who offended him where his pride or his passions were concerned, he would have risked the most imminent danger to oblige the former, or to avenge himself of the latter.

Nature had endowed him with a form marked with the prevailing propensities of his soul. His stature exceeded the ordinary height of men, and was proportioned with exactness. His countenance, though handsome, had a stern and haughty appearance, even in his mildest moments. The first view of his person generally excited admiration; but at the second, the beholder felt an involuntary dread, mingled with a sensation very near allied to disgust.

Such was Sir Martin; and when we describe his brother, it will afford matter of surprise that spirits so widely different should, even under the influence of amity, and the natural bonds of brotherly affection, move in unison.

The face of Sir Aldobrand was a lively and legible portrait of the soul which gave it intelligence. The beauty and harmony of his features could only be exceeded by that air of mingled ingenuousness and benevolence which constantly adorned them. His person was noble, graceful, and commanding. Nature to him had been unsparing of her gifts, nor did his deportment abuse them. The graces of his form were but types of his intellectual endowments. Mild as the sunniest breeze that fans the flowers—yielding to every impression of sensibility. By true valour rendered capable of enacting deeds which might emulate the darings of those heroes to whom his countrymen, in those days, paid a religious veneration.

When Sir Aldobrand heard of the passion of his brother for the lovely Editha, and the refusal of Sir Hildebrand to sanction their union, he immediately returned home, and, seeking an interview with his father, he expatiated warmly on the numerous charms and virtues of Editha, and endeavoured to persuade him to relent; but in vain, he remained inexorable, and declared that, if Sir Martin persisted in making the damsel his bride, he would never more acknowledge him for his son.

Sir Aldobrand was deeply afflicted on hearing this, and set out for De Lancy Castle, to make his brother acquainted with the unsuccessful termination of his mission.

Sir Martin was greatly enraged at his father's inflexibility, and swore that no consideration whatever, not even the bitterest hatred of Sir Hildebrand, should induce him to abandon his intentions; and that determination was greatly urged on by the death of Sir Reginald de Balfour, which left Editha without a protector. Several months were allowed to elapse for Editha to pay the proper respect to her father's memory, and then Sir Martin again renewed his addresses, and energetically urged her to consent to become his bride without any more delay.

Editha for some time hesitated, knowing the invincible dislike which the father of her lover had to the union, and fearful that it might be productive of future misery to him; but the sincerity and ardour of the passion she entertained for him, at length overcame all her delicate scruples, and she gave her consent, and the day was fixed for the marriage rites to be solemnized.

In the mean time, there were strange reports respecting the Black Tower of Bransdorf, which daily gained strength, and created quite a sensation in the neighbourhood. Frightful noises, it was said, had been lately heard to proceed from its chambers after dark, and strange figures had been seen in its casements, though it had been left uninhabited for some years.

The peasants shrugged their shoulders when they spoke of it; and not one of them could at last be persuaded to approach it after nightfall.

These reports greatly annoyed Sir Martin, and he did all he could to quiet them and to prove their fallaciousness; but with little or no effect. He and his brother examined the whole of the ancient building minutely, but without discovering the least traces of any person having been there lately, which they knew was utterly impossible, as every entrance was properly secured, and Sir Martin held the keys in his own possession. They also sat up together in the tower one night, to keep watch; and, although they neither saw nor heard anything to disturb them, they could not convince the foolish and superstitious persons with whom the reports had originated; and some of them even went so far as to say that Providence frowned upon the union of Sir Martin and Editha, and that endless misery would be the consequence to both parties if they persisted in carrying it into effect.

Sir Hiidebrand had shut himself up in his mansion, and refused to see any one, even Sir Aldobrand; and the latter remained at De Lancy Castle, resolved to be present at the union of his brother. The night before the morning appointed for the ceremony was a fearful one; there had not been such a storm witnessed in that part of the country for many years; and its terrors appalled even the stoutest heart.

It was frightful to hear the howling wind as it swept, in a perfect hurricane, over the earth; to listen to the almost incessant roaring of the thunder, which seemed to shake the earth to its centre, and to watch the lightning, as it lit up the heavens in one broad sheet of fire. Awfully was the old Black Tower of Brandsdorf reflected in its lurid glare; and those who gazed upon its glittering lofty casements might very well have imagined all kinds of fantastic and hideous shapes dancing before them. The screech-owl, alarmed by the horrors that prevailed around, sent forth her most frightful shrieks, which might, at intervals, be heard even above the furious voice of the storm.

A portion of one wing of De Lancy Castle was struck by the lightning, and it was only by a miracle that Sir Martin and his brother escaped an untimely death. All the extensive and magnificeant preparations that had been made for the celebration of the marriage, in the spacious grounds of the castle, were destroyed; and that which but a few hours before had been almost unparalleled in grandeur, now presented nothing but a scene of the wildest desolation.

Again the simple rustics, as they sat within their humble dwellings, and with quailing hearts watched the ravages of the tempest, shrugged their shoulders, and murmured to each other that it was a bad omen—a very bad omen; and then they imagined all sorts of fearful calamities which were about to happen, but more especially to Sir Martin de Lancy and his intended bride.

The storm subsided during the night, but left behind the sad evidences of the fearful

destruction it had caused.   The morning dawned, but it was heavy, dark, and gloomy
and there was a frigidity in the air, which made it come cheerless to the heart.

Most of the numerous and noble guests who had been invited to grace the marriage
ceremony with their presence had arrived at the castle several days before : but now they
seemed dull and spiritless, and it might have been imagined that they were invited to a
funeral, instead of being the attendants on the nuptials of rank and beauty.

Sir Martin himself, notwithstanding all his efforts to the contrary, felt an unaccountable
and unconquerable depression at his heart; and when the time arrived that he should hasten
to the residence of Editha, to escort her from it to the altar, a feeling of hesitation and
melancholy forboding crept over him, which he found it impossible to conquer.

The procession moved towards the residence of Editha; but although there were crowds
of persons assembled, no joyful shouts rent the air ; and even the appearance of the lovely
bride herself could not arouse them from their apathy, or dispel the universal gloom
which had taken possession of their senses. And Editha looked pale and ill, and her
hand trembled as she gave it to Sir Martin; but no particular notice was taken of this,
as such emotions were only natural on such an important occasion, upon which the happiness or misery of her future life depended.

The trying moment has arrived : they stand before the altar, and the ceremony has
commenced.   But as it proceeds, black clouds obscure the horizon; the sacred building
is almost enveloped in darkness ; and before the priest can give utterance to the final
words, terrific peals of thunder shake the lofty dome, and his voice is stifled in the roaring of the storm.

Editha clung to her husband, trembling with terror, and almost fainted. Sir Martin
felt a shuddering sensation, and looked timidly around the building, as though he expected that every moment something was about to happen.

A dreadful clap of thunder now shook the heavens ; the lightning played frightfully in
at the different gothic casements of the holy building ; and the persons present stared at
each other with ghastly looks, while not a word was spoken, and all seemed rivetted to
the spot on which they were standing, as if some fearful spell was upon them.

The thunder ceases; not a murmur, nor a sound is heard ; a dead calm seems to have
stagnated the very course and system of nature. The silence of the grave could only be
compared to that awful pause—awful, far more awful, than the storm in its most hideous
violence.

While thus all stood appalled, and staring, with vacant looks, at one another, the silence
was broken by a loud and delirious exclamation from the farther end of the chapel—an
exclamation, that it seemed scarcely possible could proceed from anything human, and
which struck with a nameless and irresistible feeling of horror all who heard it.

Sir Martin clasped the shivering form of the new-made bride to his bosom, and turned
his appalled gaze in the direction from whence the cry proceeded, in the expectation of
something terrible.

The other persons present seemed fully to participate in his agonised feelings; nor
were they long kept in suspense.

A door at the farther end of the chapel, which had hitherto been concealed by a dark
curtain, was thrown back on its hinges, and from the aperture emerged, into the centre
of the aisle, what appeared from its dress to be a female form, tall and majestic, but its
features were concealed from view by a long veil that descended to her feet.

Every one fixed their eyes with astonishment upon this unexpected appearance ; but
could not speak, or offer to move from the spot to which they were transfixed, like so
many statues. Sir Martin felt a shuddering sensation come over him. Editha became
more pale ; and even the priest seemed to be filled with emotions of mingled surprise
and consternation.

With a dignified and measured step, the strange intruder advanced along the aisle,
until she stood in the midst of the astonished group, and but a few paces from Sir Martin
and the Lady Editha.   In vain they tried to penetrate the veil that hid her features, and
more powerful did their agony and suspense become. And now again the thunder
rolled along the vaulted roof of Heaven.

The stranger raised her hand as the last peal died away in the distance, and, in a
voice which thrilled through the very veins of all who heard it, and petrified the soul of
Sir Martin, she thus spoke—

" Hark ! how the hoarse voice of offended Heaven joins that of the injured, in showering down curses on the head of the guilty.   Dost thou not hear it, Sir Martin de Lancy, and tremble?—It is the knell of judgment that sounds thy future destiny.   Listen to it, destroyer of the innocent, and tremble !''

"Woman !" ejaculated Sir Martin, with quivering lips; "who art thou that thus intrudest thyself at this solemn hour ?—and what is thy purpose?''

"To invoke the vengeance of Almighty God against thee, villain—to breathe upon thine head a damning curse !" replied the woman, in louder and fiercer tones, and advancing nearer to Sir Martin as she spoke.   Editha shrunk back, and could not repress a scream of terror; while the other spectators stood silently by, completely thunderstruck with amazement.

"The deed is done, Sir Martin !" continued the woman, in the same solemn and impressive accents—"thou art married—thou hast violated all those vows solemnly pledged to another, who gave up all her love, her innocence, her very soul to thee. 'Tis done; 'tis done; and there but awaits the dying curse of the poor deceived one to complete the tragedy—and it shall speak to thee in a voice that shall appal even thy remorseless soul !''

Large drops of perspiration stood upon the forehead of Sir Martin, and his whole frame shook with agony.

"No more of this !" he cried, in a hoarse voice; "this suspense is insupportable, Woman, though the sight blast me, reveal thyself, I command thee, and let me know the worst.''

"Ah, miscreant !" shouted the mysterious stranger, "is thine heart so insensible to shame that thou canst brave the trial ?   Take, then, thy wish.   Behold !''

Immediately she withdrew her veil, and there stood revealed to the gaze of the bewildered spectators the lovely but careworn countenance of a female, apparently not more than twenty years of age, who fixed her large, black, and supernaturally brilliant eyes, with an overpowering intensity of expression, full upon Sir Martin, while her form seemed to dilate itself, and inspired every beholder with awe.

But what strange and fearful emotions are those which agitate Sir Martin, and freeze the very blood within his veins ?   Why do his lips quiver, and his limbs totter beneath the weight of his body ?   Why that ashy hue that overspreads his features, and renders his whole aspect perfectly ghastly and unearthly ?   Had he been struck by the fierce lightning which lately blazed into the sacred pile, he could not have exhibited a greater picture of horror and overwhelming astonishment.   He tried to speak; but for a few moments his tongue cleaves to the roof of his mouth, and refuses to perform its office.

It was a moment of the most painful excitement; the numerous persons present gazed with amazement and expectation at the mysterious woman, and watched the powerful anxiety and agony of mind Sir Martin was enduring.   He evidently quailed beneath the keen, the brilliant, and expressive eye of the damsel, who marked him with a proud look of the bitterest reproach and contempt; and as she stood in the glare of the lightning, that now darted its fires in at the gothic windows of the chapel, she looked like some supernatural being, who had been permitted to revisit the earth to effect some wise purpose, and to lay bare the evil doings of the guilty.

It was clear that the feelings which predominated in the bosom of Sir Martin, were those of mingled astonishment, incredulity, and dread; and Sir Aldobrand and the witnesses of the scene awaited in the greatest suspense the result of this extraordinary adventure.

As for Lady Editha, she stared aghast at the singular visitor, and tremblingly clung to her husband, every moment expecting, but dreading, some terrible disclosure.

Little, however, was any one prepared for the fearful scene that followed.   Again Sir Martin tried to address the unknown; but still his voice faltered, and the words he would have uttered died away in unintelligible mutterings in his throat.

The strange being kept her eyes fixed upon his countenace, and it was evident, from the sardonic smile which played around, and so ill became her beauteous lips, where innocence and kindness alone should have sported, that she exulted in the misery and confusion her sudden and unexpected appearance had excited in the mind of Sir Martin de Lancy.

Once more the thunder reverberated through the sacred building, and the stranger advanced with a proud and majestic step a few paces nearer to Sir Martin, and with one hand raised towards the stormy heavens, in the same solemn and impressive accents as before, she ejaculated—

"Hark! again the voice of the Almighty in thunder utters his wrath against the guilty Dost thou not mark it, Sir Martin de Lancy, and tremble? Yes, yes; I see thou dost; and even in this awful hour, my soul feels a triumph it never expected to achieve. Oh, it is a fitting season for the fearful crisis that is approaching! It is a proper requiem over the sorrows of the deceived and broken-hearted! Thou seest me, Sir Martin, and thy blanched cheek, thy quivering lips, thy palsied frame, are unquestionable evidences that thou knowest and fearest me. Say, villain, canst thou, darest thou deny this?"

"Powers inscrutable!" exclaimed Sir Martin, and his whole frame was terribly convulsed with the power of his agony. "What fiends of darkness are at work to distract my brain? Can the charnel house give up its ghastly inmates? Away! away! horrible delusion; I must not, cannot gaze upon thee, and call thee Almira!"

"But thou shalt, thou must, deceiver!" cried the mysterious female, and her voice thrilled through the veins of all who heard her, and the expression of her countenance became more awful and unearthly than ever. "The time is come; the day of reckoning and denunciation is arrived; and here, in the presence of thy bridal guests, do I proclaim thee, monster, miscreant!—Yes, it is the deeply-injured, the broken-hearted Almira, once the pure, the innocent, the pride, the comfort of her doating parents, who stands before thee. Oh, if thou hadst not a heart of steel, the sight of this poor ruin of what was once lovely—this careworn face, thine honied tongue did once delight to flatter, would freeze thy blood to ice. Mark me, wretch, it is Almira, who, in her dying moments, with her latest breath, comes to invoke her most horrible curses on thy devoted head, and the voice of Heaven will ratify the maledictions to which her lips give utterance. 'Tis Almira de Montreville—she, who sacrificed parents, home, everything—even her very soul, for thy sake, who speaks to thee. I—I, who steeped my hands in the blood of the sweetest innocence to save thee from shame; I, whom thou thought'st had long since fallen, perished by thy commands, to conceal thine iniquity. Here I stand, before thee and thy new-made bride, to blast thee with my presence, and to give utterance to the curses which most assuredly will overtake thee!"

As the unhappy being gave utterance to these words, her countenance and whole demeanour became truly appalling; and Lady Editha, unable to endure more, uttered a frantic shriek, and sunk inanimate upon the cold pavement of the chapel; Sir Martin being too much overpowered by his own emotions to be able to support her."

Almira gazed at her for a minute or two with a look of hatred and triumph, and a hollow laugh escaped her bosom.

"Poor, wretched lady!" she ejaculated, in tones half pitiful and exulting; "it is but a prelude to the future miseries, the oppressions, and the cruelties she will have to endure. Oh, how her fair prospects shall be blighted; how her heart shall be wrung! What years of bitter anguish, what days of hopelessness and unmitigated horror, will it be her fearful lot to experience! Triumph, Sir Martin de Lancy; for behold in thy new-made bride another doomed victim to thy detestable vices."

"Heaven and earth! must I endure this?" cried the distracted Sir Martin, his eyes blood-shot, and his mouth foaming with the power of the insupportable emotions and the terrible fever which raged with all the violence of the troubled elements in his heaving bosom. "Drag this infuriated maniac, this fiend in female form, from my sight! D'ye hear?—Will none of you obey when I command?"

Some of the astonished and appalled spectators of this singular scene, scarcely knowing what they did, made a slight movement towards her; but she no sooner observed their intention, than she erected her form with more commanding dignity than before; an expression lighted up her dark eyes which inspired every beholder with a feeling of the most uncontrollable awe; and, taking a poniard from her bosom, she held it aloft in the air, with a menacing attitude, while, in a voice that commanded instant obedience, she exclaimed—

"Miscreant, wouldst thou dare to offer to lay violent hands on her thou hast already so deeply injured? Wouldst thou further aggravate that vengeance thou hast already provoked? Oh, thou art most brave, Sir Martin de Lancy. But stand off, all of ye! Venture not to approach me nearer, or, by high Heaven, this woman's hand shall deal destruction on the first who dares to molest her. Hark! once more the thunder! The moment is coming—death is already rankling in my veins—thou wilt behold the corpse of thy wretched, deluded victim, Sir Martin de Lancy, before thou quittest thy brid'al altar! Oh, it will be a gladsome sight to thee; one that shall never more quit thy memory, sleeping or waking. The death eyes, the blackened countenance, the convulsed form of the unfortunate Almira de Montreville, who, but for thee, might still have been good, and innocent, and happy, shall ever more be present to thine imagination; rising before thine appalled eyes in the hour of festivity; never absent from thy sight in thine hours of health, of sickness, and of pain. And see, and see! the blood-stained phantom of my murdered infant rides upon the blast, pointing at thee, monster, and demanding vengeance! Dost thou not see it?—Dost thou not mark the streaming blood that issues from its side? It is the blood of innocence that I shed to preserve thee from shame and the voice of calumny!—shall the spirit of that murdered innocent appeal in vain?—No, it shall not. Hear me, guilty Sir Martin, and rest assured that as certain as the just retribution of offended Heaven never fails to overtake those who have offended against its laws, the curses I now invoke upon thine head will be fulfilled. The curse of the betrayed, the curse of the broken-hearted parents, the curse of thy murdered offspring pursue thee and thine! Mayest thou, with her thou hast this day made thy bride, become a wretched wanderer on the face of the earth, loathed and hunted by thy fellow creatures, and afraid to venture in the light of day. May thy life become a perpetual hell to thee, from which thou canst not escape, nor gain one moment's respite. May all mankind shun thee as they would some savage beast. May all thine employments be turned to poison, preying upon thy vitals, gnawing at thine heart like hungry vultures; may one moment's peace never solace thee in thine hours of misery, and balmy sleep, the boon of rest to the afflicted, prove to thee but a renewal of those horrors that thou shalt experience in thy wakeful moments. May stern fate plunge thee headlong into the abyss of crime, so that in future ages mankind shall hear but the bare mention of thy name with a shudder of horror and disgust. May thy human course be long, so that thou mayest live to see thyself alone, friendless, childless in the world. And when death shall summon thy guilty soul to everlasting punishment, may no hallowed grave enclose thy remains, but may thy rotting corse moulder in the open air, food for the birds of prey; a ghastly spectacle for human beings to shudder at, and loathe, and execrate thy memory! Such, miscreant, is the dying curse that thy wretched victim, Almira de Montreville, calls down upon thine head ; and Heaven's dread voice proclaims that her curses will be realized!"

As the unhappy woman concluded this dreadful malediction, terrific peals of thunder shook the vaulted roof, and the very earth seemed to tremble beneath their feet. The persons present stared at each other aghast, unable to move or utter a syllable. The priest crossed himself, and covered his face with his hands with horror ; while the distracted Sir Martin, unable to support himself any longer, sunk down on his knees, and in his agony clenched his fists so vehemently together, that the blood started from the palms of his hands. His eyes were distended with anguish; large drops of perspiration bathed his temples ; conscience, guilty conscience, kindled a thousand fires in his brain ; his face assumed the livid hue of a corpse, and one lengthened groan of heart-bursting agony was all that he could give utterance to. Had the eternal judgment of the Supreme at that moment have been passed upon him, he could not have exhibited a more awful spectacle of horror and abject misery.

But fearful was the change that in a few minutes had come over Almira. Her features, which before had been distorted with the dreadful excitement of her feelings, while she was giving utterance to the above malediction, were now frightfully convulsed ; her countenance became black, her eyes rolled wildly in their sockets, her limbs trembled, and, with a cry of anguish, she sunk prostrate before the altar.

Sir Aldobrand and one or two others, aroused from their lethargy of astonishment and horror by this occurrence, rushed towards the unfortunate woman, and raised her in their arms. Awful was the appearance which her countenance displayed. Her eyes glared frightfully ; her features were so distorted that they were scarcely human; her bosom heaved with hysterical convulsions ; and it was evident that the hand of death was upon her. Sir Martin still remained upon his knees, with his hands still clenched, and his eyes fixed with stupefied amazement and horror upon her; but he had not the power to move; and, although he made several efforts to do so, he could not give utterance to a single word.

"Miserable woman!" ejaculated Sir Aldobrand, gazing with a look of earnest compassion upon her; "what have you done?—what rash and guilty act have you been tempted to commit?"

"It is over," said Almira, in a faint voice, and a ghastly smile overspread her features; "the deed is done—my wish is accomplished—I have invoked my curses upon his head—they—they will be fulfilled—and I die in——"

The sentence remained unfinished; she fixed one fearful look of meaning upon Sir Martin, and shook her fist menacingly at him. She then made one last convulsive effort to rise upon her feet, but nature was exhausted; her eyes became glazed and fixed; one dreadful pang seemed to shoot through her whole frame; and with a frightful groan she sunk back in the arms of Sir Aldobrand a ghastly corpse!

CHAPTER III.

THE MYSTERIOUS DISAPPEARANCE OF THE CORPSE OF ALMIRA.—THE EXTRAORDINARY CONDUCT OF SIR MARTIN DE LANCY.—THE IMPRISONED LADY.

IT would be a waste of time to attempt to describe the emotions of all present at this extraordinary scene, and the awful *denouement.* The corpse of Almira, who had evidently destroyed herself by poison, was removed into one of the rooms attached to the chapel; and the various persons who had been assembled on this remarkable occasion, prepared to leave the place, deeply impressed with what they had witnessed, and each forming their own conjectures upon it, though none of them were favourable to Sir Martin de Lancy.

Lady Editha was still in a state of insensibility, and a litter having been hastily formed, she was placed on it, and conveyed by the servants to the castle, Sir Martin taking his brother's arm, and following in a state of complete apathy, and seemingly unconscious of all that was passing around him.

No joyous festivity celebrated that extraordinary bridal. The feast remained untouched; a silence like that of the grave prevailed in the castle; the guests gradually retired from it, as though after what had occurred they were afraid to remain within its precincts; and the domestics gazed at each other, and shook their heads, with ominous looks, and forebodings which they dared not trust themselves to give utterance to.

That night it was said that awful sounds were heard to proceed from the Black Tower of Bransdorf, as though the troubled spirits of the departed were repeating the dreadful curses of the unfortunate Almira de Montreville, on the midnight air.

Immediately on their arrival at the castle, Lady Editha was conveyed to a chamber, and the assistance of a skilful leech procured; but she remained for some time in a state of insensibility, and when she was indeed restored to a state of consciousness, her mind was in such an agonised condition, that it was truly melancholy to behold her suffering.

But the conduct of his brother was of such an extraordinary description, that Sir Aldobrand was completely lost in amazement, and knew not what course to adopt under the circumstances. He found it impossible to arouse him from the lethargy which had fallen upon his senses since the fearful scene at the bridal. When he addressed him, he replied incoherently, but positively refused to visit the chamber of the unhappy Lady Editha, and appeared to evince a feeling amounting to horror at the mention even of her name.

At length he abruptly quitted the presence of his brother, and retired to his chamber, locked himself in, and peremptorily refused to be intruded upon by any one.

Sir Aldobrand de Lancy passed a restless night, for the terrible and mysterious events of the day had made an impression upon his mind, which nothing could easily efface; and he racked his brain to no purpose, to form a reasonable conjecture upon the subject.

He had never heard of the unfortunate Almira before, and he was shocked to find that his brother had been guilty of the vices which there could be no doubt he had; and deep was the sympathy he felt for the misfortunes and untimely fate of that miserable woman. He feared, also, the misery that was in store for Lady Editha; for, after what had occured, it was impossible that her and Sir Martin should ever be happy together, for he, no doubt, would be afraid to enter into any explanation of his past conduct, and she must, consequently, look upon him with suspicion, if not with absolute disgust.

What a terrible train of events did the observations and denunciations of Almira imply!

It would seem that Sir Martin had cruelly deceived her, destroyed her innocence, and by his neglect and treachery had plunged her into a vortex of crime, the bare thought of which must cause the humane heart to revolt with horror. Were her assertions true, she had shed the blood of her innocent offspring; but that idea was too dreadful even to think upon.

The night passed away; the morning came, and Lady Editha was more calm, but still she evinced a feeling of the greatest repugnance to see her husband; an objection that seemed not at all likely to disturb Sir Martin, as he was equally indifferent; and when his brother met him in the morning, he was quite astonished at the change which only a few hours had effected in him.

His countenance was very pale, and there was an occasional convulsive movement about his lips; but in other respects, his demeanour altogether was as composed as if nothing had happened. When Sir Aldobrand, however, ventured to allude to the awful events of the day before, he abruptly interrupted him, and refused to enter into any explanation whatever, or to deny or to acknowledge the truth of the dark accusations which the unfortunate Almira had made against him.

With respect to his wife, he declined to seek an interview with her, for the present, and appeared vexed with Sir Aldobrand at the sympathy he expressed towards her.

What could be the meaning of such extraordinary, such inexplicable conduct? Sir Aldobrand was surprised, bewildered, and disgusted; and the positive refusal of Sir Martin to confide in him, cnnvinced him that all of which Almira had accused him was true, and that he had been guilty of crimes, the recollection of which must ever heap upon him disgrace and misery.

This interview between the brothers was interrupted by the hasty arrival of a messenger from the priest who had performed the marriage ceremony, who informed them that the corpse of Almira, which had been removed to the room attached to the chapel, had disappeared in the night, and that it was impossible to form even the most remote idea by whom or by what means it had been conveyed away.

The intelligence caused the greatest surprise and consternation in the minds of Sir Martin and his brother; and the former almost immediately became lost in abstraction, and muttered a number of incoherent expressions to himself, which Sir Aldobrand was perfectly at a loss to understand.

What made the circumstances the more extraordinary was, that the apartment in which the remains of the ill-fated woman had been placed, had been properly secured, and the key taken into the possession of the priest; and although the body was gone, and there was no other means of gaining access to it, the door was found locked in the same manner they had left it; and there was nothing at all in the appearance of the room to denote that any one had entered it.

"What can be the meaning of this mystery?" said Sir Aldobrand; "were we inclined to be superstitious, this would certainly appear to be the work of witchcraft."

Sir Martin offered not a word in explanation, and almost immediately afterwards quitted the room, and retiring to his own apartment, remained secluded within it for the remainer of the day.

Sir Aldobrand became more and more lost in the labyrinths of fruitless conjecture, and racked his brain to no purpose to imagine the cause of these remarkable events. But what were the sufferings of the lovely Lady Editha in her lonely chamber? How cruelly had all her early hopes been blighted, and how dark and wretched was the prospect now before her. She was the wife of one who had been denounced as a villain; the betrayer of female innocence; and upon whom the dreadful and dying curse of his hapless victim rested; and if all that she had accused him of were true, most fearfully would those curses be realised. And could she love him; could she view him with any other feelings than those of loathing and disgust? She felt that she could not; that she could only view him with dread and suspicion. Nay, had he not himself already discarded her? Had he not refused to see her; which plainly showed that he no longer loved her, if indeed he had ever done so; which thought was too reasonable for her now to reject. Cruel fate! to think that they should ever have encountered each other. The prospect that opened to her eyes was of the most frightful nature, and she almost feared to contemplate it.

Such were the thoughts which distracted poor Editha, and were almost too torturing for her reason to support. But were there no means of her escaping from her present melancholy fate?—since they could never hope to be happy together, surely they had better separate; and, from the present behaviour of Sir Martin, she could not think he would object to that. Willingly would she retire into a convent, for there was nothing now left to charm her in the world; and only in holy seclusion, and the comforts of religion, could she hope to find any consolation under the severe destiny with which it had pleased Providence to visit her.

Sir Aldobrand would have been glad to have had an interview with Lady Editha; but his brother not only sternly refused it, but desired that he would never again venture to mention her name to him, or to allude to the circumstance which had taken place on the day of the union, as he considered that was a subject that concerned no one but himself, and he wonld not submit to any interference.

Sir Aldobrand naturally felt his pride mortified at this haughty behaviour, and the consequence was, that a quarrel ensued between him and Sir Martin; and, after expressing his opinions pretty strongly, the former hastily quitted the castle, and resolved to hold no further intercourse with his brother until he should have learnt to treat him with more becoming respect. All these events caused the greatest sensation in the neighbourhood of De Lancy Castle, and even those who had formerly been the warmest friends of Sir Martin, began to look upon him with feelings of doubt and suspicion. The prejudice against him was not a little strengthened when it became known that Sir Martin had caused the unfortunate Lady Editha to be removed to the Black Tower, where he kept her strictly confined, only visiting her gloomy prison occasionally himself.

Whatever could be his reasons for acting with such cruelty to one who had so recently become his wife, was a mystery no person could fathom; but it is needless to say that his conduct was viewed with the utmost indignation by every one; and there were many who did not hesitate boldly to express their opinions upon the subject. The domestics felt themselves uncomfortable in the service of a man whom they could no longer respect, and who treated them in the most haughty and tyrannical manner, and several of them resigned their situations, while most of them would gladly have done the same, had their circumstances permitted.

But great was the astonishment and excitement which prevailed when it was understood that Lady Editha and her only female attendant had suddenly disappeared from the old Black Tower; and that was increased when Sir Martin abruptly discharged all the domestics at De Lancy Castle, except an old man and his wife, and retiring alone to the tower, secluded himself in it, and would not permit any person to hold any communication with him, or to have the least chance of penetrating the mystery of his conduct.

The darkest rumours and suspicions got into circulation, and intelligence of all the circumstances having been forwarded to Sir Aldobrand de Lancy, he thought it his duty to hasten to the tower without delay, and to demanded an explanation of his brother; for it could not be tolerated that Sir Martin, by conduct so ambiguous and suspicions, should be the means of bringing a stigma and reproach upon that noble name, which hitherto had remained unsullied.

On arriving at De Lancy Castle, he was surprised at the melancholy change which had been wrought during the brief period (altogether amounting only to a few days) that he had been away from it; and he was more and more lost in amazement and perplexity, when old Simon informed him of what had taken place since his departure. Simon was also about to enter into a prolix account of the strange noises and sights which had been heard and seen at the Black Tower; but Sir Aldobrand abruptly stopped him, and gently chided him for giving any credence to such superstitious folly; then, without waiting to partake of any refreshment, he hastily remounted his horse, and, his mind agitated by the most powerful and conflicting emotions, he made his way towards the tower.

It was now evening, and the moon cast its broad beams upon the gloomy pile, only, if possible, making its aspect more lonely and cheerless.

Sir Aldobrand and his servant ascended the hill, and then looked up at the different casements; but there was no light to be seen in any of the chambers—there was no sign that the tower was inhabited by a human creature. He ordered the servant to ring the bell at the principal entrance. The sound reverberated hollowly around, and the knight impatiently awaited to hear the result; but several minutes elapsed, and no answer was returned—all remained wrapped in the same gloomy silence as before. Twice the servant, by his master's orders, repeated the summons, but with no better success; and Sir Aldobrand's impatience increasing, they removed round to another entrance to the old tower, and both knocked and rang repeatedly, but still without the least satisfactory result. Sir Aldobrand became more astonished and alarmed; but after having waited some time in a state of uncertainty what to do, he determined to procure assistance, and force an entrance to the tower, with the hope of being enabled to remove his suspense, and to unravel this most extraordinary and painful mystery.

He was about to desend the hill when a rustling sound smote his ear, and turning hastily round, his eyes, for a moment, caught a glimpse of a tall figure in white, which was hastily retreating round an angle of the building.

He called aloud, and urged his horse forward towards the spot; but though he did not occupy scarcely an instant in gaining it, when he arrived there the figure was gone, and, as far as his eyes could trace, he could not discover the least signs of it, or the means by which it could have disappeared so suddenly.

He closely examined that part of the buildings; but could find no door or aperture by which it might have entered the tower; and he was now completely lost in a maze of fruitless conjecture and perplexity.   The form had vanished so instantaneously, that he had had no opportunity of judging whether it was that of a male or female ; and he became the more bewildered the longer he ruminated upon the remarkable circumstance.

That he had not suffered his imagination to deceive him he was certain, for his attendant had seen the figure as well as himself; and being, like many others of his class in those days, prone to superstition, he was now labouring under very evident terror at the circumstances; for he immediately concluded that it was some supernatural being who had appeared to warn them against attempting to penetrate the mystery of the old tower. However, he knew the disposition of his master, and the contempt he entertained for such vulgar and vignorant ideas, and he therefore wisely kept his thoughts to himself.

After having once more looked up at the different casements of the tower, without being able to discover a light in any of them, and concluding that Sir Martin, if he were still there, must inhabit some of the interior apartments of the building, Sir Aldobrand again began to descend the hill, much to the relief of his domestic ; but resolved to return again that night with proper assistance, and at once to solve the doubts and apprehensions which agitated his mind.

In little more than an hour, he again repaired to the tower, accompanied by several persons, with proper implements to force an entrance, and in a few minutes the door yielded to their efforts, and the whole party entered the building.

All was silent and dreary, and as they proceeded through the different rooms, they presented no signs of their having been inhabited for some time ; but, on their arriving at a small apartment in the northern wing, all the tokens of its having recently been occupied were revealed to them.

A table in the centre of the room, and at which two chairs were placed, was spread with refreshments, which seemed to have been left untouched ; two goblets were filled with wine, and, from the freshness of the viands, it would appear that they could not have been left for any length of time.

Sir Aldobaand was overwhelmed with astonishment, and the mystery appeared to him to become still more inexplicable.   He was about to proceed farther in his examination of the other apartments, however, when his eyes were attracted by a strip of paper which was lying on the table, and read the following words in an unknown hand—

" Sir Aldobrand de Lancy, or whosoever's eyes these lines may reach, seek not to penetrate the mystery of Sir Martin and Lady Editha's fate, for time and circumstances can only unravel it.   Remember Almira's curse on the day of the bridal, and beware !"

Sir Aldobrand read these extraordinary words again and again, and could scarcely believe the evidence of his eyes.

" Gracious Heaven !" he ejaculated.   'Am I then still fated to remain in this insupportable state of mind and suspense?   There is a fearful import in the words here written, which bewilders and distracts me.   What—oh ! what can have become of my wretched brother, and his unfortunate and innocent bride?   But follow me," he added, " I will not rest satisfied until I have examined every nook and corner of the tower."

His companions by no means fancied the business, and would fain have persuaded him to abandon his design, although they knew not what cause they had to fear ; but they dared not to offer any objection, and Sir Aldobrand led the way, not suffering any part of the building to escape his scrutiny, but without meeting with anything to throw the least light on the mysterious affair ; and he returned to the room before mentioned in disappointment and perplexity, which was not a little heightened when he remembered the form he had seen outside the tower in the early part of the evening.   But to remain there was useless, and after some further reflection, therefore, he reluctantly quitted the ancient building.   He ordered all the doors to be again secured, and strictly prohibited every one from attempting to enter the tower, though he had no occasion to do so, as they were all too much terrified to entertain, for a moment, any such idea.

The disappearance of Sir Martin and Lady Editha from the tower, excited the utmost astonishment in the neighbourhood, and gave rise to many conjectures ; but all the efforts of Sir Aldobrand, who had now taken up his residence in the castle, to discover the fate of his brother and his lady, from that day to the time at which this narrative commenced' were unavailing ; and it was generally supposed that they were both dead, though by what means they had perished it was impossible to form even the least idea.

The fearful curse of Almira, and the remarkable and unaccountable disappearance of her body, were strongly impressed upon the memory of all who were acquainted with the circumstances; and they appeared, to the imagination of most persons, to be immediately associated with the impenetrable mysteries of the Black Tower of Bransdorf.

Having entered into this explanation, it is now necessary that we should return to the humble individuals who were introduced to the reader in the first chapter.

CHAPTER IV.

THE STRANGE APPEARANCE.—THE CHILD OF PROVIDENCE.—THE RESOLVE.

SAMPSON HEWLEY and his son, with their precious burthen, made all the speed they could to the cottage, picturing to themselves what the amazement of Margery, Barbara. and Arnold would be, on learning their adventure and beholding the little innocent whom they had discovered in so extraordinary a manner.

The child still slept as soundly as if it had rested on its mother's bosom—that mother whom Sampson feared had met with a dreadful and untimely death; and the cloak of the old man completely sheltered it from the cold.

"Poor child," said the honest and warm-hearted cottager; "Providence has sent me to thy rescue from a wretched fate, and in me thou shalt ever find a kind, though humble protector. Did I not tell thee, Hugo, that something more would come of our enterprise than thou anticipated? Had I yielded to thy fears, this unfortunate child must have perished; and it is most wonderful that the monster who has this night, too evidently, perpetrated a frightful deed of blood did not also sacrifice the life of this innocent babe.'

Instead of returning any answer to these observations, Hugo suddenly grasped his father's arm, with an expression of astonishment and alarm, and pointed significantly in the direction they were proceeding. Sampson looked, but could perceive nothing but a cluster of tall trees some distance before them.

"Why, what's the matter with thee now, boy?" he demanded.

"Did—did you not see it?" faltered Hugo, still pointing in the same direction as before.

"See what?" ejaculated Sampson; "why, by the saints, Hugo, I do verily believe that thou hast taken leave of thy senses to-night."

"No, no; indeed I have not. I saw, as plainly as I see you now, a tall figure, all in white, standing just there, and apparently awaiting our approach. It disappeared like lightning, among the trees, the moment that I drew your attention to it."

"Fancy—fancy, boy; the singular adventures of the night have given you the vapours."

"It was not fancy, father," returned the young man; "I could swear with my dying breath that I saw it."

"And what was it like?" inquired Sampson.

"As well as I could distinguish in the short time I was permitted to behold it, it seemed to be the form of a woman," answered Hugo.

"Ha, ha, ha!" laughed his father; "and you surely are not going to be frightened by a woman."

"Hush! 'tis there again. Do you not see it?"

Sampson strained his eyes, and did indeed behold the tall shadowy form of a woman, clad in white, and standing on the spot to which his son pointed. The distance was too great for him to distinguish the features; but its stature was far beyond the common height, and its whole appearance in the dim light was extremely ghastly. The attitude was erect, and one arm was extended towards them, as if to arrest and command their attention.

Sampson was at first much surprised and confused at this appearance, but he soon recovered himself, and calling aloud to the woman to stop, he took his son's arm, and moved towards it. They had not advanced many paces, however, when the strange being uttered a strange wild cry, and waving its arms in the air above its head, it immediately vanished, as it had done before, among the trees.

"This is most extraordinary," said Sampson; "I shall certainly never forget the adventures of St. Swithin's night. But come, boy, we must not suffer this mystery to remain unravelled, if possible."

They hurried on towards the place where the form had disappeared, but on arriving there, nothing whatever was to be seen. There was a wide open tract of country before them, however, and it seemed most wonderful and unaccountable how the stranger could have concealed herself in so short a space of time.

"Well, I can make nothing of it," said Sampson; "but the woman could have no business with us, and therefore we should not suffer it to disturb us. Come, we are delaying time, and your mother and Barbara will be greatly alarmed at the length of our absence."

Hugo made no reply, but he was far from being satisfied; and Sampson himself, although he pretended not to be much affected by the adventure, was excited by it in no ordinary degree, and puzzled his brain to imagine who the female could be, and what was her purpose for appearing before them. They now hurried on their way, and soon came in sight of the cottage; but when they had arrived within a few paces of it, the same figure which they had beheld before darted rapidly past it, and was out of sight in an instant, and before Sampson and his son could recover themselves from their utter astonishment.

"Is not this indeed most extraordinary?" said Hugo.

"Aye, it is so, boy," replied his father; "I am at a loss to understand it. But, perhaps, after all, it is only some poor maniac, who has escaped from confinement. Time will probably explain all."

They now approached the cottage, and were met at the door by Margery, Barbara, and Arnold, who were delighted to behold them again, for they had been afraid from their long absence that some danger had befallen them, and Arnold was just going to leave the cottage in search of them.

"Aye, aye, dame," said Sampson, returning the welcome greeting of his wife with equal cordiality, "I knew that you would be alarmed that we did not return before, but we could not help it. Hugo and I have met with such adventures to-night that will cause you to marvel at for a twelvemonth. But come, clap another log on the fire, and then I will show you the handsome present I have brought you."

"A present!" repeated Margery and her daughter in a breath.

"Yes, and such a one as you little expect; and I shall be much disappointed if you are not pleased with it."

"Now, now, Sampson," said Margery, "do not be tantalizing. What have you got so carefully concealed beneath your cloak?"

At that moment the infant, who had been aroused from its slumber, uttered a faint cry, and Margery and Barbara started back with amazement.

"Holy Virgin!" exclaimed the former, "that was surely the voice of a child, and it seemed to proceed from the very spot on which you are sitting, Sampson."

Sampson smiled, and not wishing to keep them any longer in suspense, he removed his cloak, and revealed the beauteous little innocent to their view.

The surprise of Barbara and her mother exceeded all bounds, and for two or three minutes they could only take the infant in their arms, and cover it with kisses.

"What a lovely little cherub!" ejaculated old Margery; "but, for Heaven's sake, Sampson, how did you come by it—and what would you do with it?"

"Become its protector while I have the life and the means," fervently replied her husband; "I fear the poor child has no other but the Almighty. Oh, dame, what will be your astonishment when you hear the manner in which I discovered her. But, prithee, administer to it some gentle nourishment, and then I will tell you all about it."

Margery took the child in her arms, and Barbara having made it some food, and administered it to it, it once more sunk off to sleep, and she was about to place it in a little bed, that had been made up for it on some chairs by the side of the fire, when a small scrap of paper fell from its bosom, and on picking it up, they read the following words:—

"The child's name is Mildred; seek not to discover more, for its life depends upon secrecy."

"Unfortunate infant," cried Sampson; "this shows at once the cruel destiny to which thou art exposed; but while Sampson Hewley lives, thou shalt never want a warm and affectionate friend."

He was interrupted in these observations by a shriek of horror from Barbara and her mother, and looking up he beheld them both pale and trembling, and gazing with vacant looks towards the casement.

"What is the matter?" eagerly demanded Sampson; "why, you look as scared as if you had just beheld some frightful spectre."

"Oh, Sampson," answered Margery; "we saw it, just now, as you were giving utterance to your intention towards the poor child. It was there at the casement."

"What, what?" hastily demanded Sampson.

"It was a tall figure in white," said Barbara; "and with such a frightful expression of countenance! Oh, it freezes my blood while I think of it."

Sampson and his sons hastened to the cottage door, and looked out, but they could not perceive anything. But the description of the form corresponded exactly with what they had seen, and their interest and wonder were, therefore, not a little excited.

"It was only imagination," remarked Sampson, not willing to encourage their apprehensions. "There is no one to be seen, and it would have been impossible for them to have disappeared so suddenly unless they sunk into the earth."

"Oh, no," said Margery; "I am positive I saw it, just as Barbara described it."

"Nonsense," returned her husband; "you have suffered the strange events of this night to take effect upon your fancy. But about this poor little stranger, our future protegee; do you wish to hear the particulars of the way in which I and Hugo discovered her, or shall I defer my account till to-morrow, for it is now getting late?"

Margery and her daughter conquered the fears which the late event had inspired them with, for they were both anxious to hear the account which Sampson had to give; and Arnold, at their request, having secured the door, they drew their chairs closer to the fire, and Sampson detailed to them, in as few words as he could, what had happened to him and Hugo in the tower; to which Barbara and her mother listened with the deepest attention and amazement.

"Alas!" observed the dame, when he had concluded, "it is too plain that some fearful deed of blood has been this night perpetrated in the old tower. The wretched parent of this unfortunate child has probably fallen a victim to some atrocious monster. May Almighty God bring the guilty to light, and visit him with his most terrible retribution. Oh, Sampson, you have had a most fortunate escape. But surely it was very imprudent of you to venture into the tower after Sir Aldobrand has so strongly prohibited any one from doing so; and you might incur his most serious displeasure should it come to his knowledge."

"It was providence certainly that directed me to do so, dame," observed her husband; "had I not been bold enough to venture there, this poor child must have perished. Besides, Sir Aldobrand is at present abroad, and it will be our own fault if ever he knows anything about it."

"But whose child can we say it is?" asked Margery.

"We will arrange that anon," replied Sampson. "But, come, it is time to retire to rest. The little Mildred, for so it seems she is to be called, had better sleep with Barbara, who, I know, will pay every attention to her."

After solemnly invoking the protection of Heaven on the head of the innocent little foundling, who had been so mysteriously placed under their protection, the worthy family separated for the night, Barbara cheerfully taking charge of the infant Mildred, who had remained locked in a tranquil sleep ever since the nourishment, of which, no doubt, it stood so much in need, had been administered to it.

CHAPTER V.

SIR ALDOBRAND BEHOLDS THE CHILD.—HIS EMOTION.—THE WEIRD WOMAN OF THE HEATH.

A PERIOD of three years elapsed, without anything particular occurring. Sampson and his wife were faithful to the resolution they had formed, and attended to their young charge with the greatest affections. By every one who had seen her, she was believed to be what the cottagers had represented her, namely, the orphan child of their niece; and Mildred herself was yet too young to be made acquainted with her history, so that she had no cares to oppress her early days, and was supremely happy in the caresses of her humble but generous benefactors. Even had the child been aware of the loss of her parents, the kindness and indulgence which on every side were lavished on her, would have reconciled her to it.

Mildred's artless prattle, her infantile graces, and the sweetness of her temper, won the love of all who saw her; and as for the cottagers, they could not have looked upon her with the greater affection had she been connected with them by the nearest and dearest ties.

The warning in the paper which had been found upon Mildred had prevented Sampson from again seeking to penetrate the secret of the Black Tower; but his thoughts were frequently occupied with the secrets of that night, and often had he the greatest difficulty to conquer the anxiety he felt once more to visit that ancient building, which was still lonely and neglected, shunned with the utmost dread by the inhabitants of the neighbourhood, and suffered to fall into decay. It was a matter of surprise to most persons, why Sir Aldobrand did not raze it to the ground altogether; since there were so many strange reports about the frightful noises which were heard to proceed from it; and there was no little reason to believe also, tnat those stories, wild and extravagant though they were, were not entirely without foundation.

Sir Aldobrand had been absent abroad for a period of two years, leaving his son, the interesting little Ethelbert, under the care of his faithful housekeeper, Juditha; and, consequently, he had no opportunity of knowing what took place in the neighbourhood of De Lancy Castle, but, although so many years had elapsed since the disappearance of his brother and Lady Editha, he did not the least abate his exertions to discover their fate, but entirely without success; and it seemed but too probable that the painful mystery would never be revealed: for he thought it most likely that they had both long since been no more.

There was one report that greatly perplexed and tortured Sir Aldobrand; and that was, that Almira de Montreville was still living; for several persons declared (among whom was the priest who performed the bridal ceremony) that they had seen her, and spoken to her; that they were satisfied that it was no unearthly spirit, but a human being, and that Almira, whose terrible curse had been invoked upon the head of Sir Martin de Lancy. But they added that, although they endeavoured to secure her, she always managed to elude them, and in such a manner that to them was unaccountable.

This circumstance to Sir Aldobrand was more extraordinary than all, and he in vain endeavoured to come to some conclusion upon it; for he could not doubt the statements of so many persons, although he had never seen her himself, and it was completely useless to rack the brain in seeking to form a conjecture.

Could the death of Almira only have been assumed, to answer some sinister purpose? He could not believe it possible for any one so well to counterfeit decease as to deceive so many persons; and that opinion only added to the ambiguity of the circumstance, especially while the disappearance of the body of Almira was unaccounted for. He well knew the piety and integrity of Father Paul, the priest who had solemnized the nuptials of Sir Martin and Edith, or he might have suspected that he was colleagued with Almira in carrying out her schemes of revenge; and certainly, if that could be proved, the whole of the mysterious events would be sufficiently explained; but, as it was, to speculate upon them was but to plunge into a still more intricate maze of doubt and uncertainty.

Sir Aldobrand de Lancy, previous to his departure abroad, was frequently in the habit of calling at the cottage of Sampson Hewley; for, ostentatious in his manners himself, he admired the natural good sense and manly virtues of the humble cottager, and took much pleasure in his conversation. But since his return to the castle, he had found something else to occupy his time, and therefore had no opportunity of knowing the addition which was made to Sampson's family.

It happened, however, that one evening in the summer time, when Sir Aldobrand had been taking a longer ride than customary, and was returning home, he was overtaken by a smart shower of rain, and Sampson's cottage being the nearest at hand, he sought shelter there.

His arrival was, of course, quite unexpected by the cottagers, and threw them into no ittle confusion. On the entrance of Sir Aldobrand, he started back in some amazement at the scene which presented itself.

The beauteous little Mildred was seated on the knee of Sampson, twining his silver hair round her taper fingers.

"Time had blanched the ebon locks" of the old man; but his eyes still retained their wonted fire, and his cheeks the ruddy glow of health. Perhaps youth and age were never more beautifully contrasted than at this moment, and Sir Aldobrand gazed with blended surprise and admiration on a scene so novel and so pleasing.

Sampson felt more confused than before when he beheld the emotion of Sir Aldobrand and Margery and her daughter equally partook of his feelings; for they saw that probably the time for concealment was at an end, and they felt doubtful as to what the consequences might be.

Sampson, however, arose, and presented Mildred to his master, who, as he gazed more attentively at her features, evinced more emotion than before.

"I never beheld a more lovely child," he observed; "to whom does she belong?"

Sampson hesitated, and looked at his wife.

"You had better tell his lordship all about it, Sampson," said the old woman.

"About what?" demanded Sir Aldobrand, with some surprise and interest; "is there some secret connected with this pretty little child?"

"There is, Sir Aldobrand," answered Sampson; "and I hope your honour will pardon me for not having made you acquainted with it before; but I was afraid that you would be angry with me for having broken through one of your commands."

"Tell me the truth, Sampson, and do not fear," said Sir Aldobrand, "for your observations have greatly excited my curiosity."

"I will, Sir Aldobrand," returned the old man : "but Barbara, while I am stating the facts to his honour, you had better take Mildred into the next room, for it is fit that she should not hear the particulars at present."

Barbara took Mildred (who made a graceful little curtsey to Sir Aldobrand) by the hand, and led her from the room, and the knight awaited in profound attention to hear the explanation of Sampson.

"The little angel whom your honour has just now seen," began Sampson, "has been under my care a matter now of three years; and we all of us love her as fondly as if she were our own child. She has hitherto been known only as the orphan daughter of my deceased niece, but such is not the truth."

"Indeed!" said Sir Aldobrand; "to whom, then, does she belong?"

"That, and please your honour," replied Sampson, "is more than I can tell. I found her on the night of St. Swithin's, under circumstances of great horror, alone and deserted."

"Amazing!" exclaimed Sir Aldobrand; "is there a being so lost to humanity as willingly to abandon innocence like this?"

"Alas! it is too true, your honour," replied Sampson; "but I fear that a foul deed of murder was committed at the same time."

"Ah!" ejaculated Sir Aldobrand; "by whom?—where?"

"By whom I know not; but in the Black Tower of Bransdorf."

"In the tower! How know you this?"

"It was in the old tower, your honour," answered Sampson, in a faltering voice, "that I found the little Mildred."

"Is it possible," said Sir Aldobrand, "that you ventured to enter the tower after I had so strongly prohibited any one from doing so?"

"I knew your honour would be angry; but I trust that you will forgive me when you hear the circumstances under which I was induced to break through your commands."

"Well, well, relate, them, for I am all impatience to hear."

Sampson replied, and Sir Aldobrand was so much astonished at what he heard, that he several times interrupted him to give expression to his feelings.

"Most extraordinary mystery!" he exclaimed, when the old man had concluded; "this must be strictly inquired into. And this poor child, who can she be?—and what could be the motives of the wretches for leaving her in that lonely and deserted place? Where is the paper which you say you found upon the little Mildred?"

Sampson produced it, and Sir Aldobrand perused it attentively.

"This throws no light upon the mystery," he said; "I have no recollection of the characters; but this paper shows, at any rate, that the greatest care must be taken of the child, and the utmost precaution used, or the secret of her birth will never be discovered. Sampson, I caution you never to reveal those circumstances to Mildred until you have my permission to do so."

"I will obey your honour in every particular," said Sampson, bowing.

"At present she will remain under your care," continued Sir Aldobrand; but when she is two or three years older, I will have her removed to the castle, where she will be better protected from any dangers by which she may be threatened than she can possibly be at your humble dwelling."

Sampson's countenance assumed an aspect of sorrow and regret when he heard this, which Sir Aldobrand perceiving, said—

"Do not alarm yourself, Sampson, for, although I remove Mildred from your roof, you will have every opportunity of seeing her, and receiving the marks of her esteem and gratitude, feelings which she can never cease to entertain towards you."

"Oh! thank your honour," said the poor old man; "for, indeed, it would be a sad thing for us to lose our little foundling altogether, after we have become so attached to her."

"True," coincided Sir Aldobrand; "but, upon that point, you may rest yourself satisfied."

Sampson expressed his thanks, and the little Mildred, at the request of Sir Aldobrand was again brought into the room.

He contemplated her features with deeper interest and admiration than before; and, after having sat for some time absorbed in meditation, the rain having ceased, he bade farewell to the cottagers, and telling them to be mindful of their tender charge, remounted his horse, and rode slowly towards the castle.

Sir Aldobrand de Lancy was by nature humane and charitable; yet these ennobling feelings of the soul were often obscured by the prejudices of his education. From his earliest days he had been taught to value himself on the antiquity of his family; length of pedigree, in his estimation, was highly superior even to fortune, and even merit shrank beneath the vain boast of honourable ancestry.

The diamond when hewn from its native bed, sparkles, though surrounded by the rubbish of the mine; so shone Sir Aldobrand's virtuous deeds, throwing a luminous gleam on the less noble part of his character.

The beauty, innocence, and unprotected state of the helpless little Mildred, claimed his tenderest compassion; he resolved to cherish her, to supply to her the loss of a parent, to be her friend and guardian.

Mildred, even at that early period, was a perfect model of feminine loveliness. Her face was oval, her complexion was transparently fair, her hair flowed in amber ringlets over her neck and shoulders, and her eyes dark, and animated, blanded with irresistable sweetness. Sir Albodrand thought her one of the most lovely little creatures he had ever seen, and the singularity of her fate had so deeply interested him, that he was prepared to love her with the same affection as if she had been his own offspring.

Ethelbert, the son of Sir Aldobrand, was now about nine years of age, and since the discovery of Mildred, Sir Aldobrand resolved to prohibit him from ever visiting the cottage of Sampson; he trembled lest the beauty of the little foundling, should, even at so early an age, make an impression on the susceptible mind of Ethelbert. He was sensible how harduous a task it would be to eradicate from his heart an affection imbibed in childhood, an affection which he imagined would " grow with his growth, and strengthen with his strength," and though many revolving years must pass away before any unpleasant circumstances could arise, or his son become sensible of his feelings, Sir Aldobrand resolved not to endanger his future peace by permitting him to associate with the fascinating Mildred. For this reason, he resolved that Mildred should not be sent to the castle until Ethelbert had become old enough to be entrusted to the care of a tutor, and to travel on the continent for the benefit of his education.

Sir Aldobrand was so absorbed in these meditations, that he paid no attention to the way he was travelling, until his horse happening to make a slight stumble, he looked up, and perceived that he had strayed from the right road on to a wild and barren heath, which was at some distance to the right of De Lancy Castle.

Vexed at this, for the night was gloomy, and the wind blew bleakly across the heath, he was about to turn his horse, to get into the right road again, when he was startled by hearing his own name pronounced in a strange voice, and looking towards the spot from whence it issued, to his utter amusement, he beheld, standing before him, a figure, which he supposed to be that of a woman, though such was the singularity of its dress, and the coarse and even frightful character of its features, that it was rather a difficult matter to come to any satisfactory conclusion upon that point.

She fixed her black and penetrating eyes full upon the countenance of Sir Aldobrand, and waved her long skinny arms with singular attitudes, while in a voice of the most impressive, but disagreeable character, she thus addressed him :—

" Years may speed their rapid flight,
And though thy sun of life shines bright;
Clouds thy fate shall overcast,
And thou shalt bend beneath the blast.
Hopes which in thy bosom glow,
Must to care and anguish bow ;—
Almira's curse and fell disgrace,
Still rests on all De Lancy's race !"

" Mad woman !" exclaimed Sir Aldobrand, " why dost thou seek to annoy me with thy croaking predictions ? I never injured mortal being, and why should the sins of my unfortunate brother be visited on me ?—away !"

" Not so, Sir Aldobrand de Lancy," returned the hideous being; " thou mayst mock my predictions as thou will, but they will nevertheless be fulfilled. Almira's curse hangs over the whole of the hated race of De Lancy, and think not that thou wilt be suffered to escape its consequences. Ay, and that child of mystery, in whom thou now feelest so great an interest, will be the cause of care and misery to thee, from which thou canst not escape. She will wring thine heart, and lower thy pride in spite of all thy efforts to the contrary."

"Strange being," said Sir Aldobrand, "how knowest thou my secret thoughts ?"

"Ho, ho!" returned the hag; "thou art surprised, art thou?—But thou art compelled to acknowledge that I do know them. Then scorn not my prognostications, for rest assured, that as certain as the tide of life now circulates through thy veins, they will be fulfilled. Remember Almira's curse, and beware! We shall meet again."

She said no more, but shaking her bony fist at Sir Aldobrand, and grinning upon him frightfully, she retreated across the heath, with the speed of the wind, before Sir Aldobrand could recover from the surprise and confusion into which her words had thrown him, and in an allmost inconceivable short space of time was out of sight ; the darkness hat enveloped al around quickly concealing her from the view.

CHAPTER VI.

THE ADVENTURE IN THE BLACK TOWER OF BRANSDORF.

SIR ALDOBRAND remained for a short time transfixed to the spot, completely lost in amazement at this singular adventure, which it must be confessed had considerably unnerved him ; for there was something so uncommon in the woman's appearance, that it rendered her words doubly impressive. By what means she could have become acquainted with his secret thoughts and intentions, he was at a perfect loss to conceive ; and the whole circumstance had such an unnatural appearance, that he could not help viewing it with a feeling of superstitious terror.

The woman had warned him against the little Mildred, and predicted that she would be the cause of future care and misery to him ; but such was the hold that the poor child had gained on his affections, that those prognostications failed to prejudice him against her, or to alter his generous intentions towards her. He must have acknowledged himself weak, indeed, could they have done so ; and the prophecies of the weird woman were of so extravagant a nature, that he thought them unworthy of serious consideration ; and having come to this conclusion in his own mind, he urged on his horse, and striking into the right road, pursued his way to the castle, but still with his thoughts fixed on the remarkable events of the evening.

He had arrived within a short distance of the tower, when happening to cast his eyes towards it, he was completely astonished to behold several of its casements suddenly illuminated with a glowing light ; and, at the same moment, he almost imagined that he beheld the shadow of what appeared to be human forms flitting past it, but in an instant only the lights were extinguished, and all was buried in the same intense darkness as before.

"Strange !" ejaculated the knight, "there can be no deception in this. The old tower must surely be inhabited, and the reports which have been circulated of the noises which have been heard to issue from it, may not, after all, be unfounded. I must examine into this minutely. To-morrow, I will myself make a strict search in the tower, and endeavour to unravel the mystery which has so long been connected with it."

With this resolution Sir Aldobrand made his way to the castle, and after partaking of a slight repast, he retired to his chamber.

The events of the evening occupied his mind for two or three hours before he could go to sleep ; and the more he reflected on them, the farther did he become involved in mystery. The account which Sampson had given of his discovery of Mildred in the old tower, particularly interested him, and more than all determined him to make a strict examination of that ancient building, which he resolved to defer no longer than the next day ; and made up his mind that Sampson and his son should accompany him, as he thought it would not be prudent to trust the discovery which might be made to any other persons for the present, and he knew well that his domestics were too timid to undertake the task with any degree of readiness.

The following morning, Sir Aldobrand repaired to the cottage of Sampson, and once more beheld Mildred. The beauty and bewitching artlessness of the child charmed him more than ever; and he sat for some time contemplating her features with a feeling for which he was at a loss to account.

After a short time passed in conversation upon topics of an indifferent character, Sir Aldobrand drew Sampson aside, and, after confiding to him the adventure he had met with after leaving the cottage on the previous evening, he informed him of his intention to visit the tower, and asked him whether he and his son would be willing to accompany him.

Sampson immediately expressed his willingness to do so; and indeed, he not only felt proud of the confidence which his master placed in him, but was as anxious as he was to penetrate the mystery of the tower. It was therefore arranged that Sampson and his son, Hugo, should meet Sir Aldobrand near the tower, in two hours from that time, and they were instructed to arm themselves, and also to bring with them a lanthorn, as it was the knight's intention to penetrate all the dark and subterraneous passages and dungeons of the tower.

Sir Aldobrand then took his leave. Sampson and Hugo were true to the hour of appointment, and they had not been waiting many minutes, when Sir Aldobrand joined them. He had brought with him the keys of the tower, so that there would be no obstruction to their search; and, first looking round to ascertain whether the coast was clear, for they did not wish to be observed, they ascended the hill to the tower.

Sampson pointed out to his master the way by which he and Hugo had entered, but they found that the door was secured, and it was therefore evident that some person had been there since they had. Sir Aldobrand tried the lock, but the door was so well secured on the inside, that it resisted all his efforts to unfasten it.

"This is certainly most strange," he said; "but, at any rate, it confirms the fact that some one has been here since you visited the tower, Sampson; and we must, if possible, discover, at any hazard, who the intruder is."

They were about to move away from the door, when a single sound, like the clinking of heavy chains, smote their ears, and added in no small degree to their amazement. The sound appeared as if it was passing up a flight of stairs, and gradually died away in the distance.

"There can be no mistaking that, at any rate," said Sir Aldobrand; "the tower certainly must be inhabited. Perhaps it may be necessary to have further aid, in case we might meet with more persons than we expect."

"Oh, no, your honour," replied Sampson. "I do not think we have any cause to fear; and it will be as well not to have too many in the secret."

Sir Aldobrand admitted the truth of these observations, and they then moved round to the principal entrance.

Sir Aldobrand placed the key in the lock, but it was not until repeated efforts on his part, and that of his companions had been used, that they could succeed in opening it, and they then entered the tower.

A cloud of dust, which had been long pent up, saluted them; but, pausing, they listened attentively, and all was perfectly still.

They moved round towards the other door which they had at first tried, and found it secured on the inside by a strong bar of iron, which Sampson and Hugo declared was not there on their former examination of the tower.

This again added to their suspicions, and they thought it would be necessary to proceed with the utmost caution, lest they should meet with any surprise, and should be thus rendered incapable of defending themselves from any sudden attack which might be made upon them. They only spoke to each other in whispers, and kept constantly looking about them, and listening attentively, so that they might catch the slightest sound; but nothing broke the solemn silence that reigned throughout the building, save the hollow echo of their own footsteps, or the fluttering of the bat, as he flapped his wings in passing them.

They ascended the spiral staircase, and proceeded at once to the chamber in which Sampson and his son had discovered Mildred. To his horror, Sir Aldobrand traced the stains of blood upon the flooring, exactly as they had been described to him, and which appeared as fresh as if they had only been imprinted yesterday.

On gaining the important chamber they found it involved in complete darkness, for the shutters were shut; and here was another positive proof that some one had been there since the night on which Sampson and Hugo discovered the child.

The shutters were unfastened, and then Sir Aldobrand beheld the marks upon the floor here, the blood-stained print of the hand; and Sampson pointed out to him the couch on which he had found the little Mildred lying.

"Gracious Heaven!" ejaculated Sir Aldobrand, solemnly, "what awful atrocity has been here perpetrated? Unravel, I beseech thee, this painful mystery, and suffer not the guilty to escape the punishment due to their crimes."

At this moment they all distinctly heard a solemn groan, which seemed to proceed from one of the apartments beyond that in which they were, and it was immedi a tey folowed by a similar noise to that which they had heard outside the tower, and which graldually died away in the distance.

They started, and listened in profound attention and amazement.

"Some unfortunate being must have sought an asylum within these ancient walls," said Sir Aldobrand: "let us examine farther, for I am determined that this mystery shall be solved this very day, if possible. Murder has evidently been perpetrated, and, perhaps, if we persevere, we may not only discover the authors of it, but likewise find something out to the advantage of the poor child, Mildred. Sampson, you are not afraid, are you?"

"Afraid, your honour," returned the old man, with an expression of mortified pride; "and please you, that is a feeling that I am not much acquainted with, I flatter myself, especially when I am engaged in a good cause. I do not apprehend any danger, so lead on, your honour, if you please."

They all now moved to the door of the adjoining apartment, which they found unlocked; but, on opening it, they heard a sound like the rustling of a female dress, and could almost swear that they saw a figure in white glide to the further end of the room; but although they immediately rushed in that direction, for they had all observed it at the same moment, there was nothing whatever to be seen, nor did there appear the least outlet by which it was possible for any person to escape.

"These marvels multiply," remarked Sir Aldobrand; "I could certainly have sworn that I saw a human form retreating from this room at the instant we entered."

"And so could I, your honour," said Sampson; "and yet, where could it have gone? Here is no door, and it could not have passed through the wainscot."

"Unless there is some secret sliding panel," suggested Hugo.

"A good thought," said Sir Aldobrand; "and I know there are many such means of escape in this old tower. Let us sound the wainscoat."

They did so accordingly, but discovered nothing to confirm their suspicions, and they were involved in greater perplexity than ever.

"We must have been deceived," observed Sir Aldobrand, "and suffered our imaginations, which had before been strongly wrought on, to mislead us."

"I do not see, your honour," said Hugo, "how we could all have been deceived, and fancied that we saw the same object. Surely this old tower is haunted by the troubled spirit of the murdered victim, and——"

"Psha! nonsense," interrupted the knight, impatiently; "do not encourage such idle superstitions, Hugo. Come, let us continue our search. Here is a door which is locked and barred, so that it is quite certain no one has escaped that way."

They removed the iron bar, and Sir Aldobrand having at last found a key among the bunch which he had brought with him that fitted it, after some difficulty unlocked it, and they found themselves in a winding gallery, which was only dimly lighted by a single casement at the extreme end, and which was thickly encrusted with dust, and overgrown by the ivy which clung to the walls on the outside.

Sampson lighted the candle in the lanthorn, the better to accelerate their view.

It was a gloomy place, and the heavy carved work of the panels looked grim in the glimmering light emitted by the lanthorn. The several portraits which hung around were greatly impeded by time and damp, and many of them were fast mouldering from their frames. This part of the tower had been closed up ever since it had been in the possession of the family of De Lancy; and had always been avoided by the domestics with a feeling of superstitious fear and dread.

They moved to the further end, where they found a door open, and which led into a suite of apartments, all in a state of the greatest decay, and half filled with the crumbling remains of ancient furniture.

They passed through these rooms, for there was nothing whatever to gratify their curiosity, and after descending several flights of broken stairs, found themselves on the same spot from which they had first started, so that they concluded that they must have made a complete circuit of the tower, and now paused to consider how they should further proceed.

"We have yet discovered nothing to solve this mystery," said Sir Aldobrand ; "but yet I am far from being satisfied. The lights which I beheld to issue from the casements of the tower, last night, and the noises we have heard since we have been here, require an explanation ; and seem to prove beyond a doubt that some person or persons have sought a refuge within these walls. We will not abandon our search until we have examined the subterranean passages and vaults. Follow me ; there is a flight of steps at one end of this place which lead to the underground vaults."

Sir Aldobrand was about to proceed, when Hugo suddenly arrested his arm, and directed his and his father's attention to something which had met his observation.

They both looked towards the spot pointed out to them ; and, at the instant caught a glimpse of a figure in long white flowing garments, but which glided behind a pillar with the quickness of thought, and they saw nothing more of it.

"By Heaven, that was no delusion," exclaimed Sir Aldobrand, dashing foward, followed by his companions ; "stay, mysterious being, in the name of the Almighty, I command you ; if you are the victim of sorrow and oppression, I promise to release you from your present miseries, and redress your wrongs."

No answer was returned to this, and when they arrived at the spot where the form had disappeared, they could perceive nothing whatever to gratify the eager curiosity which now filled their bosoms.

"The form was that of a female, I am convinced," said Sir Aldobrand. "Surely it must be some dreadful circumstance that can have induced her to seek shelter in this wretched place."

"It must, indeed, Sir Aldobrand," coincided Sampson ; "but is it not remarkable how she can manage to elude us so easily?"

"It is," replied the knight, "but this time I think we are upon her track, for there is no outlet by which she could effect her escape this way, and she must, therefore, have descended into the vaults. Let us not delay following her."

They immediately began to descend the steep flight of stone steps ; but they were s broken in many places, that it required the greatest caution in so doing. They, at last, however, arrived at the bottom, and then found themselves in a long, dark passage, upon which numerous vaults or dungeons opened, but the doors of which were all secure ; and it seemed evident no person had been there lately.

Having the master key that opened them all, Sir Aldobrand found no obstruction, and they minutely inspected the whole range of gloomy dungeons, without meeting with any object at all, except in one of them, where, in one corner, they found a heap of human bones, which seemed to have been there for many, many years, and had probably belonged to some unfortunate wretch who had formerly been left to perish there.

They returned disappointed to the upper part of the building.

"It is useless to search any further," said Sir Aldobrand, "for it does not appear likely that we shall make any further progress ; and still the secret is surrounded, if possible, with greater mystery than ever. I will, however, lose no opportunity of unravelling it, and for that purpose will keep a strict watch upon the tower. And do you, Sampson, make me immediately acquainted with anything that may come to your knowledge."

"Your honour may depend upon it that I will," said Sampson.

They now quitted the tower, and Sir Aldobrand having given Sampson some more instructions, left him, and returned to the castle, pondering upon the events of the afternoon.

Sir Aldobrand, a day or two afterwards, gave instructions to several workmen to close the different apertures which time had made in the tower, and having secured all the doors, it seemed quite impossible that any human being could obtain an entrance to it . but still the same noises were reported to be almost nightly heard to proceed from it' and ghastly forms were said to have been seen ; which the vulgar and superstitious readily believed, and the rumour that the old Black Tower was haunted by evil spirits' daily gained strength in the neighbourhood, much to the annoyance of Sir Aldobrand, whose mind was tortured with suspense and anxiety upon the subject.

CHAPTER VII.

THE SECRET STILL REMAINS UNREVEALED.—MILDRED LEAVES THE COTTAGE, AND IS
TAKEN UNDER THE PROTECTION OF SIR ALDOBRAND.

Two more years had now winged their rapid flight, and Mildred still remained under
the humble roof of her kind benefactors, and her sweetness and innocence of disposition
daily gained upon their love, and they looked forward with dread to the moment when
she would be taken from them, although they would still have the opportunity of daily
seeing her; and they could not but feel delighted that she had found so powerful and
generous a friend in Sir Aldobrand.

Sir Aldobrand had been most careful in preventing Ethelbert from visiting the cottage
of Sampson Hewley, so that he knew not even of the existence of the lovely little Mildred; but vigilance, however strict, is sometimes useless.

It was the custom of Sir Aldobrand to take an airing every morning. During his absence, Ethelbert employed the moments in studying his morning exercises.

It happened that one morning Sir Aldobrand had protracted his ride to an unusual
length. Ethelbert had therefore finished his studies and was at liberty to pursue his
amusements before his father's return.

Attended by Robert, an old and long tried domestic, he strayed to the most romantic
part of his father's wide domains. Flora, a favourite dog, bounded before him, and
having been at the cottage the preceeding day with Sir Aldobrand, again took the same path
Ethelbert followed till within sight of the cottage; the dog then sprang forward, and
fawned at the feet of Mildred, who was seated before the cottage-door.

"Dear Flora," she said, patting the dog on the back; when looking up, she discovered Ethelbert and his attendant. The flowers she had been cutting fell from her
hand, and she was hastily retreating, when her foot slipped, and she fell to the ground.
Ethelbert and his attendant hastened to her assistance: at that moment Sir Aldobrand arrived, and alighting from his horse, commanded his son to resign the hand of
Mildred.

His countenance, naturally benign, glowed with passion; but when he turned to Mildred, and beheld her pale and trembling and bleeding (for she had cut her hand with a
pebble), he took her in his arms and bore her to the cottage, where Ethelbert followed,
entreating she might be carried to the castle.

Sir Aldobrand, in a voice expressive of anger, ordered him to be silent; he obeyed,
but eyed, with an attentive and delighted gaze, Mildred, who now sat smiling on his
father's knee.

The event which Sir Aldobrand had so long feared, was now realised; he saw with
inexpressible regret the pleasure with which Ethelbert, though so young, contemplated
Mildred; and notwithstanding that it was natural that one child should be pleased
with another, he trembled lest the seeds of passions should find their way to the heart of
the youthful Ethelbert, and engender an affection which increasing years would only
strengthen.

These reflections awakened in his mind an ebulition of passion which triumphed over
reason, and he rebuked his son, unconscious of the cause, adding to his other reproaches,
the epithets of mean-spirited, pitiful boy, unworthy the honour of being called his son.

Ethelbert looked abashed, nor could he conceive what he had done to deserve his father's displeasure.

Mildred possessed a greatness of soul which shone forth even in her earliest days; she
was now, probably, not more than seven years of age, and though she could not find words
to express her ideas, was well convinced that Ethelbert suffered on her account—but why?
Her benefactor had always endeavoured to enrich her mind with sentiments of humanity,
and never failed to caress her for any little kindness she rendered his favourite dog, or a
dove which he had given her. Amazed at his contrary behaviour, and terrified at the
baronet's anger, she sat with her eyes bent to the ground, endeavouring to stifle her
tears till they would no longer be restrained, but rolled plentifully down her cheeks.

Ethelbert was now approaching her, which Sir Aldobrand perceiving, lifted his arm,
and would have struck him, had not Mildred sunk on her knees, and clasping his hand,
sobbed aloud, and exclaimed:—

"Dear, sir, pray do not beat the young gentleman; indeed he is not to blame—no; it was very kind of him to assist me to rise when I had fallen."

This artless address of the innocent little Mildred effectually restored Sir Aldobrand to the use of his reason; affection and pride had been struggling in his breast—the former had triumphed. He kissed with tenderness his little favourite, commended her to the care of Margery, and extending his hand to Ethelbert, walked towards the castle.

To prevent any further intercourse between Ethelbert and Mildred, the baronet determined on committing him at once to the care of his tutor, and sending him on the continent. Then he could, without hesitation, put in practice the design he had first formed, namely, to have Mildred to reside at the castle, under the care of Juditha, who, though she was now placed in humble circumstances, had formerly been in a far different station, and was a woman of good natural sense and the most amiable manners.

Sir Aldobrand's plan was soon accomplished, and Ethelbert quitted the castle, attended by his tutor. The baronet was now anxious to have Mildred under his own roof without delay; but before he removed her from the cottage, he considered that it was necessary she should be made acquainted with the real facts of her history, she having hitherto known herself only as the relation of Sampson and his wife. Accordingly he instruc ed the old cottager to do so without any more delay.

This was a task of no very pleasant description to Sampson, and he shrunk from it. He felt aware of the anguish it would inflict upon the youthful mind of his lovely young charge. But he knew well it must be done, and he therefore mustered all his fortitude to the task.

The surprise and grief with which the poor foundling listened to this extraordinary account, may be imagined, and it was sometime before they could pacify her; but at length she became more tranquil, and sobbed her feelings of gratitude upon their bosoms.

The day appointed for her to remove to the castle arrived, and the parting between Mildred and her humble friends, was as affecting as if they were about to be separated for miles, and were never likely to behold each other again; but, at length, Mildred resigned herself to the care of Sir Aldobrand, and by him was at once conducted to the castle.

A large castle and elegant furniture were so new to Mildred, that she was perfectly delighted; but, as evening approached, she wished to return to the cottage.

To divert her from this thought, the baronet led her to the picture gallery, and, with all the pompous enthusiasm of family pride, named the different personages each portrait represented.

"That portrait," he said, " Mildred, which you see at the upper end of the gallery, is a likeness of the most noble warlike Earl Ranulph de Lancy, from whom I have the honour to be descended."

The artless Mildred thought, by the solemnity of the baronet's manner, that she ought to pay some respect to this great personage, therefore, approaching the portrait, she dropped a low curtsey in reverence.

Juditha, who stood at Sir Aldobrand's side, could not forbear from smiling at the child's mistaken politeness, at which the baronet seemed displeased, saying that every respect was due to such great personages, and even their resemblances. The ruddy hue of reproach mantled on his cheek at the latter part of his speech, for Sir Aldobrand was a man of sense, though the idea which he imbibed in his early days caused him to pay deference to a noble family which nought but virtue had a right to claim.

Sir Aldobrand continued pointing out the different portraits to Mildred, and repeating to her the various titles, but was passing one without naming it, when Mildred, who had been gazing at it for some moments in speechless wonder and admiration, timidly said—

"Oh, dear, sir, who is this handsome gentleman, whose eyes seem fixed upon me as if he were living and knew me?"

"My brother!" said Sir Aldobrand, with a deep sigh.

"And was he a lord or a prince?" asked Mildred.

"He was a warrior," answered the baronet.

"And what is a warrior, sir?" inquired the innocent child.

"A warrior," returned Sir Aldobrand, "is a man who will preserve the liberty of his country, even at the hazard of his life."

"Oh," ejaculated Mildred, fervently, "I shall ever love a warrior better than a lord."

Sir Aldobrand smiled, and, bidding her good night, retired. But Mildred could not remove her gaze from that portrait which had so rivetted her attention; nor could she banish from her mind the impression that its eyes were following her, and were fixed upon her in whatever direction she turned.

Juditha led her from the gallery, but still the portrait seemed to pursue her, and she could almost imagine that its lips moved, as if it was about to speak to her.

"Dear Juditha," said Mildred, as the former assisted her to undress, "I shall always love a warrior better than any lord or prince; for, though I do not know what Sir Aldobrand meant by saying he will preserve the liberty of his country, I suppose it is something very good, because his eyes sparkled, and he smiled, just as he does when he tells me I am a nice little girl."

"But, my love," said Juditha, "if you were to see a very poor man that was good, and a very rich warrior that was wicked, you would not love the wicked man because he was a warrior, and despise the poor man merely because he was not?"

"Oh, no," returned the child; "Margery says I must love the good; but I did not think, from what Sir Aldobrand said, that a soldier was ever wicked."

"In every station of life, my dear child," said Juditha, "may be found vice and virtue; you must learn to respect virtue, though the inmate of the lowest cottage, with as much sincerity as if discovered in the stately palaces of the great, since it is that which can alone ennoble."

With these words the good Juditha tenderly embraced her, and Mildred having offered up her innocent prayers to the Supreme, retired to the little bed prepared for her, and balmy sleep soon descended upon her eyelids.

CHAPTER VIII.

THE MIDNIGHT VISIT.—THE ALARM.—THE WEIRD WOMAN AGAIN.

UNDER the care of Juditha, and the unremitting kindness of Sir Aldobrand, Mildred daily improved; her precocious mind easily received instruction, and her grateful and affectionate disposition endeared her to her kind preceptress, the baronet, and her beloved friends at the cottage. She awoke in the morning with delight, and when the hour of repose arrived, sunk on her pillow with content. No base or turbulent passion found a place in her bosom; alike a stranger to guilt or sorrow, she enjoyed the present and contemplated the future with rapture.

And yet there were moments, too, when Mildred felt a temporary shadow of melancholy steal over her youthful mind; it was in those moments when her parentless state would arise to her recollection, and the probability that she might never know who were the authors of her being, or what fate had befallen them. But she was quickly aroused by her kind benefactor from these gloomy meditations, and soon became gay and happy again.

Mildred had never forgotten the portrait Sir Aldobrand had shewn her, and as often as she could she would steal alone into the gallery, and gaze at it with feelings of the most unaccountable rapture, and until the tears would gush from her eyes, and the most convulsive sobs would agitate her bosom.

But why the contemplation of a simple portrait should have such an effect upon her she was at a loss to imagine. Daily she walked out with Juditha, and never failed to visit her old friends at the cottage; and she was allowed to gambol among those scenes to which she had been accustomed from her earliest recollection. In short, there was no restraint put upon her innocent amusements, but every one was alike studious to promote her happiness.

Mildred had now been at the castle for several months, and nothing had occurred to disturb her tranquillity; but an event was about to take place which caused her considerable alarm.

She had retired to her bed one night rather more low-spirited than usual, though for what reason she could not imagine. It was some time before she could go to sleep, and there appeared an unusual gloom about the chamber, which inspired her with a feeling of terror. She was several times half inclined to arouse Juditha, who slept in the adjoining room; but, fearing that she would chide her for her folly and weakness, she forbore tor do so, and having once more offered up her simple, but fervent prayers to Heaven, she again endeavoured to compose herself to sleep. She, at length, succeeded; but sleep was even more torturing than her waking moments, for the most frightful dreams haunted her imagination, and she fancied herself in the most alarming positions of danger. She was awakened by the old clock in the castle striking the hour of midnight; and she started up in the bed, with a strange confusion of ideas, and, for the moment, scarcely conscious where she was. But what was the appalling sight upon which her eyes became rivetted, and which froze the blood in her veins as she looked? Was she still dreaming? or were her senses disordered by the visions which had already appeared to her imagination?

No; it was no delusion of the fevered brain! At the foot of the bed stood a tall figure in white, with its bright and unearthly eyes fixed full upon the countenance of the poor child. The complexion of the face was ghastly and livid; and the features were so distorted, that they were truly hideous to gaze upon.

The horrified Mildred uttered an appalling shriek, and instantly became insensible· The cries of the poor child aroused Juditha, and she hurried into the chamber. Her alarm on beholding the situation of Mildred may be conceived; and she could only imagine that she had been terrified by some frightful dream.

She lost no time in endeavouring to restore her, but it was some time before she succeeded, and then when the poor child recalled to her memory the hideous object she had seen, she almost relapsed into her former state, and implored Juditha not to leave her.

It was several moments before Juditha could elicit from her the particulars of what had happened to alarm her in such a manner; and when Mildred did inform her, she was almost as terrified as herself, but still endeavoured to persuade her that her imagination had merely been disturbed by a dream. Still, however, nothing could shake the belief of Mildred; and Juditha had the greatest difficulty imaginable to restore her to any degree of composure. She would not be pacified at all, until Juditha removed her into her chamber; but nothing whatever could compose her mind to sleep again; and as soon as daylight dawned, Juditha was compelled to remove her from that part of the castle altogether.

When Sir Aldobrand was made acquainted with the circumstance in the morning, he was much surprised and alarmed; but still, he could not bring himself to believe but that Mildred must have been mistaken; and tried all he could to persuade her to think so likewise, but without effect.

It was several days before Mildred could at all recover from the shock which this strange and alarming adventure had given her, and it threatened to be a long time ere she would be restored to her accustomed spirits. She was afraid to move about the castle alone, and could never again be persuaded to sleep in the same chamber, but was removed to that of Juditha, who, in some measure to quiet her apprehensions; became her companion.

Time, however, greatly abated Mildred's terrors, and she entered into her accustomed sports and amusements with nearly her former alacrity and vivacity.

Notwithstanding the fearful stories that were related of it, Mildred always felt an unconquerable wish to ramble near the old tower, although it was but seldom that she could persuade Juditha to indulge her in this singular whim.

No wonder that the old tower should possess such interest in poor Mildred's eyes; it was there she had been found by Sampson Hewley and his son, and nothing could persuade her but that her future destiny would be in some way associated with that gloomy building. She would have liked to wander over its gothic apartments, and to inspect the room in which she had been discovered; but she forbore to express such a wish to either Juditha or Sir Aldobrand, for she very well knew that it would be entirely useless. She had frequently heard of the horrors of the old tower, but they only the more excited her curiosity; and such was the extraordinary curiosity which she had to explore its chambers, and particularly the one in which she had been found, that she would not have felt the least hesitation in venturing to enter the building alone, had she been permitted, or if she could have found an opportunity of doing so unknown to any one.

She took the greatest pleasure in hearing old Sampson relate again and again the adventures he had met with in the tower; and the oftener she listened to them the more did she become involved in amazement and perplexity.

Sir Aldobrand would never permit her to walk forth alone; for he knew not what secret enemies she might have, or what dangers might threaten her; and, therefore, she had no opportunity of gratifying her curiosity; and this circumstance, simple as it might appear to be, caused her many an hour of uneasiness, and the most torturing reflection.

It happened that one day, Mildred and Juditha had been to pay their customary visit to the cottage, and they were so much interested in the subject upon which they conversed, that the evening had advanced before they thought of departing.

"My sons had better accompany you to the castle," said Sampson, "for it is getting dark, and there is no knowing what ruffians might be abroad to insult you."

Juditha, who entertained no apprehensions of the kind, however, thanked the old man, but declined his offer, and her and Mildred departed, taking the nearest route, and expecting soon to arrive at home.

The night had set in very gloomy; the moon was buried in dense black clouds, and the wind blew keenly from the north, whistling among the foliage, and sweeping the fallen leaves in clouds across their path. They quickened their speed, for the night was not a pleasant one to tarry in, and they regretted that they had remained so long at the cottage.

They had to traverse a long lane, completely overshadowed by lofty, wide-spreading trees, so that the light of day could scarcely ever penetrate, and now it was so utterly dark and dismal that they could scarcely see a step before them.

They had advanced about half-way along this dreary lane, when Mildred made a sudden stop, and clung timidly to her companion, who inquired eagerly what alarmed her.

"I am certain I saw the dark shadow of a human form glide along by the side of the bushes," said Mildred, in a timid voice.

"Nonsense, child," said Juditha; "you have suffered your fears to deceive you. It could only have been one of these old trees which your imagination construed into a human form."

"Oh, no, indeed I did not," answered Mildred. "I saw it as plainly as the darkness would enable me to do; and I could almost be positive that I saw two large glaring eyes fixed upon me. Oh, I wish we had allowed Hugo and Arnold to accompany us to the castle."

"Well, it would perhaps have been better," observed Juditha; "but still, Mildred, you may depend upon it you were mistaken in what you imagined you saw. Come, let us push on our way, for I am afraid Sir Aldobrand will be alarmed at the length of our absence, and will chide us."

Mildred looked timidly around her, and her eyes penetrated as far as the darkness would permit, as though she expected to behold some terrific object; for not all the arguments her companion made use of could persuade her that she was mistaken in the object she supposed she had seen.

They walked rapidly on, and had nearly reached the end of the lane, when a dismal cry, like the moaning of some person in great agony, smote their ears, continued for a second or two, and then gradually died away in the distance.

There could be no mistake in this; they both distinctly heard it, and Juditha was almost as much astonished and alarmed as her young companion.

They paused involuntarily, and looked around them, but they could perceive nothing, and all was silent save the hollow whistling of the wind through the trees.

"What can this mean?" ejaculated Juditha; "that certainly sounded like a human voice; and yet, although it seemed so near to us at first, it was borne away by the wind in the distance with astonishing rapidity."

"Ah," ejaculated Mildred, "that more than all convinces me that I was not mistaken in the object I stated I saw."

"While we tarry here we may be involving ourselves in danger," remarked Juditha; "let us hasten, Mildred."

They again proceeded on their way, Mildred looking eagerly around her as they went, but it was quite evident that her curiosity was even more excited than her fears.

They emerged from the lane, and the castle then burst upon their view at no great distance before them. The heavy clouds had partially dispersed, so that the surrounding objects were not rendered so indistinct to them, but as far as their eyes could trace, they could not discover anything to excite their astonishment or alarm. They therefore proceeded on their way without making use of any observation to each other.

It was necessary that they should pass by the hill on whose lofty summit the old Tower of Bransdorf stood, and Mildred gazed upon the dark shadow of its black and frowning walls with the same degree of awe and interest which she ever felt on beholding them.

Strange as the impulse may seem to be in one so young, even at that lonely hour, she would gladly have availed herself of the opportunity of penetrating its dreary chambers, and wandering through the dreary scenes of that deserted building which had so often been described to her by old Sampson. The tales circulated about it had no terrors for her; on the contrary, they only excited her curiosity the more; and she felt convinced that she could never rest until that curiosity was satisfied.

"Come, come, Mildred, child," said Juditha, impatiently; "do not let us linger in this manner; remember how late it is getting, and Sir Aldobrand will really begin to fear that something has happened to us. What can there be about that black and frightful old tower to attract your attention in so remarkable a manner? We never approach it but you linger about it in the same way; and any one would think that you have a curiosity to inspect it."

"And they would think right if they did so, good Juditha," returned Mildred; "I never gaze upon its venerable walls but a strange feeling comes over me; and even now I would give anything to be permitted to wander over it, and to penetrate its hidden mysteries."

"Holy Mother!" exclaimed the astonished Juditha; "can I believe my ears? For goodness sake do not talk so, child, for you quite frighten me to hear you. For my part I wish the crazy old building was levelled with the ground; and I am only surprised Sir Aldobrand does not order it to be demolished, useless as it is."

"Oh, I should deeply regret were he to do so," said Mildred, earnestly.

"Why, Mildred," ejaculated her companion, "do you not remember the awful stories which are circulated about that ancient place?"

"Yes, I recollect them all," replied Mildred; "but they do not alter my feelings respecting it in the least; nay, they only make me the more anxious to inspect it."

Juditha was again about to express her amazement, when an exclamation from Mildred interrupted her—

"See—see!" she cried, pointing in the direction of the tower. Juditha looked towards it, and to her utter astonishment beheld every gothic casement of the building illuminated with a broad glare of light; but in another instant they all vanished as if by magic, and the tower was enveloped in the same darkness as before.

Juditha, now looking for her companion, was surprised and alarmed to behold her running hastily towards the hill on which the tower stood.

"Mildred! Mildred!" she cried; "where are you going? What strange idea possesses you? Is the child bewitched? Mildred!"

But Mildred either did not hear her, or heeded her not, and continued her flight, until she arrived at the foot of the hill, which, to the utter consternation of Juditha, she began to ascend.

"Why the poor girl has certainly gone mad," ejaculated the old woman; "and I must pursue her to that frightful old place, or God knows what harm may come of her."

Juditha now hurried as fast as her feeble limbs would carry her, still calling aloud on Mildred to stop; but she evidently did not hear her, but continued to ascend the hill; and when Juditha arrived at the foot of the hill, she was hidden from the sight.

Notwithstanding the alarm she was in, lest any danger should befal her youthful charge, she hesitated, for she could not conquer the fears she entertained of the tower, although she was a woman of natural good sense, and not near so prone to superstition as many persons in those days were. But she knew there was no time to deliberate, and she, therefore, commenced ascending the steep hill as rapidly as she could.

She had nearly reached the top, when she was alarmed by hearing a loud shriek, and, looking up, she beheld, standing on the summit of the hill, a tall and frightful figure, which had nothing of the appearance of humanity about it.

It was the Weird Woman of the Heath; but in an instant she vanished, Juditha could not perceive how or whither.

The old woman was completely thunderstruck, and for a moment or two could not offer to move from the spot on which she was standing; but, apprehensive for the safety of Mildred, she conquered her terrors, and made her way to the place where, the minute before, she had seen the awful figure of the Weird Woman standing.

She beheld poor Mildred stretched senseless on the earth, and at first fearing that she was dead. she raised her distractedly in her arms, and pressed her hand upon her heart. It beat; and the first dreadful fears of old Juditha were removed.

She now called upon her name, and did all she could to restore her, and, in a few minutes, her efforts were crowned with success, for Mildred revived, and, opening her eyes, looked anxiously yet timidly around her.

"Come, come, Mildred," ejaculated the old woman; "for God's sake, let us quit this dreadful place without a moment's delay. Oh. how could you be so foolish and so headstrong as to venture hither?"

"Did you not see it?" said Mildred, in a voice of terror.

"Yes, yes," answered Juditha, hastily; "but come, there is no knowing what danger may surround us while we remain here."

"Oh, was it not frightful?" continued Mildred. "And she grasped my wrist, and, in tones which I can never forget, while her eyes were fixed with such an awful expression upon me, she called me the doomed girl—doomed to continual sorrow and persecution."

"Horrible!" cried Juditha, "let us away, let us away."

It was not without the greatest difficulty that Mildred could sufficiently conquer her emotions to comply with this request; and, as they descended the hill, many were the fearful glances she cast behind her, to see whether any person was following them, and expecting to behold the hideous and unearthly form of the Weird Woman again.

But nothing more occurred to alarm them, and, in a short time, they arrived at the castle, where they found Sir Aldobrand most anxiously awaiting their return, he having despatched a domestic to the cottage, to ascertain the cause of their delay.

He sharply reprimanded Juditha for having kept her young charge out until so late an hour; and his astonishment may be easily conceived when he was made acquainted with their adventure. He was unable to form any satisfactory conjecture upon the subject; but he strictly enjoined Mildred to avoid the tower as much as possible, and, of course, she promised to obey him, though she did so very reluctantly, for, notwithstanding the danger that might accrue to her, she still felt as anxious as she had ever been to penetrate the mysteries of that ancient building; and many were the coversations which she had with Juditha and old Sampson upon the subject.

It was some time ere she recovered from the surprise and terror into which her meeting with the Weird Woman had thrown her, and the observations which that mysterious being had addressed to her were almost constantly present to her imagination.

CHAPTER IX.

THE LAPSE OF YEARS.—ETHELBERT'S RETURN TO THE CASTLE.—THE UNSANC-TIONED PASSION.

EIGHT years had elapsed since Mildred became a member of Sir Aldobrand's family and in that long period Ethelbert had not visited the castle, but continued his travels and education abroad; for Sir Aldobrand had deferred his return as long as possible, although he was so anxious to see him, actuated by a consciousness of Mildred's loveliness, whose charms he feared might make an impression upon the youthful and susceptible mind of Ethelbert, and thereby render abortive the ambitious schemes he had formed for his future establishment in life.

But Sir Aldobrand now received a letter from his son, earnestly beseeching his permission to return home, as he could no longer endure the pain of a separation from him.

This distressed Sir Aldobrand; he knew not how to refuse this reasonable and natural request, yet dreaded an interview taking place between Ethelbert and Mildred.

After mature deliberation, he fixed upon a plan, which, though strange, he was nevertheless determined to put in practice, and therefore requested our heroine and Juditha to attend him in his study—they obeyed his summons, wondering at the cause of it.

Sir Aldobrand desired Mildred to take a seat by his side.

"My dear girl," said he, "I have never had any reason to doubt your duty and affection; I am now going to make a trial of your sincerity; tell me, therefore, if you are ready to make any sacrifice for my comfort?"

"What sacrifice," replied Mildred, "is there, that I, the child of your bounty, can refuse to make, for you who have been my friend and father?"

"Well spoken, my sweet girl," said Sir Aldobrand, patting her cheek; "and by following my commands you will be still more dear to me. My son is about to return to the castle, though I do not intend that he shall remain here long; during his residence here, you will greatly oblige me by remaining in your own apartments, except at such times when Juditha may think it impossible for him to see you."

Mildred cheerfully acceded to Sir Aldobrand's request; yet could not imagine his reason for a conduct which appeared to her so eccentric; but Mildred held even his commands sacred, and she was therefore resolved to obey them.

The morning after Ethelbert's arrival at the castle, he strolled to the cottage of old Sampson. Its venerable master was not at home, but the lowly Margery greeted him with many a curtsey, and hoped he would be pleased to rest awhile in her habitation, which, though not fine, she assured him was as clean as hands could make it.

"I am glad to see you look so well, Margery," observed Ethelbert; "but pray where is your grand-daughter?" (For such Sir Aldobrand had styled Mildred, when Ethelbert first saw her.')

" Who does your honour mean ?" said Margery.

" The little girl who fell before the cottage door, when I was last at the castle; is she not your grand-child ?"

" No, and please your honour—yes, and please your honour—no——" faltered out the unguarded old woman.

" What do you mean?" interrupted the astonished Ethelbert.

" Oh, dear, dear ! if your honour tells Sir Aldobrand, or my husband, what I have said, why, to be sure I am ruined for ever. I shall never be forgiven ; and Sampson will say it all comes of my talking, that you knew Miss Mildred was not our grand-child ; though, for the matter of that, the king himself might be proud of such a lovely daughter."

" Then Mildred," said Ethelbert, smiling, " is not your grand-child ?"

" Lord, no, your honour; though, as a body might say, Sampson and I have been father and mother to her. It is now some years since Sampson found her in the old Tower of Bransdorf."

" The old Tower of Bransdorf?" repeated Ethelbert, with astonishment.

" Yes. I'll tell your honour a very strange dream which I had the night before—I dreamt——"

" I'll hear your dream another time, my good Margery ; I am impatient to hear this strange story."

Margery related all the particulars she could recollect of Mildred's discovery ; and was going to produce the clothes she had worn, when, looking out of the cottage, she saw Sampson approaching.

" As I hope to be saved," she said, " here comes my husband ; if your honour would but promise me not to tell him, or Sir Aldobrand, what I have said——"

" I do promise," replied Ethelbert; " make yourself perfectly easy."

During Ethelbert's walk to the castle, he pondered over Mildred's singular story in his mind ; the more he reflected on it, the more it appeared involved in mystery. There was something romantic and incredible in its commencement ; yet when he reflected that every life was filled with some circumstances which to strangers would appear improbable, he assented to the truth of Mildred's history, though " 'twas strange, 'twas passing strange."

At night, when Ethelbert retired to his chamber, his thoughts again recurred to Mildred. The sudden entrance of Sampson in the morning, he doubted not, had prevented Margery from informing him of her residence, though he thought it most likely she was still an inhabitant of the cottage.

It was early ; for Sir Aldobrand kept very early hours, and he resolved to amuse himself by a walk in the picture gallery.

The moon shone with peculiar radiance ; the hoary tops of the distant hills formed a contrast to the dark umbrage of the woods near the castle beautifully striking ; while a clear lake, whose lucid bosom not a breeze ruffled, reflected a broken landscape of polished art and wild uncultivated nature.

The windows of the gallery were formed in recesses. In one of those Ethelbert had thrown himself, and was contemplating the surrounding scenery, when the door opened, and a light figure glided up the gallery. He arose from his seat, and bending forward, discovered a lovely young woman, in whose features he immediately recognised Mildred.

Astonished at the discovery he had made, and agitated beyond expression, he leaned against the wall, and repressed his breath, lest it might alarm Mildred, who placed a lamp which she held in her hand so as its beams might fall on the portrait of Sir Aldobrand, which she began to copy.

Ethelbert thought he had never seen so beautiful or interesting an object. The sweet expression of her countenance, more than the loveliness of her person, attracted his admiration ; he found it difficult to conceal the emotions her presence excited, when an accident discovered him to the affrighted Mildred.

Mildred, when she turned from Sir Aldobrand's portrait, placed the candle on the floor, and was going to the window ; but the flame caught her gown, and she screamed for help. Ethelbert sprang forward with the swiftness of an arrow, and folding her clothes around her, extinguished the fire.

Pale, trembling, and confounded, Mildred could not find words to express her astonishment. Ethelbert politely solicited her pardon for so long concealing himself, and assured her he would immediately withdraw, adding, he hoped to have the pleasure of conversing with her at an hour more consistent with the delicacy which he doubted not she possessed.

There was an energetic sincerity in his manner which calmed her mind more effectually than the most laboured or complimentary language could have done. She hesitated for a few moments, and then replied—

"As the son of my benefactor, sir, I shall always acknowledge myself honoured by your expressing a wish to see me again. As the descendant of Sir Aldroband, I feel it my duty to decline the pleasure, since it is his request that I see and converse with none but Juditha and my grandfather."

As she spoke the word grandfather, her voice faltered, and a transient blush crossed her cheek. Ethelbert observed her change of countenance, and with strong emphasis repeated it—

"And is Sampson Hewley really your grandfather?"

"Alas!" said Mildred, "why do you task my sincerity thus highly? Of what consequence can it be to you, sir, whether Sampson is really my grandfather? By assuring you he is not, I justly incur the displeasure of Sir Aldobrand; but my heart revolts at a falsehood, and obliges me to declare I am attached to Sampson by no ties save those of gratitude and affection."

Ethelbert ventured to press her hand to his lips.

" I have distressed you," said he, " allow me thus to seal my pardon."

Mildred blushed, and withdrawing her hand, bade him good night, curtseyed and retired

Mildred's mind was too much agitated to admit of repose, and she passed the night in reflection. She had, though involuntarily, broken the promise she had given to Sir Aldrobrand, and the very circumstance he dreaded was come to pass. She thought Sir Aldrobrand's wish of secluding her from Ethelbert peculiarly singular, as she could not conceive his motive. It pained her to think she had undesignedly frustrated his wishes ; though she could not comprehend, she resolved to obey.

She sighed when she recollected she must be for ever deprived of Ethelbert's society, and wished Sir Aldrobrand had not permitted his return to the castle. Unaccustomed to concealment, she anxiously expected the morning, that she might communicate to Juditha the events of the preceding night ; the best advice that excellent woman had to bestow she knew would be offered her, and she was resolved through life to have no secrets with this valued friend.

Ethelbert, enchanted with the beauty of Mildred, determined, if possible, to see her frequently. Her loveliness had awakened his admiration, while her sentiments and address heightened his feelings to rapture.

That Sir Aldrobrand wished to conceal such a lovely girl from his sight was to him no source of wonder. He knew pride too well to be amazed at its effects ; but he flattered himself that Mildred was of a house, whose alliance would throw no stain on his own.

Could so much excellence, elegance, sense, and sweetness be descended from a plebeian tribe ? Reason checked the effervescence of pride, and Ethelbert could not but acknowledge that the daughter of a peasant might be endowed by nature with intellectual as well as personal perfection, and have an equal claim on our esteem and respect with the most opulent or noble.

Mildred rose earlier than usual, and sought Juditha in her chamber. To her she ingenuously related the events of the preceding night, and intreated that she would advise her how to act—whether to acquaint Sir Aldobrand with these circumstances, or to remain silent on the subject.

Juditha was charmed with her sincerity, though she lamented her having seen Ethelbert, as she trembled lest he should conceive a partiality for Mildred, which the affection she bore her, and the exalted idea she entertained of her beauty, induced her to think would undoubtedly be the case.

But this was a subject on which she kept a profound ignorance, not daring to express her sentiments, lest they should raise hopes in the bosom of her young friend highly impolitic to encourage. She therefore advised her to be cautious how she quitted her apartment.

"In your closet, Mildred," she said, " you will find amusement; your books, your music, and drawing, are never failing sources of instructive pleasure to mind like yours. I am convinced, my dear girl, that you would derive not even transient satisfaction from the conversation of Ethelbert, even if I were to allow his visits, which I certainly never shall, without Sir Aldobrand's approbation. We shall find sufficient time for exercise during their absence from the castle, which will necessarily take place sometimes : therefore, my dear Mildred, make yourself perfectly easy, and by all means avoid Ethelbert."

Mildred thanked Juditha for her sage advice, and they retired to the breakfast-room, where, having finished her repast, Juditha left her young charge for a few minutes, while she gave some necessary orders to the servants.

Convinced she was perfectly free from any intrusion, as it was a part of the castle appropriated entirely to the use of herself and Juditha, Mildred took her lute, and playing a plaintive air, accompanied it with her voice.

She had nearly finished, when Ethelbert entered the room. Thinking it was Juditha, Mildred finished her song, and rising from her seat, to her utter confusion, discovered Ethelbert. She started, and sunk on her chair.

"I am peculiarly unfortunate," said Ethelbert, " to have twice alarmed you ; but as my crimes are unintentional, I throw myself on your mercy for pardon. Permit me to inquire after your health this morning. I hope you received no injury from your last night's fright ?"

Mildred replied she was perfectly well, and arose to leave the room.

"Stay, Mildred," ejaculated Ethelbert. "Do not refuse me the first request I have ever made to you; but allow me the honour of enjoying your conversation a short time."

"I am sorry," replied Mildred, "you should be led to imagine, sir, that I will ever willingly disobey Sir Aldobrand's commands, or meanly deviate from truth. I have given my word not to permit your visits, and shall most religiously observe my promise."

"I admire your sentiments," returned Ethelbert, warmly, "and regret that I must be deprived of your society. I should ever have held my father's commands sacred; till now I never found them disagreeable, or dared to doubt their justice. But why should Sir Aldobrand exclude me from your conversation? What just reason can he have for immuring you from me?"

"I know not," replied Mildred, while a tear glistened in her eye, "unless it be the uncertainty of my birth. The child of charity and doubt is but a poor associate for the son of Sir Aldobrand de Lancy."

"Idle prejudice!" exclaimed Ethelbert—"ridiculous pride! Would to God your parents could be discovered."

At this moment Juditha entered the room, and surveying him with an air of anger, said,

"Ethelbert, your conduct gives me infinite pain. I thought Mildred had acquainted you with your father's request."

"And so she has, my good Juditha. I think it amazingly singular my father should exact such a promise."

"Not at all, sir," replied Juditha; "Sir Aldobrand's reasons are no doubt very just."

"I cannot conceive them in that light," said Ethelbert; "but he has given me no orders respecting this lady. I shall certainly take every opportunity of seeing her."

"Then you will oblige me to acquaint Sir Aldobrand with your determination; and I have no doubt he will effectually prevent you from putting your plan into execution."

"My good Juditha," remarked Ethelbert, "you know the warmth of my disposition; and whatever my sentiments of my father's conduct are, I respect you and your charming young friend for your attentive observance of his commands."

Ethelbert arose from his chair, and bidding Mildred and Juditha a good morning, left them to reflect on his behaviour.

Mildred immediately retired to her chamber. The late events led her into unpleasant reflections; they had touched on that string on which hung all her sorrows—the mystery which attended her fate. Till now she never felt the pangs of dependence, or the seclusion which she was obliged to live in. The new ideas which Ethelbert's conversation had infused into her mind withdrew the veil which Sir Aldobrand's former indulgence and parental tenderness had concealed from her heart, and made her feelingly alive to the sense of obligation and to the unpleasantness of her situation.

Though Ethelbert's sentiments were different from those which oppressed Mildred, yet they were not void of anxiety and suspense. He could not divert his mind from dwelling on her perfections, or prevent innumerable and disagreeable thoughts from harassing his peace.

Sir Aldobrand observed the unusual gloom of his spirts, and endeavoured to disperse it by relating some family anecdotes.

"And have you never been able to gain any clue to the fate of my uncle, Sir Martin, or his lady?" asked Ethelbert.

"Alas! no," answered Aldobrand; "and it seems as if it would be for ever buried in oblivion."

"And think you that Sir Martin married imprudently, sir?"

"Yes; because it was contrary to the wish of his father."

"But the lady Editha was worthy, was she not?"

"She was most amiable."

"Then what objection could my grandfather have to her as a daughter?"

"A family feud; but above all he considered that her family was not distinguished enough to be allied to ours."

"I should suppose, sir, that can be of very little consequence in the choice of a wife."

"Such were your uncle's sentiments. His fate, I hope, will prevent you from pursuing a similar conduct. Young men, under pretence of being liberal-minded, imagine themselves wiser than their fathers, and thoughtlessly form connections which their ripe judgments disapprove,"

Ethelbert was perfectly well acquainted with his father's sentiments respecting the engagements which he considered as improper to be formed. He knew that by marrying into a mean, or what is usually called a creditable family, his father's eternal displeasure would be incurred; yet, notwithstanding these assurances, she unfortunately became attached to a young lady who had nothing to boast of save her beauty and virtue.

Ethelbert saw that the recollection of his brother's misfortunes, and the mystery in which his fate was enshrouded, had affected Sir Aldobrand, and therefore proposed an airing, which invigorated their spirits, and Ethelbert returned to the castle to form new schemes for seeing Mildred.

CHAPTER X.

THE CONFESSION OF LOVE.—THE RIVAL.

WEEKS rolled on without Ethelbert having an opportunity of speaking to Mildred, so assiduously did she endeavour to avoid him. When she walked out it was at a time when she knew him to be abroad, and then in company with Juditha.

Ethelbert sometimes gained a transient view of her from her chamber window, and almost tortured Juditha with his ceaseless inquiries respecting her health, who represented to him the folly of his conduct, and requested (knowing the impossibility there was of his ever having any intimacy with Mildred) that he would endeavour to forget that there was such a being.

"Never!" he exclaimed. "The very means which my father has taken to prevent my knowledge of Mildred, and my wish to cultivate her acquaintance, has produced the opposite effect. Had he permitted her to remain in your apartment, and enjoy her wonted liberty, I should have been unacquainted with the refinement of her mind, and only have regarded her as a lovely girl; but now I am all anxiety—I am perfectly enchanted with her, and am resolved, let whatever consequences ensue, to see and converse with her previous to my departure for London, as Sir Aldobrand seems determined that I shall not remain at the castle."

"You are determined, then, to act in direct opposition to your father's will!" said Juditha.

"Juditha, I am unhappy, and wish to make myself otherwise."

"There was a time, sir, when you would not have triumphed in such open rebellion to your father's will."

"Nor do I now. Perhaps I ought not to acknowledge my father's defect of mind, yet I cannot be insensible how much he is prejudiced in favour of high blood and sounding titles, which are surely light and trifling in comparison with a man's happiness; and I seriously assure you, Juditha, no power on earth shall induce me to marry a woman I am not tenderly attached to."

Juditha scarcely knew in what manner to act; Mildred's spirits were depressed; her health began to suffer from unusual confinement, and she trembled lest it should endanger her life. In the evening, when she imagined Ethelbert was engaged with company, she attended Mildred on a walk.

It so happened that Ethelbert, from his chamber window, saw them enter a grove which led to the hermitage.

Resolving to profit by this opportunity, he immediately followed their steps, and arrived at the hermitage soon after they had entered it. He heard Mildred pronounce his name, and the word rivetted him to the spot, and quite entranced his senses.

"That you are of a genteel family, my love," he heard Juditha say, in answer to her fair companion, "I feel assured, and agree with Ethelbert, that while you remain as amiable as now, you will be an ornament to it. The few superficial accomplishments you have attained are of little value when put in competition with sweetness of temper, liberality of sentiment, and virtue. These, I trust, Mildred, will ever adorn your mind, and be the standard of your actions; these, whether you derived your origin from the illustrious or the obscure, will alone ennoble you."

Ethelbert had listened with intense application, while Juditha was speaking, hoping to discover Mildred's sentiments; but disappointed at his ill-success, and tortured with contending passions, he knew not how to proceed.

Mildred was dear to him, and there were moments when he would have sacrificed all the future prospects of his life to obtain her ; but when cool reason came to his aid, the idea of wounding the peace of his kind and generous father made him resolve not to marry without his consent. Piercing the veil of possibility, he looked forward with rapture to the hour when Sir Aldobrand, having either discovered her family, or no longer the victim of prejudice, would give his consent to their union. Cheered with this thought, he entered the hermitage.

Mildred shrieked ; Juditha looked displeased, and arose to retire ; but he entreated her so earnestly to hear him, that she resumed her seat.

For some moments they were so embarrassed, that they remained silent, till Juditha again rose to retire, and Ethelbert once more requested her to stay.

"For what reason," said Juditha, " do you detain me, sir ? Why are you here contrary to the command of Sir Aldobrand ?"

"Forgive me, Juditha," replied Ethelbert; "and permit me ingeniously to declare my reasons for acting thus. My sweet friend," he continued, taking Mildred's hand, "you are the innocent cause of my disobedience; I love you, tenderly love you, with an ardour which time will increase ; for I am certain that neither absence or change of scene will eradicate my affection."

" Hold, sir," interrupted Juditha, " and no longer insult a lovely and innocent girl, worthy of every one's esteem."

" By Heaven, I would not insult her for the worth of worlds," cried the impassioned youth ; " that I love her I again repeat, but never will lead her to the altar without Sir Aldobrand's consent. While he lives—and God grant him a long and happy life—it shall be my pride and study to oblige him ; a different conduct would render me unworthy the friendship of Mildred, or the favour of Heaven."

There was a solemnity in the voice of Ethelbert that could not fail of affecting his hearers.

" But what says my Mildred ? Will she pardon my presumption ? Will she return my affection ?"

" I will esteem," replied Mildred; " I will remember you as a friend ;" and rising hastily from her seat, and taking Juditha's arm, she quitted the hermitage.

Juditha, to restore the repose of her young friend, endeavoured, with that persuasive eloquence genuine friendship can alone inspire, to divest Mildred of any confidence she might repose in Ethelbert's professions of love. Not that she doubted his sincerity, but she knew him to possess violent passions, and concluded, whatever might be his present sentiments towards her, absence would most likely banish them from his remembrance, and he might then turn his thoughts on some object who would meet the approbation of Sir Aldobrand.

With these reflections, Juditha ingeniously acquainted Mildred, who assented to the justness of her remarks, yet appeared much agitated, sighed frequently, and warmly expressed a wish that her family could be discovered. In this Juditha sincerely joined, at the same time pointing out the necessity as well as duty of conquering that excess of sensibility Mildred often expressed.

" I would not wish you to be unfeeling, my dear child," she remarked ; " but surely you ought to arm your mind against a day when I may no longer be here to instruct you. Assume a fortitude on this occasion; let reason triumph over inclination ; do not, by returning ingratitude for tenderness and benevolence, wound the soul's peace of him who for so many years has been a friend and a father to you."

" Dear, dear Juditha," exclaimed Mildred, throwing her arms around her neck; " how can you for a moment imagine I would be ungrateful to my kind, my generous benefactor. No ; rather should this stubborn heart be humbled to the last state humility knows, than, by aspiring to Ethelbert's love, plunge a dagger in the bosom of my valued protector."

Juditha pressed her fondly to her bosom, bade her always preserve such sentiments, and wiping the traces of sorrow from her countenance, had soon the pleasure of seeing it adorned with smiles.

Ethelbert was now soon to leave the castle ; Mildred therefore resolved not to leave her apartment, even when she knew he was from home ; as the day of emancipation was so near at hand, she wished not to see him, fearful that she might forget the obligations that she owed Sir Aldobrand, and become equally attached to Ethelbert as he was to her.

The evening before his departure to London, distracted at not being able to see

Mildred, yet resolved to leave no means untried which might accelerate his wishes, he stationed himself under her chamber window, and pensively traversed the turfy path.

Agitated with jarring passions, he formed innumerable schemes, but quickly relinquished them to form others equally ridiculous and impracticable, till hearing a casement open, he looked up and discovered Mildred.

The night was beautifully serene; the wild picturesque scenery around the castle was softened and refined by the moon's silvery beam, which gave inexpressible lustre to the snow-clad summits of the hills, and discovered here and there a half-seen shepherd's hut among the cliffs, the distant steeple of a village church, and the whitened cottages which sprinkled Sir Aldobrand's estate, and seemed emblematic of their inhabitants—content and labour.

Mildred had for some moments enjoyed the beauty of the scene before she discovered Ethelbert, who leant against the trunk of a tree nearly opposite her window, silently gazing at her. She no sooner perceived him than she drew back, and would have closed the casement, but he entreated her so earnestly to allow him a few moments' conversation, that, notwithstanding she conceived it wrong, she bent forward, and in a tremulous voice said—

"Alas! Ethelbert, why do you wish me to pursue a conduct so disconsonant with delicacy? Consider to what censures you render me liable."

"Who shall dare to stigmatise your character?" said Ethelbert, warmly.

"Many," replied Mildred, "if they were to discover me in conversation with you at midnight."

"Oh, Mildred," said Ethelbert, "in spite of reason and duty, I cannot avoid loving you; in vain do I struggle to conquer my partiality; each day increases my affection, and I am determined you shall no longer remain in obscurity. I will implore Sir Aldobrand to sanction my love; I will implore him to receive you as a daughter. What if your family is unknown, your virtues would add lustre to a diadem."

"Seek not your father's displeasure," answered Mildred, "by making such imprudent requests; and know, sir, that I have a soul that scorns ingratitude; whether I derived my origin from a lowly peasant, or illustrious lord, I will ever study true nobility—that of the mind."

"Noble-minded girl," exclaimed Ethelbert, "how does your every sentiment charm me! My father will not long remain blinded by early prejudice; permit me then to hope that you will sometimes think with tenderness of Ethelbert De Lancy."

"I will think on and esteem you as the son of my benefactor. Adieu!—good night!"

She closed the window and retired to her pillow, while Ethelbert sought his apartment, if possible, more than ever charmed with the gentle and amiable Mildred; and the next morning he departed from the castle.

Things now began to wear their wonted appearance; again Mildred amused Sir Aldobrand with her conversation, and daily took her customary walks, and visited her friends at the cottage.

She had lost much of her lively spirits, and looked paler than usual; but this Sir Aldobrand attributed to confinement, and flattered himself exercise would recover her health: he loved her with the tenderness of a parent, and had he been certain that her origin was respectable, and that her parents were worthy, he would have looked forward to a union with her and Ethelbert with delight; but when he considered she might be the offspring of infamy, he felt his honour would be contaminated; and notwithstanding Mildred's beauty, goodness, and sweetness of temper, he resolved that Ethelbert should never marry her, unless her family should be discovered to be noble.

Juditha possessed a soul superior to disguise; she had acquainted Sir Aldobrand with the different conversations that had passed between Ethelbert and Mildred. Sir Aldobrand felt grateful to Juditha, charmed with Mildred, and not displeased with his son; as he was not surprised at the effect her charms wrought on his mind, yet sincerely hoped he would conquer his love, and learn to think of Mildred as a friend and sister.

Mildred, though she experienced every tender attention from Sir Aldobrand, could not feel herself so perfectly at ease as before Ethelbert's visit to the castle; his love had awakened her to a sense of her dependent state. When she thought of him it was with indescribable emotion, and for his sake she hoped, if ever her connexions were discovered, they might be noble.

Sir Aldobrand often expressed anxiety at her pallid countenance and dejected mind, in return, she strove, by every tender solicitude and winning action, to show she was sensible of his kindness. Often when the big tear would start in her eye, she would wipe it off with her handkerchief, and, in spite of her feelings, smile and look gay.

When Ethelbert's letters arrived at the castle, Sir Aldobrand could not avoid reading some parts to her; their easy diction delighted the father; the pleasure was doubled by communication, for poor Mildred, unconscious that Sir Aldobrand was acquainted with his son's attachment to her, artlessly amused herself, and charmed her benefactor with her judicious and elegant remarks. At such times he never failed to wish she had been the daughter of a nobleman.

To her worthy friend, Juditha, Mildred imparted those feelings she endeavoured to stifle in the presence of Sir Aldobrand, and that excellent and sensible woman left no argument untried to convince her how wrong she was to let melancholy usurp reason. She pointed out the comfort of her present situation, and reminded her that while she acknowledged her gratitude to her earthly benefactor, not to be unmindful of that Being, the first great cause of all.

Mildred was too good not to acknowledge the justness of these arguments, and had too much reason not to profit by them; in a few weeks she regained her wonted sprightliness, and peace again dawned upon her bosom.

Mildred's visits at the cottage were frequent, and, during a severe illness which had nearly proved fatal to Margery, she gave a convincing proof of the gratitude and affection she felt for her worthy friends; all the hours she could pass from Sir Aldobrand were spent in attending the good old woman. She thought it no degradation to render her the most menial services. In the sick chamber of Margery she learned a useful lesson—patience. She contemplated with admiration the mildness and humility with which Margery bore the most excruciating pain, and the submissive resignation with which the venerable Sampson beheld the partner of his heart labouring for life, which each moment seemed to be departing.

"And shall I," Mildred would sometimes exclaim to Juditha, "shall I, who enjoy such numerous blessings, weakly repine because all is not as I would wish? I blush at my own puerile mind, and am determined to copy the bright example of my lowly friends."

Margery recovered from her indisposition, and Mildred beheld with delight her restoration to health. *   *   *   *   *   *

Sir Aldobrand each day became more attached to Mildred; she was scarcely ever absent from him, and displayed every accomplishment she was mistress of to please her benefactor: he never felt happier than when she was with him; her presence seemed necesary to his existence.

But, in spite of all their efforts, nothing could banish the form of Ethelbert from her memory. It was in vain that Juditha exerted all her influence to banish the impression from her mind, for she said that it must be productive of much misery and trouble to both her and Ethelbert, for she was certain that Sir Aldobrand's pride would never suffer him to consent to their union, in spite of the distinguished virtues which Mildred possessed, unless it should be discovered that her birth was noble.

That Mildred tenderly loved Ethelbert was a truth, yet she had scarcely dared to whisper this truth to her own heart, fearful that, by encouraging a passion unsanctioned by parental authority, she might plunge into error fatal to her peace, her duty, and reason; but in vain she sought to check her innocent wishes, and many were the hours of anguish which the struggle with her feelings cost her; and deeply did she lament the mystery in which her origin was enshrouded, and which, until it was removed, must prove the only barrier to her uninterrupted happiness.

But a circumstance was about to take place which was destined to destroy the comparative tranquillity she now enjoyed.

Mildred was one afternoon seated with her benefactor in his study, engaged in conversation with him, when the loud ringing of the bell at the castle gate gave notice of the arrival of visitors, and immediately afterwards a domestic entered, and announced the Earl of Bohun, and his son, Lord Ruthlyn de Bohun.

Sir Aldobrand started from his seat, and with all the warmth of hospitality, for which he was so highly distinguished, welcomed the two noblemen to the castle.

Mildred, on beholding them, blushed, curtseyed, and was retiring, when the earl, eyeing her very attentively, requested Sir Aldobrand to introduce him, and his son made the same request.

Sir Aldobrand first presented her to the earl, then to Lord Ruthlyn, saying that he wished it had been in his power to introduce her by another name as well as Mildred; he would have added more, but that he beheld the humid drops of feeling sparkle on her cheeks, and pressing her tenderly by the hand, he permitted her to retire.

"What a lovely girl!" exclaimed Lord Ruthlyn, as she closed the door; "she looks like a glowing rose, surcharged and bending with the dew of Heaven."

Lord Ruthlyn was a young nobleman who had been bred in the great world, and with its polished manners, polished even in those early days of civilization, he had acquired many of its pernicious maxims, follies, and vices. The character of a libertine was at that time fashionable, and Lord Ruthlyn thought it impossible to avoid the beaten track of that fanciful goddess.

He had sometimes serious moments; but if any of his gay companions discovered him at these times, they were sure to stifle reflection with their noisy folly and satirical raillery.

Mildred, who was an enthusiastic lover of nature, delighted early in a morning to stray round the romantic parts of the castle, and not unfrequently her walks, accompanied by Juditha, were lengthened to the gloomy old tower of Bransdorf, which, notwithstanding all the circumstances connected with it, still maintained the greatest interest in her bosom; nor was her curiosity to explore its ancient chambers the least abated.

The morning after the arrival of the visitors, she had strayed unusually far, and feeling fatigued, she seated herself on a little eminence, from whence she had a view of that portion of the tower in which Sampson had often told her she had been found.

She sat revolving this strange event in her mind, and was completely abstracted from every other subject, when she was suddenly aroused by hearing footsteps near her, and looking up, to her confusion beheld Lord Ruthlyn standing before her.

Lord Ruthlyn, with a boldness that shocked the timid Mildred, inquired the subject of her contemplation. She made some slight reply, and arose from her seat to return to the castle; but his lordship impudently detained her, at the same time uttering a profusion of disgusting compliments, such as Mildred equally despised and was unaccustomed to.

But Lord Ruthlyn, in his vanity imagining that her taciturnity proceeded from delight at hearing her praises resounded by so great a nobleman as himself, attempted to kiss her hand; but Mildred haughtily drew it from him, and, casting on him a look of chilling superiority, asked him what in her conduct warranted such liberties.

"By the mass! fair damsel," he replied, "I intended no insult; to be insensible to your loveliness, I must be deprived of my sight."

"I am so unused to receive compliments," said the beauteous Mildred, "that I have never learned to answer or admire them."

Thus saying, she turned round and discovered Ethelbert.

Yes; Ethelbert had arrived at the castle the evening before, unknown to our heroine, and much to the displeasure of his father, whom he had not apprised of his intention, well knowing that he would most positively and peremptorily have opposed his wishes.

Surprise took from Mildred the power of utterance. Ethelbert pressed her hand. He had overheard the recent conversation, and he eyed Lord Ruthlyn with a cool and penetrating look.

"By the saints, Ethelbert," said the young libertine, "you are very polite. Have a few days made such a wonderful alteration in my features and person, that you do not recollect me?"

"I have not forgotten you, my lord," answered Ethelbert; "but it seems that you have forgotten this lady, independent of her own merits, which claim respect from all who know her, is under the protection of Sir Aldobrand de Lancy."

Lord Ruthlyn bit his lips, and could scarcely help frowning.

"I have not designedly affronted the lady," he returned; "but if through inadvertency I have offended, I now solicit her pardon, and yours too, Ethelbert."

So saying, he bowed significantly, and bade them adieu.

Mildred was astonished at beholding Ethelbert; her presence of mind forsook her, and scarcely knowing what she did, she was again seating herself.

The enraptured Ethelbert acknowledged that he had left the castle ere the morning dawned, hoping, as he knew she was an early riser, to have the happiness of seeing her before the family was moving.

He then in the most eloquent terms renewed his professions of love. Mildred's heart palpitated; warmly it beat in unison with his own; but she felt it wrong to listen to the

avowal of his hopeless passion, and therefore requested him immediately to return to the castle.

"But whither are you going, Mildred?" he eagerly inquired

"I shall breakfast at the cottage," replied Mildred.

"And will you not permit me to attend you?" rejoined Ethelbert.

"Have you forgotten Sir Aldobrand's commands when you were last at the castle?" demanded Mildred, in a gentle and melancholy voice.

Ethelbert sighed, pressed her hand, and hurried on. But several times he looked back and watched her progress with a heavy heart, and deeply lamented the fate that interposed between him and happiness.

CHAPTER XI.

THE WARNING.—THE INTERRUPTION.—A FATHER'S WRATH.

WITH a sad heart, Mildred bent her steps towards the cottage of her humble friends. The pleasure of again beholding Ethelbert was interrupted by the knowledge of the utter hopelessness of encouraging his sentiments, and the fear that Ethelbert would incur his father's displeasure by returning to the castle without his consent, and the restraint under which she would in all probability be placed.

"Dark clouds are impending o'er the head of the child of fate; the curse of Almira is working, and woe to all who come within its baneful influence. Child of the black-doomed Tower of Bransdorf, beware!"

Such were the fearful words which suddenly smote the ears of the terrified and astonished Mildred, and she beheld the fierce eyes of the weird woman (who had on a former occasion so greatly alarmed her) glaring full upon her.

The damsel was so taken by surprise at this awful and unexpected appearance, and the threatening import of the words she had uttered, that a cold shudder ran through her veins, and it was with difficulty she could save herself from sinking to the earth; but the frightful being grasped her with her shrivelled, bony hand, and seemed determined that she should not move from the spot until she had heard all that she had to say to her.

"Mark me, offspring of crime," continued the hag, and the expression of her countenance became, if possible, still more hideous than before, "thou mayest indulge in blissful hopes and ambitious desires, but evil destiny has marked thee for its own, and bitter will be the cup of sorrow thou wilt have to drain to the very dregs. Again I warn thee that the clouds are gathering which will overwhelm thee in misery, and from which no earthly power can save thee. Beware! and remember the blood-stained chamber of the Black Tower of Bransdorf!"

"Awful being!" faltered out Mildred, still trembling in the grasp of the hag, and looking eagerly around, in the hope of beholding some one near, "who art thou; and why dost thou thus appear to me, and obstruct me in my path? Oh, release me!"

"I seek not to injure thee," said the singular being; "but I came to warn thee of the danger which is in store for thee. Remember my words, and rest assured that they will be fulfilled."

"And why do you seek to alarm me by your fearful predictions?" demanded Mildred

"We shall often meet again," replied the woman, "and then thou wilt find that I have spoken the truth. In the old tower, to penetrate the mysteries of which thou hast so great a desire, we shall meet again."

Thus saying, the hag released her hold of Mildred, waved her hand menacingly towards her, and then turning round, she hurried, with inconceivable speed, towards the lofty hill on which the Tower of Bransdorf stood, and Mildred beheld her gaunt form ascending it, until the clouds which hung upon its summit hid her from her view.

For several moments the astonished and terrified Mildred was transfixed to the spot, and a variety of agonizing and bewildering thoughts crowded upon her brain, and filled her with confusion and dismay.

The words of the extraordinary and hideous being still seemed to ring in her ears, and tortured her with their intensity of import and their ambiguity.

"Good God!" she ejaculated, "for what am I reserved? What have I done that Providence should destine me to the fate which this mysterious woman has predicted? My brain turns giddy with the variety of distracting thoughts which rush upon it. Oh! all-merciful Father, reveal to me, I beseech Thee, the dark secret of my origin, that I may at once know myself and be prepared to encounter with fortitude and resignation, the troubles which are probably in store for me. And she called me offspring of crime!" she added, after a pause. "Alas! alas! is, then, my origin surrounded by shame! If so, my fate is indeed dark and dreary, and better would it have been for me had I never been born."

So great was the poor girl's emotion, that she was compelled to lean against the trunk of a tree to support her trembling limbs, and it was several minutes ere she could arouse herself sufficiently to decide in what manner to act—whether to return to the castle, or proceed to the cottage; but being in too great a state of agitation to meet Sir Aldobrand especially displeased as she knew he would be at the return of Ethelbert, she at last resolved upon the latter, and therefore slowly bent her way in the direction of the humble dwelling of Sampson Hewley, still deeply ruminating upon the strange and alarming adventure which had just befallen her.

The presence of Mildred always gladdened the worthy cottagers ; they welcomed her with fond endearments, and she returned them with almost filial tenderness.

But they noticed with deep concern the paleness of her looks, and the violent agitation of her manner ; and being convinced that something serious had happened to alarm her in such a manner, they eagerly inquired what it was.

Mildred, as well as she could, related to them all the particulars of her meeting with the hag, and they listened to her with no small share of amazement and consternation.

"It must be the same frightful being that I and Hugo beheld on the never-to-be-forgotten night that we found you in the tower, Mildred," said Sampson. "There is a strange mystery about this, which I cannot fathom. The wild predictions of this singular being are very alarming ; and yet, after all, she may only be an impostor, or some person who takes a mad delight in the misery of others. However, Mildred, let this adventure be a warning to you to avoid the tower of Bransdorf as much as possible, lest any danger should threaten you from there."

"I am lost in perplexity," said our heroine. "Still, however, I cannot resist the powerful curiosity I feel to penetrate into the hidden mysteries of that ancient building."

"The saints preserve us!" exclaimed old Margery ; "surely, my dear young lady, you can never think of venturing into that horrible place, which certainly can only be inhabited by robbers, ghosts, or devils ; or else why the dreadful noises which for years have been nightly heard to issue from it by all who have dared to approach it. I sincerely wish his honour, Sir Aldobrand, would have it pulled down, for of what utility can it be to keep such an ugly old building, unless it be to scare people out of their seven senses ?"

In spite of the anxiety of her mind, and the heavy gloom which depressed her spirits, Mildred could scarcely help smiling at the observations of the old woman.

"And probably," she said, with a sigh, "I have the greatest cause to regret that any one had ever the courage to enter the tower ; for then the worthy Sampson would not have found me, and I should not have lived to experience the troubles which I fear are now in store for me."

"Oh, do not say so, Mildred," ejaculated the old man, "it would have been a dreadful thing to have left a poor innocent child to have perished in such a manner ; and surely it was Providence that directed my footsteps to the place."

"Alas!" cried Mildred, "what can have been the fate of my unfortunate parents ? Are they still living ? And if they are, ought I not probably to dread to know them. For this singular being, whom I met this morning, told me that I was the offspring of crime."

"Oh, it cannot be, Mildred," replied Sampson ; "do not let such an idea torture your mind ; and, depend upon it, that the time will come when the mystery will be explained, and that to your satisfaction."

Mildred shook her head doubtfully, and they all remained silent for a few minutes. Mildred, however, at length felt herself somewhat consoled by the arguments of her amiable friends, and, not feeling herself in a condition to meet Sir Aldobrand at present, and also anxious to avoid Ethelbert until after he had an interview with his father, she yielded to their solicitations, and resolved to remain where she was.

A peasant was despatched with a billet to Juditha, that she might not be alarmed at her absence, and another to Sir Aldobrand, for his permission to spend the day at the cottage.

This last was delivered to Sir Aldobrand during breakfast. He retired to a window to peruse it ; and, after the repast was ended, wrote Mildred a few lines, fraught with affection, and despatched it by the messenger, whom Ethelbert contrived to overtake, and inquired of him where he was going. On hearing, he again returned to the castle, pondering a thousand reasons for this epistolary correspondence between his father and Mildred.

Sir Aldobrand felt greatly exasperated at his son's return to the castle without his permission, and severely reprimanded him for it, telling him that if Mildred was the fair object that had attracted him, he would be disappointed, for he was determined to renew his former orders, and to prevent, by that means, Mildred and him from meeting.

Ethelbert in vain remonstrated with Sir Aldobrand on the cruelty of this harsh decree, pointed out to him the gratitude and discretion of Mildred, and the irreparable injury her health, already delicate, might receive from such restraint and confinement. His father remained inexorable, and they parted on less friendly terms than had ever before existed between them.

The beauty of Mildred had made the strongest impression upon the mind of Lord Ruthlyn, and he was unable to banish her from his thoughts; he already entertained a feeling of jealousy towards Ethelbert, and after he had separated from him and Mildred in the morning, he gave vent to his rage in no very measured terms, as he retraced his steps to the castle, and fully resolved to leave no means untried to supplant him in the favour of Mildred.

It was a source of gratification to him, that the well-known pride of Sir Aldobrand de Lancy would, he was certain, be an insupportable obstacle to the encouragement of their passion, and that led him to hope that success would ultimately crown his designs.

In the evening, Sampson accompanied Mildred on her return home to the castle, and she immediately sought the chamber of Juditha, to whom she related the events of the morning.

She had scarcely concluded, when they were joined by Sir Aldobrand, who, remarking the paleness of her countenance, and the agitation of her manner, anxiously inquired the cause. His astonishment, on being made acquainted with what had happened to Mildred, may be easily imagined. He remained for some moments involved in perplexity, in reflecting upon it.

"It is most remarkable," he said. "But, my dear Mildred, do not suffer it to alarm you; for, after all, you may have nothing to apprehend. This must be examined into, and, at an early opportunity, I will make another strict search in the old tower, and endeavour to unravel the strange mystery connected with it."

After some more conversation upon this subject, Sir Aldobrand, as gently and as tenderly as he could, expressed to Mildred the uneasiness which the return of Ethelbert to the castle had caused him, and again requested that she would submit to the same line of conduct as on a former occasion, and, by all means to avoid the presence of his son.

Mildred felt hurt to think that her benefactor should apparently place so little reliance in her discretion; but she concealed her feelings as much as possible, and promised obedience; and Sir Aldobrand having embraced her, left her and Juditha to themselves.

Mildred, overpowered by the events of the day, in vain sought for sleep to relieve her spirits; but such was the situation of her thoughts, that she courted the kind power without success.

No sooner would a light slumber—the announcer of sleep—rest on her eyelids, than the uncertainty of her origin, and her parents' fate, would arouse her from repose, while imagination would present them in all manner of shapes—either as votaries of crime or misfortune, wandering cheerless and unheeded through foreign regions; or, with her "mind's eye," she beheld an unhallowed grave receive the cold remains of the authors of her being. Then, starting from these terrific visions, her senses were mocked by yet more dreadful ones; the blood-stained chamber in the old tower; the dark, unwholesome dungeons, the wretched straw bed, and the iron fetters, were presented in dreadful array. Then would the "iron enter her soul," and tears of heart-rending anguish rush from her eyes.

Again the image of Ethelbert would arise to her perturbed imagination. She beheld him pale, care-worn, emaciated; and saw his father standing over him with wrathful countenance, and heard him invoke a terrible curse upon his head.

Racked with these vagaries of the brain, it was morning ere she sunk to repose—a repose that calmed her spirits, and restored her health; and when she she awoke at noon, it was with a placidity of mind,

"Sweet as the slumbers of a saint forgiven."

Reason again re-assumed her empire, and religion, the surest soother of the afflicted, directed her thoughts to the universal Father, whose ways, however obscure and intricate to weak, presumptuous man, are founded on the eternal rock of immaculate wisdom.

To this all-merciful Being, then, she addressed her orisons—to Him she poured out the heartless language of her soul, and resigning her will to His, repaired to her generous benefactor, who had appointed to meet her in his study, so that they might not be interrupted by the intrusion of Ethelbert, with a heart glowing with gratitude, resignation, and affection, and a countenance dimpled with a thousand nameless emotions.

In vain did Ethelbert endeavour to move his father from his stern determination, and court the indulgence of Mildred's society. Sir Aldobrand would not listen to him with any degree of patience, and commanded him, on pain of his eternal displeasure, to banish all thoughts of Mildred, but as a friend, from his bosom. It was indeed an arduous task, and Ethelbert felt that it would be totally useless for him to attempt to accomplish it, and bitterly, though secretly, did he reproach his father for an act of cruelty which he had hitherto thought him incapable of.

Mildred kept herself strictly confined to her own apartments, except when Ethelbert was away from home; and then she would continue her unremitting attentions to Sir Aldobrand. At other times, when Ethelbert was engaged with his father, she would take the opportunity, accompanied by Juditha, of visiting Sampson and his wife, towards whom she felt the most lively and almost filial attachment. But could she banish Ethelbert from her thoughts? Oh, no. Sincerely she felt for the anguish she knew he was enduring, and she could not help encouraging a latent hope that the time would arrive when they might be permitted to give encouragement to their passion, without any feelings of doubt or hesitation on the part of Sir Aldobrand.

The seclusion of Mildred was a source of great annoyance to Lord Ruthlyn, and after the lapse of a few days, he and his father left the castle, the former, however, fully determined not to abandon his designs against Mildred, and to endeavour to concoct some means to put them into effect.

In spite of all her efforts to the contrary, however, Mildred at times experienced a depression of spirits that was almost insupportable, and from which the good Editha tried in vain to arouse her.

One evening, Ethelbert having, as she understood, accompanied his father from the castle on a visit to a neighbouring nobleman, Mildred, unusually pensive and restless, repaired to the library.

The sun had sunk to the ocean; the golden streaks which tinged the western horizon were quickly yielding to the pale and sober grey of twilight, while a blue vapour gradually encircled the tops of the majestic hills.

Mildred flung herself into one of the gothic windows which admitted a distant view of the old church, its whitened steeple emerging amidst the stately elms that nearly surrounded it. Mildred listened with a mild and not unpleasing melancholy to the merry bells, which now broke the stillness of even, and again the notes, wafted by the varying wind to another point, were lost in the distance.

Melancholy thoughts crowded upon her fancy, in which the gloomy mystery in which her origin was enshrouded held a prominent share; and when she reflected upon her dependent situation and the cheerless prospect before her, she covered her face with her handkerchief and burst into tears.

Her mind, relieved by weeping, soon resumed its wonted composure.

It was now nearly dark, and she arose to leave the library, when she observed a figure advancing towards her. Fear for a moment took possession of her mind, and in a hurried voice she demanded who was there.

No answer was returned; but there was a low, muttering sound, and Mildred, looking timidly in the direction where she had seen the figure, no longer beheld it.

It was strange, thought Mildred, and surely she could not have suffered her imagination to mislead her so far. A feeling of awe crept over her, and she would have been glad to leave the library, and to seek her own apartment, but she found herself incapable of moving.

She still thought she heard a rustling sound at the farther end of the library, as if some person was endeavouring to make a hasty retreat, and once more she gathered courage sufficient to demand who was there.

Still no answer. The patience of our heroine began to be exhausted.

" I have suffered my gloomy thoughts to gain such an ascendancy over my senses, that I easily become the victim of fearful delusions. I will go to Juditha."

She moved towards the door as she spoke; but still, with a slow and hesitating step. At that moment, the silvery light of the moon, which had just emerged from behind a cloud, streamed into the apartment, and for an instant startled her, as her eye caught the long shadows which its beams cast upon the polished oak floor; but chiding herself for her weakness, she again proceeded, and issued from the library.

Here she once more timidly looked around her, and her thoughts again reverted to the figure that she was almost positive she had seen. In spite of all her efforts to subdue it, a feeling of dread still beset her mind, and she walked timidly on, the sound of her own footsteps almost startling her with alarm.

In the way to her own chamber it was necessary for her to cross the picture gallery, a place which she so often visited, and in which she had lately, in particular, passed so many hours of contemplation.

A solemn silence reigned within it, and the moonbeams played upon the features of the different portraits, giving them almost the appearance of life and reality.

She paused before the portrait of Sir Martin de Lancy, on which she had so often gazed before ; and now that she did so, a more than usual feeling of awe stole over her senses, and she could have knelt in reverence to the inanimate canvas.

What could be the meaning of her emotions ? She could not divine them ; but she was completely rivetted to the spot, nor could she for an instant remove her eyes from the portrait.

The eyes seemed fixed upon her ; and once, so great was the illusion, that she could almost imagine that it smiled upon her, and that the lips moved, as if it was about to address her.

Still she continued to gaze upon it, until such was the power that a bewildered imagination had upon her senses that to her fancy the expression of the features of the portrait changed ; a dark frown seemed to lour upon the brow, and the eyes appeared to scowl upon her with such a fearful look, that she covered her face with her hands, and could with difficulty repress a scream.

She was aroused from the lethargy that had involuntarily stolen over her, by hearing a deep sigh, which was so distinct, that she was quite positive she could not have been mistaken.

She started, and looked up ; but the moon was now again obscured, and she could observe nothing but the dark shadows of the different portraits which surrounded her in their heavily carved frames. A cold shivering came over her, and she feared to move.

The moon emerged from behind the cloud which had temporarily hidden her face, and cast its beams full along the gallery ; but no object met her view, although she was certain that she had not been deceived in hearing the sigh which had but a few minutes before smote her ears. She was confident it was not the wind, for a dead calm prevailed over nature, and not a breath disturbed the stillness around.

Again the eyes of Mildred were attracted to the portrait of Sir Martin de Lancy, and once more the features seemed to smile benignantly upon her, while the lips seemed actually about to move, as if to invoke a blessing upon her head.

But what was there in his particular portrait, which should and always had so deeply interested her ? From the first moment that Sir Aldobrand had shown it to her, it had continually haunted her imagination, and she had sought every opportunity to steal to the gallery, and derived an indescribable pleasure from contemplating it.

And now she ran over in her mind the whole history of Sir Martin de Lancy, which had been in part communicated to her by Sir Aldobrand, but more particularly by Sampson Hewley, and pondered over the melancholy and mysterious circumstances connected with it. She could scarcely refrain from tears when she reflected on the extraordinary events which had attended the bridal of Sir Martin and the lovely Lady Editha, and the strange and impenetrable mystery in which the fate of them both was enveloped.

Alas ! it had indeed been a sad bridal for poor Lady Editha, and all who were acquainted with her numerous virtues could not but feel the deepest sympathy for her misfortunes, and the cruel disappointment which her hopes had received.

The hour of ten striking from the old clock in the castle-hall aroused Mildred from these reflections, and she once more moved away from the portrait, after casting her eyes along the gallery, still in fear lest they should encounter some ghastly object ; but nothing whatever to alarm her met her view, and she proceeded with more courage.

She had, however, scarcely arrived at the end of the gallery, when she heard a creaking noise behind her, and hastily turning round, her astonishment and horror may be imagined when she suddenly beheld one of the portraits glide back from its frame, and a ghastly female form, in long, flowing garments of white, with hollow yet piercing eyes, and cadaverous countenance, fill the aperture.

She was rivetted to the spot, spell-bound, as if by magic ; and such was the paralyzing effect which this awful and mysterious appearance had upon her, that she could not even give vent to any expression of terror.

It was the same awful form which she remembered to have seen standing at the foot of her bed when she was a child. But it was only for an instant she beheld it; the next moment it had vanished, and the portrait, which was that of a lady, had resumed its place in the frame.

"In a state of wild and ungovernable curiosity, and scarcely knowing what she did, Mildred rushed forward towards the place where the portrait stood; but at that instant a hollow groan saluted her ears, and overpowered by the intense horror of her feelings, she sunk on the floor in a state of utter insensibility.

CHAPTER XII.

THE PROPOSAL OF LORD RUTHLYN.—THE DISAPPOINMENT AND VOW OF VENGEANCY. THE INTERVIEW BETWEEN ETHELBERT AND MILDRED.—THE STERN MANDATE.

WHEN our heroine recovered, she found herself supported in the arms of Juditha, and Sir Aldobrand standing by her side, watching her with the most anxious looks. A cold shuddering passed through her frame, and she cast her eyes in the direction of the spot where she had seen the mysterious and awful figure.

"Dear Mildred," said Sir Aldobrand, "what is the meaning of this? What has occurred to alarm you thus? Speak—tell me."

"The portrait!" gasped forth our heroine, pointing towards it, and trembling in every limb; "the ghastly form!"

"My dear child," said Juditha, "pray endeavour to explain yourself. What mean you by these allusions?—Have you seen anything to terrify you?"

"Oh, yes—yes," answered Mildred; "indeed I was not deceived. I saw it as plainly as I now behold you. And it stood there, and fixed its hollow eyes upon me with an expression which I can never forget."

"Saw what, my sweet Mildred?" eagerly demanded her benefactor; "I do not understand you. What have you seen, or imagine you have seen?"

"Oh, it was no imagination; it stood in the frame where the portrait now stands. It was the same ghastly form that I beheld many years since, standing at the foot of my bed."

"Impossible, Mildred," said the baronet; "you really have been gazing at the different portraits in the gallery until you have suffered the illusion to make a most remarkable impression upon your mind."

"No, no," returned Mildred; "you may think me weak, but indeed I am as positive that I beheld the ghastly form of female in white, as if it was now standing before my eyes."

"And that it appeared to issue from that portrait which is that of my late mother, the Lady Hortensia?" said Sir Aldobrand.

"Yes, yes," replied Mildred.

"Most extraordinary!" cried the baronet. "You cannot surely believe in supernatural appearances, Mildred?"

"Oh, I know not," faltered out the damsel; "but for Heaven's sake let us leave the gallery."

Sir Aldobrand complied, and he and Juditha led our heroine to another apartment, where, after a short time, she partially recovered from the alarm which she had experience, and related more minutely the circumstance which had occurred to her, and to which the baronet and Juditha listened with the most mute attention and astonishment.

"Surely none of the domestics would pesume to play off a hoax upon you, in order to alarm you?" said Sir Aldobrand.

"Oh, no," answered Mildred, "I am certain it was not so; they could not have assumed a character so awful."

"This extraordinary circumstance must be strictly inquired into," observed the baronet; "in the meantime, my dear Mildred, do not alarm yourself, and let not a word of the adventure escape you to the servants."

"But is it not strange, Sir Aldobrand," said Juditha, "that the form which Mildred declares she saw should appear to issue from the portrait of Lady Hortensia?"

"It is," answered Sir Aldobrand, "and that makes me the more ready to believe that Mildred must have suffered her imagination to deceive her."

"Oh, no, indeed I did not," returned the damsel; "I was not dreaming, and therefore how could I be so much mistaken ?"

"To-morrow," remarked the baronet, "I will make a strict examination of the picture gallery, to see whether I can discover any secret entrance which I at present possess no knowledge of; but I do not think that it is at all likely."

After a short time longer passed in conversation, Sir Aldobrand affectionately bade Mildred good night, and she was conducted by Juditha to their chamber; for ever since the first alarm which Mildred had experienced when a child, they had occupied the same apartment.

Mildred for some time continued to converse upon the awful adventure of the evening, and all the arguments which Juditha made use of could not persuade her that she had been mistaken.

"It was too evident," she said, "that the form had been no mere creation of her own disturbed imagination ;" and the longer she reflected on it, the more she became involved in care and perplexity.

Juditha was also much amazed and alarmed, although she concealed her real feelings as well as she could from the observation of Mildred, and awaited the result of Sir Aldobrand's examination on the following day with considerable anxiety.

Mildred and Juditha at length retired to bed, but it was long ere sleep came to the relief of the former, and even then it was disturbed by fearful visions; and again the ghastly form which she had seen in the picture gallery was presented to her imagination.

The next morning she awoke at an early hour, and as it was particularly fine, Juditha proposed a walk before breakfast, as she thought that the fresh and invigorating air would serve to revive her young companion, and dissipate the gloom occasioned by the adventure of the previous night.

Mildred complied, and they sallied from the castle and directed their course towards the hills, from whose lofty summit they could command an extensive and uninterrupted view of the surrounding country.

As yet the sweet choristers of the woods were silent in their nests; day faintly dawned in the east, and the blue haze of morning concealed the surrounding scenery, till the bright tinge of day's gay monarch illuminated the few floating clouds, and spread a thousand enchanting graces over the face of nature.

To the west they had an expensive view of the ocean, whose lucid bosom reflected innumerable hues—the bright tinged purple, the lustrous silver, and the pallid green, till lost in the haze of distance, and added to the soft tranquillity that now stole over the senses of our heroine.

"Gratidue to the great Parent of Nature expanded the heart of Mildred as she contemplated the interesting scene around her, nor did she imagine her orisons were less grateful to Heaven for being offered from a turfy seat, than if presented in a temple made with human hands.

Convinced all space is the temple of the Supreme, reason assured her it is ardour of devotion and purity of intention that render prayer acceptable, and not particular ceremonies, forms, or places.

For some time Mildred and Juditha remained on this spot, and the latter was highly gratified to observe the beneficial effect which the pure breeze and the delightful scenery around had upon the spirits of her fair and youthful companion.

They at length descended from the lofty hill on which they had taken their station, and proceeded to retrace their steps to the castle; but they had not gone far, when their attention was arrested by hearing the voice of a man calling to them to stop.

Suprised, they turned round, and then perceived Lord Ruthlyn making hastily towards them, and by the most significant gestures requesting them to wait until he came up to them.

"Oh, let us endeavour to avoid him," said Mildred; "I do not like the boldness of his manner, and cannot listen to his fulsome and disgusting flattery. I had hoped that he had quitted the neighbourhood of the castle, and that I should never behold him again."

"I admire your prudence, Mildred," remarked Juditha; "come, let us hasten, or his lordship will overtake us."

They immediately struck into another path among the hills, and quickening their speed, they soon lost sight of Lord Ruthlyn, who it seems had abandoned the pursuit, and did not make his appearance at the castle, as they had expected he would.

Mildred felt far from easy on discovering that Lord Ruthlyn was in the neighbourhood, for her first meeting with him had prejudiced her against him, and his real character could not escape her penetrating eye. But still she thought that she probably had little cause to apprehend any outrage from him, being, as she was, under the protection of Sir Aldobrand de Lancy.

The baronet met her at breakfast with much affection, and was glad to perceive that she was far more composed in spirits than he had expected to find her after the shock she had received the night before.

He had reflected deeply on this adventure, but without being able to come to any satisfactory conclusion, and the more he ruminated upon it, the still further did he become involved in doubt, amazement, and bewilderment.

Unaccustomed as he was to give way to superstition, he could not but believe that Mildred had been mistaken; but still she was so positive, that he knew not what to think.

He had communicated the particulars to Ethelbert, who was much astonished, and became greatly alarmed lest any danger should threaten Mildred, and again he would have urged his father not to deprive him of her society, but he saw that he was in no humour to listen to him with patience, and he therefore forbore.

He requested the baronet, however, to allow him to accompany him in the examination he purposed to make in the picture gallery, to which he consented, and shortly after breakfast they repaired to the place, Mildred and Juditha anxiously awaiting the result of the adventure, though they did not anticipate that they would make any particular discovery.

On arriving at the gallery, the baronet and Ethelbert minutely examined all the portraits, particularly that of the late Lady Hortensia, but they could not perceive that they had been at all disturbed since they had last seen them.

They then sounded the canvas of the latter, and a hollow sound came from it, as though there was an opening beyond. They next endeavoured to remove the portrait, but to their astonishment they found that the frame was fixed to the wainscot.

"This is strange," said Sir Aldobrand; "there must have been some motive for this. We must not pass this over without a more minute examination."

Ethelbert again sounded the canvas.

"There certainly appears to be an opening behind this," he said. "Have you never heard of any secret entrance to this apartment?"

"Never," answered Sir Aldobrand; "although it is not unlikely, for such contrivances for escape in the hour of danger are common in all old castles."

They continued their examination, and inspected the large carved oaken frame with particular care. At length the baronet's hand came in contact with a small piece of brass, apparently fitted into the moulding of the frame.

"There is something in this," he said, and he pressed hard upon it, and at length found it begin to yield to his exertions. He increased them, and the spring (for such it was) sunk into the frame, and the portrait flew back like a door, and discovered, to their astonishment, an opening in one of the panels of the wainscot, beyond which was a narrow passage.

"The mystery is here partly unravelled," said Sir Aldobrand; "here is the means of access, and some person, with what design I am at a loss to imagine, has probably been here. We must continue our search, and endeavour to elucidate all the facts, for we cannot be safe from any secret enemy while this continues."

"It will probably be as well to have the attendance of two or three of the domestics, for we know not what danger there may be in exploring the places to which this passage leads," said Ethelbert.

"Very true," coincided his father; "and we shall also require a light to find our way. It is most extraordinary that I should never have made this discovery before, or had the least suspicion of such a secret communication."

The domestics did not much like the task, for they entertained the most outrageous fears of the dangers which might be attendant on this expedition; but of course they did not presume to offer any objection, and having provided themselves with a lantern, and such implements as were necessary to force any doors they might meet with in their progress, they entered the passage, Sir Aldobrand and Ethelbert leading the way.

The passage was short, and terminated in a stone wall, and here their examination appeared to be abruptly brought to a close, for they could not perceive anything resembling a door in the wall, and it did not seem as though there was likely to be any communication with any part of the castle beyond. Sir Aldobrand, however, was far from being satisfied, and he therefore took the lantern. and examining the floor, discovered a crevice, which on stamping on it, proved to be a trap-door.

They now applied an instrument, fitting for the purpose, which they had brought with them, and, after considerable difficulty, they raised it, and then beheld a winding flight of stone steps beneath.

Here the fears of the simple domestics were again apparent, and it was not until their master and his son set the example, that they could be prevailed upon to attempt to descend the stairs.

They at length arrived at the bottom, and then found themselves in a square stone vault, on one side of which was a low wooden door, which was fastened.

The walls were black with age, and damp with unwholesome moisture. Sir Aldobrand ordered the door to be forced, and after some labour, they succeeded in bursting it from its hinges.

Another dark passage, much longer than the first, presented itself, which they entered, and traversed with the most cautious steps. It was winding, and very low, so that in many parts they were compelled to stoop to prevent their heads from coming in contact with the roof above ; but, having at length reached the extremity, they came to another flight of stone steps, more dilapidated than the others, and which required the greatest care in descending.

" Never could I have believed that such places existed beneath this castle," remarked Sir Aldobrand; " and the discovery is a fortunate one, as it may put us on our guard against any danger that may threaten us."

They now reached the bottom of this flight of steps, and found themselves in another passage, the extent of which they were unable to penetrate, and which, from its great depth, seemed to be level with the foundation of the castle.

They proceeded along it slowly, holding the lantern above their heads occasionally to light them on there way ; but their seemed to be no end of it, and it gradually descended lower and lower into the bowels of the earth, until the dense atmosphere and confined vapours became almost suffocating.

" We must certainly now be far beyond the castle," said Ethelbert; " whither can this lead ?"

" I am at a loss to imagine," replied his father, " but at any rate we will not rest until we have made the discovery. It is of the utmost importance that we should satisfy all our doubts."

" It is," coincided Ethelbert ; and they then continued their subterranean expedition.

Several times they paused as they fancied they heard moaning sounds at a distance ; and the domestics exhibited no little terror, and evidently heartily wished themselves safe once more in the castle. But they did not venture to give expression to their fears, lest they should excite the anger of their master, and they therefore proceeded on their way with the best grace they could.

In this manner they went on for more than a quarter of an hour, and there really seemed to be no termination to this dark and dreary passage ; but at length they were all startled by beholding a stream of light, which seemed to proceed from some aperture at no great distance from them ; and now again the murmuring sounds which they had previously imagined they heard, smote their ears more distinctly than before.

" It sounds like the murmuring of the waves of the ocean," remarked Sir Aldobrand.

" Aye," returned Ethelbert; " and if it is so, we may form a pretty shrewd guess of the distance it is from the castle. I wonder much that this underground communication should never have been discovered before."

" It is indeed strange," said the baronet; " and I do believe that my father was ignorant of it, for I never heard him allude to it. It is fortunate, however, that we have now discovered it, for we might have been surprised by a secret enemy before we had the opportunity of making any resistance."

At length they arrived at the end of the passage, and then they found that their surmises were right, for that the aperture was an opening in one of the cliffs, and they had an expansive view of the ocean, and looking out, to the right they beheld the old Tower of Bransdorf at a short distance, frowning down from the lofty eminence on which it stood.

" Here, then, our search terminates," said Sir Aldobrand ; " and it is evident that the form Mildred beheld was that of a humane being, though what its purpose was I cannot form the least idea."

" Depend upon it," replied Ethelbert, " it was no good one; and I tremble to think of the danger which may be impending over her."

" Oh, now that we have made this discovery, there is no fear of it," said the baronet; " all necessary precautions must be taken to guard against it."

As it was useless to remain any longer where they were, they retraced their steps, and after some time, they once more found themselves In the picture-gallery. Here Sir Aldobrand, having given the necessary orders to a sufficient number of his vassals to guard the secret entrance to this subterranean communication, until it could be effectually and permanently secured, he left Ethelbert, and went to the apartment in which Mildred and Juditha were seated, anxiously awaiting his return, they having heard of the discovery they had made in the picture-gallery.

Mildred and her companion listened to the account which Sir Aldobrand gave of his examination of the secret entrance to the castle with the most unbounded astonishment, and it was some time ere they could recover themselves sufficiently to make any observation upon it.

" The form I beheld, then, was no delusion, that is quite certain," said Mildred.

" No, it was not; I have no doubt, Mildred," answered the baronet, " it was that of a human being ; but what could have been her purpose for visiting the picture-gallery, and who can she be, I cannot form the least conjecture."

" Oh, her countenance and whole appearance were most ghastly and awful," observed Mildred ; " I tremble even now when I think of it."

" Do not alarm yourself, dear Mildred," said her benefactor, " for I will take good care that no harm comes to you, if any is attended you. This mysterious being must be watched, and, if possible, secured, so that we may ascertain who she is, and what are her designs."

" And the secret entrance to the castle ?" demanded Mildred.

" I have placed guards over it," answered Sir Aldobrand ; " and, as soon as possible, will have it blocked up, so that we shall have no danger to apprehend from it in future. You had better remove to another wing of the castle, for probably you may feel some alarm at remaining where you are."

This was readily agreed to by Mildred, and after some further conversation, she became more composed, though she was still lost in a chaos of fruitless conjecture as to the real character of the mysterious visitor, and for what purpose she had, on two different occasions, appeared to her.

Several days elapsed, and the vassals kept a strict watch, night and day, at the entrance to the subterranean passage; but nothing whatever transpired, and workmen were at length employed to close it up, so that all intrusion by that means was prevented.

Mildred, however, began to feel the confinement to which she was subjected particularly irksome, and could not but consider the conduct of Sir Aldobrand far too strict.

Her thoughts frequently reverted to Ethelbert, and she could not help entertaining an ardent wish to behold him again, while the very course which Sir Aldobrand adopted to stifle her passion for his son, only served to increase it, and she felt, although she might never hope it would be gratified, neither time nor circumstance could eradicate it from her bosom, in which it had taken such a deep root.

Another month passed away, when she was alarmed by the sudden illness of poor old Sampson Hewley, whose days drew towards a close. Margery, unable to support the trial of beholding her beloved partner sinking to the grave, sickened with sorrow.

Mildred watched over them with the fondest attention ; each breathed their last in her arms, calmly resigned to their fate, and one grave received their cold remains.

Mildred and Juditha sorrowed for the worthy pair ; but it was that sorrow that begetteth hope. Their blameless lives bade them trust their immortal spirits were ascended to their heavenly Father.

Barbara was engaged by Sir Aldobrand to attend upon Mildred in addition to Juditha, and in the society of that amiable woman she found much consolation.

Lord Ruthlyn still resided at no great distance from the castle ; but neither him or his father had visited it lately; but the time was approaching when our heroine was to be subjected to more and much greater annoyance from his lordship's hated passion.

At first Lord Ruthlyn, considering Mildred only in the character of a humble dependent on the bounty of Sir Aldobrand de Lancy, though fascinated by her beauty, and awed by her virtue, basely resolved on plans the most dishonourable to destroy the peace and innocence of her days; but now, when he saw that the baronet looked upon her with the same regard as if she were his daughter, he began to think that she would be a proper companion for life ; and he therefore made the earl, his father, acquainted with his sentiments, and requested, if they met his concurrence, he would immediately make proposals to the baronet. Although he remembered the scorn with which Mildred had ever treated him, he flattered himself that she would entirely be influenced by the advice and persuasion of her benefactor ; and he did not doubt of achieving a triumph, especially as Sir Aldo-brand was so opposed to the passion which Ethelbert entertained for her.

The earl, notwithstanding Mildred's want of rank, approved of his son's choice, for he hoped that it would be the means of withdrawing him from his present dissolute habits, and he at once hastened to find Sir Aldobrand, to whom he communicated his son's wishes, and earnestly entreated the baronet's consent to his union with Mildred.

Sir Aldobrand, though highly pleased with the admiration which Mildred had excited, and anxious to remove the only obstacle to Ethelbert's advancement in life, felt assured that Mildred could never love, if even she should esteem his lordship ; nor could he con-scientiously advise her to give any encouragement to his addresses, so indifferent was the opinion he entertained of Lord Ruthlyn's character. Besides, he had no authority over her ; her parents might still be living, and might again come forward to claim her, and the greatest blame might be attached to him for the part he had taken.

He therefore gave no decisive answer until he had questioned Mildred on the subject.

The next morning, Sir Aldobrand requested Mildred would attend him in his apartment. She went thither with a palpitating heart, for she had heard that the Earl de Bohun had visited the castle the day before, and a fearful foreboding came over her as to the cause for which she had been summoned.

Sir Aldobrand received her with his usual tenderness, and observing her tremble, fondly kissed her cheek, and bidding her compose herself for a few moments, busied himself by replacing some books that had been removed from the shelf ; then seating himself by her side, he said—

" Mildred, I need not say how dear your happiness and honour are to me ; my conduct has evinced that I value it as highly as if you were my own child. I have, my dear girl, received from the Earl de Bohun a proposal to unite your fate with rank and station, by bestowing your hand on Lord Ruthlyn de Bohun, who will consider himself happy in being permitted to hope that you will consent to become his wife.

We need not attempt to describe the emotion of Mildred when she heard this. She turned ghastly pale, and her limbs trembled so violently that she could scarcely support herself. She burst into tears, and replied, in a hurried and faltering accents—

" Oh, my generous, my beloved guardian and benefactor, do not, I beseech you, urge me on a subject so painful and repulsive to me ; permit me to remain with you—I wish not to leave your protecting roof. I—I cannot, indeed I cannot accept the honour you offer me."

" My sweet girl," said Sir Aldobrand, " why do you express yourself with such amazing agitation of spirits ? If you do not endeavour to be more calm, I must leave the remainder of my communication till another opportunity."

" Oh, pray, sir," said Mildred, somewhat re-assured by Sir Aldobrand's manner, and his observations, " let me hear all your proposals now ; only say I shall continue with you, and I will study to show my gratitude by the strictest attention to your wishes."

" Well, Mildred," said the baronet, " for the present, then, you shall remain with me ; but I must request that you will reflect maturely on Lord Ruthlyn's offer, and do not hastily reject an alliance which undoubtedly possesses many advantages."

" I will obey you, sir," ejaculated our heroine ; " but indeed his lordship has little or nothing to hope, and I would advise him to look out for some other damsel on whom he can place his affections. I can never, never consent to become the wife of a man who has no place in my heart."

Sir Aldobrand looked at her earnestly for a moment or two. With much pain, he read the thoughts which were passing in her mind ; but he controlled his feelings, and request-ing her to tranquillise her spirits, he permitted her to retire, and then received the earl and his son, and made them acquainted with the result of his interview.

Lord Ruthlyn could scarcely help giving vent to his rage at the scornful rejection of his suit by Mildred, and he and his father almost immediately after left the castle, his lordship inwardly swearing revenge, and fully determined that as Mildred would not con-sent to become his wife, he would obtain possession of her, and make her sorely repent her refusal.

Mildred, on retiring to her own apartment, after her interview with Sir Aldobrand, for some time gave herself up to the most unbounded grief at the odious proposition of Lord Ruthlyn, and although the baronet had for the present yielded to her wishes, she could not help foreboding the greatest misery to herself and Ethelbert.

She had seen enough of his lordship to feel convinced that he was not the sort of man who would be easily induced to abandon anything upon which he had fixed his mind, and she was satisfied that he was of the most revengeful disposition, and would leave no means untried to retaliate upon her and Ethelbert.

Juditha tried to compose her, and to lead her to hope for the best, and she at last succeeded far better than she had expected.

Lord Ruthlyn's passion for Mildred was not to be cured by absence from her presence. He revolved at thousand schemes in his mind to separate Ethelbert from the object of his admiration; and though he sometimes felt the goading sting of reproach, yet such was the violence of his passion, that his penitential moments were quickly overcome, and his mind was again busily employed in laying nets to entrap the beauteous and innocent Mildred.

He well knew the deepest and best concerted stratagem was necessary to deceive Mildred, and, above all, Sir Aldobrand and Juditha, whose years and experience were so superior to her fair charge's, so that he rightly concluded that her vigilance was more to be feared than his destined victim's. He therefore, to forward his schemes, quickly returned to the neighbourhood of the castle, where he remained in obscurity and under an assumed name, resolved in this retirement to watch the issue of his dark designs.

Ethelbert still remained in the most melancholy and agitated state of mind, as he was unable to obtain an interview with Mildred; but his indignation and disgust may readily be imagined when he was informed of the boldness of Lord Ruthlyn in making an offer of his hand to Mildred, and he was determined, if ever he had an opportunity, to seek satisfaction for the insult which he considered was not only offered to Mildred, but himself.

It was some consolation to him, however, to learn how peremptorily Mildred had rejected the suit of the profligate nobleman; for it led him to hope that he held some p'ace in her affections; and he was equally gratified to find that his father had not pressed her too closely, and did not appear to wish to exercise any particular influence over her inclinations, which led him to hope that in time he would banish from his mind the foolish pride which was its only blemish, and would be induced to look upon his sentiments with a more favourable and encouraging eye.

It happened one day that Mildred, knowing that Sir Aldobrand was away from the castle, and imagining that Ethelbert was also absent, walked alone in the garden, and seated herself in her favourite retreat in the hermitage.

Ethelbert had, however, watched her from the window of his apartment, and hailing the opportunity with delight, he determined at all hazards to obtain an interview with her, and for that purpose he quitted the castle, and bent his foosteps towards the hermitage with a palpitating heart.

Mildred was absorbed in a variety of reflections of the most conflicting nature, when she was suddenly startled by hearing some one enter the hermitage, and looking up, what was her agitation and confusion on beholding Ethelbert!

The deepest blushes suffused her cheeks, and her bosom heaved convulsively with the feelings which struggled within it; but before she could collect herself in the least, Ethelbert sunk on his knee before her, and having pressed her hand to his lips in a voice which fully betrayed the powerful emotion of his feeling, he ejaculated—

"Beauteous, amiable Mildred, I throw myself upon your clemency, and crave your pardon for thus intruding upon your privacy. Oh, why should fate destine me to be so cruelly deprived of the society of that sweet being to whom my very soul is, and ever must, under all circumstances, be devoted? Did you but know what I have for weeks suffered, I am satisfied that you would pity me, and——"

"For Heaven's sake, leave me, Ethelbert," said the blushing and deeply agitated Mildred. "Alas! when you know the restraint under which I am placed—when you know the will of your excellent father, to whom, humble dependent as I am upon his benevolence, I owe every feeling of gratitude and obedience, why will you persist in placing me at the risk of incurring his displeasure?"

"By Heaven, I love, I adore you, Mildred," replied the impassioned youth, " and unless I can have the assurance from your own sweet lips of a return of my sentiments, life will no longer possess any charms for me. Do not, then, I implore you, leave me entirely to despair; suffer me, at any rate, to indulge in the hope that——"

"Hold, sir," interrupted our heroine, and her voice trembled as she spoke; "I must not, dare not listen to this. I esteem you as the son of my benefactor; but if you would have me regard you as my friend, you will cease to urge me upon a point to which the will and pleasure of Sir Aldobrand de Lancy is averse."

" I revere my father," ejaculated Ethelbert; "I have ever acted in obedience to his wishes; but I cannot consent to abide by his present hard decision, on which my whole happiness depends."

" Obstinate boy !" exclaimed a voice at that moment, and looking up, the confused and agitated Ethelbert and Mildred beheld Sir Aldobrand standing before them; his countenance flashed with resentment, and his eyes sternly fixed upon Ethelbert.

Mildred, trembling and overpowered, sunk on a seat, and covered her face with her hands, and Ethelbert started to his feet in the utmost confusion, and shrunk beneath the severe glance which his father fixed upon him.

"Disobedient boy," continued the baronet, "is it thus you reward me for the affection and indulgence I have ever bestowed upon you ? Are you entirely lost to all sense of duty ?"

" Hear me, my father, I beseech you," said Ethelbert, in a deeply agitated voice. " do not heap upon me reproaches I do not merit, until you have heard me in explanation."

"No more," cried Sir Aldobrand, passionately; "it is quite enough for me to know that you have broken through my commands, and that you would, by your future obstinate conduct, plunge both me and her you pretend to regard with so much fervour into irretrievable misery. Away, and learn repentance, unless you would incur my everlasting displeasure."

"Will you not listen to me ?" said Ethelbert, and his cheek heated with the extraordinary emotion of his feelings. "Oh! surely this is cruel, to deprive me of the only source of happiness—the society of the most lovely and amiable of her sex."

"For Heaven's sake, Ethelbert," gasped forth Mildred, and tears started to her eyes, while her whole frame was so violently agitated that she could scarcely support her trembling limbs, " if you have any regard for my feelings, forbear, and obey the will of your father. Alas! if I am thus to be made the innocent cause of dissension between you and my generous benefactor, better had it been for me that I had never entered his hospitable roof; and it would only be an act of justice and prudence towards Sir Aldobrand and myself that I should at once leave it, and in holy seclusion seek to end my days in peace and tranquility."

Sir Aldobrand kindly took her hand, while Ethelbert looked grieved to the very soul, and, in a voice of the greatest compassion and truly parental tenderness, said—

" My sweet Mildred, talk not thus, I beseech you. I have ever found you good, amiable rnd dutiful, and it is for your own welfare that I adopt the present course, however severe it may appear to be. Retire to a nunnery !—oh, never, my child; it would be cruel thus to sacrifice the days of one so young and virtuous ; and indeed your sweet society is so necessary to my happiness, that I could not exist without it."

" And yet, sir," returned Ethelbert, with a look of reproach, " of that society which you acknowledge to be so indispensable to your happiness, you deprive me. Oh, pardon me, but is not that ungenerous—is it not unjust?"

Sir Aldobrand was somewhat staggered by these observations. He could not but inwardly acknowledge their justice, yet prudential motives and inherent pride prevailed over his better feelings, and he answered—

" I have my reasons, powerful ones, Ethelbert, in which the future welfare of yourself and Mildred is involved, and it is unnecessary for me to say more than to repeat that it is your duty to submit with patience—nay, more, if you really regard the happiness of Mildred, you will do so without hesitation. Retire, sir ; I cannot permit this interview to continue any longer, and beware how in future you venture to disobey my injunctions."

" And you will not grant me the least indulgence, sir?" said his son, in melancholy accents; " you will not at all relax your harsh decree ?"

Sir Aldobrand waved his hand authoritatively. Mildred's emotion increased, and Ethelbert, bowing respectfully to her and his father, with a deep sigh, quitted the hermitage, and walked forth into the open country in a state of mind bordering upon distraction.

Juditha now entered the hermitage, having come in search of Mildred, and the baronet having spoken a few words of kindness and consolation to the latter, retired and left them to themselves.

CHAPTER XIII.

LORD RUTHLYN'S THREATS.—THE ENCOUNTER.—THE CATASTROPHE.

ETHELBERT continued to wander on, he scarcely knew whither, throughout the whole of the day, and his mind was in such a state of agitation that he had lost nearly all control over his feelings. He cursed his unlucky fate, and deprecated the severity of his father's conduct, which he could not but consider was both unjust and cruel, and he felt satisfied that h ecould not act in obedience to his mandates, let the consequences be whatever they might, but that he must endeavour to see Mildred at every opportunity.

He felt satisfied that Mildred, in spite of the harsh injunctions of his father, returned his passion, and that confidence only served to increase the ardour of his sentiments, and to induce him to hope that the time would come when there would be no further obstacle to their love, and Sir Aldobrand would see the policy and justice of relenting.

With these thoughts he endeavoured to console himself, and, as the shades of evening were descending on the face of nature, he returned to the castle. The baronet, being aware of his return, requested him to attend him in his apartment, and Ethelbert obeyed, very well aware of the subject his father wished to see him upon.

Sir Aldobrand read him a severe lecture on his conduct, and again commanded him never to repeat it, on the pain of his everlasting displeasure.

Ethelbert listened to him impatiently, and then ventured gently, but earnestly to remonstrate with him, and to beg him to relent, and not to suffer him to remain towards Mildred no more than as if he was an entire stranger. But the baronet was inexorable, and vowed that if Ethelbert did not endeavour to forget her in any other character than that of a friend, he would devise some means of effectually separating them altogether.

Etnelbert quitted his presence in despair, and retiring to his chamber, passed the night in racking thought. He saw that it was entirely useless for him to attempt to move his father from his stern resolve, and he had no alternative but to submit to his severe fate without complaining. But, alas! that was a task not easy of accomplishment.

Mildred was much grieved after the interview described in the previous chapter, and it was not without the greatest difficulty that Juditha could at all succeed in tranquillizing her spirits.

She could not deny to herself the love she entertained for Ethelbert, and when she considered the utter hopelessness of its ever receiving the sanction of Sir Aldobrand, she foreboded the utmost misery to herself and Ethelbert, and regretted that they had ever met. Her pride felt mortified at the conduct of Sir Aldobrand, and while she could not help considering that it was most unreasonably severe, she sincerely pitied Ethelbert, and mentally besought the Almighty to interfere in his favour, or to enable them both to remember each other with the regard of friendship only.

In this manner several weeks elapsed, and no change took place in the circumstances of the inmates of the castle. Ethelbert had felt compelled to obey the injunctions of his father, and had never sought another interview with Mildred; but his thoughts were constantly fixed on her, and secretly he sighed to behold her again. He could not think of leaving the castle, though Sir Aldobrand would have persuaded him to do so, for he was certain that absence from the place she inhabited would only serve to render him more miserable, and he should be in a constant state of apprehension lest some danger should threaten her, and he too well knew the character of Lord Ruthlyn to imagine that he would so easily resign all his hopes of possessing our heroine. He knew that he was impetuous and revengeful, and he was therefore constantly on his guard to frustrate any evil designs he might have in contemplation. A circumstance was about to occur which proved that there were good reasons for his fears.

One evening, Mildred being in a melancholy mood, unknown to Juditha or Sir Aldobrand, strolled from the castle, wrapt in thought, and ultimately rambled to the dire-clad cottage of her late venerable friends. When she reached its humble door, she lifted the latch, and entered the solitary kitchen, where so lately appeared seated the aged pair to whose humanity she was indebted next to Heaven for the comforts of her past years. Pale and trembling she rested on a chair, and burst into tears.

Her mind relieved by the pellucid tribute, she arose and ascended to the chambers. Here her spirits again sunk; the chilling silence that reigned in the apartment

beheld her venerated friends breathe their last sigh, rendered more dreary by the melancholy shades of evening, that gathered fast, and seemed to threaten an entire obscurity, shed
a sullen gloom over her spirits, and rendered her alive to all the horrors of superstition.

The hollow breeze sighing among the high oaks that sheltered the humble cottage from
the bleak breath of the north wind, added to the solemnity of her feelings; fearful ideas
crept through her brain, and thrilled her mind with terror.

Mildred was not subject to the weak fears which some are oppressed with; she had too
much sense to permit the idle tales of superstitious enthusiasm to deprive her of reason;
but now her spirits, weakened by sorrow, conjured up a thousand unusual visions. Some

times she started, and imagined that she still beheld her aged friends reclining on their bed, or heard the faint cough of Margery in the room below.

Terrified, yet ashamed of her fears, she determined to finish the task she had assigned herself of visiting each apartment of the humble dwelling. She had nearly fulfilled her intentions, when she was alarmed by a sound like that of a footstep on the stairs; but so often had she been mocked by imagination, that she persuaded herself her fears were only fancy, and therefore quitted the cottage.

She had scarcely emerged from the cottage door, when she perceived the figure of a man approaching. She paused; the man came nearer, and Mildred's astonishment and alarm may be imagined, when she recognised Lord Ruthlyn de Bohun.

"By the mass, this is fortunate," exclaimed the libertine, and there was an expression of boldness in his eye, which greatly added to the alarm of Mildred. "Lovely Mildred, are my eyes indeed once more gladdened by the sight of you?"

"I request that you will not detain me, my lord," said Mildred, "but suffer me to return to the castle. Prudence forbids that I should hold converse with you unless it be in the presence of my guardian."

"Nay, beauteous damsel," returned his lordship; "what have I done to merit this scorn? By Heaven, I must claim a few minutes' private conversation with you."

"Forbear, my lord," said Mildred; "this boldness is unwarrantable. Suffer me to pass. I have no secrets from Sir Aldobrand de Lancy."

"I have not a doubt," replied Lord Ruthlyn, "but the fair Mildred is perfectly ingenuous. The business I would speak of is of the greatest importance to my happiness."

Mildred was still more embarrased and alarmed. She well knew to what his lordship alluded; she saw he was determined to be heard, and again she requested that he would not detain her, as he already knew her sentiments, and that nothing could alter them.

A slight frown contracted his lordship's brow for a moment; but he conquered his resentment, and said—

"Ah, Mildred, you must be too sensible of your charms to imagine a person who has once entertained a passion for you can ever eradicate it from his breast."

Mildred blushed deep, and trembled.

"I again throw my rank and title at your feet," continued the nobleman, "on you depends my happiness or misery."

"Your lordship will suffer me to thank you for the honour intended me," answered Mildred, mildly, but firmly, "and to decline it with a hope that you will ere long meet with a woman every way calculated to fill so elevated a situation."

"I hope, beauteous damsel," said the libertine, hardly able to conceal his chagrin—"I hope that these are not your real sentiments."

"My lord," answered our herione, indignantly, "I am not accustomed to utter spurious ones."

"Pardon my warmth. I had flattered myself, since you can never hope to possess Ethelbert de Lancy——"

"Let me pass, my lord," interrupted Mildred; "I must not, will not listen to your observations. From whence did your lordship gain this information?"

"Is not all the world acquainted with Sir Aldobrand's objection to his son's passion?" said Lord Ruthlyn, with a look of exultation.

Mildred, struck to the heart, yet unwilling to betray her feelings, answered evasively, that Ethelbert de Lancy, as a friend, must always possess her esteem.

Lord Ruthlyn did not pretend to notice her unconnected reply, but again renewed his suit, to which Mildred lent a seeming attention, while, in fact, her mind was tortured with far different thoughts

Exulting at the passive manner with which Mildred heard him, Lord Ruthlyn became more importunate, and approaching closer to her, he caught her hand, and was conveying it to his lips, when Mildred, roused from the reverie which for some minutes had enveloped her senses, hastily snatched it from him, and retreated a few paces, filled with the most unbounded resentment.

"Your lordship's unwarrantable familiarity," she ejaculated, "obliges me to tell you I can no longer listen to your converation. Let me pass. I will no longer be detained."

"Stay, charming Mildred," returned Lord Ruthlyn, "and condescend to say if I may hope you will become my wife?"

"Never!" replied Mildred, firmly and emphatically.

" Beware, Mildred," he cried, " beware of driving me to madness; you may repent it."

" Your threats are vain," returned our heroine; " no power can compel me to marry your lordship without my consent."

" True," he answered with a dark look of sinister meaning; " but there are means of putting my hated rival, Ethelbert de Lancy, to eternal quiet."

Mildred trembled, and looked at him with an expression of terror.

" Good God !" she exclaimed, " you would not endanger his life !"

" It is in your power to save it."

" How ?"

" By becoming my bride."

" I have already acquainted your lordship with my unalterable determination."

" Then tremble !" cried Lord Ruthlyn, in a voice of passionate violence ; " I will be revenged !"

" I will no longer listen to you," said Mildred ; " and I set your base and unmanly threats at defiance. Ethelbert de Lancy shall be made acquainted with the savage designs you entertain against him."

She attempted to pass as she spoke.

" Nay, scornful beauty, you go not thus," said Lord Ruthlyn, throwing his arms around her, and attempting to pollute her lips with his odious kisses.

Mildred struggled, and rent the air with her shrieks of terror ; but the libertine still retained his hold of her, and attempted to force her back again into the cottage.

" Mildred's strength was almost exhausted, and she gave herself up for lost, when suddenly the sound of footsteps was heard rapidly approaching, and casting her anxious eyes in the direction from whence they proceeded, she, to her great relief, beheld Sir Aldobrand and Ethelbert running towards the spot.

Lord Ruthlyn gave utterance to a terrible oath, and then resigning his hold of our heroine, and taking to flight, endeavoured to avoid the baronet and his son ; but the latter hastened to Mildred, while Sir Aldobrand encountered Lord Ruthlyn, who had drawn his sword, and was evidently resolved to defend himself fiercely.

Ethelbert caught the almost fainting Mildred in his arms ; but they were almost immediately startled by hearing a loud groan of agony, and looking in the direction from whence it proceeded, to their horror they beheld the unfortunate Sir Aldobrand sinking bleeding to the earth, while the villain Lord Ruthlyn was flying precipitately from the spot, and was quickly out of sight.

Ethelbert and Mildred rushed towards the wounded Sir Aldobrand, whom they found perfectly insensible. The distracted Mildred knelt down, and placed her hand upon her unfortunate benefactor's heart, while Ethelbert tore away his scarf, and endeavoured to stanch the wound, which was a most desperate one, and from the effects of which they thought it would be impossible for him to recover. While they were thus occupied, two or three peasants, who were on their way home from their daily toil, approached the spot, and betrayed the greatest sorrow when they beheld the dangerous state of Sir Aldobrand. As it was necessary that his wound should be attended to with all possible dispatch, they raised him from the ground, and removed him to the castle with all possible speed, while Ethelbert and Mildred followed, in a state of mind which we need not attempt to describe.

CHAPTER XIV.

THE DANGER OF SIR ALDOBRAND.—THE APPREHENSION OF APPROACHING DEATH.—

SOLEMN INJUNCTIONS.

THE views of mortals are confined, or, if permitted to rove the boundless sea of supposition, too often founder on the rocks of credulity; while basking in the sunbeams of fancy, they notice not the approach of sorrow.

It would be a fruitless task to attempt to pourtray the extreme anguish of Mildred and Ethelbert at this unexpected and dreadful calamity. It was some time ere the baronet was restored to sensibility, and the holy man who had attended upon him and dressed his wound pronounced it very dangerous, and gave but little hope of his recovery.

The grief of Mildred, though tender and sincere, prevented her not from paying every attention to Sir Aldobrand; she hovered round his pillow, administered his medicine, and watched with anxious solicitude every unfavourable change.

Sir Aldobrand felt satisfied that his death was near its approach.   He felt no stings of remorse; for his life had been hallowed with every virtuous action: Neither the settlement of his temporal or eternal affairs was procrastinated to the last moment, since he well knew that death might come when least expected; hope shed its bright beams upon his soul, and prepared him to meet the future.

The strictest search was made after Lord Ruthlyn; but he was nowhere to be found in the neighbourhood, and the earl, his father, declared he did not know what had become of him, and he deeply lamented the dreadful calamity of which he had been the cause.

Several days elapsed, and Sir Aldobrand appeared to be every hour getting worse, and he summoned Ethelbert at last to his bedside to receive his parting blessing.

When he entered the chamber of his father, Mildred was supporting Sir Aldobrand in her arms, while with her handkerchief she wiped away the perspiration from his forehead.

It was a moment of severe trial to both our heroine and her lover. Ethelbert approached the bed, and clasping the hand of his beloved parent, remained silent and agonised with sorrow.

Sir Aldobrand turned his languid eyes, that seemed scarcely to move in their sockets, on his son, to whom he now expected he was going to bid a long farewell, and raising himself a moment, gazed mournfully in his face.   But no agony of fear distracted his bosom; he was tranquil and resigned to his fate, confident of being about to enter upon a bright eternity of bliss.

> " Sure the last end of the good man is peace;
> How calm his exit! night dews fall not more
> Gently to the ground, nor wearied, worn out
> Winds expire so soft!——"

Such are the beautiful words of the poet, and Sir Aldobrand de Lancy fully exemplified the truth of them in that solemn hour.

"Ethelbert," he said, in a clear and solemn voice, "I am going quickly to my Father and your Father, to my God and your God.   Remember, my son, virtue alone can support you in an hour like this."

He paused for a few moments, and then turned his eyes alternately, with an expression of sorrowful affection, upon his son and the weeping Mildred.

"Ethelbert,—Mildred," he continued, "you are both possessed of reason in a very superior degree; never, oh, never slight its dictates, and though this spark of Deity may sometimes urge you to actions contrary to inclination, yet remember it is the voice of Infinite Wisdom that whispers.   Obey its mandates, listen to its amiable, its persuasive eloquence, and let not blind and stupid passion lead you to destruction.   Remember the fate of your uncle, Ethelbert, and be warned not to disobey the injunctions of your parent. Guard sedulously against the first deviation from the path of rectitude.   Alas! if you once forsake virtue, your peace will be destroyed.   You entertain sentiments of affection towards each other; I know that they are reciprocal; but still the mystery which surrounds Mildred precludes the possibility of your being united, at any rate, until that mystery is satisfactorily explained.   I solemnly adjure you both to abandon all hopes of an union which might only be productive of misery and regret, till it shall please Providence to unravel that mystery, and all objection to your coming together shall be removed."

"Oh, my dear father," ejaculated the agitated Ethelbert, "surely you will not persist in this solemn hour in exacting such a promise from us?"

"They are my last injunctions," said the baronet, with increased solemnity of tone and expression; "obey them, as you would receive my dying blessing."

"Yes, yes," sobbed forth Mildred; "I promise you, faithfully promise you, that never will I consent to become the wife of Ethelbert unless under such circumstances as you would approve if living."

"Enough, enough," said Sir Aldobrand, smiling serenely upon her; "I am satisfied. Oh, my children, virtuous and charitable actions will enliven the hours of innocent enjoyment, smooth the pillow of sickness, spread tranquillity over the moments of affliction, and soothe the awful hour when those loved companions, soul and body, long linked together by the choicest ties of nature, take a long farewell of each other."

Again he paused, exhausted, and it was several minutes before he could speak again.

Ethelbert and Mildred watched him with the utmost anxiety and anguish ; but at lengt he made another effort, and turning his eyes on Mildred, said—

" Mildred, my dear child, you have from the first moment I received you beneath my roof, been all that my fondest heart could wish you. Your duty and gratitude have been exemplary ; as a small return (for those virtues will be rewarded by that Power who delights in goodness) I have bequeathed an ample sum, and——"

He could not finish the sentence ; his strength was exhausted, and he sunk back on his pillow, inanimate, and, as our heroine and Ethelbert imagined, no more.

To paint the feelings of Mildred, when she beheld, as she supposed, her generous and humane benefactor a lifeless corse, is beyond the power of the most eloquent. She placed her hand upon his bosom ; she felt his heart still throb, and it was like removing a mountain from her breast. The baronet had evidently only fainted, and the person who had been in attendance upon him during his illness pronounced that there was yet some hope left of his reviving.

Ethelbert and Mildred returned their sincere and ardent gratitude to Heaven, and continued in the chamber, and watched the sufferer, in a state of the greatest suspense.

In about a quarter of an hour, he again opened his eyes, and fixed them upon his son and Mildred with the utmost serenity. They were in a moment by his side, and leaning over him with the most anxious solicitude, they eagerly inquired how he felt.

" Better—better," he answered, in a calm voice. " I had thought that my last moment had come, and that I should never again awake to life. But God's will be done."

" Oh, may all-merciful Heaven preserve you for many years to come, my generous benefactor," ejaculated Mildred, tears of hope and gratitude starting to her eyes.

" For your sake, Mildred, and that of my son, I hope it may," said the baronet, " I feel easy now ; no pain—no pain."

The holy father, who had been examining his wound, now pronounced that it had taken a favourable turn, and that he had every hope that Sir Aldobrand, having passed the severest danger, would ultimately recover.

Again did Mildred pour forth her feelings of gratitude to the Supreme, and Sir Aldobrand, taking her hand in silence, pressed it to his heart.

The baronet now felt inclined for sleep, and Juditha having entered the chamber, gently withdrew our heroine from it, and led her to her own apartment.

Ethelbert followed her with his eyes, and would willingly have accompanied her, that he might give vent to the feelings which agitated his bosom after this melancholy and trying scene ; but the earnest looks of Mildred prevented him, and he sought his own chamber, where he could indulge in the different conflicting thoughts which agitated his mind, without any fear of interruption.

CHAPTER XV.

THE RECOVERY OF SIR ALDOBRAND.—THE EVIL DESIGNS OF LORD RUTHLYN'S PROGRESS.—THE ATTACK.—THE MYSTERIOUS MINSTREL.

VARIOUS indeed were the feelings which tortured the bosom of Ethelbert. A feeling of gratitude to the Almighty for the prospect of his father's recovery, however, held a prominent place. But he could not reflect upon the solemn injunctions of the baronet, at the very time when he thought his end was approaching, without the deepest pain and regret. It convinced him that he was determined, and that all attempts to move him from his harsh decree would be vain, unless, indeed, the mystery which surrounded the origin of Mildred should be unravelled, and she should be discovered to be connected with some noble family. He had every disposition to act in accordance with the wishes of his parent ; but he could not but deprecate those feelings of pride, which cast a dark shadow over his other numerous virtues. The solemn promise which Mildred had also made to Sir Aldobrand filled him with grief; for although he was convinced that she returned his passion, he was certain that she would never break ner word, and that it would therefore be folly for him to encourage scarcely the least feeling of hope.

Mildred's anguish also was equal to his own, and when she entered her room, accompanied by Juditha, she could no longer restrain the indulgence of the emotions which laboured in her breast, and it required all the efforts of Juditha to bring her to anything like composure.

But gratitude to the Almighty for the favourable change which had taken place in the condition of the baronet, her benefactor, at last completely superseded every other thought, and she fervently prayed that his restoration to convalescence might be quick and certain ; for, oh, she reflected, what would become of her, if deprived of the protection of him, her best earthly friend ?

At night, notwithstanding the earnest entreaties of Juditha, Mildred kept vigils in the chamber of the baronet, for she knew that there was no one whose attentions would be so grateful to him as her own.

Sir Aldobrand, though extremely ill, and very much reduced from his long suffering, lay very calm ; for his mind was invigorated by hope, and piously resigned to his fate, whatever it might be.

Mildred presaged the happiest omens from the stillness and composure of Sir Aldobrand : her heart dilated by hope, anticipated his rapid recovery, and all her other afflictions lost their former poignancy.

The web of the poor girl's reflections, however, was often broken by her anxiety, which, in spite of the delusive visions of hope, oppressed her mind.

Frequently during the night she stepped softly to the bed, and listened attentively to the short breathing of the baronet, who remained sleepless till towards the morning, when he sunk into a slumber. It was not till then that Mildred could be prevailed upon to retire, and worn out with watching and anxiety, sleep came to her relief as soon as she had stretched her limbs upon the bed.

The sleep which Sir Aldobrand obtained had the most beneficial effect on him, and it was wonderful to observe the change which had been wrought in his appearance in so short a space of time. It was indeed like the resuscitation of the dead, for no one who had seen him on the previous day could have supposed that he could have lingered many hours, nay, even minutes.

Mildred, also refreshed by sleep, arose from her couch, and having offered up her daily devotions to the Most High, hastened to his chamber, where she found Ethelbert already in attendance upon his father.

Mildred could not restrain an exclamation of delight and thanksgiving, when she beheld the extraordinary change for the better in her benefactor, and he received her with the greatest affection, and warmly thanked her for the unremitting attention she had paid him, and the solicitude she had evinced for his recovery.

Ethelbert beheld Mildred with much emotion, and it was evident from his languid eyes, and the wan expression of his countenance, that he had suffered much mental agony during the few hours' interval that had elapsed since they had before met.

The recovery of Sir Aldobrand was far more remarkable and speedy than the most sanguine could have anticipated ; his wound quickly healed, and he gathered strength so fast, that in little more than another fortnight he was enabled to leave his chamber. His greatest consolation was the society of our heroine ; and fearful that it would endanger her health, if she continued to be subjected to such restraint as she had been, and beginning to place some degree of confidence in the obedience of Ethelbert to his wishes, he no longer prevented them from meeting in his presence, although he strictly prohibited their holding any private interviews with each other.

This indulgence of his father was a great source of consolation to Ethelbert, and he endeavoured to encourage the hope that time would entirely destroy the baronet's prejudices, and that he would view the sentiments which he and Mildred entertained for each other with a more favourable eye.

And Mildred encouraged similar hopes, for she could not but acknowledge to herself that the numerous virtues of Ethelbert had created a passion in her bosom which nothing could ever eradicate.

Mildred could not conquer the terrors with which the threats of Lord Ruthlyn had inspired her. She saw that he was reckless, revengeful, subtle, and designing, and although he had been defeated in those designs which led to the almost fatal accident to Sir Aldobrand, she felt certain that he would not readily abandon his villanous schemes ; and although they had not yet been able to discover what had become of him, there was too much reason to apprehend that he was only remaining concealed until an opportunity should present itself to carry his wishes into effect. She trembled with fear lest Ethelbert and him should encounter each other, for the meeting would most assuredly prove a fatal one to one or both of them.

The conjectures of Mildred were, unfortunately, too correct; Lord Ruthlyn remained firm in his base designs, and only awaited a favourable opportunity not only to get her in his power, but to gratify his deadly feelings of revenge against her lover.

" If ever Mildred becomes my wife," muttered the haughty nobleman to himself, as he paced the gloomy chamber of the place in which he was at present concealed, " she must on her knees solicit that honour. Her pride shall be humbled—ere long this scornful beauty will sue for mercy. Ethelbert, too; oh, I will not rest until I have him in my power, and have wreaked my vengeance on his head. They little imagine the means I have of carrying my wishes into operation."

He smiled with a malicious feeling of exultation as he thus spoke, and soon became lost in deep meditation on his dark designs.

The cruel outrage committed by his son, had caused a rupture which could never be remedied between the Earl de Bohun and Sir Aldobrand de Lancy, and the former having retired to a distant part of the country, there seemed to be no likelihood of their meeting again. The baronet, however, as well as Ethelbert, were continually on their guard against Lord Ruthlyn, for they were of the same opinion as Mildred, namely, that he would not readily abandon his nefarious wishes, and that they had good reason to apprehend annoyance and danger from him.

And the time was coming when these fears were unfortunately destined to be realized.

Mildred never or seldom left the castle since the alarming adventure recorded in the previous chapter, unless she was accompanied by the baronet or Juditha; but the latter now began to feel the infirmities of age stealing on her fast, and she looked forward to the time rapidly approaching when her mortal career would terminate.

One afternoon, Mildred and Juditha had again rambled among some of their most favourite scenes, but the latter was unusually melancholy, frequently sighed, and at length, as the evening was rapidly advancing, they hastened to the castle.

Soon after their return home, Juditha complained of a head-ache, shivered violently, and retired to that bed from whence she was never to rise.

Sir Aldobrand felt greatly alarmed at the illness of his aged housekeeper, for her devoted attention and attachment to himself and Mildred made him look upon her with the esteem of a friend, and he knew not where he should supply her loss if her illness should terminate fatally. He immediately procured the attendance of a skilful apothecary, and desired him to exert himself to the utmost to save the life of his patient.

How Mildred trembled for the life of her amiable friend, for she regarded her with the same affection as if she had been her mother, and despaired of meeting with any other individual to supply her loss.

Seated by the side of the bed of Juditha, a thousand sickening and distressing images flitted through her brain.

The stillness that prevailed in the castle, the meek shades of twilight, and the melancholy screams of an owl, increased the gloom of her spirits, and conjured up innumerable vague and torturing fears.

It was not long ere the apothecary arrived at the castle. As he listened to Juditha's complaints, Mildred anxiously contemplated his expressive countenance, and in it saw all her fears confirmed. Yet willing to hear from his lips what she had to expect, she followed him into another apartment, and entreated to know what she had to hope, what to dread.

" I will not disguise my fears," said the apothecary; " if there is not a change by the morning, human skill cannot save her life."

" Gracious God!" exclaimed Mildred, lifting her fine eyes towards Heaven, "enable me to bear this severe affliction."

Sir Aldobrand endeavoured to comfort her, but she was for some time perfectly inconsolable; but at length she wiped the tears from her eyes, and once more hastened to the chamber of Juditha.

" Come hither, my dear girl," said Juditha, as Mildred entered the chamber, " and tell me, without disguise, what the apothecary says."

The tear that trembled in Mildred's eye, bursting from its lid, fell on the burning hand of Juditha, which was extended towards her.

" You do not answer, my love," continued Juditha, " you tremble, you weep, but why, my child?   I am only going to be removed from you; our separation, Mildred, will be transient to I who am about to launch into eternity, nor will it be very long to you, even should your life be extended to venerable age; for life is at its utmost length no more than a breath.   Thank Heaven that death did not deprive you of your excellent benefactor at the time you expected it, for then your situation would indeed have been lonely and wretched.   We shall meet, my Mildred, in those blissful regions where the wicked cease from troubling, and the weary are at rest.   Dry your tears, and be assured He who commanded you to exist will guard you from evil; and when I, my Mildred, am an inhabitant of a serene world, you will be blest with earthly friends who will supply the place of her who loves you with the fondness of a mother."

Exhausted with the fatigue of speaking, Juditha sunk back on her pillow and remained silent.   Mildred repressed her sighs, lest her grief should disturb her aged friend; silent and pensive, she seated herself on the bed-side, and pondered in solemn anguish on her melancholy situation.

The whole of that night did Mildred watch by the pillow of Juditha, and it was not until she had sunk into a gentle sleep, that she could be persuaded by the baronet and Ethelbert (who was greatly alarmed by the excessive grief she betrayed) to retire.

She, however, did not seek her room, as they imagined she would, but walked into the gardens of the castle to try to recruit her spirits.

Here she remained for some time, until, refreshed by the air, she returned to the chamber of the suffering Juditha, where she remained until the arrival of the apothecary, when she descended to the room in which he was, in company with Sir Aldobrand.

"My dear young lady," said the apothecary, as Mildred entered the room, "I am sorry to see you look so unwell; you appear to have rested badly."

"Alas!" replied Mildred, "while my aged friend continues in this dangerous state, I shall not enjoy much repose."

"Nay, my dear Mildred," observed Sir Aldobrand; "you must not give way to this extreme sorrow, but to try to submit to the will of Heaven with fortitude and resignation."

"Fatigue," said the apothecary, "will surely injure your health."

"I hope not," replied Mildred; "and if it does, it will be of no consequence, for, alas! I am a useless member of society."

"Mildred, this is unlike yourself," said the baronet, in accents of gentle reproach; "a useless member of society—how can you say so?   Where is there one who would supply the place of nurse to poor Juditha?"

"Ah!" sighed Mildred; "that kind friend is hastening fast to the grave."

A sign of piercing anguish stole from her bosom, and a flood of tears relieved her full heart.   Sir Aldobrand once more took her hand affectionately in his, and tried to ameliorate the agony of her feeling.   At length the damsel became more composed, and the apothecary followed her and the baronet to the chamber of Juditha, whom he found considerably worse, and he felt it his duty to acquaint our heroine and her benefactor with her extreme danger, which he did in the most gentle and delicate manner.

Heartrending as this intelligence was, Mildred received it with apparent firmness.   Hope still clung to her, and notwithstanding the assurances of the apothecary, she flattered herself that he might yet be able to administer to the comfort of her beloved friend, and therefore entreated him not to leave the castle.

Juditha well knew the hour of death drew nigh, and with mildness and fortitude awaited the result.

As she addressed Sir Aldobrand, a smile of ineffable expression stole over her features.

"I feel, Sir Aldobrand," she said, "my pilgrimage here will soon end.   Death wears not a terrific aspect, but one pang rends my heart, and that is the thought of parting with yourself and Mildred; but heaven consoles me in the assurance that in you she will ever find an affectionate protector.   To you, sir, I owe every feeling of gratitude, and accept then, I pray you, my dying blessing.   May your precious life long be spared to confer happiness on your fellow-creatures.   You see with what peace I am about to leave a world; the world where we meet grief, disappointment, sickness, and finally death. The delicate floweret of happiness cannot bloom in these chill regions of sorrow and mortality; yet, by pursuing a virtuous conduct, we may obtain contentment; but ere we arrive at this peaceful period, we must learn humility, resignation, and piety."

She paused, and the baronet, who was deeply affected, extended his hand to her, which she pressed vehemently.

A few moments before her death, Juditha requested to be raised on her pillow; her hand was clasped in Mildred's, and her eyes fixed on her with intense expression; instantly the silver cord of life ceased to vibrate, Mildred's hand was loosened from her grasp, and the suffering girl beheld her amiable and revered friend a breathless corpse.

No longer constrained by the idea of her grief alarming the object of her affection, she hung over the insensible clay in indescribable agony, till the baronet forced her from the bed of death, and, with the tenderness of a parent, led her to her chamber. He sought not to control the anguish of her mind; but, withdrawing, left her to indulge her feelings.

The baronet determined that the remains of one whom he had so much esteemed in life, whose virtues entitled her memory to reverence, should be interred in his family vault, and Mildred heard this kind resolution with the sincerest gratitude, and the compliment paid to her deceased friend increased the warmth of the veneration she entertained for her benefactor.

Mildred attended the remains of her beloved friend to their final resting-place, and

Sir Aldobrand and Ethelbert also followed ; but they were almost unobserved by Mildred, who bent over the coffin while the solemn ceremony was performing, and when it was taken for ever from her sight, she leaned on the baronet's arm, covered her face with her handkerchief, and, nearly insensible to all around, permitted herself to be led to the castle, without breaking the solemn silence that pervaded her mind. Sir Aldobrand and his son, when they returned to the castle, beheld the vacancy of her countenance with the utmost alarm and sorrow.

To arouse her from a situation so painful, they exerted all their powers of eloquence. Mildred was not indifferent to their kindness ; a flood of tears relieved the tightness of her temple, and in some measure tranquillised her heart,

* * * * * * *

The remains of Judi ha had been consigned to the tomb about a week, and her mind was still a prey to the most poignant grief. Sir Aldobrand and Ethelbert did all they could to abate it, and sometimes they succeeded ; but when Mildred retired to her chamber for the night, and was once more left to meditate on the past, her sorrows returned with all their acute anguish, and made her feel miserably lonely and wretched.

One night she sought her chamber at rather a later hour than usual, and not feeling inclined to sleep, but resting herself on the side of the bed, leaned her elbow on her knee, her head resting on her hand, and drawing a lock of Juditha's hair from her bosom, bedewed the unconscious relic with tears of pious remembrance.

Long had they flowed. The castle clock struck one, and Mildred's eye became dim, when tones of the most ravishing softness stole upon the stillness of night. She started to her feet, and listened with amazement, eager to discover from whence they proceeded. Again all was silent, and again the same enchanting notes were heard. Could they proceed from any earthly being, or was the spirit of her departed friend hovering about her to tranquillise her into hope and resignation ?

Mildred felt a powerful sensation of awe gradually steal over her senses. She could scarcely imagine that sounds so divine were breathed from mortal lips ; yet ashamed to encourage superstitious fears, she, with a trembling hand, unfastened her chamber door which opened into a gallery.

A weak light gleamed from the end, and the same mellifluous chant thrilled on her ears.

Mildred felt an irresistible curiosity to discover the musician ; yet she advanced into the gallery slowly. Cautious and trembling, half-fearing and half-resolved, it was some time before she reached the spot that could alone relieve her anxious curiosity.

It was a small chapel, on the altar of which was placed a single taper, from which gleamed a melancholy light ; but what was her astonishment to behold, kneeling before it, an elegant female form, habited in a white robe, which flowed gracefully around her. Surprise held her mute.

She had ceased singing, and was now offering before the throne of mercy the wild, but apparently sincere, effusions of her soul.

Mildred scarcely ventured to breathe, lest she should disturb her, and her feelings were bound up in an extacy of wonder and awe.

She arose at length, and as she turned from the altar, Mildred caught a transient view of her face. Grief appeared to have blanched the ruby hue of health ; but the pallid sweetness of her countenance was irresistibly interesting. Her mind seemed soothed by devotion ; yet still there was a wild lustre in her eyes allied to madness.

Before she attempted to leave the chapel, the mysterious being drew a miniature from her bosom ; a solemn smile then illuminated her features, and she fixed her eyes with such expressive meaning on the portrait, that Mildred could no longer suppress a cry of emotion, not unmingled with fear. The sound startled the unknown. She fixed her eyes for a moment on the countenance of our heroine, and uttering a wild exclamation of terror, hastily took up the taper in her hand, darted swiftly towards a door in the chancel, and the next instant was gone, and Mildred found herself left in total darkness.

Momentary terror now transfixed Mildred to the spot, for the darkness and silence of all around was sufficient to inspire dismal sensations, independent of the singular scene she had just witnessed ; but these feelings soon gave way to those of the most unbounded amazement and curiosity. The strange and interesting form she had seen she was convinced was no phantom of the brain, but life and reality. Who then could she be ? How gained she access to the castle, if it was without the knowledge of Sir Aldobrand (as she believed it was), and what was the purpose of her noctural wanderings ?

These thoughts completely bewildered our heroine, and held her for a short time inactive.

The melancholy sighing of the wind through the chapel at length aroused her, and shuddering involuntarily at the impressive gloom which prevailed around, and which was increased by the solemnity of the hour, she groped her way from the place, and, with some little difficulty, found her way once more into the gallery, and from thence to her chamber. She fastened the door, to prevent the possibility of intrusion, and throwing herself in a chair, gave way to the conflicting thoughts which the extraordinary adventure she had met with created in her breast. An unaccountable sympathy in the secret sorrows of the unknown took possession of her, and she felt an irresistible curiosity to become acquainted with her name and history.

"Sweet mourner!" said Mildred, as she rested her head on her pillow, "how do I wish to ascertain who you are, and to hear a recital of the sorrows which have apparently unhinged your mind, and driven reason from her throne? What can be the meaning of these powerful, these all-absorbing feelings which have taken possession of me? . Oh! methinks, mysterious wanderer, that could I, by participating, diminish your woes, or, by the soothing voice of friendship, calm your perturbed mind, I might again hope to know repose, and feel the thrilling sensation of joy." She raised her head hastily from her pillow, as she imagined that she heard a melancholy sigh near her; but no object met her sight, and chiding herself for her weakness, she once more reclined her head, and endeavoured to court the balmy influence of sleep.

CHAPTER XVI.

THE UNEXPLAINED MYSTERY.—THE SEARCH IN THE CHAPEL.—THE APPEARANCE, AND
THE SUDDEN DISAPPEARANCE.

REFLECTION drove slumber from the pillow of Mildred, and the sun darted his cheering rays through her chamber windows ere she sunk in the arms of sleep, so that the morning was far advanced when she made her appearance in the breakfast-room.

Sir Aldobrand and Ethelbert noticed, with much anxiety, the langour of her looks and the excitement of her manner, and eagerly inquired whether she was not well, or if anything had occurred to disturb her.

Mildred at first hesitated, and then related her nocturnal adventure in the chapel, to which the baronet and his son listened with the most profound attention and astonishment.

"This is more extraordinary than all," remarked Sir Aldobrand. "Are you certain, my dear Mildred, that you have not suffered your imagination to be worked upon by a dream?"

"Oh! no," replied Mildred; "for I had not retired to my bed when the melodious tones saluted my ears, and I heard the castle clock toll the hour of one. It was impossible that I could suffer fancy to take such firm hold of my reason."

"And you actually watched this mysterious wanderer whilst she was paying her devotions before the altar in the chapel?" said the baronet.

Mildred replied in the affirmative."

"Think you it was the same form you formerly beheld, and which so much alarmed you at the time, Mildred?" inquired Ethelbert.

"Oh! no," answered our heroine; "the appearance of this poor unfortunate, for such I feel satisfied she is, was very different to that of the form that appeared to me in my chamber, and in the picture gallery. That inspired terror; but this has excited my deepest sympathy, interest, and curiosity."

"You beheld her features?" asked the baronet.

"I did. They were most lovely, though clouded by an expression of melancholy; and from the wild lustre of her eyes, I am fearful that some deep suffering has banished reason from her seat."

"Did she appear young?" demanded Ethelbert.

"No," replied Mildred; "I should say that more than forty years have passed over her head."

The baronet and his son remained silent for a few minutes, and reflected deeply.

"I am completely lost in wonder," said the former, at length. "I cannot doubt the correctness of Mildred's statement. Can it be possible that any unfortunate being has taken up her abode in this castle unknown to me; and for what purpose?"

" May she not be befriended by some of the servants?" suggested Ethelbert.

" That is not impossible," returned his father; " but still I should hardly think that any of my domestics would venture to take such a liberty without making me acquainted with it. They must be interrogated minutely upon the subject. Did you catch a glimpse of the features which the miniature represented, Mildred ?"

" I did not, sir," answered the damsel, " but no doubt they were those of one who holds' a prominent place in her heart's affections, from the extraordinary emotions she evinced.'-

" The more I reflect on the circumstance, the more am I perplexed," observed Sir Aldobrand. " It seems impossible for any one to have remained concealed in this castle without our knowledge; and why they should seek an asylum here, I cannot imagine."

" This strange adventure, at any rate, must not be suffered to pass over without every attempt being made to elucidate it," said Ethelbert.

" Certainly not," coincided the baronet. " The old chapel has not been much used of late years, and therefore any person who had gained admission to the castle might visit it without any fear of discovery. I will interrogate the servants immediately." ;

The whole of the domestics were therefore ordered into the presence of the baronet, and he commenced a strict examination of them; but he elicited nothing from them that was at all calculated to solve the mystery, and they appeared, and doubtless were, as much astonished as any of the rest at the relation of the circumstance.

Sir Aldobrand dismissed them, satisfied that they had not attempted to deceive him, and he then proposed to Ethelbert and Mildred that they should directly repair to the chapel, to which they agreed, and followed him with impatience and expectation.

Mildred could not help feeling a sensation of awe steal over her as she entered the chapel, although the bright morning sun was shining with great splendour in at the gothic casements, and presented a striking contrast to the sullen gloom which had pervaded every object when she met with the adventure they were now so anxious to unravel. She cast her eyes towards the altar, and almost expected to behold the mysterious wanderer kneeling before it, as she had seen her the night before.

The baronet and Ethelbert looked around the chapel.

" All is exactly the same as when I last entered it," said the former.

" It is not likely that anything would be disturbed," remarked Ethelbert.

They now advanced towards the altar, and their attention was immediately arrested by something glittering upon one of the steps which led up to it. The baronet stooped, and eagerly picking it up, examined it. It was a locket containing a lock of glossy, dark hair; but there were no initials inscribed on the trinket, and nothing whatever to denote to whom it had belonged; although they had no doubt that it had been dropped by the unknown the night before.

Sir Aldobrand placed the locket in his pocket.

" This trinket," he remarked, "simple though it is, at some future period may lead to a discovery. I will carefully preserve it."

They now directed their attention to the door in the chancel, through which the unknown had vanished, and which Sir Aldobrand knew opened into a small apartment beyond. He tried it; but it was fastened, and there was no key in the lock. The baronet, however, had supplied himself with a bunch, and after some trouble, he found one that opened it.

They entered the apartment. It was cold and cheerless. The accumulated dust of years was upon the floor, and the cobwebs clung to the walls and the mouldings of the ceiling.

They passed out at a door on the opposite side, which was standing open, and entered a dark stone passage, along which they groped their way until they arrived at a few narrow stairs at the end, which having ascended, they found themselves in a vaulted gallery, which wound round the northern wing of the castle, and terminated in a chamber which had long been uninhabited, but which was elegantly furnished, and several portraits and landscapes, finely executed, depended from the walls.

This room, however, did not appear as if it had been visited by any one recently, and they therefore did not waste much time in examining it, but finding the door at one end unlocked, they entered the suite of apartments upon which it opened, and which bore all the same marks of neglect that the other rooms they had traversed exhibited.

"I wonder, Sir Aldobrand," remarked Mildred, "that you should suffer this portion of the castle to fall into decay, for the prospect commanded from the different windows is of the most romantic and pleasing description."

"Why, the fact is, my dear Mildred," answered the baronet after some hesitation, "I have my reasons, which it is not necessary that I should at present explain. One of them, however, is, that my family is not large enough to occupy the whole of the castle."

"Hitherto we have met with nothing to solve the mystery," said Ethelbert.

"And it does not seem likely that we shall," replied his father; "however, we will prosecute our search, and see whether we can find the means by which it is likely any person could obtain an entrance to the castle without our knowledge or suspicion."

They walked on through the different apartments, which presented no particular feature to excite curiosity, until they arrived at a room into which they descended by several steps, and the door of which was standing partially open.

It was only lighted by a small casement placed high in the wall, but it presented a much more cleanly and comfortable appearance than any of the chamber, they had yet seen; and there were some embers in the grate which seemed to have been formed by a fire that had recently been kindled there.

Sir Aldobrand and his son were examining one portion of the room minutely, to see whether they could discover any door or other outlet, but they could not, when they were startled by an exclamation of astonishment from Mildred, and, turning their atention to the direction in which she was gazing, found her eyes fixed upon some large characters in chalk, but in a female hand, which were written on the opposite wall. They approached nearer, and then, to their astonishment, plainly deciphered the following words :—

"Where shall the heart oppressed with grief,
Where shall the bosom torn with care,
Find generous pity—kind relief—
A spot unclouded by despair?
        Echo answers—'Where?'
"Will Sorrow's prisoner naught release?
Must still she bend fell Torture's slave?
Oh, yes, she sure will be at peace,
But only in the silent grave.
        Echo answers—'In the grave.'

"Whosoever perchance may read these lines, a wretched wife, an unfortunate outcast earnestly implores them to pray for the repose of her soule, which may then be in eternity.—E."

"Gracious Heaven!" exclaimed the baronet, "what mournful history do these words convey?" That initial, too! Ah! a painful conviction flashes upon my mind. Could these lines have been traced by the unfortuate Lady Editha, my misguided brother's much-injured wife—and is she still in existence?"

"That supposition is most probable," said Ethelbert; "and it is not at all unlikely that it was her whom Mildred last night beheld."

"I dare scarce venture to encourage that idea," ejaculated the baronet; "surely, if it was indeed my unhappy sister-in-law, whose fate is enshrouded in so much awful mystery, she would be certain to receive my protection and sympathy."

"At any rate," remarked Mildred, whose feelings were greatly excited, "it is evident that some unfortunate being has sought a shelter in this part of the castle, and it could not be any one who was not well acquainted with it."

"True," coincided Ethelbert; "and now, since we have made this discovery, we must not relinquish our task until we have further penetrated into the mystery. Have you no recollection of these characters, sir?"

"None," answered the baronet; "but it is so many years since I saw the hand writing of Lady Editha, that I do not think I should be able to recognize it again What had we best do?"

Sir Albobrand meditated for a minute or two, and then, taken up a piece of chalk which he found on the floor, he wrote the following words under the incription on the wall—

"The unfortunate sufferer may find the kindest sympathy and assistance if she will confide in Sir Aldobrand de Lancy, whose heart is never closed to the sorrows of his fellow-creatures.''

"That appeal may induce the poor wanderer to reveal herself," said Ethelbert; "and Heaven send that we may be able to afford her relief. But should it prove to be my unfortunate aunt?"

"Oh, I dare not trust myself with that supposition," said Sir Aldobrand; "alas I fear that both her and my wretched brother have long since perished."

"But the initial E.," suggested Ethelbert, "and the words upon the wall, all serve to strengthen the idea. At any rate, it fully corroborates the account which Mildred has given of her meeting with the mysterious woman in the chapel last night."

"It does," observed our heroine; "oh, I am quite certain I was not deceived."

"But there appears no means of egress from this apartment, only by the way we have come," said Ethelbert.

"There does not," coincided his father; "and had we seen her instead of Mildred and pursued her in her flight, there can be but little doubt she could not have escaped us. I am all anxiety until this extraordinary secret is unravelled."

"And what plan do you propose?" demanded Ethelbert. "It is useless our remaining here."

"Certainly; but you and I will repair to the chapel at night, and keep watch. The poor wanderer may again venture on her nocturnal mission."

This arrangement was agreed to, and after having again strictly examined the walls and the flooring of the apartment, to make sure that there was no secret outlet, but without being able to discover any, they quitted the place, and retraced their steps to the chapel, leaving everything in the same state as they had found it.

They returned to that part of the castle they inhabited, if possible, more bewildered and involved in doubt and mystery than they had been before they had entered on the examination.

All the circumstances gave rise to the most perplexing reflections in their minds, and they awaited the arrival of night with the greatest impatience.

When Mildred quitted Sir Aldobrand and his son, and retired for awhile to her own apartment, she gave herself up entirely to the thoughts which the events of the last few hours naturally excited in her breast; and she awaited the result of the adventure with the utmost anxiety. She felt the most indescribable interest and curiosity to discover who the mysterious wanderer could be, and that was greatly strengthened by the inscription, which every way corresponded with the behaviour of the fair unknown at the altar.

But why should she seek an asylum in the castle, or by what means had she hitherto contrived to remain concealed, she was at a loss to conjecture; and the longer she racked her brain with the subject, the more she became lost in the intricate mazes of perplexity.

She had frequently heard the strange and melancholy history of Sir Martin de Lancy and the beauteous Lady Editha, related by the late Sampsom Hewley and others; and many a time from her sensitive heart had she shed tears of sympathy over the misfortunes of the lady, and shuddered with horror at the fearful curse which Almira de Montreville had invoked upon them, and which, it seemed, had been so terribly fulfilled. She felt the greatest anxiety (and she scarcely knew why) to ascertain whether Sir Martin de Lancy and Lady Editha were still in existence, and what had been the reason of their sudden and unaccountable disappearance from the old Tower of Bransdorf, that ancient edifice, with which she was herself so immediately connected, and whose dark mysteries she had ever been so solicitous to penetrate.

The initial on the wall, which corresponded with the name of Editha, also filled her mind with a variety of conflicting thoughts and surmises; but it was to no purpose she sought to come to some satisfactory conclusion on the subject.

The day wore tediously away, and ten o'clock had chimed from the old clock in the castle hall, when Ethelbert and his father prepared to start on their expedition to the chapel, having supplied themselves with a light in a small lantern, in case they should stand in need of it.

Mildred was anxious to accompany them, but they thought it was better that she did not, and she therefore yielded to their advice, but did not retire to rest, as she was eager to know the result of their adventure might be. She sat in her chamber buried in profound meditatien, but still listening attentively to catch the smallest sound that might be heard in the castle.

All, however, was still as death, except at intervals, when the wind might be heard murmuring along the different avenues, or hastily banging too a heavy door which had been left open. An intense, but not unpleasing melancholy stole gradually over her senses, and she pondered over all the events of her past life, and formed a variety of anticipations for the future.

In the meantime Sir Aldobrand and Ethelbert had entered the chapel, over which a solemn stillness pervaded. They walked to the altar and examined it, and then the door in the chancel, and peeped into the room beyond, but all remained the same as when they had left them in the morning, and it did not seem as if any one had been there except themselves. They were all impatience, anxiety, and eager curiosity, and they both foreboded some extraordinary discovery, which the events of the morning, and Mildred's previous night's adventure had given them cause to expect.

Ethelbert at first suggested that they should retrace their steps to the apartment in which they had seen the inscription on the wall, and there conceal themselves and keep watch; but Sir Aldobrand overruled that, and considered that they could not do better than to await patiently where they were, lest they should, by their over eagerness, frustrate the plans they had in view.

"Probably," said the baronet, "if it is the custom of the unknown to visit this chape to offer up her devotions, although Mildred has not seen her before, she will not fail to do so this night, and then we can watch our opportunity, and starting forth from the place of our concealment, seize her before she has any chance to elude us."

"But may not what you have written on the wall alarm her if she really seeks concealment," said Ethelbert, "and cause her to abandon what may have been her previous custom?"

"You were of a different opinion in the morning, Ethelbert," returned the baronet; "and I do not see what cause you have to alter it now."

"But our sudden appearance may alarm her, and be productive of the most serious consequences."

"We must run the risk of that, and shall be the better able to judge in what manner it will be most prudent for us to act when the moment arrives. Let us hide behind these pillars, from whence we can have a good view of her features should she emerge from the door of the chancel."

Ethelbert offered no further objection, and shading their lantern, they took their place behind the pillars, and only ventured to hold converse with each other in subdued whispers.

The time passed tediously away, and still all remained quiet and undisturbed in the chapel, and the patience of Sir Aldobrand and his son began to be exhausted, and the latter again endeavoured to persuade the baronet to make their way at once to the chamber, without having the least effect upon his resolution.

The wind began to blow keenly in at the casement of the chapel, many of the squares in which were broken, and the baronet and his son felt cold and cheerless for want of exercise; at the same time they regretted that they had not deferred the commencement of their adventure until a later hour.

Mildred too was quite as anxious and impatient as themselves, and had two or three times walked to the end of the gallery, and peeped into the chapel, but without being able to discover were they were secreted.

Eleven o'clock now struck, but still nothing occurred to gratify the curiosity of the watchers, and they began to think that the task shey had come upon would turn out to be a fruitless one.

Another hour elapsed, and still the same, and Sir Aldobrand, now shading the light of the lantern, followed by Ethelbert, with noiseless steps left the place where they were concealed, and advanced towards the door of the chancel, where they listened attentively, but all was perfectly still. The silence of the grave reigned on all around.

Suddenly, however, Ethelbert cluthed his father's arms, and directed his attention to a faint murmuring sound, which, though low, audibly met their ears, and gradually seemed to grow louder and louder, until it swelled into a beautiful strain of melody that held their senses in astonishment and delight.

They scarcely dared to breathe, lest they should lose a single note of the sweet and plaintive air, and at length they distinctly heard the following words, which they had seen on the wall in the morning :—

"Where shall the heart oppressed with grief,
Where shall the bosom torn with care,
Find generous pity—kind relief—
A spot unclouded by despair ?
Echo answers—'Where?'

"Will Sorrow's prisoner naught release ?
Must still she bend fell Torture's slave ?
Oh, yes, she sure will be at peace,
But only in the silent grave.
Echo answers—'In the grave.'"

"Hush !" whispered Sir Aldobrand; "there is a glimmering light approaching !—She comes !"

With the speed of lightning they retreated once more behind the pillars which had before concealed them, and then with breathless attention and expectation awaited the appearance of the unknown midnight wanderer.

Nearer and nearer the twinkling light seemed to advance, but not the least sound of footsteps met their ears.

They were not long kept in suspense ; the door in the chancel was thrown gently and silently back on its hinges, and the tall figure of a female, clad in white, and bearing a taper in her hand, emerged from it into the chapel, and with slow and solemn steps approached the altar.

Sir Aldobrand and his son gazed at her graceful and dignified figure with amazement and admiration, but her features were now concealed beneath a long white veil, and therefore, in that respect, they were disappointed.

Ethelbert's feelings were so excited, that it was with the greatest difficulty the baronet could prevent him from rushing forward at once ; and Mildred, who had heard the voice of the unknown from her chamber, had again ventured to the entrance of the chapel, and watched the approaching figure with the greatest attention and the utmost interest.

Solemnly the unknown advanced to the altar, and once, on the way, they could hear her heave a deep sigh, and her steps seemed to falter.

How anxious was Sir Aldobrand that she would remove her veil, so that he might obtain a view of her features, and thus gratify his burning curiosity before he ventured to disturb her ; but he imagined that she was now secure, for she could not possibly escape, and he therefore tried to await the result of the adventure with patience.

The same feelings of awe and reverence which she had experienced the night before, again stole over our heroine, and her heart palpitated so violently against her side, that she was afraid its beating would be heard.

The unknown had now arrived at the altar, and solemnly kneeling before it, she appeared mentally to offer up heartfelt prayers to Heaven. Heavy sighs then escaped her bosom, and she seemed totally absorbed in the agony of her grief.

Still the attention of Sir Aldobrand and Ethelbert was so completely arrested by the conduct of the mysterious woman, and the impressive solemnity of her actions, that they could not move from the spot on which they were standing.

She now took the miniature from her bosom, and gazed intently at it through her veil and her sobs increased in intensity of anguish. Now was the moment Sir Aldobrand thought for action : he nudged his son significantly, and they both darted with noiseless steps from the place of their concealment. But fate was against them ; they had not advanced half-a-dozen paces, when the foot of Ethelbert came in contact with something, and he stumbled and fell heavily to the ground, his sword belt making a rattling sound on the pavement.

The sound immediately caught the ear of the unknown. With wonderful agility she started to her feet, and beholding them, she uttered a cry of alarm, dashed the taper from her hand, and sprang through the doorway of the chancel, closing it after her. and was lost to sight before Sir Aldobrand and his son, who had hastily gathered himself up again, had reached the altar.

"Quick —quick! This is a cursed misfortune,' said the baronet; "but it is impossible that she can escape us even now."

They burst open the door, and looked eagerly into the room beyond ; but not the least sign of the fugitive did they perceive, and the place was involved in darkness, except from the faint light emitted by the lantern.

They continued to traverse the different passages and apartments with no better success, and arriving at the door of the chamber, to their vexation and dismay, they found it fastened.

They had no key with them by which they could unlock it; but, determined not to be easily defeated in their object, they made several ineffectual attempts to force it, and then listened for a moment or two, to ascertain whether they could hear any sound.

They were almost positive they heard a footstep moving in the apartment, and then the baronet exclaimed—

"Unfortunate being, whoever you are, do not seek to avoid us, for we are friends, who would serve you all that lies in our power.''

No answer was returned to this, and all was perfectly silent in the room. The patience of Sir Aldobrand and Ethelbert was quite exhausted, and again applying all their strength to the door, they burst it open, and entering the room, gazed around them.

The object of their search was not there.

"Confusion!" exclaimed the baronet. "Are we then disappointed in our wishes after all? This looks like the work of magic, or some supernatural agency. How is it possible that the mysterious being can have escaped, since there are no means of egress from this aparsment?"

"It is quite evident she is not here," said Ethelbert. "We are foiled. There must be some secret means of escaping from this room."

Again they examined the walls, and the flooring; but no signs of any secret trap or door met their observation.

"This is a mystery which I cannot penetrate," said Sir Aldobrand. "I am lost in amazement."

"And so am I," remarked Ethelbert; "and see, the writing is removed from the wall."

And so it was, and that the more increased their bewilderment and surprise.

"It is no use remaining here," said the baronet, after a pause; "we shall not see the mysterious woman any more to-night, whatever we may do on a future occasion, that's certain. It was a most provoking thing, your falling; for she otherwise could not have avoided us."

"Yes, it was unfortunate," coincided Ethelbert; "but I could not help it; it was to be, and it seems that the fates have conspired to involve us in still greater doubt and perplexity."

"It does; but I will not rest until I have penetrated this most extraordinary secret."

"I fear it is too late to do so," observed Ethelbert; "for, after the alarm which this strange being has this night experienced, it is not very likely that she will venture to this spot again."

"I will have a more minute search made in all the other apartments besides this," said the baronet; "for it is evident that one of them must contain a secret door or trap, which has hitherto escaped our detection."

"That certainly appears most probable," returned Ethelbert; "and I would advise that a strict and secret watch should be kept in the chapel."

"That shall be done," answered his father. "But come, the light in the lantern will soon expire, so we had better make our way back again without delay."

Casting another suspicious glance around the chamber, Sir Aldobrand and Ethelbert now proceeded to retrace their steps, much disappointed at the frustration of their wishes just at the very moment when they seemed about to be gratified.

CHAPTER XVII.

THE MINIATURE.—THE REMARKABLE DISCOVERY.—THE FRUITLESS ATTEMPT TO
UNRAVEL THE MYSTERY.

ON the return of Sir Aldobrand and his son to the chapel, they found Mildred anxiously waiting there to hear the result of the adventure; and when she was informed of the singular and unaccountable escape of the unknown, she was both surprised and disappointed.

"We shall never behold her again, nor be able to ascertain who she is, depend upon it," she observed.

"I am afraid not," answered Ethelbert; "this state of mystery and suspense is most intolerable."

"This disappointment," remarked the baronet, "has only excited my curiosity in a stronger degree than ever, and I am determined to gratify it, if possible."

"I am fearful there is but very little chance of your being able to do so, sir," answered Mildred.

"At any rate, I will not give way entirely to despair. But we will talk further upon the subject to-morrow; but it is now late, and you must need rest, Mildred; you had better retire to your chamber, unless you are afraid of a visit from the mysterious lady, in which case I should advise you to sleep with your maid Barbara."

"Oh, no, sir," replied Mildred; "the feeling I entertain towards this extraordinary and unknown being is of a very different description to that of fear. I could, indeed, almost reverence her, even surrounded as she at present is by mystery."

"It is strange," said Sir Aldobrand; "but good night, Mildred, and Heaven send that your rest may not be disturbed by troublesome dreams."

They were passing by the altar when the foot of Sir Aldobrand kicked against something which was lying on the pavement. He stooped, and picked it up.

It was the miniature which the unknown had dropped in her flight.

Sir Aldobrand took the lantern from his son's hand, and eagerly held the light so that he might scrutinise it narrowly. But Ethelbert and Mildred marked with astonishment and curiosity the extraordinary emotion which immediately agitated his features. His countenance became ashy pale; his lips quivered, and his eyes became fixed upon the lineaments which the miniature pourtrayed, with an intensity of expression that plainly shewed the feelings which were passing in his bosom.

"For Heaven's sake, my dear father," demanded Ethelbert, hastily, "what do you see in that portrait to agitate you thus?"

"God of Heaven!" exclaimed Sir Aldobrand, as he still continued to gaze upon the miniature, and his emotion increased; "can it be possible, or is it only some vision conjured up before my eyes to delude my senses?"

"What mean you, father?" said Ethelbert, impatiently; "speak, I conjure you."

"No, no," cried the baronet; "it is no deception. Every feature is the same, and rendered as distinct as if they were beaming in life upon me. It is the likeness of my unfortunate brother, Sir Martin de Lancy."

"Of Sir Martin de Lancy!" repeated the astonished Ethelbert and Mildred in a breath.

"Yes, yes; behold," ejaculated Sir Aldobrand; "Ethelbert—Mildred—you have seen the portrait in the picture-gallery—look! look!"

He held up the miniature to the light before their eyes, and in the likeness they beheld the same features so ably delineated in the portrait in the picture-gallery.

Surprise rivetted their attention, and rendered them speechless, while the baronet continued to gaze with intense earnestness upon the miniature, and tears trembled in his manly eyes.

"Almighty God," he at last cried, "how wonderful are thy ways! Never did I expect to behold this impressive relic again; and to come into my possession in such a remarkable and mysterious manner! This is the very miniature my ill-fated brother presented to Lady Editha before their unfortunate nuptials. The initial and the other writing on the wall is now explained; the mysterious being we have this night seen, can be no other than Sir Martin's deeply-injured wife."

To attempt to describe the feelings of Ethelbert and Mildred, but more particularly those of the baronet, at this discovery (for that the female they had seen was no other than the unfortunate and ill-fated Lady Etitha there could be very little doubt), would be an arduous, if not altogether fruitless, task. All the painful and mysterious circumstances of the past rushed upon his recollection, and his manly fortitude almost gave way beneath the weight of them.

"Oh, surely this cannot be, my dear father," said Ethelbert; "if the strange and evidently deeply afflicted wanderer we have seen be really my unfortunate aunt, would she not, knowing the esteem you ever felt towards her, and your otherwise amiable and benevolent character, have at once boldly thrown herself on your protection, rather than thus secretly seek an asylum in the castle? And why should she thus avoid you, as if she had occasion to fear you?"

"I am lost in astonishment and perplexity," returned Sir Aldobrand; "but I feel satisfied that this unhappy being can be no other than your hapless aunt, whose extraordinary disappearance, many years since, has caused me so many bitter hours of anguish and fruitless conjecture. Who else could have obtained possession of the miniature of my misguided and I fear guilty brother? And why should she feel such deep emotion in the contemplation of it, as that we have witnessed? May Heaven solve the mystery, and reveal to me the whole circumstances of the fate of Sir Martin."

"I trust it will, my father," said Ethelbert; "at any rate, this strange being must be discovered. In what manner she could have effected her escape I cannot conceive, especially as we have not hitherto been able to detect any secret door or trap in the apartment. There must, however, be some means of egress of that description, for it is evident that she was in the room at the time we arrived at the door. A more minute search must be made, but for this night we must abandon our design, and await patiently the result of some future discovery."

The baronet remained silent and buried for a few moments in deep reflection.

"Alas!" he said at length, with a sigh, "I fear that there is little chance of this painful business being elucidated at present; and it is most likely, after what has occurred to-night, that this unknown individual will not appear again in the castle. Oh, will the cause of Sir Martin and Editha's disappearance, and the fate which has attended them, whether they be living or dead, never be explained?"

He cast a melancholy glance around the chapel, and then embracing Mildred, and begging her not to be alarmed, he and Ethelbert retired, and our heroine, in a most agitated and bewildered state of mind, once more sougl t her chamber.

But for some hours rest was a stranger to her; the remarkable evei. s of the night continued to occupy her mind, and to fill her with a variety of conflicting and unsatisfactory thoughts. She could not but feel the deepest interest in the fate of Lady Editha and her husband, so nearly related as they were to her kind benefactor and Ethelbert; and most glad would she have been could any elucidation of the mystery be obtained.

The discovery of the miniature led her strongly to imagine that the conclusions of Sir Aldobrand were correct, and that the mysterious unknown was no other than Lady Editha; but why she should act with so much secrecy, and take such pains to elude Sir Aldobrand, whom she must be sure was sincerely her friend, and deeply sympathised in her misfortunes, Mildred was completely at a loss to conjecture.

She listened attentively, with the hope of once more hearing the voice of the unknown, but all was silent; scarcely a breath disturbed the stillness around. She no longer entertained any feeling of dread of the object of her curiosity and anxiety, but she felt the greatest wish to behold her again, and to ascertain who she was, and whether the conjectures of the baronet were indeed correct.

At length, wearied with thinking, and the adventure of the night, Mildred did sink off to sleep, and did not wake again until the morning sun was darting his brilliant rays in at the casements of her chamber.

Sir Aldobrand had passed a restless night, for nothing could alter the opinion he had formed as to who the wandering being who had so much excited their curiosity was, and the miniature fully confirmed him in the belief that it could be no other than Lady Editha. But where was her husband? What had been the cause of their extraordinary disappearance from the old tower; and where had they been to all this time, and why should she seek to elude him? Why did she not at once throw herself upon his protection, and explain the whole of the singular circumstances? Altogether, it was a mystery of the most complex and inexplicable description, and the more he endeavoured to fathom it, the deeper did he bceome involved in doubt and perplexity. He was resolved, however, to leave no means untried to penetrate it, and to unravel the secret of the unknown's remarkable disappearance from the chamber to which Ethelbert and himself had pursued her, and which had about it altogether the appearance of magic.

When the baronet, Ethelbert, and our heroine met in the breakfast-room in the morning, they continued to converse for some time on the remarkable events of the previous night, but they were still at a loss to come to any satisfactory conclusion upon the subject; Sir Aldobrand, however, continuing to entertain the supposition that the unknown was the unfortunate and much-wronged Lady Editha, which the melancholy words they had heard her sing, the writing on the wall, and the likeness of Sir Martin de Lancy, which she had dropped at the altar, all seemed to tend to confirm.

The repast being over, the baronet and his son arose with the intention of visiting the chamber about which their curiosity was so much excited, and at Mildred's earnest request, she was permitted to accompany them.

As they made their way through the different avenues and chambers, the circumstances of the previous night arose to their recollection in the most vivid colours, and deeply interested their thoughts. All remained precisely the same as they had last visited them, nor was it at all likely that any one had penetrated them during the few intervening hours.

They at last arrived at the door of the chamber of mystery, and entered. Mildred looked around her with much curiosity, and again a feeling of awe and solemnity stole over her senses.

Once more Sir Aldobrand and Ethelbert closely inspected the walls, but could not discover the least signs of a secret door; and they were about to examine the boards of the floor, when the baronet's eye fell upon a small scrap of paper which was lying on a table in one corner of the room. He hastily took it up, and read the following words in a female's hand:—

"To Sir Aldobrand de Lancy.

"A wretched woman has been in the habit, for some time past, of visiting this castle, which is endeared to her by many tender yet melancholy associations. But there is another and far more powerful attraction which has led her wandering footsteps hither, and which she dare not at present reveal. You will see me no more, until fate shall permit me to discover myself, and the persecution to which I have so long and cruelly been subjected, shall be at an end, if such is ever destined to take place; therefore, it is useless to search for me. Oh! bestow your sympathy on the unparalleled misfortunes of a wretched wife, whose only hope of peace is in the grave!"

"Unfortunate sufferer!" ejaculated Sir Aldobrand, when he had perused these lines; "deeply do I, indeed, sympathise in the sorrows which evidently oppress you. What a strange and sad destiny that must be which renders such mystery imperative! This more than all convinces me—I am satisfied that the writer of this epistle is none other than the wife of Sir Martin de Lancy."

"It is strange," exclaimed Ethelbert; "it does indeed appear likely to be as you conjecture, my dear sir; but why should she hesitate to confide in you, and to claim that protection which would be so freely and so generously awarded her?"

"In vain do I rack my brain to form the least idea," said Sir Aldobrand; "nor does there appear to be any chance of this impenetrable mystery being solved. Alas! I fear that we shall no more behold her. At least, so it appears from the tenor of this note. It was most unfortunate that she should have been alarmed, and that she eluded us last night, for then all our doubts would have been at once satisfied, and we probably might have been able to have rescued her from the extraordinary misfortunes with which she is at present too evidently surrounded."

"Unhappy lady!" ejaculated Mildred, who felt a pang shoot through her bosom which she found it impossible to conquer, but for the extraordinary nature of which she could not very satisfactorily account; "it appears but too evident that she is the victim of some cruel fate, and that she fears to be discovered, lest that fate should be aggravated or completed. But in what manner could she have effected her escape from this room, for it is quite certain that she has been here since you pursued her last night."

"It is," coincided Ethelbert; "and that satisfies me that there must be some secret means of egress. Let us examine the boards."

"It is all but useless, only for satisfaction sake," remarked the baronet; "for we shall not find the object of our search. She, it seems, does not intend to visit the castle, for the present, at any rate."

"But still we may discover something in our researches that might tend to throw a light on the subject," said Ethelbert.

The baronet assented, but without expecting to make any discovery; and stooping down, they examined the floor minutely. They at first did not perceive anything to excite their curiosity, and were about to give up the task, being involved in still greater wonder and bewilderment than before, when Ethelbert found that one of the boards was more loose than the others, and this confirmed his suspicions. He placed the point of his sword in the crevice, and after some little difficulty it yielded, and raising it, they perceived an aperture, and a flight of steps beneath.

Here, then, everything was explained, and they were surprised that they had not discovered the secret trap before, although, in the confusion of the moment, it was certainly not to be wondered at.

The noise they had heard in the room the preceding night was now fully accounted for. It had been from the falling of the trap in its place on the retreat of the unknown, and they were only astonished how she had found strength to raise it.

It was very dark below; but they had taken care to bring a light with them, and Sir

Aldobrand began to descend the steps, followed by Ethelbert ; and Mildred, whose curiosity was as much excited as their own, also accompanied them.

The steps were rather difficult of descent, for they were steep, and considerably impaired by time ; but when they reached the bottom, they found themselves in a well-paved passage, lighted at the farther end by a small casement, beneath which was a door. The key was in the lock, and opening it, they beheld themselves in the court-yard of the castle.

Thus, then, their search was at an end, for the means by which the unknown had effected her escape was fully explained, and the baronet was surprised that such an entrance to the castle had never become known to him before : but of course, it was entirely owing to that part of the castle having been left uninhabited so long before.

" Our adventure is at an end," said the baronet, "and we are left in as great a state of doubt and perplexity as ever, any further than that we have discovered the means by which the unknown was enabled to elude us. But still I am determined that a strict watch shall at all times be kept in the chapel, and this part of the castle, in the hope that the unfortunate wanderer may yet be seen again, and that we may be able to discover who she is, and what are the sorrows which have compelled her to take to such a miserable and singular course of life. Should it indeed be the Lady Editha, I hope that Providence will prompt her to disclose herself, and to unravel the mystery that has so long enshrouded her fate, and that of my brother, Sir Martin de Lancy."

" Alas ! poor lady !" sighed Mildred. " Many a time have I wept over her extraordinary and sorrowful history, connected as it is too, so closely with the old tower of Brans-dorf, in which I was found in so wonderful a manner by the late honest and kind-hearted Sampson Hewley."

Sir Aldobrand took her hand, and pressed it in silence. They then walked into the castle.

This additional adventure served them to converse about during the remainder of the day ; but they were still involved in the same state of uncertainty as at first, and saw no prospect at present of the torturing mystery being elucidated. Sir Aldobrand, however, was still firmly of opinion that the unknown was Lady Editha, a conclusion to which all the circumstances seemed to warrant them in arriving.

For several weeks after this, the baronet had a strict watch kept in the chapel, and the other places which led to the chamber, but without anything transpiring to gratify their curiosity, or to throw the least light upon the bewildering subject; and at length they gave it up in despair, and began to think that all chance of their making any further discovery was at an end.

The circumstances cost no one more reflection than they did Mildred, and many a time did she long to be made acquainted with the sorrows of the interesting stranger, and to behold her again; and she could not help imagining her wishes would some time or other be gratified, although what reason she had for thinking so she could not conceive.

She had not removed from that part of the castle which she slept in at the time she beheld the fair unknown. She had become attached to it, in fact, from that circumstance ; and frequently she would wander forth into the chapel of an evening, when the pale moonlight streamed through the old gothic casements, and listen attentively near the door of the chancel, with the hope of hearing once more those mellifluous and impressive strains which had before so rivetted her attention, or to see that graceful, majestic, yet sorrowful form, again kneeling, in pious devotion, before the altar. But after an hour or two passed in this manner, she would return disappointed to her chamber, wondering that the unknown should have taken such a powerful and unaccountable hold upon her feelings.

CHAPTER XVIII.

ST. SWITHIN'S NIGHT AGAIN.—THE STORM.—THE PLOT.—THE SEIZURE.—THE DUNGEON IN THE OLD TOWER OF BRANSDORF.

IT was St. Swithin's eve, and the weather was just as tempestuous as on that memorable night described at the commencement of this narrative.

The afternoon, however, had been fine, and Ethelbert, feeling in a low, desponding state of mind, with the hope of shaking off the gloom of his spirits, had taken a ride accompanied only by one domestic, to the residence of a youthful friend of his, about ten miles distant from De Lancy Castle.

The time had passed so agreeably in each other's society, that the evening had set in before Ethelbert thought of departing, and at that time, the clouds assuming a lowering, portentous aspect, his friend endeavoured to persuade him to remain for the night at his mansion, or, at any rate, until the threatened tempest should have abated. Ethelbert was, however, anxious to get home, as he had promised his father particularly to do so, they having some business to transact together in the morning; and not supposing that the storm would come on until he had completed the journey, he declined the invitation of his friend, and shortly afterwards took his leave.

The nearest route to the castle was none of the most pleasant, and lay on the borders of a forest, which, even in the most beautiful season, was gloomy and cheerless; but Ethelbert and his attendant pushed on their way, regardless of the aspect of the scenery around them, and only anxious to reach the place of their destination before the tempest should come on.

They had proceeded about two miles on their journey, when the moon was suddenly completely obscured by the dense clouds which had long been gathering in the heavens, and the domestic, riding up to his master, observed—

" The storm will overtake us directly, your honour, I'm thinking. It would have been better had we taken the advice of Lord Gervase, and at least have waited awhile until we saw the result.'

" If we push on our way at our present speed," replied his master, "we shall even now I think, arrive at the castle before the tempest commences."

He had scarcely uttered these words, however, when they felt large drops of rain descending, and a heavy peal of thunder rattled along the sky, which plainly shewed that the forebodings of the servant were about to be verified in good earnest; and Ethelbert was half inclined to retrace his way to the mansion of Lord Gervase, as there was no place of shelter at hand; but, upon second consideration, he thought he might as well push on his road, as he could reach the castle nearly as soon as he could regain the mansion of his friend.

The storm now pelted down in right good earnest, and yet Ethelbert and his attendant were several miles from home, and the prospect before them was most gloomy.

Ethelbert was at length induced to diverge from the road, and to seek a temporary shelter beneath the shady canopy of some trees, until the rain should haply have abated somewhat of its violence. He now regretted that he had not taken the advice of Lord Gervase, for it seemed as if there would be no alteration in the weather for some time, and to remain there was both tedious and annoying.

While they were thus standing, they were aroused by hearing a trampling as if of many horses approaching the spot; but they felt no surprise or alarm, as they imagined that the sounds only proceeded from travellers like themselves. They were not long kept in suspense, for in a few moments afterwards seven or eight men, of ruffianly appearance, came up to the spot on which they were standing, and Ethelbert and his servant could then perceive that they were all well armed and mounted, and the idea of robbers then, for the first time, forced itself upon his imagination.

The lightning now glared full upon the persons of Ethelbert and his companion, and the foremost of the men, fixing a keen and penetrating look upon the former, said, with an oath—

" Ah, I told ye I was not mistaken. It is he we seek; secure him.'

" Who are ye ?—and why do ye seek to molest us ?" demanded Ethelbert, sternly, at the same time laying his hand upon his sword; but, before either he or his attendant could offer any resistance, they were seized by the ruffians, disarmed, their cloaks drawn so tightly over their heads that they could scarcely breathe, and being bound on their horses' backs, felt themselves forced away at a rapid rate through the forest.

We need not describe the emotion of Ethelbert at this outrage, and the apprehensions he entertained as to the intentions of the villains. He tried to shout; but his voice was completely stifled by the cloak, and he was rendered entirely incapable of offering any resistance.

The rain still continued to fall rapidly, and Ethelbert was soon drenched to the skin; but not a word was exchanged between the ruffians, and he was totally at a loss to imagine whither they wereconveying him, or what they intended to do with him. That their design was not robbery, however, he felt all but certain, or they would have committed it at once, and he therefore had good reason to believe that h e had something more serious to fear from them.

They had proceeded in this manner more than half an hour, as well as Ethelbert could guess, and then they slackened their pace, and he could feel a strong current of air, and the murmuring sounds which saluted his ears convinced him that they were near the ocean.

Suddenly they stopped altogether, and Ethelbert found himself lifted from his horse's back by two or three of the men, and carried along in their arms, without his having the power to oppose them, or to ask whither they were conveying him. The hollow echo of their footsteps, however, convinced him that they were traversing some vaulted subterranean passage, and the idea of a robber's cave then occurred to him.

At last they stopped. The cords were unfastened which had bound his limbs, the cloak removed from his head, and he then, to his utter amazement and alarm, found himself in a large stone vaulted apartment, dimly lighted by a lamp suspended by a chain from the roof, and surrounded by the fellows who had seized him, and several others of equally daring and suspicious aspect.

Astonishment, for a moment or two, held Ethelbert speechless; but he quickly recovered himself, and demanded in a stern voice, where he was, and for what purpose he had been brought there.

"Oh, you will know the purpose for which you are brought here soon enough," replied one of the men; "but if it will afford you any consolation to known, I don't mind informing you that you are in one of the dungeons of Tower of Bransdorf."

Ethelbert started, and could scarcely believe the evidence of his senses. In the Tower of Bransdorf, the building belonging to his family, and which they had, in spite of the extraordinary stories circulated about it, supposed to be uninhabited; it seemed almost incredible. And for what purpose could he have been brought there? He looked in the dark faces of the men, and augured the worst. It was quite clear that they had brought him there, not for the mere purpose of plunder, but upon the instructions and at the pay of a superior.

All these thoughts passed rapidly in his mind, and made him feel very wretched, not so much on his own account as the danger which might threaten Mildred.

"Villains!" he demanded, "by whose orders have ye presumed to lay violent hands upon my person, and to bring me hither? Reveal the name of your base employer, and the purpose for which ye have seized me."

"Ethelbert de Lancy," said the man, who had spoken before, "it is useless for you to attempt to offer any resistance, as you must be aware. Here you are secure; but as you have before been told, you will ascertain all the particulars so interesting to you quite soon enough. Good night; we leave you to your reflections. Here are provisions for you, and some wine, which is not bad fare for one who is a prisoner, and at the mercy of——"

The man hesitated, and Ethelbert, wound up to a pitch of frenzy, not only by the outrage that had been committed on him, but the coolness of the man, started forward from the spot on which he had been standing, and would have seized him by the throat, had he not been grasped rudely by the arms by a couple of ruffians, and held at bay.

"Release me instantly, villains," he cried, struggling in the grasp of those who [held him. "Mean ye murder? Cowards! recollect that, although ye may at present appear to triumph, ye will have to answer dearly for all this."

A rude laugh again escaped the villains, and the man who only had spoken thoughout made a sign to his companions, and they moved towards the door of the vault or dungeon,

"Stay!" exclaimed Ethelbert, as he looked round for his servant, and did not see him; "you do not mean to leave me here? What have you done with my domestic?"

"Oh, we have taken care of him," answered the fellow; "as to yourself, you will understand more by-and-bye."

He said no more, but followed by his associates, he hastily quitted the place, bolting the door after him, and left the discomfited Ethelbert to his own thoughts.

He threw himself on a stone bench that occupied one corner of the vaulted apartment, and for some time became completely absorbed in the multiplicity of conflicting and torturing ideas which rushed upon his brain, and not the least important to him was the fate which had pobably befallen his domestic.

It was quite evident that the fellows who had seized him acted from no minor

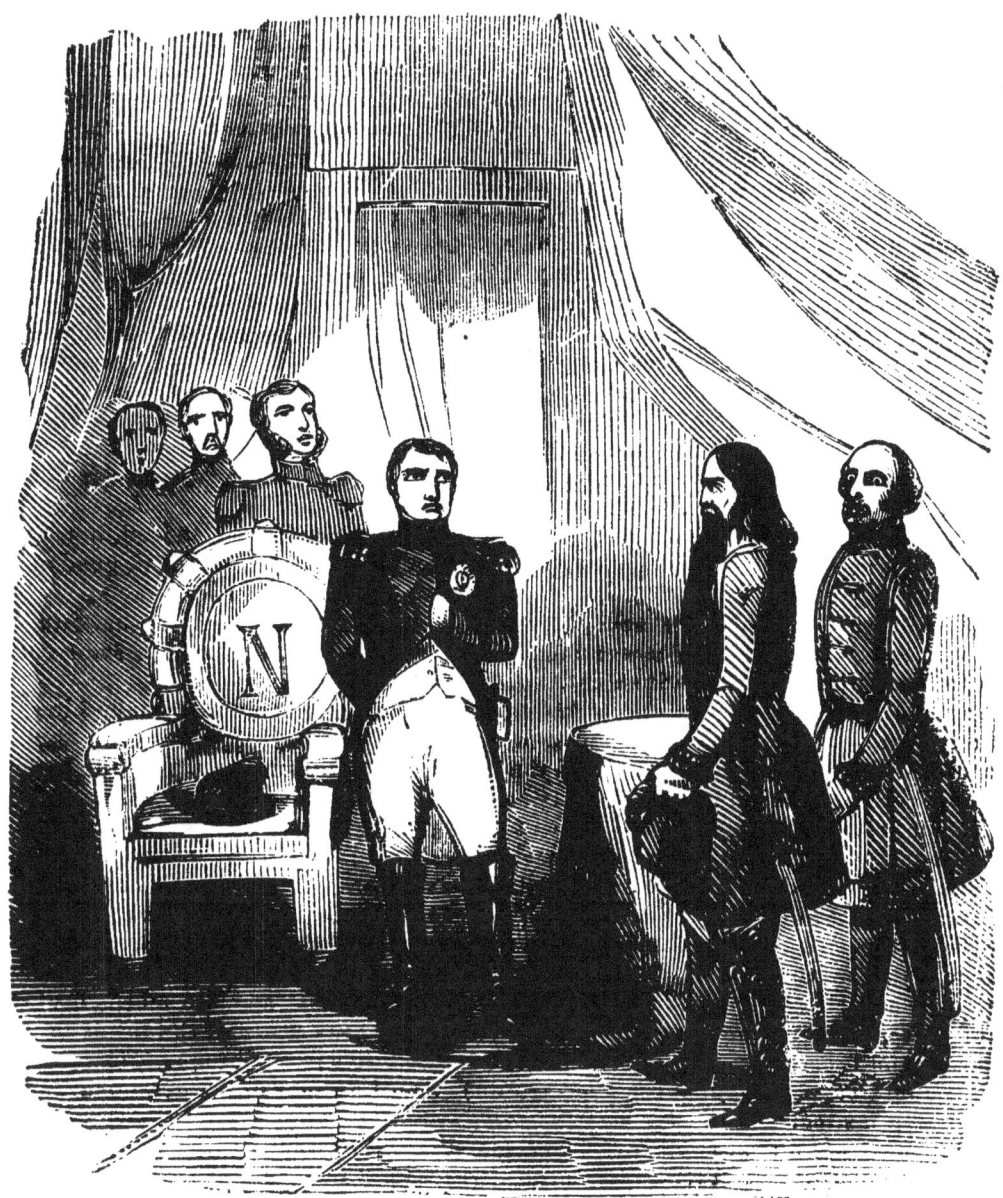

authority; and to find himself so completely trepanned, and without any possible means of offering resistance, or the least prospect of escaping the unknown power in which he was now held, was a source of greater misery to him than all.

How often did he regret that he had not taken the advice of his friend, Lord Gervase, and remained at his mansion for the night; then the plans of the ruffians might have been defeated. It was quite clear that it was a pre-concerted design, and that the men must have been employed to watch his motions, or how could they have surprised him in the manner they had? But still it never occurred to him for an instant who the author might be.

He arose from the rude seat on which he had thrown himself, and traversed the vault. He gazed round upon its blackened walls with a despairing eye, and the most gloomy thoughts were suggested to his mind. Here, in this dismal tower, had the most extraordinary and mysterious events occurred, that were also so closely connected with his family, and upon the revelation of which so much depended.

It was in this old tower, too, that Mildred had been found by Sampson Hewley—Mildred, his beloved Mildred, in whose destiny, and the discovery of whose origin, his own hopes and happiness were so deeply involved. There was a sort of charm, if we may be allowed the observation, about the ancient building, which, even under all the painful circumstances of his seizure, held him, as it were, in a sort of spell. And yet he blamed himself for not having, in spite of his father's injunctions, endeavoured to fathom the mysteries of the old tower more minutely than he had hitherto done, especially after the remarkable stories which had been continued to be promulgated about it.

But every other thought was absorbed in the danger of his present situation, the singular manner in which he had been captured, and the uncertainty of who the individual was upon whose instructions the men had acted.

To find himself placed in such a position, and without the least chance of effecting his escape, or of making his friends aware of where he was, was a severe trial of his patience, and he again traversed the dungeon (for such, indeed, it could only be called), and beating his breast, gave way to a paroxysm of rage, cursing his unfortunate fate, and making the place resound again with his exclamations and demands for liberty; but, at the same time, he felt well assured that it was all useless, as the ruffians were not the sort of men to be moved either by his supplications or his threats, if they should even hear him, or were at all in the tower."

He examined every part of the place, but found it quite secure; and, indeed, it would have been folly for a moment to imagine that the fellows would not have taken good care of that before leaving him.

Ethelbert, however, amidst his own fears, felt considerable anxiety for the fate of Arthur, who was an old attached servant, and whose society would have been some consolation to him in his present confinement.

At length Ethelbert once more threw himself upon the stone bench, and gave himself up entirely to the silence of mental agony and despair.

He could distinctly hear the howling of the tempest outside, and at times the heavy fall of some portion of the old tower that yielded to its fury. Save this, a stillness like that of death prevailed throughout the ancient pile, and there were no signs of its being inhabited by a human being excepting himself.

The strange sights which had been reported to have been seen at the windows of the tower, and the noises said to have been heard to issue from the building, were now accounted for; it seemed evident that robbers or other ruffians had made it their retreat, and had adopted that means of alarming the persons in the neighbourhood, and thus saving themselves from detection. He regretted that his father had not adopted more effectual means of preventing such an occurence, or, as no use had been made of the tower for so many years, and it certainly was no ornament to the estate, but a source of great alarm (and, as it appeared, not without very good reason) to most persons in the neighbourhood, of annihilating it altogether.

In this manner more than another hour passed away, certainly the most tedious and miserable that Ethelbert had ever experienced. He would have given anything for the company of Arthur, to whom he might have communicated his thoughts, and thus have found some little relief from his anxiety and suspense. The observations of the ruffians on leaving him, convinced him that the designs of the villain in whose power he was, were desperate, but he was unable to form even the most remote idea as to who he was, or what they were. But to be thus so easily betrayed into the power of some unknown enemy, aggravated him more than all; and it was in vain that he endeavoured to find patience to bear it calmly.

And how powerful must be the anguish and fears which Sir Aldobrand and Mildred would doubtless experience at his mysterious and unaccountable disappearance; and what course could they take to discover what had become of him? He even felt more for the anxiety he was confident they would endure, than the danger and uncertainty of his own situation. Notwithstanding the opposition of his father, he was satisfied that Mildred returned the passion which he felt for her, with an ardour that was equal to his own, and consequently that her mind would be the more deeply afflicted at his loss.

To attempt to bribe any of the men who had seized him to favour him, and to aid him in escaping, he felt confident would be a useless and fruitless task, for they were evidently not to be moved from their purpose easily, if at all, and he therefore gave up the thought in despair.

" Oh, why was I so obstinate as to leave the mansion of Lord Gervase?" he cried, as he once more paced the dungeon with hasty and disordered steps ; " had I not done so, the plans of the villains would have been frustrated, and I should now have been at liberty. But how was I to foresee this? How was I to be aware of, or even to suspect the dark plot of treachery that was being contemplated against me? It is evidently the deed of some crafty miscreant, and his myrmidons have been set to watch my actions. But who can it be? Who is there that can be inspired with such feelings of enmity towards me? Ah! Lord Ruthlyn de Bohun! He who seeks possession of my peerless Mildred, and whose hatred and revenge must naturally be excited against me. It can be no other than he, and if so, I have everything to fear from him, for he will not fail to take every cowardly advantage of his rival, now that he has him in his power."

It was the first time that this idea occurred to him, and it seemed so probable, that it made the most vivid impression upon him, and he was unable to divest his mind of it.

The rage and suspense of Ethelbert, however, increased, and he gave free vent to his feelings in the most agonised expressions. But it was all to no purpose, for nothing whatever suggested itself to him to ameliorate his despair.

And then the danger which might threaten Mildred, now that he was deprived of the means of protecting her. This thought, if possible, tortured him more than all. He beat his breast, and groaned in the bitterness of his insupportable anguish.

At length, completely tired out with thinking, he stretched his limbs upon the bench, and endeavoured to gain even a temporary respite to his suffering in sleep.

Sleep! it was madness even to think of it ; and the more he courted its influence, the more miserable he became.

A piercing shriek aroused him from the lethargy into which he had almost unconsciously fallen. He started to his feet with astonishment, and looked around him.

The sound seemed to proceed from some dungeon immediately contiguous to that he was in. But all was now silent again, and he began to think he had suffered his perturbed imagination to deceive him ; but presently it again smote his ears, and louder and more distant than before. It was followed by a clanking noise, as if of heavy chains or fetters being dragged across the floor ; and then all was perfectly still again.

Ethelbert knocked loudly against the wall, and shouted at the top of his voice, but no answer was returned, and the same dead stillness prevailed as before. He was lost in amazement, and would have given anything to have had the mystery explained ; but it appeared beyond a doubt that some other unfortunate individual was confined there as well as himself, and, from the voice it seemed to be a female.

It was useless for him to endeavour to form any conjecture upon the subject, and he at last gave it up in despair, and once more he made an effort to sleep, as it did not seem likely that he would again be disturbed by any of the ruffians that night, and repose might afford some relief to his agitated mind.

This time he was more successful than before, for sleep presently fell upon his weary eyelids ; but then his imagination was disturbed by all kinds of frightful visions, so that it could not be called anything but a mockery of rest.

When he awoke, he could form no idea of what time it was, for daylight never entered that gloomy place. The lamp suspended from the vaulted roof was still burning, and emitted a sickly ray upon the black and cheerless walls.

Ethelbert arose and looked around him. He endeavoured to tranquillise his mind, but in vain ; the horror of his situation was too great for that.

His thoughts reverted to his father and Mildred, and the idea of the agony they must now be enduring, tortured him almost to madness. He continued to traverse the dungeon for some time, uttering the most bitter lamentations and execrations against the unknown enemy in whose power he was ; and no idea, no hope could suggest itself to him to alleviate his suffering in the smallest degree.

He was at last aroused by hearing the door of his dungeon being unbolted, and he looked anxiously towards it, to see who was about to enter.

It was soon opened, and three of the ruffians who had seized him the night before, made their appearance, and Ethelbert beheld that they brought with them a heavy chain and an iron belt. One end of the chain they proceeded to secure to a staple in the wall, whilst Ethebert watched them with speechless amazement and disgust ; having a pretty shrewd idea as to what were their intentions, but rendered so completely powerless by the variety and torture of his own feelings, as to be totally incapable of offering the least resistance, or even uttering a word to them.

The chain was secured to the staple in the wall, and before Ethelbert had time to recover from his confusion, the men rushed upon him, fixed the iron belt round his waist, secured it with a padlock, and the distracted and exasperated Ethelbert found himself incapable of moving to any greater distance than the length of the chain would permit.

The reader may well imagine his rage and indignation. His eyes flashed with resentment, and he made a violent but ineffectual effort to disengage himself.

He tried to give utterance to his feelings. but for a time, so powerful were the passions which raged in his bosom, he could not articulate a syllable.

The fellows stood smiling at him with malicious triumph, and this tended to exasperate him the more ; and he stamped in the very fury and madness of his passion.

" So, so, my gallant master," said one of the men, " we have you fast enough now, and you are now in a proper condition to be introduced to your friend. No doubt he will shortly honour you with his presence."

"Dastardly villains!" cried Ethelbert; "dare ye thus add further insult to the ruffianly outrage ye have already committed ? Release me, or dread the vengeance that will some time or other overtake ye!"

" You do well to talk of vengeance, my young spark," returned the man, "a prisoner, and powerless as you are. You are at the mercy of one who, no doubt, will know how to deal with you; no one can discover where you are, or what your fate may be; so you might as well spare your breath, and resign yourself to circumstances—rather unpleasant I must confess, but from which you cannot escape."

" Oh, bitter curses light upon ye all, miscreants !" exclaimed the infuriated Ethelbert ; " but ye shall repent this, powerless though I now am."

" Well, we shall see," remarked the man, placing some provisions and a jug of water within the reach of Ethelbert ; " at any rate, we have faithfully executed our orders, and now leave you to your own enjoyment."

With these words the villains quitted the dungeon, before their unfortunate prisoner could make any reply, and he listened to their heavy footsteps until they died away in the distance.

The agony of Ethelbert's feelings was now worked up to the highest pitch, and he struck his forehead in despair. His situation before had been terrible enough, but now was ten times more torturing. To be treated worse than the commonest felon ; to be chained to the wall like a dog, and to be subjected to the insults of the most degraded villains; the thought was enough to drive him to frenzy. He raved in the most distracted manner, until he was completely overpowered, and sunk down on the bench (which the chain enabled him to do) exhausted, almost heart-broken and despairing.

Hours passed away, and still no one visited him again; and notwithstanding he was faint from long fasting, he could not partake of the provisions which the men had left for him on the previous night.

The lamp had now expired, and to add to his misery and despair, he was left in total darkness, and he had nothing in the least to relieve the horror of his thoughts.

Night must be again approaching from the time which had evidently elapsed, and now the unfortunate Ethelbert was so tortured by hunger, that he was compelled, even against his will, to partake of the provisions ; but he did so sparingly, and he did not venture to drink of the water in the pitcher, lest some deadly poison should have been mixed with it.

He felt a little refreshed, but still his anguish exceeded all bounds, and again he bemoaned his hard fate, and thought of the sufferings which Sir Aldobrand and Mildred were now undoubtedly undergoing. Then he reflected on the shriek he had heard on the preceding night, and which had seemed to be uttered by some poor persecuted being like himself, or the troubled spirit of some former murdered victim. He could not but anticipate the worst, but still he prayed fervently to Heaven to keep him no longer in suspense, but to let him know at once the villain who held him in his power, and what his purpose was with him.

He was again aroused by hearing the bolts of his dungeon door withdrawn, and his heart swelled high, thinking, as he did, that the crisis of his fate was approaching.

The door, however, opened, and one of the ruffians appeared only. He cast a look of derision upon Ethelbert, and then having placed some more food near him, he proceeded, to replenish and light the lamp, and was about to retire from the dungeon without speaking a word, when Ethelbert, in a more subdued tone of voice than he had hithertofore assumed, demanded—

"Oh, tell me, man, if you are not destitute of every spark of feeling or humanity, how much longer am I to be kept in this intolerable state of suspense?"

"Oh, you will know all to-morrow," answered the man; "when you will receive a visit that you little expect."

"And my faithful servant," eagerly inquired Ethelbert; what has become of him?"

"He is secure enough," returned the fellow; and without waiting to give any further explanation, he left the dungeon, and Ethelbert to his own harassing thoughts.

The observations of the man, uncouth though they were, had in some measure relieved him, and he looked forward to the morrow with impatience and fearful expectation. He also felt a hope that the villains had not sacrificed the life of his domestic, although it was quite certain that for their own sakes they held him in as strict confinement as himself.

The light from the lamp rendered his situation somewhat less dismal, and he seated himself once more upon the bench, and made a desperate effort to compose his spirits. This was, indeed, a most difficult task, and he succeeded but very indifferently. The chain prevented him from lying down, and thus his situation was most irksome, and entirely drove sleep from him.

Again he heard that mournful shriek which had so appalled him the night before, and apparently at the same hour, and once more he shouted as loud as he could, but received no answer, and the same dismal and unbroken silence succeeded, and was not again disturbed during the night.

He was confident it came from some dungeon near, if not adjoining that of his own, and he became lost in a labyrinth of busy conjecture upon the mysterious circumstance.

How that, the second night of Ethelbert's confinement, passed away, we need not attempt to describe. It was, if possible, still more terrible than the first. Sometimes, as seated upon the cold stone bench, quite worn out with fatigue and anguish of mind, he did drop off into a troubled doze; but he started from it with feelings of terror, and endeavoured to keep awake, for that was far less fearful.

CHAPTER XIX.

THE MEETING IN THE DUNGEON.—THE THREAT.

WE will not weary the reader by minutely describing the thoughts which further racked the mind of Ethelbert during that day, which, as well as he could guess, must have been considerably advanced, when suddenly he was aroused from the gloomy and bewildering reverie into which he had naturally enough fallen, by hearing the slow and distant sound of footsteps advancing along the passage that led to the place in which he was confined, and the next moment they stopped at the dungeon door. His heart beat rapidly; his indignation swelled to its utmost pitch, and he prepared himself to meet the tyrant who had dared to commit such an outrage upon him, and to hold him prisoner, although he had no right to expect to see him until the following day, according to the statements of the ruffian who had visited him in the dungeon.

His doubts were quickly removed. The door of the dungeon was unbolted. Ethelbert started to the full distance that the length of his chain would allow him to do, his whole frame convulsed and thrilling with emotion, and his feelings, his wrath, and ungovernable resentment may very readily be conceived, when the rays emitted by the lamp revealed to him the form and countenance of his rival, Lord Ruthlyn de Bohun.

The blood rushed to his head, his eyes glared with disgust and indignation, and he clenched his fists, and he made a mad and futile effort to release himself from the heavy chain which confined him, whilst his bitter enemy, coolly closing the door behind him, and advancing to the centre of the dungeon, folded his arms, and confronted his powerless victim with looks of the most malignant triumph.

Several times did Ethelbert attempt to speak; but the intensity of his rage choked his utterance, and he could only bite his lips, knit his brows, and glare upon his unprincipled enemy with the same expression of resentment and reproach that he had done when he first entered.

Lord Ruthlyn's exultation at length found vent in a rude laugh of scorn, and Ethelbert, aroused almost to madness, then gave expression to the feelings which swelled his bosom almost to bursting, in the following words—

"Cowardly misereant! treacherous knave! base mockery of man and of nobility! is it then indeed you who have dared to inflict this indignity upon me? Oh, villain—villain! But you shall yet pay dearly for your conduct."

"Aye, probably I might," answered Lord Ruthlyn, in the most scornful accents, "if I were fool enough to suffer you to escape me now that I hold you securely in my power. Restrain your rage, Ethelbert de Lancy, for it is all useless, and only serves to add to my triumph. I hold you at my mercy, here, in the dungeons of the Black Tower of Bransdorf, the property of your father, the weak Sir Aldobrand, and defy discovery or defeat. Even in a moment could I strike you dead at my feet, and it will be my own fault if I suffer you again to quit this place alive, to pay your suit to the fair but scornful beauty, Mildred, who presumed to reject my honourable offers."

"Hold, heartless scoundrel!" cried the infuriated prisoner; "dare not to pollute the virtuous and beauteous maiden of whom you speak by giving utterance to her name."

"Ha, ha, ha!" laughed the villain; "and yet that fair and gentle damsel shall be mine, my mistress, not my bride, unless upon her knees she sues to me to make her so. Even now my plans are in full operation, and ere many days have elapsed, Mildred will be as much in my power as you are at present."

"Forbid it, all merciful Heaven," exclaimed Ethelbert, with extreme agony, clasping his hands, and raising his eyes. "Thou surely wilt not permit such a dreadful sacrifice of innocence. Thou wilt not permit this cowardly and unmanly ruffian thus to triumph in all his diabolical plans."

"I defy the power to which you appeal," said Lord Ruthlyn. "I have succeeded thus far, and fear not the completion of my triumph. Oh, it is a double triumph to me to know that I hold you at my mercy and my will. You were anxious to find me out, Ethelbert de Lancy, and I hope that you have now done so much to your satisfaction. Oh, you do not half know Lord Ruthlyn de Bohun yet; but you will doubtless understand him sufficiently by-and-by."

"Heartless ruffian!" cried Ethelbert, fixing upon him a whithering look; "release me from this degrading chain if you dare, and if you have the least spark of the courage of a man, give me the means of defence, and and let us decide the mortal difference between us. But no; I see you fear to meet my challenge; you dare only to beard the lion when he is rendered powerless to resist."

"Oh, most bravely, most boldy spoken," replied Lord Ruthlyn, with a sarcastic grin; "but I heed it not; it only serves me to mock at, aud to and to my feelings of exultation. It suits me not to accommodate you, most noble *lion*. Ha, ha, ha!"

"God of Heaven! give me patience to endure this. Are you a man, or a fiend in human shape?"

"Whichever you please to consider me," answered his lordship; "it matters not to me I am your keeper, and you cannot help yourself. Oh, it pleases me vastly to see the pangs you suffer; but they will be greater yet; when you shall have undoubted proof that I hold the lovely immaculate Mildred in my power."

Ethelbert groaned, and struck his forehead with his clenched fist, in the almost insupportable agony of his utter despair, and the conviction of his complete helplessn Again he made a desperate but fruitless attempt to release himself from the chain, and then he fixed upon Lord Ruthlyn a look which was enough to move the most stubborn heart to relent; but it made no other impression upon that hardened libertine and tyrant than to add to his satisfaction, and to goad him on to fresh schemes of vengeance.

"Lord Ruthlyn De Bohun," at length said Ethelbert, "again I warn you to beware; for great as your triumph may at present appear to be, mark me, the time will come when my wrongs will be redressed, and a terrible retribution will overtake you."

"I defy all, everything," returned the villain; "I am not that weak child you seem to take me for, to be moved by your vain and empty threats. Again I tell you that I. hold you at my mercy, and that no one can ever discover your fate. What, then, care I for your idle observations? You were the only obstacle to the gratification of my desires and I now hold you powerless, and fear not but I will keep you so. In a few days, if it will be any gratification for you to hear it, I promise you that you shall again behold you beloved Mildred, just to convince you that I have made no empty boasts, but, that she, as well as yourself, is in my power."

"By Heaven, this can never be!" exclaimed Ethelbert, with a burst of the most overpowering anguish; "that Almighty Power which ever watches over innocence will prevent it."

"Indeed! think you so? However, mark my words, my confident hero, you will soon be convinced how much you deceive yourself with false hopes. I never promise anything that I fail to perform. Reflect upon what I have said, and console yourself if you can."

"Exulting scoundrel, dare not to proceed too far, lest the vengeance of offended Heaven should overtake you sooner than you expect."

"Bah! you do but waste your breath in giving utterance to these feelings of rage and disappointment. Think you that aught you can say can induce me to relent now I have proceeded thus far? Once more I tell you that my plans are in full operation, so darkly, deeply, insidiously laid, that their success is certain; no power on earth can frustrate them. I set every means which may be employed to do so at defiance, and here I swear that I will not rest until all my wishes are gratified and my schemes are accomplished."

"And will you dare to detain me here a prisoner?"

"I have dared to make you one, and it would be strange indeed if I did not dare to detain you," replied Lord Ruthlyn, and again a savage look of triumph overspread his features. "Oh, it is a source of much satisfaction to me to think that I have my hated rival so secure, and your sufferings make that satisfaction doubly great."

"God of Heaven!" cried Ethelbert, writhing with agony, "give me strength to release myself, that I may wreak my vengeance on the head of this heartless and cowardly miscreant."

"Fool!" returned Lord Ruthlyn, still standing before him, with his arms folded, and mocking the anguish he was enduring; "of what avail are your struggles? They are equally as useless as your threats. Oh, I have no doubt that I shall very soon be able to tame that indomitable courage of which you now boast so much, and I will yet have you cringing and begging at my feet. But I leave you now to reflect upon what I have said, and much joy do I wish you in your present enviable situation, and the promising aspect of your prospects."

"May damning curses light upon you!" cried Ethelbert, clenching his fists, and shaking them menacingly at him. "May all the tortures of hell speedily overtake you and crush you in the midst of your inhuman and nefarious hopes. And my wishes will be fulfilled; mark me, they will, much as you appear to triumph now."

"Ha, ha, ha!" once more laughed the hardened and reckless nobleman. "How much it amuses me to hear your idle predictions. But I heed not your wild ravings. I can allow you to talk, since you are powerless for anything else."

"But I shall not always be, dastardly miscreant; no, I feel convinced that the time will come when I shall be released from your power, and then may you well tremble to meet the vengeance of the man whom you dare not encounter in honourable combat."

"Oh, most boldly, most courageously spoken, doubtless," retorted Lord Ruthlyn; "but do you not recollect that I have at once the power to prove the fallacy of your threats? Idiot! is not your life in my hands?—and could I not this instant sacrifice it? Of what use, then, are your empty boasts? Pshaw? they serve me but to laugh at and revile."

Ethelbert covered his face with his hands, and groaned in the agony of his wounded feelings. The observations of Lord Ruthlyn were too fatally true, and he could only lament his cruel fate, and mentally invoke the protection of Heaven for Mildred.

He turned one look of the utmost reproach upon his cruel enemy, who treated it only with a smile of derision, and then, before Ethelbert could find power to make another observation, he quitted the dungeon.

For some time the wretched prisoner stood transfixed to the spot, and gave himself up entirely to the most racking thoughts. To find himself in the power of that man whom he had such reason to dread, was more torturing than all; and his pride was deeply mortified by the degrading insults he had heaped upon him, and his utter incapability of resenting it.

But above everything else, the danger which threatened his beloved Mildred grieved him the most. The villain, Lord Ruthlyn, he felt confident, must have good reason to rely upon the success of his diabolical scheme, or he would not have expressed himself in the confident manner in which he had; and there was no one to put her upon her guard against him, or to protect her from his power.

And oh, God! he reflected, what would become of her in the hands of such a heartless and determind miscreant as Lord Ruthlyn? Urged on by his guilty passion and revenge, even her beauty and innocence would fail to move him; he would show her no mercy, and there was nothing but misery and destruction before her, unless Providence should interpose to rescue her.

These thoughts were maddening, and for hours Ethelbert remained in a complete state of distraction, and nothing could afford him even a moment's consolation, or inspire him with a feeling of hope.

"But the villain," he cried at length, "he dare not, surely he dare not proceed to such guilty extremities. He must be less than human if he be not awed into forbearance by the innocence of that lovely being. Heaven will never permit him to triumph in his atrocious designs! Let me not, then, gloomy and terrible even as the prospect is, entirely despair."

But it was in vain that he tried to buoy himself up with hope. Alas! what cause was there for it?—None that in his reasonable reflections he could see. Drearily the hours wore on, and the man who had attended him all along once more made his appearance to trim the lamp for the night, and to bring Ethelbert some provisions, which were of the coarsest description. A thought struck him, and almost hopeless as it was he determined to try its effect upon the ruffian. He looked in his face for an instant; but its forbidding character daunted him, and he was half induced to abandon the resolution he had formed; but even if he failed in his object, he could be in no worse situation than he was at present, and he theretore determined to proceed.

"Stay," he said, in a tone of supplication, as the man was about to quit the dungeon.

"Well, what now?" gruffly demanded the latter.

"I would ask you a few questions," answered Ethelbert eagerly.

"Oh, I have no time to answer questions, if even I had the inclination," returned the fellow, "so you may save yourself the trouble."

"But surely you will not refuse me?"

"And why should I not?"

"Because, although your manners are uncouth, there is something about your that convinces me it is not in your nature."

"Oh, I want no flattery; it does not agree with me."

"But I implore you," said Ethelbert, earnestly. "But a few minutes; I will not detain you long, and you can do no harm by listening to me."

"I don't know that," answered the man.

"Oh, I am convinced you cannot, and it is the voice of common humanity that urges you to comply with my request."

"Humanity! ha, ha! It is many a day since I listened to its voice. I never found it very profitable."

"But it may prove so on the present occasion," urged Ethelbert.

"Oh, indeed," said the man, with a sarcastic grin. "Well, I am never against earning a trifle, if I can do so *honestly*. What is it you have to ask? Speak it quick, for I am in a hurry, and have other business to attend to."

"Is Lord Ruthlyn now in the tower?"

"Is that all you want to know? Oh, then, to be sure it will not take me long to answer that. He is not. Good night."

"Nay, do not leave me yet, I pray you,' said Ethelbert. "Release me from my present situation, and I will not only hold you harmless for all that has happened, but reward you with gold sufficient to keep you in comfort and honesty for the rest of your days."

"A very modest request, truly," said the ruffian; "but I'm sorry to say that I cannot comply with it. No, no, you have got hold of the wrong man for that business."

"You will not consent, then?"

"Certainly not."

"But if you will not yield to that request, I have another to make."

"If it is anything like the former, you may save yourself the trouble."

"Let but my father, Sir Aldobrand, be made acquainted with my situation, and I will give you the same reward."

"What! would you have me betray that man by whom I have often before been

employed ?" said the fellow. "No, no, I will do nothing of the sort, so you need not entertain any such a hope."

"But the peace, the innocence of one fair being, who is dearer to me than my very existence, is threatened," said Ethelbert, in distracted tones.

"I know that," answered the ruffian, carelessly; "and before many days have elapsed she will be in the power of his lordship."

"Oh! forbid it, Heaven! Will you not interpose to save her, if I reward you well for your trouble?"

"It is not very likely," said the fellow. "You must take me for a rogue or a madman."

"Will nothing prevail upon you?"

"Nothing."

"Remember the danger you at present run."

"Oh, I am not one to fear danger."

"But you may save yourself from ruin."

"I decline the offer."

"Nay, I implore you," said the wretched Ethelbert, clasping his hands, and looking in the forbidding countenance of the ruffian with the most supplicating expression, " do not, oh, do not turn a deaf ear to my entreaties."

"There, I have listened long enough to this foolery," said the inflexible ruffian; "you have heard my mind, and might have understood me sufficiently before, not to have given yourself all this unnecessary trouble."

"Alas! alas!" sighed Ethelbert, when he found that all attempts to move the man were entirely useless; "in the mercy of Heaven, then, is my only dependence."

The fellow fixed upon him a look of contempt and insensibility, and then left the dungeon, without making use of another word.

Ethelbert seated himself on the stone bench, covered his face with his hands, and unable longer to retain his manly fortitude, he gave vent to his feelings in the most convulsive sobs. It was long ere he could arouse himself in the least degree from his lethargy of agony and despair, and then his mind was so bewildered that he had scarcely any idea as to where he was.

All hope was at an end. The miscreant, Lord Ruthlyn, he feared, would remain firm in his determination, and he had no doubt that he had so well concerted his nefarious designs, that he could calculate upon the certainty of their accomplishment, and the terrors of his own situation sunk into comparative insignificance when he reflected upon the probable fate that awaited poor Mildred.

The tortures endured by Ethelbert that night may very well be imagined. Consolation or rest he could find none, and frequently did he lament that he had ever been born.

How fervently did he pray to Heaven that it would interpose to save his beloved Mildred from the power of the villain who threatened her with destruction; and how often did he invoke its curses upon that depraved and remorseless nobleman's head, until completely worn out, he fortunately sunk into a state of happy unconsciousness.

But it is now time that we should return to Mildred and her benefactor.

CHAPTER XX.

THE ANGUISH OF SIR ALDOBRAND AND MILDRED AT THE DISAPPEARANCE OF ETHELBERT.—THE FURTHER VILLANY OF LORD RUTHLYN.—MILDRED FALLS INTO HIS POWER.

MILDRED and Sir Aldobrand were sitting together on the evening of Ethelbert's disappearance, anxiously watching his return.

A powerful foreboding of some approaching calamity had possessed the mind of Mildred throughout the day, and, in spite of all her efforts to the contrary, she could not banish it.

The baronet noticed the melancholy of her spirits with some concern, and tried all he could to banish it, but without effect, although she could assign no cause for it; and the time passed tediously on.

Sir Aldobrand wondered that his son should remain so late from the castle, as it was not his custom to do so; but when the storm came on, he expressed no surprise, but concluded that Lord Gervase had persuaded him to remain at the mansion until it should have abated; and when hour after hour elapsed, and the tempest still raged with unabated violence, he was satisfied that Ethelbert would never be so foolish as to venture through it, but would continue with his friend until the morning.

Mildred affected to entertain the same opinion; but notwithstanding all her endeavours, her mind was still doubtful and restless, and when she retired to her chamber she threw herself in a chair, and gave herself up to the most dismal reflections. She listened to the howling storm, and all kinds of horrible imaginings presented themselves to her brain. Yet she could contemplate the fury of the tempest without the slightest feeling of terror, so much was her mind preoccupied by other thoughts, and of much greater importance, at least in her estimation.

She found it utterly impossible to relieve her bosom of the weight of unaccountable care that at present oppressed it, and which had done so all the day, and she found herself involuntarily engrossed by the melancholy retrospection of the events of the past, and conjuring up numerous gloomy anticipations of the future.

But above all other thoughts which arose in her mind was an apprehension that some accident had befallen Ethelbert, and which had been the cause of his not returning to the castle. She would fain have attributed it to the same reason as the baronet—the tempest and that he had remained at the mansion of Lord Gervase until the morning ; but the same powerful foreboding that had affected her during the whole of the day prevented her, and she felt an anxiety and restlessness, a sensation of almost insupportable doubt and suspense, which he found it utterly impossible to banish.

Solemnly she invoked the protection of the Supreme for Ethelbert, and never before had she so powerfully felt the tender influence which he possessed over her heart. And what could banish that influence from her bosom ? Nothing! The object that had inspired it was worthy of her heart's warmest and purest aspirations, and notwithstanding the objection of Sir Aldobrand, and the present hopelessness of that passion being gratified, she felt satisfied that she could never love any other man than Ethelbert de Lancy, and that her affections must daily increase in strength.

And yet, how happy would she have felt could she but have conquered her love; for she was acting in opposition to the wishes of her generous benefactor. But why should he object to her as a daughter to whom he had always behaved and considered worthy as his own child ? The painful anxiety of her origin answered the question, and tears started to her eyes at the state of dependence in which it had pleased Providence to, place her arose so vividly, so palpably to her imagination.

"Alas!" she sighed, " better would it have been for me, and, perhaps, more for the peace of others, that I had perished in the old Tower of Bransdorf. For what was I reserved?—Only, it seems, to be the victim of continual vexation, doubt, perplexity, and sorrow. Oh, Heaven! will the mystery of my destiny never be unravelled?"

Her thoughts now reverted to the strange events which had so recently occurred at the castle ; the singular being whom she had first seen in the chapel, and who had been followed to the secret chamber, where it appeared, she had sought a refuge ; and she felt a burning interest to discover who she was, and what had now become of her. Was she indeed the unfortunate Lady Ethitha, and ill-fated wife of the mysterious and evidentl y guilty Sir Martin de Lancy, over whose head the ban of Almira de Montreville hung ? The fact of the discovery of his miniature, which had been in her possession, seemed to offer good reason to suppose that she was. And what a strange history was theirs ! What could have been the cause of Sir Martin's singular and cruel conduct to his young, beautiful, innocent wife ? Why had he acted so harshly and unjustly towards that fair being for whom he professed so ardent an affection, and which had caused them to disappear so suddenly ? It was altogether inexplicable. And yet, our heroine marvelled that she should feel such an extraording interest in their fate and history ; but whenever she did think of it, the tears would rush involuntarily to her eyes, and she experienced a sensation at her heart which was perfectly unacountable.

How often had she wandered to the picture gallery, and found herself lost in a variety of powerful and pleasing sensations, whilst contemplating the portrait of Sir Martin de Lancy. Proud and haughty as was the expression of the nevertheless handsome features of that portrait, as she gazed and gazed, she could almost believe that the eyes beamed with kindness upon her, and that the lips moved as if in the act of addressing her. This idea frequently wrought so powerfully upon her, that she could almost fancy that she could hear the portrait whisper a blessing upon her head, and she knelt in reverence before it, and could have worshipped it as if it had been a resemblance of her father. What could be the cause of these feelings ? She was at a loss to account for them; and yet, she would not for the world have been deprived of the felicity of indulging in them. Mildred was aroused from this singular train of reflections by a heavy boom of thunder, that seemed to shake the castle to its very foundation, and inspired her with a feeling of terror which she could not readily overcome. She started to her feet, and involuntarily approached the window, and at that moment a vivid flash of lightning darted across her eyes, and almost blinded her.

It was a few moments before she was able to recover herself from the shock ; but then, in spite of all the terrors of the storm, she again directed her gaze towards the window, and looked placidly on the horrors which raged beyond.

It was indeed a fearful night. The thunder pealed in awful majesty, and the vivid flashes of the lightning appeared to set the whole face of nature in a blaze. The rain at the same time poured down in unmitigated and overwhelming torrents.

" Heaven preserve those unfortunate beings who are exposed to its fury," said Mildred energectically. " It was just such a night as this, I have heard poor old Sampson Hewley frequently say, that he discovered me in the old Tower of Bransdorf ; and this is, too, the anniversary of that event. What can be the cause of the feelings which are coming over me?" She shuddered, she knew not why ; but was unable to remove her eyes from the window.

Flash after flash of lightning darted across the heavon's in rapid succession, and ever and anon the thunder roared with deafening intensity ; but still was Mildred attracted to the window by a powerful and inscrutable influence, which she was herself at a loss to understand. The raging of the tempest, in fact, seemed to possess charms for her instead of terror, while, at the same time, her whole thoughts were wound up in expectation of some remarkable event which was that night about to take place.

To retire to rest she could not think of, for her thoughts were too much excited to allow her to hope for sleep ; and again the fearful idea that something serious had befallen Ethelbert arose to her mind, and in spite of all the arguments which Sir Aldobrand had made use of, she could not divest herself of it. And yet, she was compelled to acknowledge to herself it was a great weakness ; for the only reasonable conclusion to come to was, that Ethelbert, seeing the violence of the storm, and his time not being important, had been induced by his friend, Lord Gervase, to remain at his mansion till the morning.

The window at which she was standing commanded an unterrupted view of the Tower of Bransdorf, soaring above its lofty eminence, and the eyes of Mildred became immoveably fixed upon it, as its venerable walls were revealed to her distinctly by the broad glare of the lightning. Rude and gloomy as it was, it possessed a sort of charm for her, and recalled to her memory many strange, melancholy, but, at the same time, not unpleasing recollections.

While she was thus engaged, and with her eyes still fixed upon the tower, between the pauses of the thunder, she was suddenly startled by hearing a piercing shriek, which it seemed, was scarcely possible to be uttered by anything human, proceed from the very direction of the building itself, and the next moment lights blazed from every gothic casement, and Mildred was positive that she saw strange forms flit hastily past them ; but it was only for an instant ; the lights and the figures (at least of her imagination) disappeared, and all was again involved in darkness, except at intervals when the ethereal fire flashed across the heavens.

Mildred felt a shuddering sensation of astonishment and terror come over her, but found herself, as it were, transfixed to the spot on which she was standing, and could not remove her eyes from the direction of the tower.

She was quite certain that she had not suffered her imagination to deceive her ; and from whence, then, could that fearful cry have proceeded, and what was the cause of it ? There was something supernatural in its tone, and was just such a cry as she had heard Sampson Hewley frequently describe that he had heard on the night, the memorable night, when he discovered her.

What could it mean? Was it a harbinger of approaching evil? Mildred, notwithstanding all her efforts to the contrary, strongly inclined to this opinion ; and again her thoughts reverted to Ethelbert, and she longed for the morning, that her painful doubts and suspense might be removed.

Trembling with nameless and ungovernable fears, Mildred was about to quit the window, when she was suddenly startled by hearing a shrill, unnatural laugh, and turning her eyes quickly in the direction from whence it proceeded, what was her astonishment and terror to behold, standing in the centre of the ground below, the same awful being she had met upon several occasions before, and whose strange manners and observations were so indelibly impressed upon her memory. It was the weird woman of the heath !

Yes, there she stood, apparently having a distinct view of Mildred, as she stood at the window, and with her black piercing eyes fixed full upon her countenance. There was a malicious grin upon her savage and unnatural features, as she waved her bony hand towards Mildred, as if to signify that she saw her ; then once more she laughed aloud, and with an expression that struck horror to the bosom of our heroine, who could not remove from the spot, although her fears would have induced her to alarm the servants, so that they might secure the singular unknown, and ascertain the cause and purport of her appearance.

The woman remained a few moments gazing up at Mildred, as she stood at the window, then pointed significantly towards the Tower of Bransdorf, and once more waving her hand in a menacing manner, she bounded away, and was immediately out of sight leaving Mildred lost in astonishment at the speed with which she had vanished.

She moved from the casement, and throwing herself in a chair, for some moments was entirely lost in the racking train of thoughts that crowded upon her brain, and almost overwhelmed her with their intensity.

More terrible than ever were now the forebodings which racked her mind, and the appearance of the weird woman seemed almost to realise them. She almost dreaded to remain in her chamber. But where could she go? The inmates of the castle were all at rest, and it would indeed be thought singular and childish if she disturbed them; but how anxiously she longed for morning, that she might see Sir Aldobrand, and communicate to him what had happened.

She went to the room door, and fastened it securely; for her mind had strange misgivings of some intrusion and impending evil, and then she sunk upon her knees, and supplicated the protection of the Almighty for herself and all those who were so truly dear to her. As the name of Ethelbert rose to her lips, tears started to her eyes, and she found it impossible to dismiss the apprehensions she entertained of his safety.

She did, however, feel somewhat more relieved and composed after she had thus poured out her thoughts to the Supreme, and the storm having in some measure abated, she threw herself on the bed without undressing, and endeavoured to compose herself to sleep.

It was some time ere she succeeded; but at length nature was completely exhausted, and sleep descended upon her eyelids; but troublesome dreams tormented her imagination, and destroyed the balmy influence of slumber.

How long she had slept she knew not, but she was suddenly aroused by hearing, as she imagined, a deep and melancholy sigh, breathed immediately in her ear, and starting up, she was almost positive that she beheld a tall figure in white glide like a shadow behind the curtains.

She could not repress a faint scream of terror, and looked in the direction where she thought she had seen the figure, but nothing met her eyes. She chided herself for her momentary terror. It must have been imagination—the effects of some frightful dream, for how was it possible that any person could have gained access to her chamber, and then have vanished so suddenly? Still she felt it difficult to do away with the impression that had seized upon her mind. She recollected the form which she had, she was certain, when a child, seen standing at the foot of her bed, and this incident was so similar, that she could not easily convince herself that it was otherwise than correct. Could she believe in supernatural appearances? She was not prone to superstition, yet this adventure was almost calculated to inspire her with such a feeling.

She arose from the bed and examined the door: it was fast, as she had made it on retiring to rest, and it was, therefore, utterly impossible that any person could have entered the chamber, or have disappeared so suddenly. There was no secret means of their entering or escaping, she was certain.

"It must have been imagination," said Mildred; "and yet I could almost swear that I heard the sigh, and saw the form glide away. What a strange and inscrutable mystery attaches itself to all these events!"

She passed her hands across her forehead, and remained for a few minutes buried in reflection.

The storm had entirely subsided, and the morning was fast beginning to dawn. Mildred did not feel inclined to go to sleep again, and she therefore walked to the window and taking a seat by it, she looked out upon the scenery beyond, as yet but indistinctly revealed in the grey mist of early morn. Still her most anxious thoughts were of Ethelbert, nor were her fears in the least diminished; still the same melancholy forebodings occupied her bosom.

"Oh! would that he would return," she ejaculated, "and banish from my mind this horrible feeling of suspense. Alas! alas! should anything have happened to you, how deeply shall I lament, not only for your sake, but that of your amiable father, whose sufferings will be so great. But why should I suffer these extraordinary forbodings to obtain such a powerful influence over me?"

She could assign no reason, yet they became every moment more powerful, and her anguish increased in the same manner.

Tired of sitting at the window, she determined to leave the room, and try to divert her mind by rambling over the other part of the castle.

She opened the door, and gazed timidly into the gallery beyond; but there was nothing to create her alarm—all was silent. She walked from the room, and traversing the gallery, she entered the old chapel, where had recently occurred so many strange events and which were so forcibly stamped upon her memory.

The aspect of the chapel appeared more than usually gloomy, in the faint light emitted through its dust-covered casements, and Mildred could not but feel a sensation almost approaching to fear stealing over her; but she quickly banished it from her breast, and looked towards the altar. Did her busy fancy again deceive her? Surely it could not.' At the moment she turned her eyes in the direction of the altar, she was almost positive that she once more saw a similar form to that she had seen, or believed she had seen, in her chamber, glide behind it; but it was only for an instant, and although she never removed her gaze from the spot, when she scarcely had time to think, it was gone!

"Mysterious being, if such you are," she exclaimed, "oh! reveal yourself to me, and convince me at once that I am not suffering any delusion of the senses!"

The echo of her own voice was the only answer she received, and she remained in a state of the utmost doubt and perplexity. She conquered her fears, however, and advanced to the altar.

She saw nothing there to gratify her curiosity, and on examining the door of the chancel, she found that it was padlocked in the same manner it had been for several weeks. It was, therefore, evident that nothing human could have escaped that way, and Mildred again endeavoured to persuade herself that she had been mistaken.

She remained in silent contemplation of all around her for some time, but at length, feeling a chilly sensation stealing over her from the damp atmosphere of the place, she walked away, and bent her footsteps towards the picture-gallery, which she had not visited for some days.

She stood before the portrait of Sir Martin de Lancy, and once more fixed her earnest gaze upon it; and again the eyes appeared to look upon her with an expression most life-like and affectionate. A feeling of awe and reverence came over her, and she could not remove her eyes from it for several minutes. She could almost have knelt before the unconscious canvas, so strange and irresistible was the influence the features had upon her. But why was this? She could not account for it.

She passed some time in the picture gallery, and then rambled over several of the other apartments of the castle, in order that she might pass the time away which hung so tediously on her hands, until the family should be stirring.

She at last returned to her chamber, and gave herself up to reflection.

In this manner two more hours elapsed, and Barbara entered her chamber to assist her in dressing.

"Bless me, miss," said Barbara, who noticed the paleness of her looks and the langour of her eyes, "you look very poorly, and any one would imagine that you had not been t bed."

"I slept but badly, Barbara," said our heroine, not feeling inclined to satisfy her curiosity.

"Indeed I am not surprised at that, Miss Mildred," remarked Barbara, "for I don't know who could sleep in such a storm—it was a dreadful night."

Mildred assented to this, and then changed the topic of conversation. The time wore away, and Mildred hearing Sir Aldobrand leave his chamber and descend into the breakfast-room, she proceeded to join him.

The baronet greeted her with his usual urbanity, but immediately remarking her languid appearance, he eagerly inquired the cause. Mildred at once made him acquainted with everything, and he listened to the circumstances she detailed with no little astonishment and attention.

The breakfast hour had passed away, and still Ethelbert returned not; and Sir Aldobrand, almost distracted by his fears, mounted his horse, and rode to the mansion of Lord Gervase. Here, of course, his worst fears were confirmed; and when he learned that Ethelbert had left for home on the previous night, the most fearful forebodings of evil filled his mind. He returned to the castle, accompanied by Lord Gervase, but no Ethelbert had been seen; and then collecting all the servants who could be spared, a search was commenced over the country. Two or three days passed on, and still there were no tidings of the missing youth, when a suspicion suddenly entered the mind of Sir Aldobrand that Lord Ruthlyn (of whose feelings towards Ethelbert he was aware) might be concerned in his mysterious disappearance, and he resolved that they should visit the castle of the Earl de Bohun and make inquiries.

Mildred waited with the most painful and heart-sickening anxiety for their return, and at length Sir Aldobrand, melancholy, heart-broken, came back, accompanied by Lord Gervase. He was met affectionately by Mildred, who took his hand, which was feverish with the excitement and despair of his feelings. She looked in his face, and saw enough expressed there to convince her that her worst surmises were realized. He had met with no intelligence of his son.

He sunk in a chair, and covering his face with his hands, convulsive sobs heaved his manly breast.

Mildred approached him, and in her sweetest accents, which had received tenfold influence from the intensity of her anxiety, said—

" My dear guardian, my only earthly friend, oh, relieve the terrible feelings which oppress and distract my brain, and tell me, have you heard anything of your son—of Ethelbert?"

Sir Aldobrand looked up tenderly in her face for a moment, and shaking his head, once more covered his face with his hands, and relapsed into his former state of utter despair. Mildred needed no more to render her completely wretched, and she also sunk in her chair, and burst into tears, when she found it impossible any longer to restrain. Lord Gervase respectfully approached her, and after having allowed her several minutes to indulge her grief without interruption, requested that she would honour him with a few minutes' conversation, and he would explain everything.

" Sir Aldoorand," he added, " I know I have your permission."

The baronet slightly nodded his head, but without altering his position, and Mildred arose and accompanied his lordship to an ante-room.

" Miss Mildred," said Lord Gervase, when they were alone, " this is really a most melancholy and mysterious affair; but I must beg of you, for the sake of Sir Aldobrand (a stronger appeal to your feelings I know I cannot make) to try to meet it with fortitude, and to keep up the hope that something will yet, and before long, transpire to throw a light upon the subject, and restore Ethelbert de Lancy to his home."

" Oh, my lord," sighed Mildred, " you impose upon me an arduous task ; but, indeed, I see the necessity of endeavouring to do as you advise. My noble-minded and amiable benefactor, I fear, will sink under this dreadful misfortune."

" Your tender solicitude can bear him up, Miss Mildred," suggested his lordship, " Besides, we must ever trust to the goodness and mercy of Providence, who, depend on it, will not desert you on the present occasion."

" But your interview with the Earl de Bohun, my lord," said our heroine, eagerly, " Has nothing transpired from that ?"

" Nothing."

" Did Sir Aldobrand and the earl meet in a friendly manner?"

" They did."

" Thank Heaven for that !"

" In fact," added Lord Gervase, " the earl appeared as much surprised as ourselves at the disappearance of Ethelbert ; declared his entire ignorance of the place where his son had gone to, and solemnly protested that so far from sanctioning him in any iniquitous proceeding as that of which we suspected him, he would, if he discovered that he could so far have disgraced himself, discard him altogether. He also declared his fervent wishes to assist us in our search after Ethelbert all that lay in his power."

" But think you, my lord, that he was sincere?" asked Mildred.

" I feel satisfied that he was," answered his lordship.

" But is it not strange that the earl should be in ignorance of the present locality of his son ?"

" It is."

" Alas ! I fear that he is indeed the author of this evil."

" It would be wrong to judge him too hastily."

" I cannot forget the threats he held out, my lord."

" Very true."

" And it appears to me," added our heroine, " that Lord Ruthlyn is not the man who would readily abandon his projcts."

" Probably not ; but still it does appear somewhat unreasonable to suppose that th would so boldly venture to gratify his mere revenge, when he must at the same time be assured that retribution would be certain to overtake him."

" Alas ! would that I could think so, my lord."

" Nay, Miss Mildred, you must endeavour to banish such ideas from your mind. Even now, Ethelbert may return. He may have met with some accident certainly, which has detained him——"

" Where, my lord ?" interrupted Mildred, hastily ; " you say that you have made inquiries at every place where he was likely to go to or be taken, on his route from your mansion to the castle, without success ; have we not, then, an undoubted right to form the most unfavourable conclusions ?"

Lord Gervase scarcely knew what to answer, for he could not deny the truth of our heroine's observation.

" It is altogether a mystery of the most painful and impenetrable description," he said at length ; " but still I am not without my hopes that everything will, ere long, be satisfactorily explained. At the same time; I must beg of you, Mildred, to keep up your spirits, as much depends upon that ; and Heaven knows that Sir Aldobrand de Lancy stands greatly in need of your sweet consolation."

" I will try to do so, my lord," sighed Mildred ; " for my benefactor's sake I will ; but alas ! I fear, that I shall be ill able to succeed. How unfortunate it was that Ethelbert should have persisted in leaving your mansion, my lord, on the night of the storm."

" It was, indeed," coincided Lord Gervase ; " there seemed to be a fatality in it."

" And he may have been attacked and murdered by robbers," said Mildred, with a shudder of horror.

" Dismiss such apprehensions from your mind, Mildred," said his lordship.

" Would that I could," she answered ; " but, unfortunately, they are far too probable. Ethelbert would not voluntarily absent himself in this manner. Besides, what reason could he have for so doing ?"

Lord Gervase remained silent, for he could not but admit to himself, the justice of Mildred's observations, and he scarcely knew what to say to compose her, and put her in a fit state of mind to tranquillise the feelings of Sir Aldobrand.

" Ethelbert will return, depend upon it, Mildred," he said at last, " I feel convinced that he will, and the reason of his present mysterious absence will be fully explained But come ; let us return to Sir Aldobrand, who much needs our consolation and advice."

Mildred hastily brushed the tears from her eyes, and then reurned to the room in which Sir Aldobrand was seated, still absorbed in overwhelming grief. She approached him and laid her fair hand gently on his shoulder. He looked up at her touch, and the melancholy despairing expression of his countenance stung her to the heart.

" Ah, Mildred," he sighed ; " thou art now my only comfort—my poor boy, my Ethelbert, is lost to me for ever."

" Oh, say not so, my dear sir," said Mildred compassionately, and making a powerful effort to subdue her own apprehensions ; " Providence will surely not allow such a dreadful calamity to befall you."

" Alas ! alas ! he is murdered, Mildred !" groaned the distracted baronet.

" Oh, Heaven forbid !" ejaculated our heroine, and a cold shuddering sensation of horror seized her frame. " Who could have perpetrated so inhuman an act ?"

" I know not, unless it were robbers, for he deserved not a single enemy."

" And yet he has one, I fear," sighed Mildred.

" Lord Ruthlyn de Bohun ?"

" Alas ! and through me—I am the innocent cause. Had I not attracted, unfortunately, the attention of Lord Ruthlyn, no enmity would probably have existed between him and Ethelbert. Oh, I have been most unfortunate in being made the cause of so much misery to my only, my best earthly friends."

" My sweet Mildred," said Sir Aldobrand, pressing her hand to his lips, and looking up affectionately in her face, at the same time that he endeavoured to conquer the emotion which struggled in his own bosom ; " you reproach yourself unjustly. But compose yourself, pray ; I will endeavour to hope, though Heaven knows, there is but little cause for it. Poor Ethelbert, where are you ? Surely you would never voluntarily absent yourself !"

" Oh, no, no !" ejaculated Mildred, fervently ; " he could never be guilty of such an act of cruelty. What reason could he have for it ? Let us both continue to hope, my

benefactor ; let us both hope that some unforeseen accident has detained Ethelbert from us, and that he will return, and everything will be satisfactorily explained."

"My sweet pleader," remarked the baronet, in melancholy but subdued accents, "I will indeed try to be soothed by your arguments ; though, alas ! when I view all the circumstances, there seems to be but little room for hope."

Sir Aldobrand struggled with his feelings, and Mildred exerted herself to the utmost to overcome the anguish of her mind, to which purpose Lord Gervase also did his best ; but in the midst of such utter despair it was impossible for them to gain anything like a degree of composure, and as the time passed away without their being able to gain the least intelligence of Ethelbert, although every course that would be suggested by reason to do so had been adopted, their misery became really insupportable.

Another wretched evening passed away, and Sir Aldobrand was at last worn out by the intensity of his feelings, that he could hold up no longer, and was compelled to retire to his chamber.

Lord Gervase and Mildred separated with melancholy forebodings, and when the latter reached her chamber, she threw herself upon her bed, and, completely exhausted by the fatigue of mind and body she had so long undergone, she sunk into a sort of lethargy (sleep it could not be called) from which she did not arouse for several hours. And yet, although the body reposed in this unrefreshing state of inactivity, the mind was busy and active, as in its most healthy moments, and agonising were the thoughts which rose to disturb it.

The morning came, and Mildred started from her sleepless pillow as though she had awakened from a frightful dream. All the terrible reality was in a moment presented to her. She sunk on her knees, and earnestly supplicated the Almighty to dispel the dreadful doubts which at present occupied their minds, and to watch over the safety of him who held so dear a place in her affections.

She descended to the breakfast-room, and there met Lord Gervase, and was grieved to hear from him that Sir Aldobrand was too ill to leave his room. Mildred was greatly alarmed at this intelligence, for she anticipated the worst, knowing the ardent affection which the baronet bore for his son; but his lordship endeavoured to quiet her, and, in some measure, succeeded.

"It is natural to suppose, Miss Mildred," he observed, "that the anxiety Sir Aldobrand has endured for the last day or two will prostrate his energies for a time; but I do trust that in a day or two all our fears will be removed, and that Ethelbert de Lancy will be restored uninjured."

"Oh, my lord," replied Mildred, "believe me, I am obliged to you for endeavouring to inspire me with such hopes. Would that I could encourage them. But, alas! I fear that my beloved guardian will never be able to support this terrible shock to his feelings."

"Then by a struggle of your utmost fortitude, my dear miss, I am confident you will try to enable him."

"All that I can, I will do; Heaven aid me in the task!" said our heroine.

For three days did Mildred, with the most unremitting care and anxiety, attend upon Sir Aldobrand, and it was truly wonderful how she was, delicate as was her constitution, enabled to support the fatigue, especially when the racking agony of her own feelings are taken into consideration, and the torturing mystery of the fate which had attended Ethelbert still remained unravelled. But all was as dark and as impenetrable as ever, and Sir Aldobrand quitted his chamber a heart-broken, disconsolate man, his only comfort being in the society of Mildred.

Much as he had respected her, never had he discovered her real worth till then, and, for the first time, he regretted that he had suffered his foolish notions of pride to present any obstacle to the virtuous passion of her and his son. He thought to himself, if that son were restored to him, how gladly would he sanction it, and could not help attributing the present calamity that had befallen him to a just visitation of the Almighty.

Alas! how ready are we to form resolutions in moments of sorrow and severe trouble, which, when the clouds are dispersed, and all appears as fair and as promising as it formerly did, we are equally ready to forget.

Every inquiry had been made to endeavour to find some clue to the fate of Ethelbert. There was not an individual who knew him that had not exerted himself with the same object, but without effect; and despair settled itself upon the minds of Sir Aldobrand and Mildred, which no force of argument could tend in the least way to alleviate. Sir Aldobrand wandered about the castle like a man insane, and Mildred was in such a state of mind that she could not even attempt to offer him any consolation.

Lord Gervase, in the mean time, who had kindly remained at the castle, was the only person who was capable of giving the necessary instructions to prosecute the inquiry into this strange affair; but still the fate of the unfortunate Ethelbert de Lancy continued to be involved in the same impenetrable state of mystery.

The Earl De Bohun also exerted himself, apparently earnestly and honestly, to unravel it, and was in constant communication with the inmates of the castle; but not the slightest light could be thrown upon the subject, neither could it be discovered what had become of Lord Ruthlyn. The earl declared that he had disappeared from him suddenly, and after the unfortunate circumstance by which Sir Aldobrand had nearly lost his life; but still, although he admitted his wild, reckless, and impetuous character, he could not believe him capable of being guilty of secretly injuring any person, against whom he might be never so much excited and exasperated. Still the disappearance of both Ethelbert de Lancy and Lord Ruthlyn, at the same time, naturally caused the greatest surprise and suspicion.

A week had now elapsed since the disappearance of Ethelbert, and still not the least intelligence could be obtained to afford them the smallest hope or consolation. Sir Aldobrand concluded that he was no more—that he had fallen beneath the dagger of some vile assassin—and his joys were all annhilated. He wandered about the castle like a ghost, and shunned all society, even that of Mildred.

And, oh, how sad and lonely was she! How incessantly did she bemoan the unknown fate of Ethelbert, and implore Heaven to banish their terrible doubts and suspense. Even to know the worst, however dreadful it might be, would be far less agonising than to have to form the numerous vague and torturing conjectures they were now constrained to do. She dared not to think that she should never behold Ethelbert again; and yet, to what other conclusion could she come?

It was wonderful how she could keep about at all; but she did, and at every opportunity sought an interview with Sir Aldobrand, and endeavoured to inspire him with that hope which she herself was far from sincerely feeling.

It was night, and Mildred had for several hours retired to her chamber. All was silent in the castle, for the inmates had gone to rest; but that blessing had long been a stranger to our heroine.

It was a fine, tranquil night, and the moon was shining brilliantly in at the window of Mildred's chamber. A gentle melancholy succeeded the intense agony she had endured throughout the day, and she approached the casement in order that she might try to divert her mind in some measure by the contemplation of the surrounding scenery, which, on other and far happier occasions, had always excited her warmest admiration.

She gazed upon the old Tower of Bransdorf, which was revealed to her distinctly in the broad moonlight, and her thoughts reverted to the extraordinary scenes which tradition stated to have been enacted within its walls. She viewed it with mingled feelings of awe and interest, almost amounting to veneration; she viewed it almost as the place of her birth, for it was where she had been found, and with it she felt certain that her fate was deeply associated. What would have been her emotions, had she known that, at that very moment, the object of her anxiety, Ethelbert de Lancy, was a wretched inmate of one of its dungeons!

The atmosphere in the chamber was dense and sultry, and she therefore opened the casement, and looked out, in order that she might inhale the cool air that gently wafted amongst the foliage.

While she was thus occupied, she beheld at a short distance, a form advancing, which as near as she could distinguish, was that of a female. It came nearer, and at last stood, underneath the window, and then, to her astonishment, but not with such feelings of alarm as she had before experienced, she recognised the weird woman.

She was differently clad to what she had been when she before saw her, and her countenance did not betray so forbidding and revolting an expression.

Mildred could not remove her eyes from her, and she felt even a strange inclination to speak to her, and to ascertain who she was, and what was the object of her visit.

The weird woman fixed her eyes intent'y upon her, and then said, in a tone of voice which was entirely divested of its former harshness—

"Come down, maiden. I have that to impart to thee which concerns thine happiness, and likewise that of those who are dear to thee."

"Who and what are you?" demanded Mildred, in a tremulous voice. "If you have anything to reveal, why cannot you do so without my leaving my chamber?"

"Reject my information if you please," returned the woman; "you might afterwards sorely repent it. You have nothing to fear; I intend you no evil, but good. Will you come?"

Mildred hesitated.

"Quick!" cried the woman, "for time is precious, and you may not have another such opportunity. I will not detain you long."

Mildred still hesitated; but there was a something so impressive, and at the same time so persuasive in the mysterious woman's manner, that she was half induced to comply with her request.

"Cannot you," she demanded, "impart what you have to communicate at a more seasonable hour?"

"No," was the answer; "now is the only fitting time; at any other somthing might occur to thwart my plans, which I once more tell you, girl, are for your benefit."

"What guarantee have I for my safety?" asked Mildred.

"My word, which never yet was broken," replied the weird woman.

"And something might occur to——"

"Nothing can occur to injure you, whilst I am your companion," retorted the woman, interrupting her. "There is no time to deliberate. Will you do as I desire?"

"Cannot you state to me now what you have to tell me, without my leaving the castle?"

"No; it must not be here."

"Then—then—I cannot comply with the request of a stranger, made under such ambiguous circumstances, and at so strange and suspicious an hour. Even now I know not but that I am acting imprudently in holding converse with you."

"Indeed!" returned the woman, and a strange expression of mingled rage and pity overspread her features. "Use your own will, then, obstinate damsel; but take the consequences. I would have served you; but you reject my offers, and I can have no more to say than this, that before the sun shall light the summits of the eastern hills to-morrow, such a calamity shall befall you and all that you hold most dear, you cannot now form the smallest conception of. The——"

"Oh, hold, hold! for mercy's sake!" interrupted the terrified Mildred. "Heaven guide me how to act. What can be the purport of your visit to me at this extraordinary hour, and in so questionable a manner?"

"I would give you some information of him you love," answered the woman; "of Ethelbert de Lancy."

"Ah!" exclaimed our heroine, eagerly; "you do not attempt to deceive me?"

"Deceive you!" repeated the weird woman, with a look of scorn; "what think you I could gain by that?"

"But why not forward your intelligence to Sir Aldobrand?" asked our heroine. "Why seek out me, and at such a time, to give the information, if you have really any to impart?"

"It is enough, damsel, for you to know that my motives are just. It is useless thus trifling. Farewell! Remember what I have said. I came here with the intention to serve you; but you refuse my proferred friendship, and, it seems, are determined to provoke the consequences which most assuredly will follow. Adieu!"

"Stay, stay! but a moment, most singular woman," said Mildred. "You assert that no harm is intended me?"

"I have before asserted it. Ulrica is not used to state that which is not true, as many have found, both to their cost and to their advantage."

"I will trust to you," remarked Mildred, "and may Heaven protect me, as I act with the best intentions, and for the welfare of those whom I hold as dear to me as my very existence."

"'Tis well, Mildred of the old Tower of Bransdorf," replied Ulrica (for so she had called herself), and at the same time she folded her tattered cloak around her tall, bony figure more closely, and crossed her arms over her breast. Mildred fixed one more scrutinising glance upon her, and again for a moment she hesitated; but the idea of hearing some intelligence of Ethelbert urged her on, and having hastily offered up a prayer to Omnipotence for protection in the object she had in view, she hastily put on her hat and cloak, and gently unlocked the chamber-door, traversed the gallery of the castle, and descended the stairs, with noiseless steps, which led to one of the private entrances.

The family were all at rest; but having secured the key, which was placed in a small recess contiguous, she gently, but not without some difficulty, unbolted the door, and emerged into the broad moonlight.

Ulrica was standing there in the same attitude as when Mildred had seen her at the casement of her chamber, and seemed to be conversing with her own thoughts, and not to observe our heroine. She timidly approached her, and, aroused at her footsteps, the mysterious woman turned her large, black, piercing eyes full upon her, with an expression that might have been constructed into satisfaction.

"Ah, 'tis well, 'tis well," she ejaculated. "Thou hast acted prudently, maiden."

"Heaven grant that I may," answered Mildred. "Now, mysterious woman, what is it you would say to me?"

" That which affects not only your own welfare and future prospects, but the lives of your benefactor, Sir Aldobrand de Lancy, and his son Ethelbert."

" Oh, tell me, does Ethelbert still live ?" impatiently asked our heroine.

" He does," answered Ulrica, " and you shall behold him if you obey my instructions."

" Oh, where, where ?"

" This is not the place to inform you."

" And why not ?"

" Much more depends upon it than you seem to imagine."

" Well, well."

" This way—this way, Mildred."

" I once more begin to suspect you. I will go no further."

" Foolish girl ! you know not what danger you incur, and to those whom you affect to be so dear to you, by this rejection of my good-will towards you—this silly hesitation. Will you follow me ?"

" Whither would you lead me ?"

" But a short distance from hence," answered Ulrica, " where you will hear that which would deeply and irreparably afflict you not to be informed of. See, the moon now shines brightly. Should clouds obscure it, all hope is o'er. Come, come; you have not a moment to spare. In pity to you I have already wasted too many of the precious moments I am allowed to communicate that which I desire to do to those whom I would serve."

Still Mildred doubted; for there was a singular expression about the woman's countenance, especially as she made use of the last observation, which inspired her with a feeling of dread and suspicion, and she was half inclined to return to the castle; but then the threats which Ulrica had uttered respecting Sir Aldobrand and Ethelbert, and the irresistible curiosity she felt to fathom the whole of this mysterious adventure, strongly combatted her other objections, and she resolved, whatever the consequence might be, to see the result of it."

" I will follow you," she said to the woman; " lead on."

Ulrica returned a look of satisfaction, and pointing significantly with her hand, led the way across the lawn towards the path that conducted to the old Tower of Bransdorf."

They had not advanced many yards, when a strange shuddering presentiment that all was not well, crossed the mind of Mildred, and she suddenly stopped, and was still irresolute whether to proceed or retreat. Anxious as she was to penetrate the mysteries of the tower, she could not but feel a dread of approaching that ancient building at such an hour, and in the company of one of such questionable character, and she repented that she had quitted the castle at all.

" There can be no listeners to what you say here," she observed, " if that you have to state requires secrecy. I will go no farther."

" Nay, nay," returned Ulrica, grasping her arm, and looking triumphantly in her countenance; " it is too late to retrace your steps. You must go with me now."

" Strange being !" ejaculated the affrighted Mildred, " you have deceived me, mad that I was to entrust myself to you. Release your hold of me, or I will scream for help."

" And what would that avail you ?" replied Ulrica. " It would not bring you any assistance; there is no one at hand to help you; and if there was, what would they be able to accomplish against me, when I have the immediate means, as you see, to offer any resistance."

As she said this, she produced a brace of pistols from beneath her cloak, and still kept her hold of Mildred's arm, who felt so much alarm, that she knew not how to act.

" Your looks and threats terrify me," she said; surely you do not wish to harm one who never intended, and never could have injured you, by word or deed."

" I have told you again and again," replied Ulrica; " but no more delay, my patience is exhausted."

" Whither do you wish to lead me ?"

" You will see."

The singular being released her hold, and once more advanced a few paces forward; motioning Mildred, with looks half persuasive, half commanding, to follow. She dreaded to disobey, yet would she have given the world that she was once more safe within the castle, and she deeply regretted that she had been induced to leave it by the pursuasions of Ulrica, whose purpose, notwithstanding her asseverations, she could not help still suspecting. How would Sir Aldobrand reproach her for conduct so imprudent ; and after all, it might only be a plot to effect her or her revered benefactor some serious injury. She was, however, constrained to follow Ulrica, who still advanced towards the hill on which the tower stood, every now and then turning her head to see whether or not she was behind her, and moving with a gliding kind of motion, rather than walking.

Mildred's doubts gained strength, and she once more paused, and demanded whither Ulrica was leading her.

"Girl," she returned, "we have not much further to go; but do you still entertain those silly doubts and fears?"

"Have I not a right to do so," said Mildred, "since your conduct is so strange, and the hour at which you have chosen to perform your mysterious mission is so late? There surely can be no necessity for us to proceed so far away from the castle for you to give me the intelligence you say you have to tell me."

"But there is—there is," returned Ulrica; "but a short distance further, and then you shall know all. Come, come; recollect, I promise you that the lives of your benefactor and his son depend upon your courage and obedience to my wishes."

"And may not danger threaten me on my return to the castle?" asked Mildred.

"No; I promise you that nõ harm shall befall you; I will see to your safety."

Our heroine feared to disobey, for the looks of her conductor convinced her that she was not to be trifled with; but she trembled with suspense and apprehension, and wondered that she could have been so mad as to be prevailed upon to leave the castle on such an ambiguous errand, and in the company of an entire stranger to her, and whose behaviour, to say the least of it, was of the most extraordinary and suspicious description.

They had now got some distance from the castle, when Ulrica deviated from the path which conducted to the tower, again looking back to see whether Mildred was following her, and took the way which led to a woody glade.

The moon was now entirely obscured by a dense black cloud, and the shadow of Ulrica's tall figure had a strange, unearthly appearance in the gloom of the moment.

A shuddering sensation came over her, and pausing, she once more looked back in the direction they had been traversing. A shrill whistle startled her, and in an instant she found herself seized by several persons. She looked up, and to her horror beheld herself in the power of five or six men, whose features were concealed beneath black masks, but Ulrica was gone.

She shrieked aloud, and struggled violently, but all to no purpose; she found herself hurried along in spite of her efforts to the contrary—her strength then became exhausted, and she remembered no more.

CHAPTER XXI.

THE NOCTURNAL JOURNEY.—THE INTERVIEW BETWEEN LORD RUTHLYN DE OHUNB
AND MILDRED.

WHEN Mildred was recalled to recollection, she found herself in a travelling vehicle, in the power of the men who had seized her, and proceeding at a rapid rate.

They were surrounded by darkness, for the moon had entirely disappeared, and, therefore, the poor girl had no opportunity of distinguishing the road they were journeying; but it was quite sufficient for her to be satisfied that she was in the power of some fearful enemy, and that the hag, Ulrica, had betrayed her, and her agony of mind was almost too great for endurance.

The fierce countenances of the ruffians who were seated on either side of her, filled her bosom with terror, and she feared to speak to them, well convinced that she was likely only to be insulted by them, and she had nothing to do but to submit in silence to her fate, and to trust in Providence to interpose to rescue her from the danger which evidently threatened her. To that power, then, she mentally offered up her prayers, and then throwing herself back in the vehicle, gave herself up to the painful reflections which naturally tortured her mind.

Foolish, imprudent girl that she had been, to yield to the pursuasions of Ulrica, and to trust to her promises, when her very appearance at such an hour, and her conduct both on that occasion and previously, ought to have been enough to have excited her strongest suspicion, and to have put her on her guard. What agony would not Sir Aldobrand experience when he discovered her disappearance, especially in his present state of mind, which was almost laid prostrate by the loss of his son? This reflection increased her torture tenfold, and she could no longer restrain her feelings, but burst into a paroxysm of convulsive sobs and tears, which appeared not, however, to move the compassion of the ruffians in the least, who, having removed their masks, gazed at her with perfect indifference.

In one of their countenances Mildred was almost certain she discovered the features of one of the domestics who had attended upon Lord Ruthlyn while he was at the castle of De Lancy; and this impression strengthened her in the idea that his lordship was the author of this infamous plot; and if, indeed, she was in his power, she had everything to dread.

"Oh, where are you conveying me?" she cried, wringing her hands, and addressing herself to one of the men. "Why am I thus cruelly torn from my home, and for what purpose?"

"We have not much further to go, young lady, and you will then know all about it, so you may as well be quiet, and submit to that which you cannot control or alter," replied the man to whom she had spoken.

"God help me!" groaned Mildred; "I see it all plain enough now; this is the diabolical plot of Lord Ruthlyn de Bohun. Oh, coward that he is, thus to take advantage of an innocent, unoffending girl. But, although he may triumph now, the vengeance of Heaven will not fail to overtake him."

Neither of the ruffians returned any answer to this, but exchanged glances one with the other, and Mildred relapsed into silence, and gave herself up to despair, seeing that it was perfectly vain for her to endeavour to struggle against her fate, whatever it might be, and which had been partially provoked by her own folly and imprudence in yielding to the persuasions of the woman Ulrica, who there could be no doubt was the myrmidon of the villain by whose orders she had been seized.

Terrible were indeed the reflections which agonized her mind, but she felt more for the suspense and agony Sir Aldobrand de Lancy would endure on discovering her loss, a trial which, following so speedily upon the one he had recently experienced, might be productive of the most fatal consequences; she had been his only source of consolation under that heavy affliction, and how he would be enabled to support it she dreaded even to think.

She could form no conjecture how long they had been travelling; but at length, by the light emitted at intervals by the moon, she could perceive the faint outline of some lofty building amid the trees; and from the observations which the men exchanged with one another, she was able to ascertain that that was the place of their destination.

Mildred trembled with apprehension, and again wrung her hands in the intensity of her anguish and despair. The men seemed to take no notice of her, and the vehicle, having passed along an extensive avenue of trees, at last stopped before the entrance of a large gothic building, which, as well as our heroine could distinguish, had a most sombre and forbidding appearance. There was a light burning in one of the windows above the ancient porch, and it was evident that their arrival was anticipated, for no sooner had the carriage stopped, than the door was opened by a tall bony man, who held a lamp in his hand, and greeted the man who had approached him.

The other men descended from the vehicle, and assisted Mildred to alight also, who knowing it would be perfectly useless to attempt to offer any resistance, remained passive, and was conducted by her uncouth and repulsive companions into a spacious but gloomy hall, and from thence up a flight of winding stairs, all being so quiet in the building that nothing could be heard save the sound of their own footsteps.

They stopped at the door of an apartment which was partially open, and in which a light was burning; and the men, having ushered our heroine into the room, in which a fire was blazing, and which otherwise presented a greater air of comfort than she had expected to find, abruptly left her, and locked the door after them.

Mildred, completely overwhelmed by the agony and despair of her feelings, threw herself on a chair and burst into tears. She was now, indeed, a prisoner, and, unless Providence should interpose, nothing whatever could rescue her from the deep laid machinations of her secret enemy or enemies. But what enemy had she any reason to believe she possessed, or had cause to apprehend, unless it was Lord Ruthlyn? What conduct of her's had ever given cause for the jealousy or bad feeling of any one? She knew not of any; and yet there might be those who were acquainted with her origin, who were jealous of her being at liberty, or even of her life.

She clasped her hands frantically together, and looked anxiously, yet timidly, around her. The room was spacious and lofty, and opened into another, in which there was a bed. Mildred arose from her seat, and for some minutes traversed the apartment with the most disordered steps, whilst her brain was distracted and bewildered. Then she advanced towards the door and listened, but all was quite still, and any one would have been led to suppose that the mansion was not inhabited by any one but herself. The suspense she was placed in at the time which elapsed without any one coming near her or informing her where she was, and for what purpose she was brought there, was most intolerable; and to have known the worst at once, even though it should be ever so dreadful, would not have been half so torturing as this state of uncertainty.

At length she did hear the sound of footsteps ascending the stairs, and they stopped at the room door, which was shortly opened, and a female, apparently about her own age, and of rather a kind expression of countenance, bringing some refreshments with her, entered.

The sight of her was some relief to Mildred, and she hastily advanced towards her, and with tearful eyes and supplicating looks, exclaimed—

"Oh, stranger, for the love of Heaven, I implore you to take pity on a poor innocent girl, and inform me where I am, and for what purpose I am thus mercilessly torn from that home which has so long sheltered me? Oh, I beseech you, do not keep me in suspense; your looks are kind, and I do not believe that you can help pitying one of your own sex."

The young woman did indeed appear moved by her words, and, after a pause, said—

"Do not so violently agitate yourself, miss, for, although all appears gloomy and threatening enough at present, something may occur to rescue you from the danger with which you are threatened."

"Threatened!" repeated Mildred, eagerly; "oh! by whom?"

"Speak lower, lady," said the girl, "for it must not be known that I pity you, or I know not what the consequences might be."

"You do pity me, then; oh, thanks, thanks! And you will assist me to defeat the plans of my cruel enemies? Say that you will."

"Alas! miss," returned the girl, in a voice of sympathy and regret, "that, I fear, will not be in my power; but all that kindness and commiseration can effect, you may expect from me."

"To whom does this mansion belong?" demanded Mildred, impatiently.

"To Sir Godwin Singleford," answered the girl.

"Sir Godwin Singleford! I never heard of his name before. What can he want with me, or why has he dared to tear me from my friends?"

"Sir Godwin is the friend of Lord Ruthlyn de Bohun; and it is by the orders of the latter you are brought hither."

"Lord Ruthlyn de Bohun!" cried our heroine, clasping her hands together in despair. "Am I in that heartless nobleman's power? Then am I indeed lost."

"Be calm, miss," returned the attendant; "for his lordship may repent of his intentions, or something may occur to defeat his plans."

"But Sir Godwin Singleford will not, surely, dare to detain me here against my will," ejaculated Mildred. "I demand to see him immediately, that I may remonstrate with him on the diabolical act at which he has connived, and——"

"Neither Sir Godwin or Lord Ruthlyn are at present within the mansion," interrupted the young woman, "and they are not expected here till to-morrow."

"Oh, God! and must I then remain here? Will no one have any compassion for me, or the sufferings of my good, kind benefactor, whose heart has been sufficiently wrung by the loss of his son?"

"I wish that I could assist you, lady, but I cannot. Endeavour to await the result with patience and fortitude, and who knows what may transpire? The hour is now late, and had you not better retire to rest."

"To rest!" replied our heroine, in the most melancholy accents; "oh, how think you I can rest in this strange place, where I know not what danger may be impending over me?"

"You have nothing to apprehend at present, miss," returned the young woman, whose name was Annie; "no one will attempt to harm you that is at present in the mansion; and if it will afford you any satisfaction, I will sleep in the same room with you."

"Oh, you are very kind," said Mildred, pressing her hand; "I will, indeed, most thankfully accept your offer."

"Then compose yourself, lady, I beg of you," said Annie; "partake of these refreshments which I have brought you, and I will return to you again in a short time."

Annie then quitted the room, and Mildred, who did, indeed, feel somewhat more tranquillized after the assurances which the young woman had made her, and the sympathy she expressed towards her, having commended herself to the protection of Heaven, tasted slightly of the refreshments, and tried to await with some degree of patience and fortitude the result of her abduction; for surely Providence, she reflected, that Providence which she had never consciously offended, would not desert her at so trying an occasion; certainly, all good and merciful as it was, it would not permit the guilty Lord Ruthlyn to triumph in his iniquitous designs.

But still it was a hard, a very hard task she imposed upon herself; for when she thought of the anguish of mind Sir Aldobrand would be subjected to when he discovered her loss, coupled with the mysterious disappearance of Ethelbert, her emotion was still greater than that which was occasioned by her own captivity.

To Ethelbert, too, her thoughts were devoted in the most painful manner. What was his fate? Alas! she had every reason to dread the worst; and bitterly did she bemoan the misfortunes which had befallen him, she had too much reason to apprehend, on her account. She was now more strongly impressed with the idea than ever that Lord Ruthlyn was also the author of the infamous plot by which he had been borne away; and if such was indeed the case, she had every reason to tremble for the consequences that had befallen him.

She was interrupted in these reflections by the return of Annie, who expressed her satisfaction, in unaffected terms, at seeing her more composed than when she had left her. She again urged her to seek some repose, and assured her of her safety, as she would secure the doors which opened to the apartments, and there were no other means of entrance to them.

Mildred expressed confidence in her assertions, and promised to do so presently, as she really felt worn out with the fatigue of her unexpected journey and her anguish of mind.

"But, tell me, Annie," said she; "what is the name of this place?"

"It is called Singleford Hall, miss, after the name of the proprietor," answered Annie. "It is a strange, gloomy, old place, and is seldom inhabited by Sir Godwin."

"And I need not ask the character of Sir Godwin," observed Mildred; "for his friendship for Lord Ruthlyn, and his connection with this diabolical plot against an innocent girl, sufficiently testify it."

"Why, miss," replied Annie, "I cannot but strongly condemn my master's conduct on this occasion, and I wonder that he should run the risk of the responsibility he may incur, knowing that Sir Aldobrand de Lancy, of whom I have ever heard so much praise, is your protector. But Sir Godwin Singleford has his good qualities, as well as his bad ones."

"Is he married?" inquired Mildred.

"Sir Godwin was never married," replied Annie. "He was disappointed in love, and that, I believe, has soured his temper, and rendered him worse than he would otherwise probably have been. I am much indebted to him, for ever since the death of my poor parents (who were both in his service, and I have not another in the world), he has been to me a friend and benefactor."

"Oh, it is indeed wonderful, that a man who possesses so many noble and generous qualities, should connive at the ruin and misery of one whom he has never seen, and against whom he cannot possibly have any cause for prejudice. Surely he will not turn a deaf ear to my supplications, but will endeavour to atone for the wrong he has done me, by opposing the plans of Lord Ruthlyn."

"Sincerely do I hope he may, miss," said Annie; "but, alas! I fear he is so prejudiced against our sex since his own disappointment, that your persuasions will have but little effect on him."

"And can he be so lost to feeling and honour," demanded our heroine, her bosom swelling, and her whole frame trembling with fear and indignation, "as to aid the villain Ruthlyn in his designs against the peace of an innocent girl? Oh, if such, indeed, is his character, I have ample reason to apprehend the worst. Heaven help me!"

She again clasped her hands, and sobbed bitterly. Annie endeavoured to soothe her, and once more to persuade her to retire to rest.

"The men who brought you hither have gone to their chambers, miss," she remarked; "and you have nothing whatever to fear from them. Besides, I am with you, and although you know as yet nothing of me, I trust that you will believe me sincere in my professions of sympathy towards you. Come, come, a few hours' rest will refresh you, and who knows what to-morrow may produce?"

"Alas! alas!" sighed Mildred, "who, indeed, knows what it may be productive of? Perhaps, my eternal shame and misery. Oh, Annie, you who appear to have so much feeling towards one of your own sex, surely you will not turn a deaf ear to my supplications; you will not refuse to aid me?"

"All that lies in my humble power I will do, miss, rest assured," answered Annie.

" Every person has retired to rest in the hall, you say," eagerly rejoined our heroine. " Oh, why could you not set me at liberty, and accompany me ? Sir Aldobrand de Lancy would not only bless and reward you for the inestimable service, but would protect you from the consequences. Oh, in pity yield to my solicitations, for although the hour is late, and the way is lonely, what is there that I would not brave to escape from the horrers which now surround me ?"

" Alas! it is impossible, miss," returned Annie. " All the doors of the hall are secured, and one of the men who conveyed you hither has the keys in his possession. Besides, I could never deceive one, who, at least, has been to me a friend, in such a manner. I would assist you, lady, but I fear, as I said before, that my means will be found to be only limited."

" Then there is no hope for me," sighed Mildred, looking at her companion with an expression of disappointment. " Oh, God ! what have I done that such a fate should befall me ? Oh, my beloved guardian, how insupportable, how maddening will be your anguish when you discover my loss. What conjectures can you form upon the dreadful subject ? What means adopt to recover me ?"

She covered her face with her hands, and rocked herself to and fro with the intensity of her mental sufferings.

Annie was much affected, and gently approaching her, she again earnestly tried to pacify her distracted feelings.

" Something may eccur, miss, to prevent the evil you now apprehend. You may be able to move the compassion of my master, and he will, I am convinced, prevent any act of violence on the part of Lord Ruthlyn. Besides, I believe that his lordship only seeks to gain your consent to become his wife, and ——"

" Become his wife !" interrupted Mildred, with a feeling of the most ineffable disgust and indignation; " sooner would I perish than become the wife of that detested man. He already knows my sentiments, and has he the presumption to think that conduct such as this will have the power to change them ? Does he think that force will ever compel me to become the bride of one whom I must ever loathe, whom I must ever look upon with horror ? No ! Heaven will not permit so inhuman a sacrifice, and he shall see me a corpse at his feet sooner than I will yield to his wishes. Oh, Ethelbert, where are you now ? What would be your agony and distraction did you but know my present situation ?"

" Pardon me, miss," said Annie ; " but if I have heard aright, Ethelbert de Lancy is the successful rival of Lord Ruthlyn in your affections. But he has disappeared from the castle of his father, has he not ?"

" Alas ! alas !" sighed Mildred, almost choked by the power of her emotions ; " or this would never have happened. But what know you of him ?" she added, hastily, and fixing a penetrating look on the countenance of Annie ; " tell me, quickly, what know you of Ethelbert de Lancy ?"

" Nothing more than I have told you, miss."

" The villain, Lord Ruthlyn, his the cause of his disappearance," cried our heroine ; " I feel satisfied that he is. May the vengeance of offended Heaven pursue him. But tell me, Annie, and in mercy do not attempt to deceive me, do you know nothing more of the fate of the unfortunate Ethelbert de Lancy than what you have stated ?"

" Most solemnly I declare before high Heaven, that I do not, or I would readily, believe me, reveal it to you."

" Think you not that Lord Ruthlyn has been the cause of his disappearance ?"

" It is not for me to form an opinion upon so important a subject, miss," replied Annie.

" Are there any other prisoners in this hall besides myself ?" demanded Mildred.

" I know not," replied Annie ; " in fact, I am convinced that there are not, or I must have become aware of it."

" But, alas ! alas !" continued our heroine ; " why do I ask ? Poor Ethelbert has ere this perished by the hand of his secret and cowardly enemy."

" Nay, miss," returned Annie, " it may not be so ; and something may yet transpire to restore you to each other. Come, come, do not give way entirely to despair, dismal as your fate at present seems to be."

" In vain you talk, girl ; what else is there but despair before me ? What reason have I to hope ? Oh, my kind benefactor, could you but become acquainted with my situation, how quickly would you hasten to release me from it. Annie, if you have the humanity you profess to have, you will at least not refuse my earnest entreaties to apprise him of it."

"Ah, miss," said Annie, "you know not the difficulty of that which you request me to do. But—but I will think further upon it, and at some future period——"

"No—no—do not delay; some future period may be too late. Promise me that you will immediately yield to my supplications, and set my distracted mind at rest. Oh, there is no reward that Sir Aldobrand will hesitate to give you."

"Indeed, indeed, I cannot promise you, miss."

"Then you do not pity me."

"Oh, do me not an injustice, miss," said Annie, fervently. "Indeed, indeed I do; and this I will promise, namely, that I will do everything in my humble power to save you from the fate you apprehend. Let this for the present satisfy you; try to compose your feelings, and to seek rest; an hour or twos' repose will serve to strengthen you, and give you fortitude to meet the man you dread to-morrow."

"Alas! alas!" sighed Mildred, "how shall I, indeed, meet him? Disgust and terror will render me completely powerless."

After some further persuasion on the part of Annie, she was induced to allow her to assist her to undress; and at length, after having again besought the protection of Heaven, she retired to bed, Annie occupying a mattress by her side.

But, notwithstanding the extreme fatigue she had undergone, it was some time before she could go to sleep; and her tears flowed unrestrained when she thought of the melancholy and painful situation in which she was placed. Nature, however, could hold out no longer against the all-subduing influence of the drowsy god, and she gained a brief respite to her sufferings.

The sun had long arisen before she awoke, and she started up in her bed and gazed vacantly around her, for a few minutes having but an imperfect recollection of where she was; but the fearful reality soon burst upon her memory, and she wrung her hands in despair.

Annie still slept, and Mildred did not attempt to arouse her, for she was anxious for a while to give free indulgence to her thoughts; and terrible, indeed, they were. Probably by that time, Sir Aldobrand had discovered her disappearance from the castle; and she pictured to herself his maddening state of anguish, with no one at hand to afford him any hope or consolation. The idea was horrible, and her reason almost sunk beneath the weight of it. He would never be able to sustain himself beneath this additional trial, for she knew that he loved her as fondly as if she had been his daughter, and to be thus deprived of all that he held dear—to be left alone, was sufficient to sink him to the lowest depths of misery and despair.

And in what manner could he imagine her abduction had been accomplished? The more he might endeavour to penetrate the mystery, the deeper he would be sure to become involved in perplexity.

Again and again did she reproach herself for leaving the castle at the pursuasion of Ulrica. She could not but blame herself for all that had happened. She might have been certain that the hag had some sinister designs in view, or why should she seek her at such an hour of the night; and why did she not impart that which she had said she had to communicate to her on the spot, where there was no one near to overhear them?

But the mysterious contrivance of the plot bewildered Mildred more than all; how Ulrica could calculate upon seeing her at such a time, and the ruffians be ready to seize her, as if they were before certain of success, she could not imagine. Her actions must indeed have been most closely watched, and great must have been the skill and power of Ulrica to carry the nefarious stratagem into effect.

But from these torturing thoughts, her ideas turned to subjects equally as painful. The morning had dawned on which she had been told she must be prepared to meet her dread enemy; and every moment that elapsed increased her fears. Alas! what might transpire at that meeting? To what insolent lengths might not the odious and guilty passion of Lord Ruthlyn lead him, now that he had her entirely at his mercy, and she had so little power to offer any resistance to him? Alas! what could a weak, defenceless woman do against one who was goaded on by passion and revenge?

She shuddered, and for a few moments became lost in the agony and perplexity of her thoughts. Never had she expected to experience such a severe trial of her fortitude as this; and now that it had come upon her, how little was she prepared to meet it.

She listened attentively, and all was silent—no one was yet stirring. A thought suddenly flashed across her brain, and for a moment it inspired her with hope. Annie slept; could she secure the key of the chamber, she might yet effect her escape before any one was about.

But this thought was only transient: she remembered what Annie had told her in respect to the doors of the hall being secured, and the keys being in the possession of one of the ruffians who had brought her there, and, therefore, all chance of escape was rendered impossible. She threw herself back on her pillow in despair, and for some time remained in a state of the most racking anguish. But at length she arose, and was preparing to dress herself, when Annie awoke, and, looking up and beholding her stirring, she kindly and respectfully inquired after her health.

"Alas!" sighed Mildred, shaking her head mournfully, "think you I can be well either in mind or body, and know myself a wretched prisoner in the power of the depraved Lord Ruthlyn de Bohun? Oh, Annie, my heart will break under this terrible persecution."

"Heaven forbid, miss," replied Annie, sincerely; "come, come, courage, or you will give your enemy an advantage. You know not what effect your remonstrances and supplications may have upon him."

"Oh, no," returned our heroine; "it would be absurd to entertain such a thought for an instant. Neither remonstrances nor supplications can have any influence over the callous heart of a miscreant who could so overstep the bounds of honour and humanity as Lord Ruthlyn has done. And must I, shall I so far degrade myself to supplicate to him? It is he who should bend the knee to me, in contrition, and to sue for forgiveness for the injury he has done me, for the agony he has inflicted upon the heart of that venerable man whom I revere as a parent."

"And he may repent, miss," suggested her companion, "and a few hours may see you restored again to liberty."

"The villain who could proceed so far," observed our heroine, "must be determined. He is not likely to relent. And well do I remember his threats on the occasion when we last met. But you, Annie, have it in your power to save me."

"I, miss!"

"Yes, yes; only contrive some means of letting Sir Aldobrand know the place of my confinement, and may the blessings of Heaven alight upon your head."

"Indeed I have no means of doing so, miss."

"The willing heart never lacks the power to render service to the injured and the persecuted, Annie. I fear that even in you, one of my own sex, I cannot expect to find much sympathy."

"Oh, my dear lady," returned Annie, how great is the injustice you do me. I pity you from my very soul, and only hope that the opportunity may speedily occur to convince you how anxious I am to serve you. But I am at present surrounded by more difficulties than you can imagine. Come, miss, do not thus give way to grief; for, depend upon it, that Providence will avert the dangers you now apprehend."

Mildred shook her head, and once more relapsed into dismal thought. People were now moving in the hall, and, after again begging of Mildred to conquer her emotions, Annie left the room to prepare the morning's repast. Our heroine paced the apartment with the most disordered steps, and nothing could dissipate the distressing thoughts and apprehensions which arose in bewildering haste upon her imagination. That Annie possessed a kind heart, and pitied her, she felt satisfied, but she was fearful that, as she had stated, she had not the power to serve her, and therefore she had little reason to hope anything from that quarter.

Again she reflected upon the state of agony her beloved benefactor would now be in, he having, probably, by this time, become acquainted with her loss. She could scarcely contain herself as the picture of his sufferings arose to her imagination, and many were the tears she shed.

"Oh, my more than father!" she sighed, "was it not enough that Heaven should deprive you of your son, but that this additional calamity must befall you! Alas! it will drive you to madness; and you have no one left to offer to you the balm of consolation under your sorrows. May every misfortune attend the villain who has been the cause of this!"

Annie now re-entered the room, bringing with her the morning's repast, which having spread upon the table, she requested our heroine to be seated, and to partake of it, hoping that it would tend to revive her.

Mildred was but little disposed to eat; but she felt faint, and therefore complied, and the breakfast passed off in silence, except when interrupted by the deep sobs and sighs which escaped from the bosom of Mildred.

"At what hour are Sir Godwin and Lord Ruthlyn expected to arrive at the hall?" she inquired, in a melancholy tone.

"I know not," answered Annie, "neither am I acquainted with the cause of their absence."

"And are the ruffians still here?"

"They are; but you have nothing to fear from them. They would not dare to offer to insult you."

Another gloomy interval elapsed. The apprehensions of Mildred increased, as every moment she anticipated the arrival of Lord Ruthlyn, and Annie tried in vain to compose her.

At length the hall bell was heard to ring violently, and Mildred started to her feet, and turned ghastly pale, trembling at the same time all over.

"They are here!" she ejaculated. "Oh, Heaven! give me strength, for the moment of my trial is at hand."

"Courage, miss, courage," expostulated her companion. "I will go and see; and in the meantime, let me beg of you to endeavour to tranquillise your feelings."

She quitted the room as she spoke, and Mildred sunk on her knees in an agony of grief and terror. She tried to offer up a prayer to Heaven; but the words died away upon her lips before she could give utterance to them; and she remained in a state of almost utter unconsciousness until Annie returned.

"Now speak, speak," she said, turning hastily towards her attendant; "tell me, has he come?"

"My master has returned alone," replied Annie.

Mildred felt a dead weight removed from her heart.

"Alone!" she repeated. "Where, then, is Lord Ruthlyn? Has any accident befallen him?"

"No, miss," answered Annie; "but some business has detained him, and he will not be here till the afternoon. But Sir Godwin has desired me to inform you, that, with your permission, he will have an interview with you after he has partaken of breakfast."

"Oh, yes, yes, I will see him," eagerly ejaculated Mildred; "and if he have indeed the least feeling of humanity existing within his breast, he will not turn a deaf ear to my supplications, or any longer degrade himself by acting as the colleague of Lord Ruthlyn in such a base act of cruelty and oppression. Tell him so, good Annie."

"I will," answered Annie, "and I only hope that you may succeed in moving him to interest himself in your favour."

Annie once more retired from the room to make her master acquainted with the answer to his message, and during her absence, Mildred experienced mingled feelings of hope, doubt, and suspense. Surely, if Sir Godwin Singleford possessed the many amiable qualities which Annie had represented to her that he did (and Mildred, from what little she had seen of her, and the candour of her manner, had no reason to doubt her), he could not be insensible to the injustice that was being done to her, and would try to make all the atonement in his power for the part he had taken in the affair, by resisting the persecution of Lord Ruthlyn, and restoring her to her friends.

With these hopes Mildred flattered herself, and awaited impatiently her interview with Sir Godwin, trusting that her tears and entreaties would have their due effect on him, and that, in spite of the guilty designs of Lord Ruthlyn de Bohun, a short time would witness her release from his power, and that such steps would be taken as would most effectually render all his plans abortive.

"God grant," she ejaculated, "that my supplications to Sir Godwin may prevail; for should I longer be detained from my beloved benefactor, the consequences, I have too much reason to apprehend, will be fatal to him. Oh, Sir Aldobrand, may Heaven give you fortitude to support this heavy trial till I am restored to you again!"

Sincerely she hoped that Sir Godwin would see her without delay, for then he might be induced to release her, and restore her to the castle, before the arrival of Lord Ruthlyn at the hall, and thus his plans would be defeated, and the disappointment to his nefarious hopes would be a just punishment for the pain he had already put her to.

Annie at length returned, and to the eager inquiries of Mildred she answered—

"Sir Godwin will be here presently, miss, and from what he said in reply to the observations I ventured to make to him, I anticipate the most favourable results."

"Oh, thanks, thanks, my good girl," said our heroine, energetically; "believe me, you will not find me ungrateful for any services you may render me."

"Do not mention that, miss," returned Annie. "I shall only be too happy if I be made the humble instrument of rescuing you from the dangers which at present seem impending over you. But be firm, I beseech you, and trust to Providence for the result, which I strongly hope will be all that you can desire."

"I will, my good girl, I will, and if Sir Godwin possess the good qualities you have said he does, he will not, cannot treat my supplications with indifference. Most freely will I pardon him for the part he has taken in this guilty transaction, and I know that Sir Aldobrand will readily accord the same forgiveness on my restoration to him. What can your master hope to gain by becoming the accessory to the destruction of an innocent and almost friendless girl?"

"I know not what his motives may be, miss," replied Annie, "and I beg of you to reserve your opinion until after your interview with him."

"I will, Annie," said Mildred; "and may all the hopes you have so kindly expressed be realized. Alas! should they be disappointed, my courage will entirely sink under the misfortune. My heart will break at the terrible prospect before me."

"Cheer up, miss; view everything on the brightest side, and Heaven will not desert you."

"Your words inspire me with hope, dear Annie," said Mildred. "I will endeavour to follow your advice."

"'Tis well, miss," remarked Annie, "and humble as it is, I trust that you will, notwithstanding, find it to be not unworthy. But I must leave you now."

"And why so, Annie?" demanded Mildred.

"It was the order of my master, miss," replied the latter; "besides, I have some domestic duties to perform. When the interview between you and Sir Godwin is at an end, I will return to you, and hope to have to congratulate you on the successful issue of the same."

Mildred once more returned her thanks to the kind-hearted attendant, for her good wishes, and the interest she took in her welfare, and Annie then left her to her reflections.

She continued to wait with the utmost anxiety the appearance of Sir Godwin, and her breast was filled with alternate hopes and fears. She listened attentively to catch the sound of his footsteps, and her heart palpitated violently with the strength of her mingled feelings.

At length she heard a door close below, and immediately afterwards some person ascending the stairs which led to the apartment in which she was confined; and when the individual stopped at the door, she felt convinced that it was he she expected.

The door was unlocked, and the commanding figure of a man stalked into the room; and no sooner did he fix his eyes upon the pale and anxious countenance of our heroine, than he uttered an exclamation of astonishment, and started back, as though he had encountered something fearful.

Sir Godwin Singleford (for he it was) was a man verging upon fifty years of age. His hair was partially grey; but evidently more with thought and melancholy than time. His features were still handsome and expressive; but the almost constant contraction of his black eyebrows gave a forbidding and sinister expression to his countenance. His eyes were now fixed with a penetrating and almost withering glance upon our heroine, and various emotions of the most powerful and unpleasant nature appeared to agitate his bosom.

Mildred trembled as she gazed upon him, and marked his singular and repulsive demeanour; but quickly recovering herself, and feeling that her liberty, her happiness, depended upon the result of this meeting, she sank upon her knees at his feet, and with clasped hands, gazed up in his face with such imploring and impressive looks that might have moved the sternest heart to pity.

Sir Godwin, however, seemed to shrink from her, as though he was appalled; but he never for a moment removed his eyes from her countenance.

"Girl, who are you?" he at last demanded, in a hoarse voice.

"Alas! sir," sobbed Mildred, "you must know full well I am your prisoner—the prisoner of Lord Ruthlyn de Bohun, who seeks my ruin, and the misery of my benefactor."

"By all my hopes!" ejaculated Sir Godwin, "those features cast a deadly horror and hatred to my very soul, kindling up the degradation of the past, and adding fresh strength to passions which I have not power to subdue.

"Oh, Sir Godwin," cried the alarmed and astonished Mildred, "why do you exhibit, such strange and fearful emotion on beholding me? We have never met before, and——"

"No—no," hastily interrupted Sir Godwin, in a most singular tone of voice, "*we* have never met before; but a likeness such as that you bear has never been absent from my imagination for years. It has been the bane of my peace, the poisoner of all my hopes, and it will continue to be so to my dying hour."

"Oh, sir," said our terrified heroine, "what mean those fearful words? I would implore your pity; I would supplicate you not to suffer me to be sacrificed to a villain. Oh, take compassion on a poor girl, who never injured you or other mortal being."

"Your voice is torture to me," said Sir Godwin. "But—but—your name?"

"Mildred."

"Mildred what?"

"I know no other."

"'Tis false! 'tis false!" cried Sir Godwin. "You would deceive me, girl."

"Oh, Sir Godwin," exclaimed the more astonished damsel, "why should I attempt to do so? Lord Ruthlyn must have told you that I am an unfortunate foundling, supported by the bounty of Sir Aldobrand de Lancy. Parents I never knew. For Heaven's sake, then, do not turn a deaf ear to my supplications, but suffer me to return to that home from which I have been so cruelly, so unjustly taken."

"It is—it is the very same!" exclaimed Sir Godwin; "and but for the age, I could swear that her who deceived me now knelt before me. Oh, it would be glorious revenge to behold that haughty and scornful being in this suppliant posture before me. Girl, your features have condemned you; you plead in vain. I hold you my prisoner, and at the mercy of Lord Ruthlyn de Bohun."

Mildred started to her feet, and gazed at Sir Godwin with the most speechless amazement and consternation. His behaviour was more that of a madman than a rational being, and it was some moments ere she could give utterance to a syllable, until Sir Godwin was preparing to leave the chamber, when, worked up to a pitch of frenzy and despair, she flew towards him, and clasping his arm, while she fixed her eyes with the greatest intensity of anguish upon his countenance, she said—

"Sir Godwin Singleford, what have I done to deserve this? By what right do you deprive me of my freedom, and threaten me with the cruelty and persecution of Lord Ruthlyn? You will not, you must not detain me here. But you will relent; you cannot be so lost to all sense of shame and honour as to add to the outrage you have already committed. No, no, you will not, you——"

"Unhand me, girl!" vociferated Sir Godwin. "Every word you give utterance to but adds to the fearful passions that rage within my breast. I tell you it is useless for you to sue to me; for nothing whatever can move me from my purpose."

"Good God!" cried Mildred, still clinging imploringly to him, "how shall I act? what can I say? Cruel man, stranger as you are to me, why should I have excited your enmity? Have you no respect for my sex?"

"Your sex!" repeated Sir Godwin, fiercely; "they are deceitful, treacherous, all of them. They assume the smiles and graces of angels, and possess the hearts of devils— ay, very devils. Such was the one whose likeness you bear. You think me mad, girl; yes, the recollection makes me so. Release your hold. When I gaze upon your features no earthly power could induce me to pity you."

"The vengeance of offended Heaven will most assuredly pursue you for this, Sir Godwin Singleford," solemnly ejaculated our heroine, as she released her hold of him, and sunk disconsolately in a chair. "This unexampled cruelty to an unprotected girl, who never knew you till now, and therefore could not have offended you, will not go unpunished. Whatever may be my fate, you will be called to a severe account. But, you will repent; you will not, cannot consign one to misery and shame, who never injured you."

"I tell you, girl," returned Sir Godwin, "you plead in vain. Oh, what torturing thoughts has the sight of you rekindled in my breast. No more; I will not listen. My mind is made up!"

Thus saying, the singular man rushed out from the room, and left Mildred in a state of the most unspeakable amazement, alarm, and agony.

For a few minutes she was too much bewildered by the extraordinary events of this meeting to collect her thoughts; but when she did so, the nature of them may very readily be conceived. Sir Godwin must certainly be insane, or he could never have acted in such a manner towards one who was an entire stranger to him. And yet, the observations he had given utterance to had made a most powerful impression upon her. The terror, the violent agitation he had evinced when he first beheld her, all tended to fill her mind with anguish, and to involve her still more in perplexity.

Annie had told her that Sir Godwin had been disappointed in love; and it would appear, from what he said, that she bore a striking resemblance to the object upon whom he had fixed his affections. But why should that excite him in such a fearful manner against her?

The disappointment to the hopes she had encouraged, from her interview with Sir

Godwin, was almost more than she could support, and had not tears come to her relief she must have fainted.

Alas! how dreadful indeed was her situation, to be placed in the power and at the mercy of two such men as Lord Ruthlyn and Sir Godwin! She saw nothing but ruin an misery before her, unless Providence should interpose to save her, and restore her to Sir Aldobrand, or she could induce Annie to try some means to make him acquainted with the place where she was confined. And even amidst her own sufferings, and the fate which at present seemed inevitably to await her, her thoughts wandered to Ethelbert, and sad were the forebodings that she should never behold him again.

"Alas!" she thought, "perhaps he now lingers in some wretched dungeon, shut out from the light of day, and with no one to pity him in his persecution. Or even before now he may have fallen beneath the dagger of the assassin, and his fate may ever remain involved in mystery. Oh, surely the Almighty will not permit the wretches who have been the cause of this to escape punishment! Poor Ethelbert! our sad destinies are indeed similar."

And now once more the horror that Sir Aldobrand must be suffering forced itself upon her imagination, and increased the intolerable anguish she was herself enduring. She traversed the apartment with hasty steps, and uttered her lamentations aloud.

She was interrupted by hearing the door once more being unlocked, and Annie entered the room, and affectionately, and with a look of the deepest commiseration, advanced towards her. Mildred dropped her head upon her shoulders, and burst into tears.

"Do not take on so, my dear lady," said Annie, soothingly. "I did not think Sir Godwin could have been so cruel; but, from his own manner, and the grief you evince, I am fearful that the meeting between you has not been productiue of any favourable result."

"Alas! alas!" sighed Mildred, "all is over; all hope is at an end. But the strange conduct of Sir Godwin has distracted me. He behaved to me with absolute ferocity from the first moment he beheld me—I, an entire stranger to him. Surely, Annie, he cannot be in his right senses."

"Why, I do really think that at times he is not, miss," said the attendant; "but compose yourself, I pray you. Come, sit down, and tell me all about it."

As well as her emotion would permit her, Mildred complied with her request, and Annie could not help frequently interrupting her to give expression to her astonishment.

"It is very strange," she said, when our heroine had concluded; "but I can only account for it by supposing that he recognised some likeness between you and the lady on whom he formerly placed his affections."

"Did you ever hear that lady's name?" asked Mildred.

"Never," replied Annie. "But although this interview is very disheartening, still I would have you not entirely despair; for Sir Godwin, when he comes coolly to reason with himself, may relent and be inclined to save you. He can have no reason for persecuting one who is an entire stranger to him."

"He cannot; but I fear, from his observations, that he will show me no mercy. Oh, Annie, imagine what my feelings, what my sufferings must be, torn from my aged protector, and threatened with a fate which humanity shudders at."

"Indeed, miss, I can, and do truly appreciate and sympathise in your feelings, and sincerely hope that the plans of your enemy may be defeated."

"There is no chance of that; he holds me entirely at his mercy, and Sir Godwin, your master, has declared his determination to aid him in his diabolical designs."

"But Lord Ruthlyn will not dare to take any other course if you still persist in refusing to become his wife."

"Oh, what is there that a villain like Lord Ruthlyn will not dare?" said Mildred. "It is not likely, since he has proceeded so far, that he will abandon his purpose. I shudder with horror when I reflect upon it. But you, Annie, might surely aid me."

"How, lady?"

"I have told you," replied Mildred; "by making Sir Aldobrand acquainted with the place of my confinement. He would immediately hasten to my deliverance, and you would be protected from the consequences of having served me, should the same reach the knowledge of Sir Godwin and Lord Ruthlyn."

"Ah, miss," returned Annie, "how willingly would I do so if it were in my power; but it is not."

" And wherefore not ?"

" I have no means of leaving the hall, neither do I know any person to whom I could entrust such an important communication.''

" Oh, God ! then," exclaimed Mildred, with agony, " I am indeed without hope."

She gave herself up entirely to the most absorbing grief, and it was in vain that Annie used all the efforts she had at her command to appease her.

Shortly afterwards Annie was obliged to leave her, and when she was alone the anguish of her feelings found vent in the most convulsive sobs and tears. All was the most absolute horror and despair, whichever way she directed her thoughts, and her brain was completely bewildered and distracted with the weight of care that oppressed it.

Time passed on, and Mildred remained without interruption, for Annie did not return, and thus she was left without the solace of the only sympathising breast to which she could confide her sorrows, the only being to whom she could look for the least hope of consolation.

And now her agitation increased, as the time flew on, and she might shortly expect the arrival of Lord Ruthlyn. Yet did she struggle with her feelings as much as possible, and try to collect all the fortitude and resolution she could to meet him. And she even succeeded better than she could have expected ; a feeling of womanly pride took possession of her bosom, and trusting in the protection of the Supreme, she did not entirely despair of being able even to awe this heartless libertine into forbearance.

Inspired by these thoughts, she felt more composed than she had done since she had been taken from the castle, and when Annie re-entered the room (which she did shortly afterwards, with the dinner) she was both surprised and gratified at the change which had taken place in her appearance in so short a time.

" Ah, miss," she remarked, " depend upon it, if you maintain a proper firmness, you will yet defeat the base designs of your enemy, and shortly be restored to liberty and your friends."

" May your predictions be verified, Annie," replied our heroine ; " but there is not much prospect of their being so at present. Still, why should I entirely despair, when there is a just God above who never fails to protect the innocent."

" Very true, miss, and he will not desert you on this very trying occasion.''

" But your master, Annie—oh ! tell me, is he less terribly excited than he was when he left me?''

" He has just retired from the hall ; but his brow was gloomy and his manner agitated, as he passed out of the door, miss," answered Annie.

" Alas! I fear that he contemplates some evil design," observed Mildred.

" He is frequently subject to these fits, miss," said her attendant, " and I am so used to them that I take but little notice of them.''

" But his observations to me I shall never forget ; they have made a deep impression on my mind."

" Endeavour to think no more of them. lady," said Annie. " When he has recovered from his present state of excitement, he will probably repent of his conduct towards you, and be inclined to listen with a compassionate ear to your supplications."

" Oh ! no ; I cannot entertain such a hope," returned Mildred ; " he seems stern and inflexible, and, whatever he may have been formerly, now almost a stranger to the common feelings of humanity."

Mildred partook but sparingly of the meal, for her mind was too much oppressed with its numerous cares and anxieties. It was scarcely over when a horse was heard to gallop up to the hall door, and immediately afterwards the bell was rung.

Annie hastened to the window, and looked out.

" It is Lord Ruthlyn, who has just dismounted," she said.

Mildred turned pale, and a faintness came over her even at the mention of her enemy's name.

" Now Heaven give me fortitude," she ejaculated, " to meet the villain with becoming firmness , so that I may abash him in his diabolical designs."

" Form a strong resolution, miss, and you will, you must succeed," said Annie.

" I will," returned Mildred, as fresh courage seemed to nerve her, and her bosom swelled with resentment at the thought of the indignity which his lordship had already inflicted upon her. " He shall find, at least, that I am as firm in virtue as he is practised and hardened in guilt."

At this moment a bell rung to summon the attendance of Annie below, and after having bestowed a look of encouragement on our heroine, she quitted the room.

A feeling of confidence now came over Mildred, which she had not expected to experience, and she awaited the entrance of Lord Ruthlyn with perfect calmness.

She had not to wait long. A heavy footstep ascended the stairs ; the door was opened, and the villain, Lord Ruthlyn, stood before her.

CHAPTER XXII.

THE SCENE IN THE CHAMBER.—MILDRED'S REPROACHES.—THE LIBERTINE REPULSED.—HIS RAGE AND THREATS.

FOR a moment Lord Ruthlyn stood near to the door, as if almost afraid to advance, and Mildred met him with a steady, scornful, and reproachful eye. Feelings of the utmost scorn and indignation swelled her bosom, and imparted such a withering tone to her whole demeanour, that the libertine was conscience-stricken and ashamed ; for at that moment, if he had never done so before, he fully felt the degraded and despicable position in which he stood, and shrunk abashed beneath the dignified glances of her whom he had intended to make his victim. He was half tempted to abandon his designs, and to make a hasty retreat ; but his guilty passions prevailed, and he quickly recovered himself, and advanced into the centre of the room, and with looks of the most ardent admiration, thus addressed himself to our heroine, whose attitude still remained unchanged—

"Beauteous Mildred, why look with such freezing coldness upon one who loves you beyond all earthly beings ?"

"If the spirit of my feelings, the utter disgust and loathing I feel towards you, tyrant, be imparted to my eyes, their flashes should strike shame to your breast," replied Mildred with a voice and manner that again absolutely startled Lord Ruthlyn, and for a minute or two completely dumbfounded him.

"I was prepared to meet your scorn and reproaches *for a time*, sweet Mildred," he said, at last ; "but, at any rate, it must be some satisfaction to me to know that I have succeeded in my plans."

"Yes," retorted Mildred, with increasing courage ; "the satisfaction that every heartless villain feels in the success of his nefarious projects for the time being. Oh, it is most brave, Lord Ruthlyn de Bohun, to exult over a defenceless female, whom you have marked for your prey. But though you hold me in your power for the present, I defy you. I am so strong in virtue that all your artifices will prove unavailing ; they will recoil upon yourself. I have just Heaven on my side, and as surely as you now stand before me and disgust me with your presence, its retribution will ere long overtake you for this cruel, this monstrous outrage."

Lord Ruthlyn bit his lips with vexation. He had not, although he had so boasted, been prepared to find our heroine so firm and resolute, and for a short time he was at a loss how to proceed.

Mildred observed her advantage, and determined not to lose the opportunity, she thus continued—

"By what right, Lord Ruthlyn, have you dared to tear me from my home, and thus to make me a prisoner ? But I will not ask the question. A man like Lord Ruthlyn de Bohun is insensible alike to the feelings of honour and humanity."

"Beauteous Mildred," said his lordship, recovering himself, and, as he advanced nearer towards her, assuming all the airs of the practised hypocrite, "I pray you not to judge me too harshly. I am the devoted slave of your all transcendent charms, and it was only the madness of my despair at your rejection of my suit that induced me to take this desperate course. Promise me, pledge yourself that you will endeavour to love me, to return the ardent, the unconquerable passion I feel for you, and to become my bride, and not another hour will I detain you."

"Even though a certain and lingering death should be the consequence of my refusal, you should not extort from me a promise so utterly hateful, so revolting to my feelings," answered our heroine. "You have before heard my sentiments, my decision, and a man of honour would have been satisfied. He would rather have sacrificed his own feeling than the happiness of a damsel, who might have esteemed him, but now can only view him with contempt and detestation."

"These words are bold, scornful beauty, for one who his entirely at my mercy," said his lordship, with a frown.

"They are the dictates of virtue," replied our heroine, "and why should I fear to utter them to a villain ?"

"By Heaven, damsel, you may proceed too far, and have cause to repent. Seek not to exasperate me."

"Then render me justice and reparation for the injury you have done me," replied Mildred. "Dare not longer to detain me a prisoner ; abandon your guilty designs; repent of that which you have already done, and then I may learn to pardon you, and to look upon you with respect, though never with love."

"You would exact too much from me, fair Mildred," said Lord Ruthlyn, with a sarcastic smile, "and indeed I cannot comply with your demands. But why this scorn ? Is not Lord Ruthlyn de Bohun as noble a match for an unknown girl as the much favoured and headstrong boy, Ethelbert de Lancy ?"

"Ethelbert de Lancy possesses virtue and nobleness of soul," retorted Mildred, and her voice faltered when she thought of the uncertainty of Ethelbert's fate, "which your lordship's conduct proves you do not possess."

"Indeed !" said Lord Ruthlyn, with a malicious grin of triumph that did not escape the observation of our heroine, and all but confirmed her worst surmises. "But yet, with all these qualifications, 'tis a pity that he should be lost to you for ever."

"Ah !" ejaculated Mildred, fixing her terrified eyes with a penetrating glance upon him. "I see it all now. It is you, oh, most designing and heartless of men, who is the author of all this. You smile with exultation. You do not deny it. Tell me, Lord Ruthlyn, as you value your soul's future welfare, what have you done with Ethelbert de Lancy ?"

"No doubt you are most anxious to ascertain his fate," returned the libertine, coolly, and giving undisguised expression to the feelings of triumph which possessed his breast.

"You mock me, cruel man," said our heroine, and her anxiety almost overpowered her. "Oh, you are indeed lost to every sense of shame and mercy. '

"Nay, nay ; calm yourself, sweet Mildred ; harsh words are not likely to move me to compassion. You have accused me of being the cause of Ethelbert's disappointment ; and what if your surmises should be correct ?"

"Then would you prove yourself to be even a greater villain than I now take you to be," replied Mildred, with firmness.

Lord Ruthlyn again bit his lips ; but he tried to stifle his rage as well as he could, and observed—

"Well, I must e'en bear with you for awhile, I suppose. But mark me, Mildred, if you would secure your own happiness, and no further endanger him on whom you have placed your affections (curses light on him !) you will be more circumspect in your language and behaviour towards me."

"Ah !" ejaculated Mildred, eagerly, and grasping his arm. "You acknowledge, then, that by your treacherous artifices, Ethelbert de Lancy has been torn away from his friends ?"

Lord Ruthlyn returned no answer, but his looks expressed everything.

"Tell me, Lord Ruthlyn," continued his fair prisoner, with almost breathless emotion, "what have you done with him? How far have you suffered your feelings of hatred and revenge to carry you ?"

"Ethelbert de Lancy," coolly but triumphantly replied Lord Ruthlyn, "like yourself, is in my power."

"Oh, God ! oh, God!" groaned Mildred, "then, indeed, is his fate, certain. Heaven protect him, and defeat the plans of this cruel man."

"It is in your power, Mildred, to induce me to abandon my designs."

"How ?"

"I have told you ; by consenting to renounce Ethelbert for ever, and becoming my bride."

"Never ! the very thought strikes horror to my bosom ; the sight of you is now odious to me."

"Beware, Mildred; you may try my patience too far, and urge me to do that I would fain refrain from putting into execution. The sentiments I feel for you are not those of a day; they are not evanescent; neither time nor circumstances can change them; but your scorn may drive me to desperation, and I will not answer for what the consequences might then be. I am ready to be the slave of love, of adoration, but will not submit to become the victim of your caprice and haughty disdain."

"And think you, my lord," said Mildred, "that it is by conduct such as this you can hope to win my heart? But I will not deceive you; under any circumstances, Lord Ruthlyn de Bohun can never possess the heart of Mildred."

"Then look to it," returned the enraged Lord Ruthlyn; "remember, Ethelbert de Lancy is in my power."

"You will not, you dare not harm him," gasped forth our heroine, and looking imploringly in her persecutor's face.

"His liberty, nay, his very life is in your hands," answered his lordship. "Say that you will become mine, and that moment shall unbar his prison doors."

"Lord Ruthlyn," returned Mildred, after a pause, and almost suffocated with the intensity of her emotions, "you surely will not persist in hopelessly endeavouring to exact a promise from me which is so repugnant to my feelings, and which nothing can ever induce me to give. Are you so lost to all sense of feeling and humanity as to continue io torture me thus? At least, have some consideration for my sex; and reflect what the ultimate consequences must be to yourself, should you persevere in your plans."

"I am ready to brave them all," replied the libertine; "and since I have advanced so far, nothing shall tempt me to recede. I have made you a fair offer, and it is for you to accept it or not; but I would have you understand me properly; my plans are all well matured; no power on earth can frustrate them; and either you consent to my wishes, or you shall become mine by force."

"Oh, spare me! spare me!"

"You have heard my decision, Mildred; repent of this foolish obstinacy before it is too late, and accept the honour I offer you. All the happiness that wealth and love can procure you, shall be yours. I will study your every thought, and you shall not have a wish ungratified. As for Ethelbert and his father, a reconciliation can be effected with them, and we may afterwards live in harmony and friendship with them. Reflect on what I have said, and let us no longer continue this fruitless altercation."

"Oh, my lord," ejaculated Mildred, now completely overcome by her terror, and the utter hopelessness of her situation, and that of Ethelbert, if Lord Ruthlyn spoke the truth (which she had too much reason to fear he did), "have mercy on me, I beseech you, and do not persist in a persecution which can afford you no real gratification, and which must terminate in my madness and despair. Why should you seek to possess yourself of an unknown and probably humble girl like me, who has no heart to bestow on you? Why seek to injure the son of my benefactor, who never did you wrong?"

"He has," cried Lord Ruthlyn; "has he he not won your affections, Mildred? and that is enough to inspire me with hatred towards him."

"His virtues had won my heart long ere I beheld your lordship," said the blushing damsel.

"And he therefore presented the only obstacle to the accomplishment of my hopes," said Lord Ruthlyn.

"He did not."

"Ah! say you so?" hastily demanded his lordship. "Explain yourself."

"Had I never known Ethelbert de Lancy, Lord Ruthlyn de Bohun could not have possessed my affections," answered Mildred, firmly.

"Now, by all my hopes, this is too much!" said his lordship, stamping with rage. "Scornful damsel, think not to move me to abandon my resolutions by language such as this. In spite of all—notwithstanding all your obdurate resistance, you shall be mine."

"Have you no fear of the wrath of Heaven?" solemnly demanded Mildred.

"None! I will brave everything to accomplish the end I have in view," he answered determinedly.

Mildred covered her face with her hands, and sobbed aloud in the anguish of her despair. Lord Ruthlyn contemplated her for a few minutes with indifference, but a length his heart seemed moved with something like a feeling of compassion, and he advanced towards her, and even attempted to take her hand, but she started back appalled, and gazed at him with an expression of fear and disgust.

"You shrink from me, Mildred," he said, "as though I were something loathsome. Come, come, banish this disdain, which cannot avail you anything. I would behave to you all that man should do towards a woman; but you work me up to desperation by your freezing coldness, and the reproaches which you heap upon me."

"Dare you look upon me? Dare you address me, after the brutal threats you have just given utterance to?" demanded Mildred. "Can nothing make any impression on your heart?"

"Yes, sweet Mildred," replied the hypocrite, quickly; "the assurance of your love. That will make me your fondest, your most devoted slave for ever."

"Cease!" cried the indignant damsel; "I will not listen to you. Heaven will yet give me power to resist your hated importunities."

"But you will find yourself deceived, mark me. Remember what I have said; the liberty, the life of Ethebert de Lancy, are in your hands."

"This is but a falsehood concocted to frighten me into a promise repugnant to my feelings," replied Mildred; "I will not believe you; Ethelbert is not in your power."

"Oh. indeed; you flatter yourself he is not," returned Lord Ruthlyn, with a triumphant smile. "Would you, then, have proof?"

"Oh, yes, yes," eagerly ejaculated Mildred; "confirmation of the worst would not be half so torturing as this state of suspense."

"Behold, then," said Lord Ruthlyn, showing her a ring which had been taken from the finger of Ethelbert, when he was conveyed to the Tower of Bransdorf; "know you this?"

"Oh, God!" exclaimed Mildred, and her heart sunk within her; "it is Ethelbert's ring. Then, alas, it is too true, and my misery is complete. Oh, Lord Ruthlyn, how could you become so guilty as to perpetrate this cruel outrage? But tell me, as you hope for mercy, does he still live?"

"He does," answered Ruthlyn; "and you have the power, I once more tell you, to release him from confinement."

"Then Heaven protect him," solemnly implored Mildred, "for that alone can save him; he would not accept his liberty at the price that you would exact. But once more, Lord Ruthlyn, I warn you not to persist in your diabolical designs; for though you may triumph for a time, rest assured that punishment will overtake you."

"Your predictions will have little effect on me, beauteous Mildred," replied Lord Ruthlyn; "I am not easily daunted or diverted from the prosecution of anything upon which I have fixed my mind. Besides, my plans have all been so nicely managed, that I can set detection at defiance."

"Oh! repent, repent," supplicated our heroine, clasping her hands together; "spare me—spare the son of my benefactor, whose heart must now be almost broken at the heavy loss he has sustained."

"And yet, by your obstinacy, you will determine his fate. But I will leave you for the present to ruminate on what I have said to you, and trust that you will, ere long, see the necessity of changing your mind. Remember, I offer you rank and wealth, and a heart which will be all your own. If you reject my offers, then am I resolved to obtain that by force, which I may not by persuasion."

"Oh, monstrous!" sighed Mildred, gazing at him with the most indescribable sensations of horror; "how base must be that heart which could ever conceive such cruelty as this."

"It is you, sweet Mildred, that drives me to it by your scornful rejection of my vows. But for the present, farewell; it is useless to protract this interview any longer. You have heard my determination, and if you act prudently, you will not oppose it."

"Oh, stay, stay one moment," said the distracted Mildred; "and tell me, if the unfortunate Ethelbert is indeed your prisoner, where is he confined?"

Lord Ruthlyn hesitated for a moment or two, and then replied—

"In one of the dungeons of the Tower of Bransdorf."

Mildred started when she heard this, and turned very pale. The very name of that ancient building struck an indescribable sensation to her heart.

"The Tower of Bransdorf," she repeated; "the possession of his father—and so near the castle?"

"Even so, fair Mildred. There are secrets connected with that tower, in which you are not wholly uninterested."

"Oh, what could be your reason for conveying him there?" demanded our heroine, wrapt in amazement.

"This is not the time to enter into a discussion of my motives," returned Lord Ruthlyn; "it is sufficient for you to know that he is there, from whence it is in your power alone to release him."

"And do you not fear his future vengeance?"

"I am unused to fear," briefly replied his lordship. "Adieu till we meet again."

He fixed one look of mingled triumph and admiration upon her as he spoke, and then retired from the room, leaving Mildred in a state of mind which it is needless to attempt to pourtray to the reader. The fortitude she had maintained in such an extraordinary manner at the interview, now entirely forsook her, and, giving herself and Ethelbert up for lost, after what Lord Ruthlyn had said, she sunk into despair, from which Annie, on her return to the room, which she did a short time after his lordship had left it, could not, without the greatest difficulty, arouse her.

CHAPTER XXIII.

THE REMORSE OF SIR GODWIN SINGLEFORD.—HIS SYMPATHY WITH MILDRED, AND TALE OF SORROW.—THE ESCAPE.

THREE more dreary days of suffering to the hapless Mildred wore away, and still no change in her prospects for the better occurred. Lord Ruthlyn had twice visited her since the interview recorded in the former chapter, and on each time his importunities became more determined and disgusting, and the threats which he held out, and which she had no doubt he would, ere long, put into execution, unless Providence interposed to save her, filled her with terror. But greater even was the agony of mind she endured when she reflected on the sufferings of Sir Aldobrand and his son.

From Annie she learnt that a most extraordinary change had come over Sir Godwin; he was more melancholy than ever, and seemed to take less pleasure in the society of Lord Ruthlyn, than he had done before; and although he affected to enter into his views with his former acquiescence, Annie declared that she thought in his heart he really repented of the part he had taken in the infamous plot; in which opinion she was strengthened by the frequent inquiries he made, almost in accents of kindness, after the health and spirits of the fair prisoner.

All these circumstances inspired our heroine with some degree of hope, and she awaited the result with the greatest impatience.

"Oh, that I could see him again," she said; "for in his present state of mind I might probably be enabled to interest him in my favour. Oh, why will he thus continue to degrade himself by becoming the tool of so unprincipled a villain as Lord Ruthlyn?"

"From what I have been given to understand, miss," said Annie, "my master is under some obligations to his lordship, and is therefore fearful of offending him. But still I hope that in a day or two he may be induced to visit you again, and that he will then turn a favourable ear to your supplications."

"Oh, if I could really think so, what a weight, what a terrible weight would be removed from my heart," said Mildred. "If something does not quickly take place to release me from the power of the miscreant, Lord Ruthlyn, my ruin is inevitable; for what can my resistance effect against his brutal determination?"

"Be of good heart, miss," said Annie, "and depend upon it that you will yet be restored to liberty and happiness."

The day after this conversation had taken place Annie hastily entered the apartment in which Mildred was confined, and she could see by the expression of her features, that she had something particular to communicate; and her heart foreboded that it was good news. She hastily inquired what it was.

"You will be released from your persecutor for the present, miss," answered Annie; "he has received information that his father, the Earl de Bohun, is seriously ill, and not expected to recover, and he has therefore resolved to depart for the castle immediately."

"Oh! thank Heaven for this respite, however brief it may be," ejaculated Mildred, fervently.

"Aye, miss," returned Annie, "and so say I, with all my heart; and who knows but that while his lordship is absent something may fortunately turn up to favour your escape?"

"God send that your wishes may be realised, my good girl," ejaculated our heroine.

In a short time after this they had the pleasure, while they were standing at the window, to witness Lord Ruthlyn's departure, and Mildred now felt lighter of heart than she had done ever since her incarceration.

Shortly afterwards Annie received a summons to attend her master, and our heroine awaited her return with impatience, and with mingled hopes and fears.

It was some time before she came back; but when she did, Mildred could perceive that she was even in better spirits than before.

"Sir Godwin is in one of his most amiable moods, miss," said the kind-hearted attendant, "though very melancholy, and he has desired me to inform you that you may expect to see him in about an hour, when he has something of importance to communicate to you."

"To me!" said Mildred, with a look of astonishment; "oh! what can it be? If his behaviour should be the same as on our former interview, I shall dread to see him."

"Oh, no, miss," replied Annie, "do not alarm yourself, for I feel confident it is something for your good."

"And what makes you think so, Annie?" asked Mildred.

"Because there was such a peculiar expression of kindness upon his features when he delivered his message to me," answered Annie. "Ah, my lady, mark my words, some good will most assuredly arise from this."

"I thank you, Annie, for your good wishes; for I feel confident, from your behaviour towards me throughout, since I have been here, that you speak with sincerity."

"Indeed I do, miss," returned the girl; "and I'm sure no one would be more thankful than myself to see you restored to liberty and to your friends. Lord Ruthlyn, I am certain, is a thorough bad man, and I wonder that my master, who, in spite of his eccentricities, as I have often told you, possesses many excellent qualities, should have become on such terms of intimacy with him, or suffer himself in any shape to be the panderer to his vices."

"You have said, Annie, that Sir Godwin Singleford is under certain obligations to his lordship, and is fearful of offending him."

"Very true, miss; I had forgotten that. You see, the secret sorrow which preys upon Sir Godwin's mind, and renders him at times so uncouth and disagreeable, led him into extravagancies, by which, as I am told, his fortune became greatly impaired, and he was involved in difficulties, from which Lord Ruthlyn recently *conditionally* released him."

"Ah," observed Mildred, "I understand you perfectly. Then, such being the case, what reason have I to hope that Sir Godwin will venture to interest himself in my favour?"

"I know not, miss," answered Annie; "but, notwithstanding, the impression on my mind is that he will, and I shall indeed be disappointed if he does not. In fact, from certain observations he made use of, and which I overheard, though he evidently did not intend that I should do so, I am almost positive that he is disgusted with Lord Ruthlyn, that he is stung with remorse, and is determined at all hazards to throw off his trammels, and to render you an act of justice."

A feeling of joy and hope darted through the bosom of Mildred on this assurance of Annie.

"But are you positive, my good Annie," she asked eagerly, "that you have not put a wrong construction upon the observations of your master?"

"Why, my dear young lady," she replied, "of course I cannot be certain; but the strong impression upon my mind is that I have not. He mentioned your name in talking as it were to himself."

"Ah!" ejaculated Mildred, "and what did he say?"

"Why, I cannot exactly recollect the words, miss; but they were to this effect,

"'The poor girl! she never injured me, and shall I see her sacrificed—nay, become the instrument of her destruction by a heartless scoundrel, because of her extraordinary likeness to her who doomed me to misery by the disappointment to my hopes?'"

"The words are significant, good Annie," remarked Mildred, "but most extraordinary."

"Do you not see, miss, that they are calculated to inspire you with hope?"

"Oh, yes, I cannot deny that they are; but still, I must not be too sanguine, lest I should be disappointed, which would be a more severe trial to my fortitude than anything. God grant that your anticipations may prove correct, Annie. How grateful shall I be for my restoration to liberty and my beloved benefactor, who, at the present time, must be suffering so severely. But should this fortunately take place, will you not accompany me, Annie? Your kindness to me since I have been confined here has endeared you to me, and I should deeply regret if we were separated again."

"I cannot leave my master, Sir Godwin, miss," replied Annie, "to whom I am so much indebted."

"But what if he should give his consent?"

"Then would I willingly accept the honour you offer me, miss; for nothing could give me greater pleasure than to be constantly near so amiable a young lady as yourself."

"Enough," said Mildred; but recollecting herself, she added, "but, alas! I am speculating too hastily. Sir Godwin, after all, may not be disposed to serve me, and then the disappointment will be more severe than I think I could patiently endure."

Annie was about to reply, when she was interrupted by their hearing footsteps upon the stairs, and immediately afterwards Sir Godwin Singleford made his appearance.

He gently waved his hand for Annie to retire, which she did, and he having closed the door, confronted Mildred; but no sooner had his eyes become fixed upon her than the violent emotion displayed upon his countenance was painfully visible. His frame was at the same time agitated by a convulsive tremor, and he averted his gaze, as though the sight of our heroine recalled to his memory some agonising recollection.

Mildred viewed him with the greatest sympathy and amazement, which was not unmixed with anxiety, when she thought that upon him depended, most probably, her future misery or happiness.

"Young lady," said Sir Godwin at last, in a gentle voice, and turning his gaze once more towards our heroine, "doubtless you think me a strange and an uncouth being, and certainly my behaviour to you upon our first interview was every way calculated to excite such an idea in your mind; but it is a heavy grief—disappointment that admits of no consolation—that has changed me, and caused me to assume a character which is foreign to my nature. And then your likeness to that one individual, your extraordinary resemblance to her who has been the destroyer of my peace, took me by surprise, and brought all the reminiscences of the past more vividly to my brain. Even now, as I gaze upon you, a strange shuddering sensation, almost amounting to horror, comes over me, and I tremble in your presence."

"Oh, sir," ejaculated Mildred, in her most sweetly persuasive accents, "banish those thoughts. Why should I, a poor unknown girl, cause such emotions in your breast?"

"That voice!" gasped forth Sir Godwin; "I could almost imagine that *she* was addressing herself to me. Such were the silvery accents, falling upon the ear like a magic spell, and entrancing and bewildering the senses. Do not speak to me, maiden; and yet, I could dwell for ever upon the tones of your voice, and dream of the days that are gone, never, never, to return. At times I think I am mad, damsel. But—but—I have injured you, deeply injured you. I have become a villain despicable to myself. Oh, maiden, time was when I would have shuddered with horror and repugnance at the bare idea of that which I have now done."

He sunk on a chair, and covering his face with his hands, resigned himself entirely to the racking thoughts which distracted his brain.

Mildred's heart palpitated with mingled feelings of hope and sympathy in the agony which she saw that Sir Godwin was undergoing, and for a short time she remained silent, and did not offer to interrupt him in his painful train of thoughts. But at last she ventured to approach him, and her footstep, light even as it was, aroused him, and he looked up in her face with a mingled expression of admiration, remorse, and fear. He tremblingly took her hand, and Mildred knelt respectfully before him, for she saw that his heart was melted in her favour. She commiserated his unknown sorrows, and at once her generous heart forgave him all the misery to which he had been an accessory in inflicting upon her. He seemed at once to understand her feelings, and pressing her fair hand in heartfelt gratitude to his lips, he gently raised her, as he said,—

"Nay, beauteous, much-wronged damsel, this posture becomes you not; it is I, who have so deeply injured you, and made myself the tool of a heartless villain who has doomed you to destruction. I should blush to look upon you; I should shrink appalled from your gaze, to think that I, Sir Godwin Singleford, who was once the very soul of honour and integrity, should so unman myself."

"I pray you, Sir Godwin," said Mildred, who was much affected by his manner, and impatient to hear the purport of his visit, "do not reproach yourself so severely. For my own part, I sincerely forgive you for the part you have taken against me. But you will no longer suffer me to remain confined here? You will restore me to my friends, will you not, and thus defeat the diabolical plans of Lord Ruthlyn?"

"Yes, yes, I will," answered Sir Godwin. "I have made my mind up to that, and also to enter into the peaceful seclusion of a monastery for the rest of my days; there, haply, I may find that tranquillity of mind which the world cannot now afford me."

"Oh, thanks, thanks!" cried the delighted Mildred, again sinking on her knees. "What a weight of anguish have you removed from my breast. My dear benefactor, I shall then behold you again! and Ethelbert de Lancy, it may not be too late to save you! But has Lord Ruthlyn told me the truth? Is Ethelbert indeed in his power?"

"It is true," replied Sir Godwin; "Ethelbert de Lancy was waylaid and seized by order of Lord Ruthlyn, and is at present confined in the Tower of Bransdorf."

"Are you certain that he lives?"

"Yes," answered Sir Godwin. "Lord Ruthlyn, I am convinced, great villain as he is, and notwithstanding his threats, would not dare to embrue his hands in the blood of his fellow creature."

"And what could be his reason for confining Ethelbert in the old tower?" asked Mildred.

"I know not, unless it was that he thought he would be more secure there than anywhere else."

"Then he will be saved," exclaimed our heroine, joyfully. "But, tell me, Sir Godwin, when will you suffer me to depart from hence? Oh, I am all impatience till I once more behold Sir Aldobrand."

"This very day shall see you restored to him," said Sir Godwin. "I will myself conduct you to the castle, where I must leave you."

"Not until you have seen Sir Aldobrand, and received his thanks," said Mildred.

"His thanks!" repeated Sir Godwin; "I merit them not, and must not see him. The sight of him would fill my breast with anguish."

"Oh, why, Sir Godwin?" demanded Mildred.

"Ah, damsel," sighed Sir Godwin, "I have reason to hate all those who bear the name of De Lancy."

"Why so, sir? Sir Aldobrand surely could never have injured you."

"Not he; but his brother, Sir Martin de Lancy, was the cause of all my misery, and has made me the wretched being that I am."

"And how did he that?" inquired Mildred.

"By supplanting me in the affections of one whom I loved more dearly than my own existence," replied Sir Godwin.

"The Lady Editha?"

"The same. And it was your extraordinary likeness to her which caused my violent agitation when I first beheld you. Oh! even now, as I look upon your countenance, I could almost imagine that Editha stood before me in her youth and loveliness, when I believed her heart to be all my own."

The emotion of Sir Godwin increased, and our heroine could not but feel the greatest astonishment at the assertions he had made.

"Ah, maiden," he continued, "there was a time when I knew not what sorrow was. Then I believed that I possessed Editha's love, for often had I drawn the sweet avowal from her lips. But Sir Martin de Lancy came, and my dream of joy was over. He tried all the consummate art which he so abundantly possessed to insinuate himself into Editha's favour, and he succeeded but too well. Editha forgot the solemn vows of everlasting affection she had made to me, and gave her hand to my rival. But she was severely punished for her cruelty and deceit. No doubt, young lady, you have heard the history of her and her husband, and the extraordinary mystery with which their fate is still enveloped?"

"Oh, yes," answered Mildred; "but tell me, Sir Godwin, know you anything as to what became of them?"

"I do not," replied the latter, "though I have tried hard to discover it; for even now, should Sir Martin cross my path, notwithstanding the many years which have elapsed since last we met, I would have ample vengeance for the wrongs he did me."

"Oh, sir," said Mildred, "you surely would not seek to injure him now?"

"Nothing can stifle the feelings of hatred I bear towards him," returned Sir Godwin. "But why should I obtrude my sorrows upon you, maiden? I will leave you to make preparations for your departure. I will send Annie to you."

"Once more I thank you from my very soul, Sir Godwin," ejaculated our heroine, tears of gratitude and joy starting to her eyes; "but I would speak to you of Annie. To her I am much indebted for the kindness she has shown me since I have been here, and I have every reason to believe that she has formed an attachment to me. You have

stated it to be your intention to retire from the world, and the poor girl, who, I understand, is an orphan, would then be left without a friend or home. If she is willing, will
you consent to her accompanying me to the castle, where I know she will be most kindly
received by Sir Aldobrand ?"

"I can offer no possible objection," replied the baronet, "and will leave Annie to use
her own discretion, as it is my intention to make a provision for her. I have arranged
my affairs for some days, and immediately after I have seen you safe to the castle of your
protector, the walls of a monastery will close upon me for ever."

"And may Heaven bring consolation to your lacerated mind, my dear sir," said
Mildred, fervently.

Sir Godwin pressed her hand in silence, and abruptly quitted the room.

When our heroine found herself alone, she fell upon her knees, and poured forth her
gratitude to the Most High for her promised deliverance, and earnestly she prayed that
her loss might not have been the cause of any serious consequences to her revered
benefactor.

The story of Sir Godwin Singleford had deeply affected her, and her interest was also
excited in no ordinary degree from its immediate connection with the family of Sir
Aldobrand, and the remarkable likeness which Sir Godwin said she bore to Lady Editha.

Annie shortly made her appearance, and her animated countenance showed the joy she
felt at the deliverance of Mildred being so near at hand.

Our heroine made her acquainted with what had taken place between her and Sir Godwin, and his consent to her accompanying her to the castle, if she was willing to be her
companion.

"Oh, miss," said Annie, "how grateful am I to you for your kindness, and how gladly
will I avail myself of your generous offer ; for since my poor master, it seems, is resolved
to enter into seclusion, I should have been without a friend in the world, had I not found
one in you."

"Your kindness to me, Annie," said Mildred, "since I have been a prisoner here, has
greatly endeared you to me. But for you, I must have sunk entirely beneath the weight
of my despair. To you I am much indebted."

"Oh, do not mention it, Miss Mildred," said Annie; "for indeed I have done no
more than my duty towards my fellow creatures, especially one of my own sex."

"Sir Aldobrand I know will receive you with kindness," continued our heroine.
"Oh, how impatient I am to behold him again. and to see Ethelbert released from his
dreary confinement in the Tower of Bransdorf. There is not a moment to lose ; for
should Lord Ruthlyn be apprised of my escape, he would be sure to take immediate steps
to secure him in some other place, or, perhaps, he would even sacrifice his life to his
vengeance."

"Indeed, miss, there is no fear of that," returned Annie, "for you will have reached
the castle of your benefactor long before his lordship can become acquainted with your
escape, and the deliverance of Ethelbert de Lancy will, of course, immediately follow.
Come, let us prepare for our departure without any more delay."

"Are the men who brought me hither still in the house ?" asked Mildred.

"They are not, miss; they departed yesterday."

"That is well," said Mildred ; "so that there is no one to prevent my departure."

"No one," answered Annie; "we have nothing whatever to fear ; and before many
hours have elapsed, you will be safely restored to the arms of your benefactor."

Mildred raised her eyes in gratitude towards Heaven, and her and Annie being
quickly prepared for the journey, they descended into the parlour of the hall, where they
found Sir Godwin in readiness and awaiting them. He started on beholding Mildred,
and a convulsive expression passed over his features, but he quickly recovered himself,
and approaching her, respectfully took her hand.

"Miss Mildred," he said, "I cannot but again implore your forgiveness for the guilty
part I have taken in this nefarious transaction, and which has caused you so much
misery. I can never cease to remember it without the deepest remorse and shame."

"Oh, do not mention it, my dear sir," replied Mildred; "your present conduct
more than atones for your former error. May Heaven reward you, and restore you to
happiness."

"Happiness is not for me," sighed Sir Godwin, with a melancholy look ; "if I can
find tranquillity during the few short years I may be permitted to live, it is all I can

hope for or expect. But come, my poor girl, the vehicle is ready, and, therefore, the sooner we depart the better."

The moment of deliverance had now arrived, and Mildred's agitation was so great, that she could scarcely contain herself. It came so suddenly and so unexpectedly, that she could scarcely believe in its reality, and in a state of almost unconsciousness, she suffered Sir Godwin to take her hand and lead her to the door, and it was not until she was seated in the vehicle, and it was proceeding at a rapid rate from the hall, that she awoke to recollection. Annie was seated by her side, and Sir Godwin occupied the other, but he appeared to be lost in melancholy meditation; and Mildred, much as her heart prompted her to pour forth her feelings of gratitude, did not offer to interrupt him. The looks of Annie fully expressed the feelings which animated her breast, and Mildred pressed her hand in silence, for her heart was too full to allow her to speak at present.

It was a lovely day, and never had the face of nature appeared so smiling to the imagination of Mildred, as farther and farther they progressed from the place of her late confinement, and the nearer they approached towards the castle of her beloved benefactor. From Sir Godwin she had learned that it was not more than a three hours' journey, and how her heart palpitated at the certainty that so brief a space of time would restore her to that excellent man who had been to her more than a father. She regretted that a messenger had not been dispatched to the castle, to apprise Sir Aldobrand of the joy that was in store for him, for she was fearful that the shock might be too much for him; that the sudden transition from utter despair to joy might be attended with dangerous consequences; but she put her trust in Providence, and at last entertained no fear of the result.

Sir Godwin at length aroused himself from his lethargy of thought, and conversed with Mildred more freely than she could have expected he would have done. He appeared fully to have made up his mind as to his future course, and, in fact, he stated that he had already disposed of his estates, and had fixed upon the monastery, in which he had determined to pass the remainder of his days, in the hope of finding that consolation in religion, which he could not meet with in the world. Mildred felt the greatest sympathy for him, for she saw plainly that he naturally possessed a noble mind, which had been wrecked and distorted by disappointment, and most sincerely did she hope that he might meet with that tranquillity which he sought.

To Annie he communicated the provision which he had made for her, and delivered to her the necessary documents, and the poor girl ardently and sincerely expressed to him gratitude for the kindness he had ever shown her, and for this act of generous consideration now that they were about to separate.

From the window of the vehicle, our heroine anxiously watched their progress on the journey; and as the scenes which they passed through seemed to become more familiar to her, and to announce their approach towards the Castle of de Lancy, her heart bounded with a feeling almost amounting to extacy. But a short time, and she would once more be clasped in the arms of her venerable benefactor, whom she had never expected to behold again.

The thought was, indeed, transporting, and tears of gratitude chased each other down her cheeks. And yet, at times, a feeling of dread would come over her, that Sir Aldobrand had been unable to withstand the severe trial to which he had been put; but she exerted herself to the utmost, and endeavoured to dissipate such gloomy apprehensions, and to hope for the best. Providence would not surely doom her to such a disappointment, especially after the many troubles to which she had already been subjected, and she therefore banished the idea from her mind, and tried to divert her thoughts by entering into conversation with Sir Godwin and Annie.

They stopped but once on the journey, and at length the well-known scenes which surrounded De Lancy Castle burst upon the delighted view of Mildred. The black towers of Bransdorf were revealed to her sight, soaring high above the summits of the loftiest trees; and need we attempt to describe her feelings as she gazed upon them? What would be the thoughts of Ethelbert could he be aware of her approach, and that his own deliverance was, in all probability, so near at hand? She could not restrain her tears as this idea arose to her imagination; but when they passed by the hill, on the summit of which the tower stood, and the Castle of De Lancy was fully revealed to her view, her emotions became indescribable.

Sir Godwin now suddenly ordered the driver of the vehicle to stop, and turning to our heroine, he said, with a melancholy expression of countenance, and in a faint voice,—

"I must now leave you, fair damsel; I have performed my promise, and you can reach the castle in safety. Farewell; may every happiness attend you, and sometimes, in your prayers, I beseech you not to forget the unfortunate Sir Godwin Singleford."

"But you will not leave us now," said Mildred, looking anxiously in the baronet's face; "you will see Sir Aldobrand, and receive from him his thanks for the kindness you have rendered me; for the service you have done me in rescuing me from the power of that man who meditated my destruction."

"Not for worlds," replied Sir Godwin energetically. "I respect your benefactor, although he bears the name of De Lancy, and it is that feeling which compels me to decline an interview with one who must conscientiously deprecate my conduct in, unfortunately, becoming the instrument of Lord Ruthlyn. Miss Mildred, I can take no credit to myself for having performed an act of justice. Adieu; may you possess every happiness."

Mildred was about to reply, but he gently waved his hand, and having assisted her and Annie to alight, he motioned to the driver of the vehicle, and in a few minutes it was out of sight.

Mildred and her companion stood for a few minutes and reflected; there were many thoughts suggested themselves to both of their minds, and particularly the parting with Sir Godwin Singleford left a melancholy impression upon them. But Mildred was quickly aroused to other thoughts more immediately important to her; and as the lofty turrets of De Lancy Castle burst upon her view, her heart bounded with the excitement of her feelings, that she could with difficulty only keep herself within the means of reason.

And was she indeed so near the residence of her benefactor, whom she had never expected to behold again? The transition from almost absolute despair to hope, was so sudden and so unexpected, that she could scarcely believe in the reality. But at the same time, a melancholy presentiment came over her mind, that Sir Aldobrand had sunk under the extraordinary affliction of the loss he had sustained, in the bereavement of his son and her, and she almost dreaded, although she was so anxious, to approach the castle, for the sudden shock upon his feelings might be productive of the most serious results.

"It will not do to enter the castle suddenly, and unannounced to Sir Aldobrand," she observed to her companion; "I wish that Sir Godwin could have been prevailed upon to accompany us. But we will retire into one of these cottages, where we may learn the condition of Sir Aldobrand, and likewise apprise him of our arrival."

It was the humble dwelling of one of the tenants of Sir Aldobrand, whom she had often befriended, to which Mildred alluded, and Annie coinciding with her opinion, they entered the cottage, much to the astonishment of honest Dame Yardley, who started back on their appearance, as though she had encountered something frightful, and with upraised hands ejaculated,—

"Gracious Heaven, Miss Mildred, is it you or your spectre?"

"Myself, I hope, good dame, in *propria personæ*," replied our heroine, with a faint smile; "I have escaped from a villain of the blackest dye; but tell me—Sir Aldobrand—how is he?"

"Ah, poor gentleman," answered the old woman, "he has suffered severely, and is now confined to his chamber; but since you have returned, Heaven be thanked! I trust ——"

"Is your husband at home?" interrupted Mildred, who saw that the garrulity of the old woman was likely to tire her patience, and at the same time to retard her meeting with her benefactor.

"Yes, miss," answered the dame; "but, dear me, how rejoiced I am to see you; and oh, what pleasure it will afford to my good master, Sir Aldobrand, to see you restored to him; for, lack-a-day, after the loss of his son, it was enough to break his heart."

"His son will quickly be restored to him, my good dame," said our heroine.

"Ah, say you so, miss?" said the old woman; "well, I am so astonished and delighted by your unexpected return, that it almost deprives me of my senses. Oh, how rejoiced will the good baronet be, and ——"

"Let me see your husband, good dame," once more interrupted Mildred; "I wish him to go on a message for me to the castle."

"Oh, yes, miss," replied the dame, and leaving the room, she summoned her husband, who was at work in his little garden. Mildred felt the utmost anguish at the situation of Sir Aldobrand, though she had fully anticipated it, and saw the prudence with which she had acted in not abruptly making her appearance before him. Old Yardley was a sensible man, and Mildred knew well that there was no one to whom she could better entrust the conveyance of such joyous, unexpected, and delicate intelligence.

On beholding her, the sincere pleasure of the old man was respectfully, but fervently evinced, and he was immediately despatched to the castle, with instructions to break the news to the baronet as gently as possible.

During his absence, Mildred endeavoured to collect her thoughts, and to prepare herself for the trying and interesting meeting that was to take place. Such was the change, from utter despair to joy, that she could scarcely persuade herself that it was not a dream. But the moments that elapsed during the absence of old Yardley, were tedious, for every one seemed fraught with danger to Ethelbert, who was still lingering in his gloomy dungeon in the Tower of Bransdorf, and exposed to the vengeance of Lord Ruthlyn, who, notwithstanding all that Sir Godwin had said to the contrary, she firmly believed would not hesitate to go to the most desperate extremes to appease his wrath, on the discovery of her escape.

The humble cottager, however, was absent but a very short time, and returned with his countenance animated by pleasure. Mildred augured the best from it.

"Now, my good old man," she said, "tell me, how is my excellent guardian, and how did he receive the intelligence?"

"Oh, miss," answered the old man, "you may imagine how. He is better now than he has been for some days; but I really thought, when I told him, that he would have taken leave of his senses; and it was only from want of strength that he was prevented from hastening to see you. He will not be convinced that you are alive, and that I have not been deceiving him, until I escort you to him."

"Oh, let me hasten to him," ejaculated Mildred, rising from her seat, and her heart bounding with joyous anticipation; "my revered benefactor, what must you have suffered under this terrible calamity! May you be able to support the sudden and pleasureable intelligence I have to impart to you with fortitude. Come, Annie, let us immediately depart, You will attend us, Mr. Yardley?"

The old man bowed his assent, and they left the cottage. What a variety of feelings rushed through the mind of Mildred, as they bent their way to the castle; and how she dreaded, although she was so anxious for, the meeting with Sir Aldobrand! Her heart palpitated so violently, that it seemed as if it would quit her side, and it was not without the greatest difficulty that she could support herself.

Sir Aldobrand, whom the joyful and unexpected intelligence had aroused from the lethargy of his despair, was standing at the window of his room, and on beholding her approaching along the avenue which led up to the castle, he could contain himself no longer; he rushed forth, and with the greatest transport clasped her to his bosom, whom he had never expected to behold again.

The scene which took place we must leave to the imagination of the reader. The looks of the aged baronet, and his attenuated form, sufficiently shewed how deeply he had suffered during her absence; but her sudden and unanticipated restoration seemed to impart new life to him, especially when she informed him of the place wherein Ethelbert was confined.

"Gracious Heaven!" he exclaimed; "so near to me, and on my own estate! What could induce the villain, Lord Ruthlyn, to such a course? But another hour shall not elapse before he is restored to us. Oh, Almighty Providence, even in the midst of all thine afflictions, thou hast been most merciful to me. My child, my sweet Mildred, whom I love as fondly as if you were mine own, do I indeed once more clasp you to my bosom? Heaven has been kind to me, or my heart must have broken under the severe trial."

Mildred looked up in his face affectionately, and tears started to her eyes. The joy of this meeting was almost too much for her to support with becoming fortitude.

"Oh, my dear, my generous benefactor," she ejaculated, "how grateful am I to that

beneficent providence that has restored me to you, and has enabled you to bear up against the trials with which it has been pleased to visit you. Never, never did I expect to behold you again. But Ethelbert—oh, do not delay a moment in unbarring the doors of his dungeon."

"No, no," replied Sir Aldobrand; "this instant will I dispatch persons to release him. But the circumstances are so astonishing, and so unexpected, that they quite bewilder my senses. And Sir Godwin Singleford; why did he not accompany you?"

"I have told you, sir," replied our heroine.

"I never injured him," remarked Sir Aldobrand, "however much my unfortunate brother may have done so, and I fear that his statement is too true. To Sir Godwin I am much indebted for his restoration of you to me, and I freely forgive him for the part he took in the plot against you. He has made ample compensation for it, and I should have liked to have acknowledged to him my sentiments upon the subject."

Again did Sir Aldobrand embrace our heroine with parental fondness and delight, and it was some time before they either of them could compose their feelings so as to converse with calmness. Persons, however, were immediately dispatched to the Tower of Bransdorf to release Ethelbert, and then Mildred recounted to Sir Aldobrand all that had happened to her since they had been separated, to which he listened with the deepest attention and disgust, perfectly astonished at the villany and effrontery of Lord Ruthlyn, and vowing that he would not rest until he had ample satisfaction for the same.

With what impatience did both he and Mildred await the return of the men who had been dispatched to the tower to release Ethelbert; and, in spite of the assurances of Lord Ruthlyn, the fact of his being confined in that building seemed so improbable, that their minds were filled with mingled doubts and fears.

That Ulrica was an agent of Lord Ruthlyn, and was an enemy to their peace, was now evident, and Sir Aldobrand was anxious to get her in his power, for it was clear that they would not be safe a moment while she was at large; there was a mystery, too, in her behaviour, which was sufficient to inspire them with alarm, and they could not rest until it was explained. One thing was certain, that the reports which had been circulated respecting the Tower of Bransdorf, were not entirely fabulous, and Sir Aldobrand determined to leave no means untried to unravel it, and to take such steps as would prevent any future danger to be apprehended from it, and to discover and banish from it the wretches, who, in spite of his precautions, had apparently made it their resort.

CHAPTER XXV.

ETHELBERT IN THE TOWER OF BRANSDORF.—THE MYSTERY INCREASES.—THE MANUSCRIPT OF ALMIRA.

NEED we attempt to describe the sufferings of Ethelbert whilst these events were taking place? How drearily did the hours pass away in his gloomy and loathsome dungeon; how racking were the fears which constantly beset his mind, but more so on account of his father and Mildred (who he had every reason to fear would fall a victim to the designs of Lord Ruthlyn) than his own. The trial was so severe to him, that his fortitude almost sunk under it, and he was unable to gain one moment of tranquillity. And to be bound there, fettered like a felon, and without the least hope of making his friends acquainted with his situation—to be entirely at the mercy of the villain Lord Ruthlyn, who would not hesitate to go to any length to gratify his revenge, was surely a trial too great for the patience of any one to endure. He invoked the bitterest curses on his cruel enemy, and formed the most fearful conjectures of the sufferings which were yet in store for him and Mildred.

Lord Ruthlyn had threatened to have her in his power, and he had no doubt, from the conduct he had hitherto pursued, that he would keep his word. And what means had Sir Aldobrand of even suspecting him, or thwarting his designs? Alas! should Mildred indeed fall in the power of that abandoned villain, he had every reason to apprehend the worst. Days and nights passed away, but rest Ethelbert could obtain none. His senses almost sunk under the severe trial to which they were put.

The only person who visited him was the man who brought him his meals, and he had had sufficient proof to know that it was completely useless to appeal to his mercy or humanity.

That the tower was inhabited by the ruffians who had brought him there he was satisfied, and he was surprised that, notwithstanding the efforts of his father, and the reports which had been circulated, they had hitherto escaped detection; but he was more than all astonished to think that Lord Ruthlyn should have selected it as the place of his confinement.

In this manner a week passed away, and Ethelbert saw no more of Lord Ruthlyn, and to the anxious inquiries he made of the man who attended upon him, he could gain no satisfactory answer; but from the observations which he inadvertently let drop, he had every reason to apprehend that he was engaged in some nefarious plot against the peace of Mildred; and he had no doubt that he would prosecute his designs against her with perseverance.

His punishment was at last in some measure ameliorated, by the man releasing him from the chain, and he was thus allowed the liberty of traversing the limited precincts of his miserable cell.

He passed his time in bitter lamentations against his cruel destiny, and in offering up prayers for the preservation of Mildred, who, he feared, was doomed to experience much persecution from the villany of Lord Ruthlyn, and against whose artifices there was now no one to warn her or protect her.

Every night, and at about the same hour, he heard the melancholy cry, which seemed to proceed from a dungeon adjacent to the one in which he was confined; but although he called upon her (for it was evidently a female), and begged of her to inform him who she was, he could obtain no answer from her, and he was thus left in the same state of painful mystery and doubt.

He frequently questioned the man who attended upon him on the subject, but he could obtain no satisfactory answer from him. All that he could elicit was, that there certainly was another unfortunate individual confined in the tower like himself, and it seemed very clear that it was at the instigation of Lord Ruthlyn, and that his villany was far deeper than he could at first have conceived. Sometimes his fears even went so far as to lead him to imagine that it was Mildred; but the utter improbability of this was soon apparent to him, and he dismissed it at once from his mind. Had it been Mildred, she would at once have answered him; besides, it was not likely that if she had been in his power, Lord Ruthlyn would have failed to apprise him of it, and to have exulted in his triumph, and in the misery which he must be aware it would cause him.

In one corner of the dungeon, in which Ethelbert was confined, was a heap of rubbish, the remains of an old bedstead, and a mattress, which had no doubt, at some former period, been occupied by some unfortunate victim of cruelty and oppression like himself, but many years had doubtless elapsed since that had taken place. Ethelbert had frequently felt a strange curiosity to examine this heterogeneous mass, though what prompted him to it he could not conceive. Now he was released from the chain which had bound him to the wall, he had an opportunity to gratify his curiosity, and in order to wear away the tedious time, he accordingly made an inspection of it. He had not proceeded far, when a bundle of papers, tied together, met his sight, which he opened, and by the light of his lamp, the first line that met his observation, was the following :—

"CONFESSION OF ALMIRA DE MONTREVILLE."

The name immediately struck him, being so closely connected with the fate of his uncle, Sir Martin, but he was completely astonished to meet with the papers in such a place, and wondered that they should have been suffered to remain there, according to their appearance, for such a number of years. His curiosity was naturally excited, and seating himself, he devoted his whole attention to the perusal of the singular story which the manuscript revealed, and which was in the following words, written in a delicate, but perfectly legible hand.

"THE MANUSCRIPT OF ALMIRA.

"If fate should ever destine these lines to meet the eyes of the humane and charitable, the unfortunate but guilty writer (guilty through the treachery of one whom she was persuaded to imagine to be all perfection) most earnestly implores them to sympathise with her misfortunes, and to pray for her soul, which probably may then be in eternity.

"But, alas! what hope is there for the wretched sufferer; what chance of her heavy wrongs and sorrows being revealed? Here, in the Black Tower of Bransdorf, where so many revolting crimes have been perpetrated—confined in this loathsome dungeon, at the instigation of that man whom I was infatuated enough to believe loved me more fondly than man ever loved woman before, what hope is there for me that this melancholy history of my troubles, and the villany which has, and is now being practised towards me, will ever come to the knowledge of my fellow-creatures? Possibly, ere many hours have elapsed, I may have fallen a victim to the nefarious designs of that man on whom I bestowed all my heart's fondest, warmest affections; and to whom, confiding in his deceptive vows, I sacrificed my innocence, and became a thing to be loathed, despised, execrated. God of Heaven, how shall I write the dreadful acknowledgment? A *murderess!* The murderess of my innocent babe, the offspring of my shame, and his black-hearted villany!

"My brain burns! and yet 'tis stubborn, or madness would surely seize upon it. How shall I attempt to detail the dark catalogue of my crimes (crimes into which he has plunged me) in this gloomy abode of hidden horror? But Heaven, oh, in thine infinite mercy, give me power and fortitude to make the only small atonement that is left me by a confession of my guilt.

"How dark and gloomy is all around; what terrors surround me on every side; how busy is conscience to kindle up fearful imaginings, and to add to the sufferings of my anguished, despairing soul! Hark! what dismal cry breaks upon the solemn stillness of the midnight hour, and reverberates through these awful subterranean dungeons? It is the wailing shriek of helpless infancy in its dying agony. It is the voice of my murdered infant. I know it well—oh, never can I forget it, as it rang in my ears on the night that the hellish deed was perpetrated. And hark! that hollow plash, as the deep waters of the well receive its beauteous, tender form. Horror! horror! can I listen to this, and still live?"

*　　*　　*　　*　　*　　*　　*　　*

Ethelbert laid down the manuscript for a minute or two, for the fearful nature of its commencement, and the knowledge of his being the occupant of the same dungeon in which it seemed the unfortunate but guilty writer had been confined, made a most powerful and sickly impression upon his mind; the more so, when he remembered that Almira was so intimately connected with his uncle's history, and he had every reason to suppose that he it was to whom she alluded as the betrayer of her innocence, and the primary cause of her crimes. The fearful events which had taken place at the union of Sir Martin with the unfortunate Lady Editha; Almira's terrible curse, and the circumstances which had subsequently occurred, and which he had so frequently heard related, were now reproduced to his memory in more glowing colours than ever, and a cold, shuddering sensation came over him which he could not repress. He cast a cursory glance round the dungeon, as if he almost expected to behold the phantom of Almira standing before him; yet that she was really dead there was no satisfactory proof to shew, when the mysterious and unaccountable disappearance of the supposed corpse was taken into consideration.

Irresistible curiosity, however, on a subject in which he was so deeply interested, quickly overcame his other feelings, and trimming his lamp, he once more took up the manuscript.

Part of the writing was rendered almost illegible, either from the effects of time, and the damp of the dungeon, or the tears of the unfortunate author. They comprised a few broken, unconnected sentences, but nothing out of which he could make anything; but at length the characters became more distinct, and he was enabled to proceed with the singular and interesting document as follows :—

"Ulrica, the faithful, the old domestic of my parents, has supplied me with the materials for leaving these documents behind me. She was permitted to accompany me, under the supposition that my seducer was about to render me justice, but is now only suffered to visit me occasionally. Alas! she is powerless to render me any assistance, and even I am deprived of the blessing of her consolation under my unparalleled misery. Would that she could supply me with the means of terminating my wretched existence, for what can life now be to a poor guilty creature like me but a curse?

"And yet I cannot, dare not die! How dare I meet that Eternal Judge, against whom I have sinned so frightfully? Oh, conscience, conscience, terrible monitor, how awful are the torments thou dost inflict upon me!

"And why does he not take my life? It would be a mercy to me. Why does he permit the poor wretch to live whom he says has now become hateful to him, and by whose death he might save himself (for a time at least) from that exposition of his black-hearted villany he has so much reason to dread?

"But, no; there is a fate in all this; an instinctive voice tells me that I shall yet live to see the hour of retribution; to invoke my deadly curses upon his guilty head, and to see them realised, too. It is that one thought, that hope, which alone sustains me under this dreadful trial.

"It is now, as near as I can guess, the hour of midnight. How awfully silent and dreary is all around, save the dismal shriek of the owl, or the sweeping blast of the wind, as it seems to shake these old towers to their foundation, muttering, as it were, strange legends of the crimes which have been perpetrated within its blackened walls, in times long past. The voices of the troubled spirits of the dead appear to murmur their sad plaints in mine ears, and all, in this, my living tomb, is darkness, misery, and despair.

"Be calm, my wandering mind, and let me at once proceed to the task I have imposed upon myself.

"Know, then, all who may hereafter, perchance, peruse these lines, that my name is Almira de Montreville, and that the author of the guilty circumstances they detail, is Sir Martin de Lancy, of De Lancy Castle, and of this, the Tower of Bransdorf!"

Ethelbert again paused at this part of the manuscript, which was so direct a confirmation of his first surmises; and he could not but shudder at the thought of the dark career of iniquity his uncle had pursued, and which these papers, so singularly placed in his hands, would reveal to him. The circumstance also of Mildred having been found in the tower, and in such an extraordinary manner, flashed most vividly upon his recollection, and, for a short time, bewildered his brain in a chaos of conflicting and painful conjectures.

There were more horrors connected with the Tower of Bransdorf, he was certain, than he had hitherto formed any conception of, and most fervently he wished that he might be rendered the humble instrument, in the hands of Providence, to unravel them. That would, he considered, more than sufficiently repay him for the misery to which he was now put, and might be the means of unfolding the mystery now connected with the origin of his beloved Mildred, and restoring her to her proper position in society.

But was it possible that Lord Ruthlyn should be unacquainted with some, if not all, of these facts? He was the more perplexed the longer he reflected upon it.

He remembered the dismal cry he had so often heard since he had been confined in the tower, and it seemed quite evident to him that there was some other unfortunate individual imprisoned there as well as himself, of which Lord Ruthlyn, it stood to reason, could not but be fully aware. And might not that unhappy being be the wretched Almira herself?

The thought was not unreasonable. Still, for what reason could she be now there confined?—by whose orders? and how had she so long escaped discovery? All these were problems which Ethelbert was totally unable to solve, and he gave up the thought in despair, and once more resumed the perusal of the manuscript, bound up as his interest was in its melancholy recital, from its peculiar connection with his own family, and the hope he entertained that it would disclose the mystery that had so long enshrouded the fate of Sir Martin de Lancy, his uncle, and the Lady Editha, who, they had so much reason to believe, was the solitary wanderer whom they had followed in the chapel of the castle, but who had eluded them in so unaccountable a manner.

Thus the manuscript went on to say:—

"The hapless writer of these lines was the only child of virtuous parents, in respectable, but not affluent circumstances, natives of one of the most ancient towns of Normandy, and her early days were passed in tranquillity and delight, every attention being paid to her education, and all those precepts of virtue being instilled into her mind, which she afterwards, by the insidious arts of the villain who destroyed her, so much abused.

"Oh, memory, how torturing art thou to me! With what bitter pangs of remorse dost thou afflict my heart. When I recall to my recollection the scenes, the innocent scenes, of my childhood, the endearments and indulgencies of my parents, the retrospection almost drives me mad. Why did it not please Heaven to take me to itself when I was good and virtuous, instead of permitting me to live to become the degraded, the wretched being I now am?

"The past appears to me a bright vision, too bright, too joyous, in contrast with my present misery, to have been real. Oh, God! why from that blissful dream did you ever suffer me to awaken? Why arouse me to this sense of shame, of degradation, and horror?

"Hark! again that piercing cry of agony! It rings in my ears; it is the voice of the murdered—of my murdered innocent—of my child! Yes, it was I who did that hellish deed. But my senses were bewildered at the time. It was at the instigation of the monster, my seducer. Sir Martin de Lancy, the blood of that innocent child is upon your head; it calls aloud for vengeance. Oh, Heaven! dare I pray to you for forgiveness? My pen refuses its office; I have imposed a task on myself which I cannot accomplish. I am unable to proceed."

The manuscript again abruptly broke off, and Ethelbert laid it down for a minute or two, and became absorbed in meditation. Was it possible that his uncle could have been the guilty villain he was here represented to be? Could he really be the instigator and the author of the crimes there attributed to him? It seemed scarcely probable; and yet, from the circumstances which were connected with his history, and which had come to his knowledge, it seemed but too likely to be correct.

What an irremediable obloquy was then cast upon his family name! Already he felt himself degraded, and dreaded the effects this confession would have upon his father, if it should ever meet his sight.

A feeling of awe came over him, as the impression of what he had already perused in the singular and interesting documents which had fallen into his hands gained strength upon his mind. The death-like silence of all around increased the gloom of his thoughts, and he could not help yielding to something like a feeling of superstitious fear. He, however, quickly overcame this temporary weakness, and once more taking up the manuscript, resumed the perusal of the extraordinary narrative it detailed.

" My time passed away in a round of uninterrupted happiness, until I had attained the age of seventeen, and then the black clouds of my evil destiny obscured the horizon of my days, and fate conspired to render me as wretched a being as I had before been blest and contented. The gloomy retrospect brings nothing but horror and remorse. May my errors prove a warning to others, and guard them against the insidious arts of the tempter!

" Possessing, as I have been flattered to believe, at that time, many personal and intrinsic attractions, it may readily be supposed that I was not without my admirers, and indeed I had a host of suitors, who made overtures for my hand; but I saw not one whom I could view with any warmer sentiment than esteem, and my parents would not attempt to bias my inclinations, feeling a fond confidence that whenever my choice was made it would fall upon a worthy object. Alas! alas! how cruelly did I deceive them! and how could they imagine that I would ever be the cause of such a bitter disappointment to their hopes.

" It was my usual custom to ride out of a morning, sometimes alone, but generally accompanied by an old and faithful male servant of my parents', who had been in their service for many years.

" It was on a beautiful morning in the spring of the year that I took my customary ride, attended by Theodore, the faithful domestic above alluded to.

" The morning being so particularly fine, I prolonged my ride to a much further distance than usual; but suddenly my horse took fright at some noise created by a group of peasants close at hand, and before Theodore could come up to me, it started off with frightful speed.

" I was a skilful horsewoman; but I was so unnerved at the unexpected event that I lost all my presence of mind, and was in danger every moment of being precipitated to the earth, old Theodore, although he exerted himself to the utmost, not being able to come up to me.

" The horse continued its rapid flight, and I know not how I maintained my seat; but my terrors were so great that I almost became insensible.

" I was now being hurried towards a frightful precipice, and Theodore's cries of horror and despair rent the air, for my fate seemed inevitable. Nothing but an awful death appeared to await me.

" I have often regretted since that I was rescued from that fate; for then I should at least have perished in my innocence, and not have been spared to endure the dreadful pangs of remorse and conscience I am now suffering. Then the tear of regret and pity would have been shed to my memory, whilst now it can only excite disgust and horror.

" The frightened animal continued its course with undiminished speed, and now I was within a few yards of the precipice. My brain turned giddy; a sickly sensation fell upon my heart; I breathed a short prayer to Heaven for mercy; I closed my eyes, and remembered no more.

" When I was restored to consciousness, I found myself supported in the arms of Theodore, who was bathing my temples with some water, which had been procured from a neighbouring spring. By his side, and anxiously watching my recovery, was a young and handsome stranger, who, by his costume and features, I immediately knew to be an Englishman, and who eagerly inquired after my health, after the imminent peril and the severe fright to which I had been exposed.

" His voice thrilled upon my heart, and I could feel the crimson blushes glowing in my cheeks. Alas! this was the fatal moment that sealed my doom.

"This was Sir Martin de Lancy, and it was to him, the future destroyer of my peace, my present brutal persecutor, that I was indebted for the preservation of my life. Oh, fatal hour that ever I saw him! Better, far better, would it have been for me had I been suffered to meet the fate with which I had been threatened.

"I timidly, but artlessly, expressed to him my acknowledgments for the service he had rendered me, and he replied to me in a manner which plainly showed the admiration he felt; but still, his demeanour was most respectful, and too powerfully won upon my favour.

"In stopping the horse he had severely strained his shoulder, and I could see, notwith-standing he endeavoured to conceal it, that he was suffering much pain. I could not help inviting him to the residence of my parents, that he might receive their thanks, and some remedy for the hurt he had sustained; and he accepted the invitation with a pleasure he did not attempt to conceal. He mounted his horse, after having assisted me to mine, and taking his place by my side, while old Theodore followed at a respectful distance, we proceeded on our way towards the residence of my parents.

"It would be fruitless for me to attempt to deny that the handsome and gallant young Englishman had excited the warmest emotion in my breast from the first moment I had beheld him, and that feeling was naturally strengthened by the recollection of the service he had rendered me; but still, it was not unmingled with a peculiar sensation, almost amounting to fear and regret, which at that time I was at a loss to understand.

"Sir Martin de Lancy was, at the fatal period when we thus accidentally encountered each other, not more than twenty-two years of age, and, in addition to a noble figure and commanding and handsome countenance, few men could boast of a greater store of accomplishments, or a more flattering and captivating tongue. He had the art of ingratiating himself immediately in a person's favour, and it was few who could divest their minds of the favourable impression he so powerfully made upon them from the first moment of his introduction. Alas! too well he knew how to play the hypocrite! and how great was the misery he was enabled to cause in consequence of it!

"He conversed with me freely as we pursued our way, and I confess that there was a charm in every word he uttered, which, although he was a perfect stranger to me, irresistibly rivetted my attention, and afforded me the greatest pleasure. I could not but consider within my own mind that he was the most agreeable man I had ever seen, and that idea soon gained the most powerful and fatal ascendancy over me.

"He informed me that he had been travelling for some months on the continent, and was at present staying at the castle of a friend, only a short distance from the place where he had encountered me.

"This information also afforded me considerable pleasure; for I trusted that this would not be the last time we should meet; and I fancied that Sir Martin could read the thoughts which were passing in my mind, for his countenance became more animated than ever; and, fearful that I had betrayed myself, and surprised at my own feelings, I blushed deeply, and remained silent for a few minutes.

"At length we arrived at my residence, and my parents were not a little surprised to behold me with such a companion; but when they were made acquainted with the particulars of his having preserved me from a shocking death, they expressed to him the gratitude of their feelings in the most unbounded terms.

"A surgeon was quickly called in, who examined the injury he had received, and having applied an effectual remedy to it, the inflammation was quickly reduced, and he gave it as his opinion that no serious consequences would result from it.

"Sir Martin remained at the house of my parents for more than a couple of hours, and seemed loth to depart. They were evidently almost as much captivated with his conversation and manners as myself, and when he took his leave they most cordially assented to his request to be permitted the pleasure to call again.

"When Sir Martin was gone, my parents were most lavish in their praises of his noble demeanour, and the numerous accomplishments he evinced, and every word they gave utterance to forcibly accorded with my own feelings, and increased the interest I felt in the handsome stranger; but I concealed my real thoughts as well as I could, lest they should create their surprise, and, in fact, I almost blushed to acknowledge them myself. Alas! what a fatal infatuation it was to take possession of my senses! and what an easy victim did it render me to the artifices of the tempter. But it was my evil destiny; and even if my efforts had been ever so great, and however good my will, I could not have avoided it."

CHAPTER XXV.

THE MANUSCRIPT OF ALMIRA CONCLUDED.

" THE same busy thoughts that had racked my mind ever since my meeting with Sir Martin, pursued me to my chamber, and when indeed I sunk into the arms of sleep, his form was presented in a vision to my imagination, and I again, in fancy, listened to his elegant conversation, and beheld the looks of admiration he had bestowed upon me. I could not believe for a moment that a guilty heart could be enshrined in so manly and noble a form, and I waited impatiently for the time to arrive when he would pay us another visit, according to his promise, and which I fondly anticipated he would not fail to keep, especially after the pleasure he had evinced on our first interview.

" The next day and the subsequent one, however, passed away without Sir Martin paying us his promised visit, and during that time I suffered the greatest uneasiness of mind, and had a difficulty in concealing my real emotions from my parents, though they were, in fact, as anxious to see him again as myself, such was the impression that Sir Martin had made upon them. They frequently conversed upon him, and expressed the grateful sense they entertained of his heroic conduct on the occasion of my accident, and their admiration of those brilliant attainments he had so pre-eminently displayed.

" Every word that my excellent parents uttered in praise of Sir Martin de Lancy created in me a sensation of delight and gratitude, and added to the irresistible anxiety I felt to behold him again.

" Ah! little did the authors of my being imagine the fatal consequences that were about to follow their encouragement and admiration of the hypocrite cruel fate had brought in our way. Had they done so, with propriety they might have regretted that even I had not been destined to perish by the awful means which had threatened me, rather than that I should live to become the unfortunate victim of his villany to bring shame and misery upon their aged heads, and to be left to linger out a wretched existence, the scorn and hatred of all mankind. Oh, God! and with the damning weight of blood upon my conscience, the blood of my innocent offspring, and that of him whose treachery lured me from the paths of virtue!

" Again that cry! that fearful shriek of suffering infancy! It rings more distinctly than ever in mine ears! By Heaven, it is no delusion! It is the voice of my murdered babe! It shrieks! its sainted spirit calls for vengeance on its unnatural parent! Its cry will not be in vain. Oh, no! I terribly feel it now! And see!—ah, it is no delusion of the disordered imagination. The form of my child rises up before mine eyes! Its cherub features as they were in death, that terrible death to which I consigned it! Dreadful! My guilty soul is appalled at the sight! Whither can I fly to escape it? Oh, hell! thou canst not possess greater tortures than those I now endure! Mercy! mercy! It is gone; but a convulsive tremor shakes my every nerve; my hand can no longer guide the pen; the flickering ray of my lamp expires; I am surrounded by darkness and horror. Oh, that I could find even but a temporary oblivion of my sorrows!"

*   *   *   *   *   *   *   *   *   *

Here the manuscript was again interrupted, and so great was the excitement which the dismal recital caused in the mind of Ethelbert, that he even felt a kind of relief (notwithstanding his interest and curiosity were wound up to the highest degree) in the pause which had thus ensued.

So far, too, had the narrative wrought upon his imagination, that he could almost realise the description of the unfortunate Almira, and believe that he heard the appalling shriek of the murdered infant, and visions of horror for a minute or two seemed to flit before his eyes, and gradually to fade away in the obscurity of his dungeon.

He laid down the painfully interesting records, and for a short time paced his gloomy dungeon with folded arms, and wrapt in meditation. He could not but feel the deepest sympathy in the misfortunes of the misguided Almira de Montreville; and when he reflected that in this very cell she was confined, and had probably died, a feeling of awe came over him, which he found it impossible to control.

The dreadful curse which she had invoked upon the head of Sir Martin (if all that she stated in her narrative was true, and he certainly had no reason at present to doubt it),

was sufficiently explained; and he shuddered to think that one so nearly allied to him by blood, should have been guilty of such villany.

"But is it possible," he soliloquized, "that my uncle could really have been guilty of the black-hearted treachery that is here attributed to him? Notwithstanding all that I have been enabled to elicit respecting him, I can scarcely believe it. It seems impossible that there should be such a marked difference between two brothers as him and my amiable father. And yet, all the circumstances attendant upon his marriage with Lady Editha, his alarm on the unexpected appearance of Almira at the altar; his inability to deny the charges she made against him; his reserved behaviour afterwards; his cruel conduct to the unfortunate lady he had so recently united, and their extraordinary disappearance from this ancient tower, where, it seems, so many dreadful crimes have been perpetrated, all serve to corroborate the truth of the statements, and to excite the worst surmises in my mind. Oh, my uncle, of what unparalleled misery have you been the cause!"

But still his brain was bewildered in endeavouring to think what had been the reason that the rubbish collected in the dungeon, and which had been there evidently for such a number of years, had not been removed by the persons who had made the tower their retreat, and the confession of Almira consequently discovered; and it seemed as though it had been ordained by the special will of Providence, to fall into his hands, who was so immediately connected with the facts which it recorded.

Ethelbert was interrupted in the course of these reflections, by hearing the bolts of his dungeon door being removed, and he hastily concealed the manuscript in his bosom, and had no sooner succeeded in doing so, than the man who attended upon him entered, bringing with him his usual supply of provisions.

Ethelbert imagined that his looks were less repulsive than usual, and he was, therefore, induced to interrogate him further, with the hope of eliciting from him what it was intended ultimately to do with him, and whether it was at all probable that he would be released from his present state of insupportable misery and confinement.

The fellow listened to him with an expression of countenance so totally inflexible, that it convinced him he had nothing whatever to hope for, and when he had concluded, said,—

"You ought to have been satisfied, young gentleman, from what you have heard from me before, that it is totally useless to put any questions to me. It is not very likely that Lord Ruthlyn would have been at all the trouble he has to secure you, to let you escape so easily. As for your ultimate fate, that entirely depends upon his lordship's will, and probably your own conduct."

"The villain!" exclaimed the enraged Ethelbert; "he surely will not dare to detain me in his custody."

"He will not dare!" repeated the ruffian, with a look of scorn; "these are bold and presumptuous words, Ethelbert de Lancy, for a prisoner like yourself to make use of, and who is entirely at the mercy of him who holds you in his power. Think you, Lord Ruthlyn is a weak child, to be intimidated from the completion of those designs upon which he has so boldly ventured, especially when it is impossible for any one to discover them or counteract them."

"Secure as he may think himself," remarked Ethelbert, and his bosom at the same time swelled with indignation, "depend upon it, that vengeance, a terrible vengeance, will speedily overtake him, and that, too, when he the least anticipates it."

"Bah!" replied the man, contemptuously. "But I leave you to the indulgence of such hopes, and much consolation may they afford you."

"Stay one moment," said Ethelbert, eagerly; "but another word with you."

"What would you now?" demanded the man, sternly; "be quick, for I have no time to waste."

"Where is Lord Ruthlyn at present?"

"Far away from hence. More interesting business occupies his time, at present, than attending upon you, whom he knows he has secure enough."

"What mean you?"

"Oh, I don't know why I should trouble myself to explain to you," answered the fellow, with consummate insolence; "but methinks the fair Mildred ——"

"Ah!" interrupted Ethelbert, and a fearful pang shot through his heart as he noticed the expression of the man's countenance, and the tone in which he uttered the observations he had made use of. "What of her? Speak!—tell me, in mercy, what do your words insinuate?"

"That your beloved Mildred," replied the ruffian, with a sarcastic and sardonic grin, "is at present in the power of your rival, Lord Ruthlyn de Bohun."

"No, no; it is impossible!" cried Ethelbert; "my Mildred in that miscreant's power, and at his mercy—it is false! Heaven cannot have permitted him to triumph so far in his diabolical schemes. It is only a plan to torture me. You would deceive me—I will not, cannot believe you."

"Well," coolly replied the fellow, "you can do as you think proper; it is a matter of total indifference to me; but no doubt you will soon have sufficient proof of the fact."

"My God!" exclaimed the distracted Ethelbert, striking his forehead in despair. "Can this be true? My Mildred in the power of the heartless libertine, Lord Ruthlyn! Oh, horrible thought! I could have endured anything, even death itself, rather than this. But tell me, man, if you have any humanity at all left within your nature, by what means did your guilty master get the innocent and unfortunate damsel within his power, and where is she confined ?"

"That I must leave you to discover in the best manner you can," replied the man ; "it is not my place to inform you ; it is enough for you to know that she is in the power of Lord Ruthlyn de Bohun, and has been for some days. His lordship's triumph is complete."

Without saying another word, the ruffian quitted the dungeon, and Ethelbert remained for a few minutes completely astounded by the intelligence he had received ; but at length he started from his lethargy, and beating his breast, groaned aloud in the intensity of the anguish which the unexpected intelligence he had received naturally excited in his mind.

To resume the manuscript again, in the present agonizing state of his thoughts, would have been impossible, and he traversed his dungeon for a considerable time completely distracted, and giving utterance to expressions of the wildest despair.

"My Mildred," he cried, "my own gentle and innocent Mildred in the power of the miscreant Lord Ruthlyn, then is his triumph, indeed, complete. Oh, God ! this blow is worse than all. What has that poor, helpless maiden done, that she should thus be made the victim of so cruel a destiny ? But Thou wilt not, surely, permit him to complete his diabolical designs ? Alas! to what dreadful sufferings she is now exposed, and there is no one near to assist her, or to pour the balm of hope and consolation in her ear. Heaven help me, or I shall go mad. And by what means has the villain been able thus triumphantly to accomplish his diabolical designs ? Alas! alas! and what must be the anguish of my poor father, thus deprived of all that he loved on earth ? He can never survive so terrible a calamity. Oh, had he given his sanction to my union with one who was every way so worthy of me, all this might have been prevented."

The violence of his anguish choked his utterance, and for a few minutes he could only pace his gloomy dungeon, and give vent to his emotion in groans and sobs.

"And perhaps ere this," he continued, "she has fallen a victim to his brutal and disgusting passions. The thought is madness, and freezes the very blood within my veins. Oh, may the bitterest curses that human being can invoke, descend upon his head for this monstrous conduct. Better would it have been for me had I expired before I could have received such revolting intelligence."

"But yet, after all," he resumed, after a pause, "may it not be a base fabrication to torture me ? It may, and I will still endeavour to hope, until I have received more satisfactory proofs of the truth of this ruffian's statement. I cannot believe that Sir Aldobrand would have been so careless of Mildred's safety (especially after my disappearance) as to suffer her to fall in the power of one whom he was fully aware sought her destruction. He would not permit her to leave the castle, and Lord Ruthlyn could not have dared to make an attack upon it. I will try to hope, and to meet the result with fortitude."

It was, however, a most arduous task that he had imposed upon himself, and he succeeded but indifferently. He threw himself on the seat, and for some time he gave himself up to the most bewildering and torturing thoughts ; then he started up in a state of distraction, and once more traversed the cell with hasty strides, and was scarcely able to contain himself within the bounds of reason.

The time wore heavily on, and it was now getting late ; a death-like silence reigned around ; but still Ethelbert could not think of attempting to sleep, nor could he find patience (much even as his interest was excited) to resume the perusal of the manuscript, so that he might have diverted his thoughts from the melancholy and torturing subject that now so entirely engrossed them.

Fervently he supplicated the interposition of Heaven to prevent the calamity which he dreaded, and to save Mildred from the power of her cruel and remorseless enemy ; but still, in spite of all his efforts, nothing could abate his fears. How anxious was he once more to behold Lord Ruthlyn, that he might, at least, obtain a confirmation or contradiction of the ruffian's assertions, and until then his suspense would be even more terrible than certainty.

At length, however, by dint of great exertions, he became somewhat more tranquillised, and, worn out with fatigue, and the anguish of thought, he stretched his weary limbs upon his rude pallet, and sleep speedily came to his relief.

In the morning he awoke much refreshed, but still the assertions of the man continued to distract and perplex his mind ; and he could not, notwithstanding he endeavoured to do so, banish from his bosom the painful impression they had made, and the fears they had created.

Once more he implored the mercy of the Supreme, and while he was thus occupied, the door of his dungeon was unbolted, and the ruffian, whose name was Osrand, entered. He merely brought with him his morning meal, and having placed it by his side, he was about to retire without speaking, when Ethelbert, in his agony of excitement, thinking it was possible he might elicit something more from him, begged that he would stop, and answer him a few more questions that he had to put.

"Of what use is it your teasing me with your idle questions?" demanded Osrand, with a forbidding look. "I have already answered more than I had any right to do, and you must be satisfied."

"Oh, tell me," said Ethelbert, looking most anxiously and imploringly in his face, have you told me the truth?"

"I have; and if you do not believe me, I care not. Probably you may not be so incredulous before many days have elapsed."

"And is the unfortunate Mildred really in Lord Ruthlyn's power?"

"I have told you so."

"It is not a story got up to aggravate my torture?" demanded Ethelbert.

"It is not," answered Osrand; "but you can continue to think so if you please. It matters not to me."

"Oh, Heaven! can I endure this?" groaned Ethelbert; "and here am I confined, without the least means of rendering her any assistance, or of avenging the diabolical outrage committed against her."

"And if you were this moment at liberty," remarked Osrand, "you would be equally powerless. The girl is secure enough, and it would be impossible for you to discover her. Lord Ruthlyn does not his business by halves."

"But by what means did he accomplish his infamous designs?" asked the distracted Ethelbert.

"Oh, you will know all by-and-bye, I dare say," replied Osrand; "I have nothing more to tell you."

He left the dungeon as he spoke, and Ethelbert clasped his forehead in despair, while his brain became giddy with the racking thoughts which overwhelmed it.

It was some time before he was enabled at all to calm his feelings, or to arouse himself from the gloomy lethargy into which he had sunk; but at last hope and fortitude fortunately came to his aid, and he once more took up the deeply-interesting manuscript of Almira, and continued the perusal of it.

*   *   *   *   *   *   *   *   *

"Once more I resume my melancholy task, and endeavour to detail my numerous and unparalleled misfortunes. But, alas! of what use is it my doing so? These lines may never meet the eye of mortal being; and even should they do so, the wretched writer of them will probably have long ceased to exist, and will be beyond the reach of confession or assistance.

"Still it helps to wear away the tedious hours in this loathsome dungeon, and affords some trifling relief to my guilty conscience, and I will proceed with my task to the end, should strength be permitted me to do so, or my cruel oppressor allow me to live. And oh, should they at some future period meet the eye of one of my own sex, may she be warned by my terrible example to avoid the paths of vice, and to turn a deaf ear to the voice of the tempter.

"The absence of Sir Martin excited a fear in my breast that the injury he had received in rescuing me had taken a more unfavourable change than the surgeon had apprehended, and this idea increased my uneasiness; and my parents were not without the same idea, and were half inclined to send a messenger to make inquiries at the castle of the gentleman where he was residing; but our anxiety was removed on the third day after the accident by Sir Martin making his appearance, and to find that he was perfectly recovered.

"My parents received him with the greatest respect, and, for my own part, I could not without the greatest difficulty conceal the extreme pleasure I felt in beholding him again. Sir Martin must have perceived from my blushes and the confusion of my manner the thoughts which were passing in my mind, and indeed the pleasure he evinced on seeing me was equal to my own.

"By degrees, however, the diffidence of a first acquaintance wore off, and before Sir

Martin had been long in our society, we conversed as freely as if we had been on intimate terms for some time.

"His conversation, as I have before said, was brilliant and captivating; there was not a subject with which he was not familiarly acquainted, and his wit was sparkling, pure, and abundant. He had travelled much, and he had treasured up in his mind a rich fund of information; and no one could listen to his graphic and glowing descriptions without delight and admiration.

"Sir Martin remained with us the whole of the day, and oh, how sweetly passed the time. Never had I experienced such perfect happiness before; it could only be equalled by the regret I felt when the hour arrived for him to depart. And Sir Martin was evidently quite as loth to go, and prolonged his departure to the latest moment. Alas! it was a fatal day for me; my doom was sealed; and the triumph of the deceiver was all but complete. So favourable was the impression that he made on my parents, that, on his rising to depart, they most warmly requested him to renew his visits as often as was convenient to him while he remained in that part of the country; and Sir Martin accepted their invitation with equal pleasure. No doubt he in that moment marked me for his own, and considered his success as almost certain; and surely he had every reason to entertain that idea, both from my looks and demeanour.

"When Sir Martin had quitted our residence, my father and mother were again most warm in the eulogiums they passed upon the handsome young Englishman; and I listened to them with a feeling of rapture and satisfaction. Alas! they little thought of the danger of their praises; they could not (how could they?) anticipate the dreadful consequences which were destined to arise from my introduction to the object of their admiration. Oh, that they could have done so, then might I have been rescued from the fearful gulph into which I was afterwards plunged.

"Again that night, little did I sleep; but my waking moments were those of pleasure; for I recalled to my memory (in fact, they had never been diverted from it) all the eloquent observations of Sir Martin; and the more I reflected on them, the stronger became the influence he had already gained over my feelings, the less the command I possessed over my passions, which had never been excited before, for no one had I ever seen who, in my estimation, possessed the attractions, both of head and heart, of Sir Martin de Lancy.

"Fatal delusion!—unfortunate infatuation! It led to the abandonment of those precepts of virtue and strict integrity which had been so strictly and prudently instilled into my mind by the most excellent of parents.

"In fact, I had set my whole soul upon winning his admiration. Could I have thought that any behaviour of mine could have lessened the admiration which I flattered myself I had inspired in his breast, I should have been the most miserable being in existence. No wonder, then, that the triumph of the libertine, over so inexperienced and innocent a girl, was rendered so complete. Accomplished in the arts of seduction as Sir Martin de Lancy was, it would indeed have been wonderful had he not so fatally well succeeded in his diabolical and unprincipled designs as he did.

"But why do I dwell upon this subject, so revolting and so torturing to my present fevered brain? It is only in the full sense of mine own shame, and his duplicity, and with the faint hope that, should these papers ever come under the perusal of the younger branches of my own sex, it may prove a warning to them to avoid the snares that are laid for the destruction of their innocence by the accomplished libertine.

"I fear that my remorse of conscience renders me tedious; but, alas! what else can the weary heart do than to dwell upon the misery which oppresses it? What other relief can it find, than in pouring forth its sorrows, even though, as I now do, to the black walls of a gloomy dungeon, and without the prospect of their ever meeting the eye of sympathy or generous commiseration?

"Week after week wore away, in a blissful state of delusion to me, for Sir Martin was almost our daily visitor, and every day, every hour, did he obtain more influence over my heart by the accomplishments and manly perfections of heart he was so great an adept at assuming. He had not attempted to disguise the admiration he felt for me, and I—poor credulous fool—took all he said for truth, and not only received his attentions very graciously, but in the simplicity and candour of my heart, and never for a moment suspecting his sincerity, took no pains to conceal from him the sentiments with which he had inspired me. Had I even attempted to do so, the language of my eye, whenever I m d him, would have revealed all; and it was not many weeks from the time of our first i et
n-

troduction to each other, ere he confessed the most ardent passion for me, and elicited from me an avowal of a return. And Heaven knows that I believed in his sincerity, and felt myself the happiest of human beings in possessing the love of one whom I thought to be the perfection of his sex—the very soul of honour, and who could sooner have sacrificed his own existence than have attempted to deceive any mortal being, much more one of that sex whom he professed to admire so much.

"The tempter had succeeded—he had entrapped me into the snare he had laid for me, and from that fatal moment I was lost.

"Oh, God! little did I dream of the fatal consequences which were about so soon to follow; little did I anticipate that, from the very moment when I had sacrificed my confidence to the man who had implanted himself so deeply in my heart, I had plunged at once into the very vortex of destruction and crime.

"My dreams were now those of bliss; I flattered myself that I had gained a heart of which any one might have been envious, and of the possession of which I was far unworthy, and my joy, my pride were unbounded.

"It was some time ere I awoke from this vision of felicity, and then how terrible were my thoughts! Even now I fear to look back upon them.

"But I am wandering from the main thread of my melancholy narrative. From the moment that our mutual sentiments were communicated to each other, the restraint which had hitherto marked my conduct towards Sir Martin was thrown aside, and I met him with confidence and undisguised pleasure.

"He saw his triumph, and he took advantage of the power he had gained over me. He elicited from me the most candid and ample acknowledgement of my sentiments, and I admitted that nothing whatever could diminish the passion which he had excited in my bosom.

"Weak, foolish girl! And yet was I not so much to blame, unsophisticated and inexperienced as I was, and so little prepared to combat the powerful and flattering arguments of an accomplished libertine.

"My life hitherto had been one of comparative seclusion, seeing no one but the persons who were confined within the limited circle of our acquaintance; and although my parents had taken every care to inspire me with feelings of the strictest virtue, their own confined experience of the arts and deceptions practised in the busy world, from which they had been, as it were, estranged almost from childhood, rendered them very inadequate to the task.

"Destitute of guile themselves, they suspected it not in others, and least of all were they likely to imagine it in one who knew so well how to play the hypocrite, and to ingratiate himself into the good graces of even the initiated, as was Sir Martin de Lancy.

"Thus were we all made the innocent victims of his treacherous designs.

"My parents could not be blind to the marked attentions which Sir Martin paid me, and the evident pleasure with which I received them. They often questioned me upon the subject, and elicited the truth; and so far from expressing any disapprobation of the sentiments which they imagined had sprung up between us, they gave them every encouragement; they were anxious to see me settled in life with a worthy man, and believing firmly that Sir Martin was that individual, they rejoiced in the prospect of my happiness, before it might please the Almighty to deprive me of their protection.

"Fallacious hope! Oh, my poor, my excellent, my beloved parents! What scalding tears of anguish fall from my eyes while I write these lines, and reflect upon the manner —the cruel manner in which your fondest wishes for your darling child, on whom you had bestowed so much care, so much anxiety and attention, were doomed to be disappointed.

"Myself and Sir Martin daily took long rambles in the romantic neighbourhood of my dwelling, where I paid a ready and attentive ear to all the honied accents and protestations he made, and reciprocated his vows and sentiments with equal ardour, but, oh, how much more sincerity. These were the most delicious hours of my existence that I had ever experienced, and I fondly flattered myself that they were destined to last for ever— that nothing could occur to disturb that blissful dream. Oh, God! how fearfully have I been deceived! What a horrible reality am I awakened to now.

"It was in the course of one of those fatal rambles that he obtained from me my consent to his acknowledging to my parents the mutual sentiments we felt for each other, and of requesting their permission to his paying his addresses to me, declaring that that once gained he would only await the approbation of his father, before making me his bride; and that, even should he fail in doing that, he would run any risk, even that of his eternal displeasure, sooner than he would be false to the vows he had made to me. On the possession of my hand and my affections, he added, depended his only hope of happiness in this world, and without securing them, all he had to do was to die.

"Oh, the heartless villain! That the treacherous words should not have scorched his tongue as he gave utterance to them. No wonder that he should have imposed upon so artless and inexperienced a girl as me! Yes, I believed every word he spoke, and felt myself the happiest of human beings, while, alas! I was upon the very brink of destruction.

"Having received my consent, and finding that I reposed every confidence in him, Sir Martin seized the earliest opportunity of throwing himself at the feet of my parents, and confessing the love that he pretended to bear towards me, and the honour of his intentions to implore them to sanction his addresses to me.

"They listened to him with pleasure, for, like me, they firmly believed in the sincerity of his protestations; and hearing not only from his lips, but mine own, that my heart beat in unison with his, they expressed very warmly their approbation of the passion that had sprung up between us, and not only gave every encouragement to it, but entertained the most sanguine hopes of the happiness that would accrue to me from such a desirable alliance; and, whilst the insidious villain was contemplating the basest designs for my destruction, and flattering himself with the certain prospect of their success, anticipated the brightest scenes for the future.

"From that time forward, Sir Martin never missed a day in visiting me at my residence, and we were left to the free and uninterrupted indulgence of our thoughts. Every hour the ardour of his passion seemed to increase, and mine gained proportionate strength and confidence. When he was away, I was truly miserable, and when he was present my eyes brightened with pleasure, and my heart bounded with a feeling which I find it almost impossible to describe.

"A thousand times I blessed the accident which had introduced us to each other. Oh! had I known all, what good cause had I indeed to curse it.

"At length Sir Martin informed me that he had received a letter from his father, demanding his immediate presence in England, and that in a week, at the farthest, he must depart in obedience to his wishes.

"Need I attempt to describe the anguish, the unconquerable apprehensions with which I received this intelligence? I was for a time completely inconsolable, but Sir Martin endeavoured to quiet my fears, by assuring me that he would return as speedily as possible, and, having won the consent of his father, which he felt satisfied of doing, make me his bride. He knew the power he possessed over my credulity, and exercised it accordingly. He succeeded too well.

"My parents, on hearing of Sir Martin's summons to England, were no less grieved than myself; but still they placed every confidence in the honour and integrity of his promises, and endeavoured to comfort me, and inspire me with hope.

"As for myself, I was almost broken-hearted, and, as the time drew near when Sir Martin was to depart, my despair increased, and I turned a deaf ear to all attempts at consolation. Sleep never visited my pillow at night, and the only respite I gained from my sorrows, was when I was in the company of my lover, or, rather, my deceiver.

"The fatal moment of my destruction was at hand. The evening arrived prior to the morning on which Sir Martin was to depart; and oh! what an evening of anguish was it to me. We had been together the whole of the day, and my parents left us almost entirely to ourselves. Never did experienced hypocrite so powerfully exercise his eloquence and arts of deception as Sir Martin de Lancy did on that occasion. Again and again he repeated the vows he had made on former occasions, and expressed in glowing and affectionate terms the agony he felt at even a temporary separation from me; but declared that no power on earth should prevent him from returning as speedily as possible, and making me his wife.

"The hour arrived when he must take leave of me, perhaps for ever. Oh, never can I forget the anguish I felt at that moment. He strained me to his bosom, and pressed the most ardent kisses upon my unresisting lips; whilst the convulsive sobs which agitated my bosom completely choked my utterance. It was to me as severe a trial as parting with life and soul; and, even had I the will, I could not have restrained the expression of my emotions. The villain must have seen the advantage he had gained over me—that he held me entirely in his power; and no doubt he exulted in his triumph; for at that moment he must have seen that his diabolical plans were all but accomplished.

"At length he uttered the melancholy word—farewell—and tore himself away. I sank in a paroxysm of uncontrollable anguish on a seat, and covering my face with my hands, I remained in a state of utter unconsciousness, until I was aroused by my parents, who led me into their apartment, and tried all that affection could suggest to console me, but for some time without the least effect. At length they persuaded me to retire to my chamber, and there to endeavour to gain repose. I was glad to avail myself of the opportunity of being alone, that I might give uninterrupted indulgence to my own thoughts and sorrows; but, as for sleep, I knew well that in my present dreadfully agitated state of mind, it would be impossible for me to obtain any.

"I threw myself on a sofa, and for some time I gave way entirely to the excessive violence of my grief, and deplored the cruelty of my destiny. Oh, had I but known the villanous designs of my betrayer, how thankful ought I to have been that he was taken from me—how heartily should I have prayed that I might never behold him again.

"I must have sat in this state for some time; for suddenly I was aroused by the clock in the mansion striking the hour of ten, and it was early when I had quitted my parents.

"I started up, looked around me, and listened. All was perfectly still in the house, and I was satisfied that my parents and the rest of the family must have retired to rest.

"It was a beautiful night, and the moon was shining brightly in at my window, and imparted a sensation of tranquillity to my agitated feelings.

"I breathed a prayer to Heaven for the safety of my lover, and then advanced towards the window, and gently opening it, gazed with undiminished delight and admiration at the scenery, of which it commanded so extensive a view.

"I had not been long thus occupied when I heard a rustling noise beneath my window, and directly afterwards my name was repeated in a subdued but impressive voice.

"'Be not alarmed, dearest Almira,' said Sir Martin; 'and, oh, pardon me for this boldness; but indeed I could not resist the temptation of once more beholding you, and bidding you again farewell ere we part for Heaven knows how long.'

"'Oh, Martin,' I faltered out, 'what a dreadful trial is this! And now that I again behold you, and know how soon we must separate, perhaps never to meet again, all my anguish is renewed with tenfold violence.'

"'My Almira!' said Sir Martin, and he looked up in my countenance with an expression of persuasive eloquence and tenderness, 'I almost fear to put the question, only that I am certain that you cannot put a wrong construction upon my motives, and that you can well imagine the feelings which prompt me to this step; but will you not descend to me, if only for a few minutes, that I may whisper in your ear the tender emotions which now agitate my soul, and once more permit me to press the kiss of love upon your beauteous lips at parting. Oh, what a sweet solace will it be to me in this hour of trial, and I know that my Almira will not refuse me.'

"And could I refuse? Oh, no! My own heart and inclinations urged me on. I thought not of the impropriety of granting this clandestine interview; fondly as I loved him, and confident as I was of his honour and integrity, I could not entertain the least fear. I therefore whispered my consent, and retired from the window.

"Oh, blind infatuation! Fiends of darkness hovered around me at that moment, and contemplated the certainty of my destruction with exultation. My doom was indeed sealed, and nothing could save me from it. I gently opened the door of my chamber, and stepping lightly to the head of the staircase, I listened with breathless attention; but not a sound disturbed the silence which reigned around. My parents and the domestics were evidently all at rest, and there was no danger of my being observed or interrupted.

"I descended the stairs, unfastened the outer door, and the next moment was clasped to the throbbing bosom of my secretly exulting betrayer.

"For a few minutes we were so overcome by the different feelings which agitated our breasts that we could neither of us speak; but at length, Sir Martin having gently released me from his embrace, and looking affectionately in my face, ejaculated in those impressive tones he so well knew how to assume,—

"'Beloved, adored Almira! how can I ever sufficiently thank you for this sweet condescension? Oh, had it not been granted me, what tenfold misery would have accompanied me in my dreary journey.'"

"' Alas! dear Martin,' I sighed, 'and must we indeed part so soon? Oh! how shall I be able to support the dismal hours during your absence ?'

"' Be comforted, my sweet Almira,' he answered; 'Providence will watch over you, and I trust quickly restore us to each other. But we might be observed here; let us retire to the summer-house, where we can confer for a few minutes without fear of interruption.'

"My thoughts were so bewildered and distressed, that I scarcely knew what I did; but I offered no objection, and taking my arm, he gently led me to the summer-house, in which we had often passed so many happy hours; and here we gave vent to our feelings without restraint.

"Oh, let me hurry over the fearful and guilty scene which followed. Even now, after the lapse of time, as I recall it to my memory, burning feelings of shame and remorse agitate my breast. Suffice it that that hour marked my ruin; madness must have seized upon my brain; the villain, Sir Martin de Lancy, triumphed, and I fell!

"My God! how can I record the shameful, the disgusting truth? The bare recollection should sink me into the earth; and 'tis well that I am hidden from the world, and no longer permitted to contaminate the pure and virtuous by my presence. My heart is sick! my hand trembles, and I must again pause in my melancholy recital of shame and sorrow."

    *   *   *   *   *   *   *   *

"Unfortunate woman," said Ethelbert, when he had arrived at this part of the confession: "your's is, indeed, a melancholy history; and how deeply are you to be pitied, greatly even as you have erred. Sir Martin de Lancy, my uncle, you must have been a bad man, and your treacherous conduct to this poor, confiding woman, must ever fix disgrace upon your memory. I blush to own you for my relative."

After a pause, Ethelbert continued the manuscript to its conclusion.

"Great God!" the manuscript went on to say, "how can I properly depicture the horror, shame, disgust, and remorse, to which I was awakened from this guilty scene? Even now the remembrance curdles the blood in my veins. I must have been a hardened, callous wretch, or the sudden knowledge of my fallen, degraded state, should have struck me a corpse at the feet of the destroyer of my innocence. True, a fearful mist was removed from before mine eyes, and I started from his embrace, and for a few moments gazed at him with an expression of shame and remorse which I find it impossible to describe. The villain felt his triumph; he knew that he had completed his infamous task, that he held me in his power, and he stood before me unabashed.

"Oh, he must, indeed, have been a hardened scoundrel, otherwise the sense of the enormity of his offence, the wretched being he had made of that poor, confiding girl, who before was innocent, would have struck him dumb.

"But no; he again snatched me to his bosom; pressed warm and deceptive kisses upon my lips, and by all those artifices in which he was so thoroughly accomplished, endeavoured to sooth me into composure. He repeated his former vows; assured me that he would speedily return from England, and make me his bride; and that what had now taken place between us but increased his love, and that nothing whatever should induce him to prove faithless to me.

"Weak fool that I was, how readily was I deceived; how easily was I persuaded to believe his false and flattering asseverations. I returned his caresses with equal ardour; repeated my fatal vows; and when the moment arrived for us to separate, I still clung to him with mad fondness and regret. Indeed, such was the influence that my seducer had gained over me, even though I knew he had sunk me to the level of the most degraded of my sex, that I was willing to become the partner of his journey, and could have abandoned home, parents, everything, and resigned myself entirely to his power, had he made the proposition.

"The libertine, no doubt, saw the triumph he had gained over me; and how greatly must he in secret have exulted at the ruin he had caused, and the further misery which he contemplated. At length the farewell word was uttered; with sobbing anguish I tore myself from his arms, and he conducted me to the house; then snatching from my lips one burning kiss, he bounded from the house, and was out of sight long before I had recovered from the state of confusion, agitation, and perplexity of mind into which I had been thrown by the fatal and shameful events of the last hour.

"What a miserable being did he leave me; how fallen; how much to be pitied, yet how greatly to be despised. I paused on the threshold, and all the horrors of my situation burst in burning fervour upon my brain. I was lost, ruined for ever! The seducer had triumphed—my innocence was destroyed, and what could ever restore the peace of mind I formerly enjoyed.

"Yes; Sir Martin de Lancy had triumphed; he had achieved his diabolical object; he held me completely at his mercy, and probably I might never behold him again. He would, perhaps, smile at my degradation, and despise and loathe me for so easily becoming a victim to his nefarious plans. Horrible thought! what torturing, what insupportable pangs it inflicted upon my bosom when it occurred to me, and yet it was by far too probable for me easily to reject it.

"Still I paused at the door, and my heart palpitated violently, whilst the blood seemed to rush like liquid fire through my veins. My limbs trembled, and I was ready to sink down upon the earth. Would to Heaven that I could have done so and died; what years of suffering, remorse, and shame, would it have saved me.

"How could I again meet the searching eyes of my affectionate parents? Oh, what an ungrateful return had I made for the years of love, and attention, and anxiety they had bestowed upon me. What disgrace, what irremediable disgrace had I brought upon their hitherto unsullied name; and what would be the horror of their feelings when the dreadful truth could no longer be concealed from them?

"This thought alone was enough to overwhelm me, and it was wonderful how I could find fortitude to support it. A death-like faintness came over me, and I still hesitated at the door, fearful to re-enter that home which I had by my misconduct rendered miser-- able, and whose amiable inmates slept in utter unconsciousness of the shame which their only and beloved child had within the last short hour brought upon them.

"The old clock striking the hour of twelve aroused me, and opening the door, I traversed the hall and ascended the stairs which conducted to my chamber, with noiseless steps, like those of a thief.

"When I had gained my room, I threw myself on my knees, and burying my face in my hands, for some time became completely lost in the agony of my feelings. I awoke to a terrific certainty of the degradation which had fallen upon me; of the villanous part which Sir Martin had played; and the almost certainty that now he had triumphed, I should never behold him again; and madness almost seized upon my brain. One moment I was half tempted to lay violent hands on myself, and thus to end at once my misery; and then again some instinctive power withheld me, and, in spite of everything, inspired ...e with something like a feeling of hope. Sir Martin surely could never be so great a miscreant as to deceive me, after the solemn vows he had made? Alas! what a poor, weak fool I must have been to imagine that the man who could have had the heart to take advantage of my innocence, would hesitate at anything. He could never have loved me sincerely, or he would have shrunk with horror and disgust from the bare contemplation of such a crime.

"It would be a completely fruitless task for me to attempt to describe the horrors I endured on that fatally memorable night. I raved and wept by turns; sometimes reproaching, in the most bitter terms, myself and Sir Martin for what had happened; and at others, calling in the most affectionate accents upon his name, invoking blessings upon his head, and imploring Heaven to restore him quickly to me, that he might fulfil the promise he had made to me, and make me his lawful bride. But I never attempted to undress myself, and though I threw myself upon the bed, slumber came not to my relief. It was, indeed, madness to think of it.

"What racking thoughts flitted across my brain! they were sufficient to drive me to madness, and, indeed, I was at times quite delirious, raving in the wildest manner. It was fortunate that no one was present to overhear me, or I must undoubtedly have betrayed the whole dreadful truth.

"The morning found me in a high fever, and unable to rise from my bed, and when Ulrica entered my chamber, which was her custom, she was greatly alarmed at my appearance, and eagerly inquired what had occurred to place me in this situation. I threw myself sobbing in her arms, and was unable to return any answer. The feelings which overpowered me at that moment I can never forget, but my principal horror was at the thought of beholding my parents, whom Ulrica considered it necessary immediately to make acquainted with my alarming condition.

"My God! how could I encounter their searching glances, knowing myself the guilty, fallen creature that I was? My brain whirled round at the thought, and when my father and mother entered the chamber, they found me in a state insensibility.

"In this condition I remained for several days, only reviving for a brief period at intervals, and it was wonderful that I did not, during that time, betray myself; but I did not, although, as I was told, I raved almost incessantly of Sir Martin; and my parents, therefore, concluded that it was in consequence of his departure, that I suffered so severely.

"But when I was restored to something like reason, and beheld my affectionate parents hanging over me with anxious solicitude, how I shrunk appalled from their tender glances, and hid my blushes of shame, self-reproach, and compunction, beneath the bed-- clothes. I felt as if my heart would burst; and it would have been a mercy to me had it done so at that moment, and have buried for ever in oblivion the knowledge of my guilt and degradation. But Providence had ordained that I should live for further punishment.

"It was several weeks before I was sufficiently restored to convalescence to leave my chamber, and then I had lost all my former cheerfulness, and was not at all like the same being. I trembled in the presence of my parents, and sought retirement at every opportunity, where I brooded over my secret sorrows, and passed my time in prayers to the Almighty, and in the most bitter self-reproaches.

"My poor parents attributed my sufferings entirely to the departure of Sir Martin, and exerted themselves to the utmost to console me; but their endeavours only added to my anguish and regret, feeling, as I did, and that most acutely, how utterly unworthy I was of them.

"Another week passed away, when I received a letter from Sir Martin. With what trembling haste, with what mingled hopes and fears I broke the seal, and for a few moments my eyes were so dimmed with tears, that I could not trace the characters. But when I did, hope was revived within my bosom. Sir Martin breathed the same ardent protestations of love and constancy which he had so often whispered in my ears, and declared that he was one of the most miserable of human beings in his absence from me. He assured me that I was constantly in his thoughts, and that he looked forward to the time when we should meet again, and he should once more enfold me in his arms, with the most eager impatience. He implored me to keep up my spirits, and assured me that our separation should not be for long.

"He said that he had not yet had an opportunity of revealing his passion to his father, but that he would do so without delay, and that he had not the least doubt of his success, and that he should shortly have the felicity of returning to Normandy to make me his bride.

"Alas! how was I deceived by this specious epistle; fresh hopes animated my breast; I placed every reliance on his truth, and the sense of my shame lost half its weight.

"I shewed the letter to my parents, for there was nothing in it that could excite their suspicions, and they congratulated me on his constancy, and encouraged me to hope that he would not fail to fulfil the promises he had made, and that the time was not far distant when my happiness would be made complete.

"Oh, how the words went to my heart! and how bitterly I reproached myself when I knew, I felt, that the time was not far distant when the full extent of my guilt could no longer be concealed from them. What then would be their misery, their disgust, their despair! I shuddered at the thought.

"It was several days before I could find fortitude to return an answer to my seducer, and then I revealed to him the whole truth; that I was in a condition shortly to become a mother; and implored him by all his vows of unalterable affection, by every law of justice and humanity, not to deceive me, but to snatch me from the shame and misery of which he had been the cause, and to save my hitherto spotless character from the opprobrious voice of scandal.

"A fortnight elapsed before I received an answer to this letter, and the agony and anxiety of mind I endured during that interval may readily be imagined. In fact, I was worked up to a pitch of almost utter despair; for a dreadful thought came across my brain that Sir Martin, on receiving the delicate intelligence it had been my painful duty to communicate to him, had resolved to abandon me altogether, and to leave me to my fate.

"But surely, I reflected, he could not be so heartless a miscreant! I could not believe that there could be so base an hypocrite in the world. Alas! how inexperienced was I in the guilt and treachery of mankind at that time; but it was not long that I was permitted to remain in that state of ignorance.

"In the moments of my deepest anguish and despair, how sincerely, how fervently did I pray that I might die ere my shame should become apparent; for how could I ever meet the reproaches of my amiable parents, whom I had so cruelly deceived?

"At length, however, I did receive another letter from Sir Martin. It was a very different one to the former; but he again repeated his vows of unalterable affection, and begged of me to keep up my spirits, for that he would return to Normandy as soon as he could, though the time when he should be able to do so was at present uncertain. He added that he had confessed his passion to his father, but he had unfortunately expressed his entire disapprobation of his contracting a matrimonial alliance at present; however, he urged me not to despair, for no power on earth should prevent him from fulfilling his promise at the earliest opportunity.

"This last announcement was a death-blow to my hopes, notwithstanding Sir Martin's protestations. I saw plainly that he could never be mine, and the whole horror of my fate burst at once, with overwhelming force, upon my imagination. The letter fell from my hand, a giddiness seized upon my brain, and I dropped upon the floor insensible.

"In that state I was found by my mother; and, picking up the letter, she became acquainted with the whole painful and disgraceful truth.

"How shall I describe their anguish—their poignant despair? Oh, that I should ever recover again to behold it! But they heaped upon me no reproaches; their hearts were ready to burst with the torture of the unexpected discovery, but they could only weep scalding tears of agony and regret over their poor fallen child, and reprobate the dark designing treachery of my destroyer. Their commiseration in my melancholy fate was far more agonizing to me than even their resentment would have been, for I felt how ill I deserved it, since I had brought such eternal disgrace upon their hitherto unsullied name. Alas! what atonement was it in my power to make? I wished myself dead, for I felt as if I had become a scandal upon society.

"I could see plain enough that my parents placed no confidence in the promises of Sir Martin, especially since his father had refused his sanction to his paying his addresses to me, and this added to the despair and agony of my mind. I again became seriously ill, and for some weeks my life was despaired of.

"In the meantime my father wrote to Sir Martin a letter, in which he bitterly reproached him for the misery he had caused, but implored him, if he possessed one spark of the honour he professed to have, to make all the atonement in his power, by redeeming the promise he had so solemnly pledged to me, and not to suffer me to sink entirely into shame and disgrace.

"Weeks elapsed, and to this letter we received no answer, and the black-hearted villany and hypocrisy of Sir Martin were now apparent. It became evident that the vows he had made were all false, and that he had no intention whatever of fulfilling his promise. The veil was torn from before my eyes, and I became distracted. The sufferings of my unhappy parents were almost equal to my own; but still they endeavoured to console me, and offered not one word of reproach towards me.

"No language could describe in adequate terms the remorse I endured—the bitter remorse I felt for the misery and shame I had caused—the reproaches I heaped upon the name of my heartless seducer. How I continued to exist with all this weight of care upon my conscience, I know not.

"But at length I did again recover sufficiently to be able to leave my room, and when I could muster resolution enough to perform so painful and arduous a task, I sat myself down, and wrote another letter to my betrayer. The forcible appeal I there made to him surely must have moved him, had he possessed one spark of feeling or honour; but Sir Martin was destitute of either, and therefore I might have expected to have been disappointed.

"With what insupportable anxiety I awaited his reply, after I had despatched this letter! but days, weeks, passed away, and it came not, and my despair and misery were rendered complete. It was certain, too fatally certain, that he had abandoned me, and left me to bear the whole weight of disgrace which he had brought upon me. My parents had no consolation to offer me; for how could they attempt to deceive me by leading me to hope for justice from one who had proved himself a heartless and unprincipled scoundrel?

"They became seriously alarmed at my condition; but, for my own part, I viewed it with indifference, for life had become a curse to me, since I could no more show my face in the world without a blush. The finger of scorn and opprobrium would be pointed at me, and I trembled at the thought. Death would indeed be a happy release to me from my sorrows, and I prayed for it hourly. But little did I imagine that I was reserved to endure still greater torture, and to become the perpetrator of a crime at which humanity shudders.

"Oh, God! how fearfully have I been punished, for only in my woman's confiding weakness lending too ready an ear to the voice of the seducer! My brain maddens! My murdered child, oh, why were you ever permitted to see the light of heaven!

*   *   *   *   *   *   *   *   *   *

"The agony of my bodily and mental sufferings brought on premature labour, and I gave birth to a lovely girl. Oh, what excruciating torture wrung my soul, when its innocent cry smote my ears, and convinced me that the offspring of my shame lived! In the frenzy of my despair, I reproached Heaven for not having killed it in my womb; and when I first beheld its cherub face, even then so like its guilty father, it was with no mother's feelings that I gazed upon it, but I shrunk from it with horror, as though it was something hideous.

"My confinement was long and dangerous, and it was not expected by any one that I could possibly recover. Oh, how affectionately did my poor mother constantly attend upon me, and how many were the tears of anguish she shed as she pressed my unfortunate infant to her bosom, and invoked the blessings of Heaven on its head. God forgive me! but at that moment her blessings seemed like a bitter mockery to my distracted imagination, and curses even would have been more congenial to my ears.

"Again my father wrote to Sir Martin, informing him of my accouchement, and reproaching him for his cruelty, at the same time that he eloquently appealed to his honour and humanity (if he possessed the smallest particle of either, which there was too much reason to suppose he did not), to redeem the promise he had so solemnly made to me, and not to leave me entirely to the shame and degradation of the world. He assured him that, notwithstanding his cruel conduct, I still loved him with undiminished fervour. And he spoke the truth—poor weak fool that I was!

"To this letter also, like the others which had been forwarded to my heartless betrayer, no answer was returned, and my anguish increased to such a degree that it would be impossible for me to describe it properly. Heaven only knows how I was enabled to exist under such trying, such unparalleled circumstances.

"As I gazed upon the innocent face of my babe (God forgive me!), I could not help secretly wishing that it was dead, and frequently such dreadful thoughts entered my mind that, when I was recalled to reason, I myself shuddered at their contemplation, and exerted myself to fly from them.

"Oh, Sir Martin! remorseless man! could you then have beheld me and your innocent offspring, surely your heart must have been moved to pity and repentance. And yet, how can I imagine so, after what subsequently occurred?

"Oh, never can I cease to remember, with feelings of the most unbounded gratitude, the affectionate sympathy, solicitude, and attention, with which my parents watched over me during this painful period. And yet, to think that I afterwards should make so cruel a return for all! Oh, I have indeed been a most guilty wretch, and richly do I merit the punishment I am now undergoing.

"I recovered sufficiently to be able to leave my room; but I never quitted the house. I was ashamed to meet the eyes of my former companions; for I thought that they must look upon me with shame and disgust—poor, fallen, degraded creature as I felt myself to be. I sought seclusion, that I might brood without interruption over my sorrows, and I would, if I could have done so with any show of reason, have avoided even the society of my parents. I loudly prayed for death, and nothing whatever could impart the least consolation to me. Yet even amidst all this, and with the constant recollection of the cruelty and deceit of Sir Martin present in such vivid colours to my mind, I could not conquer the love with which he had inspired me. How bitterly I wept when I reflected on the disappointment to the brilliant and sanguine hopes I had formed, and pictured to myself the misery which was, probably, yet in store for me.

"That Sir Martin had entirely abandoned me—that he could never have loved me with the ardour and sincerity which he had professed to do, now became but too fearfully certain to me; I must indeed have been blind and deluded to have entertained for a moment any other idea. And what was there left to me but utter despair?

"But I am becoming tedious, and must hasten to a conclusion of my dreadful narrative. God give me strength to do so! for the most appalling part is left for me to relate. And why should I repeat the revolting horrors?—why should I not seek to bury them for ever in oblivion?

"My father, determined to leave no means untried to see justice rendered to me by my seducer, now addressed a letter to his father, making him acquainted with all that had happened, and demanding from him that justice which his guilty son had denied.

"In about a week an answer was returned by Sir Hildebrand, which was at once calculated to dissipate any hopes which we might have previously entertained. It was cold, formal, and decisive. He regretted that Sir Martin should have been so "imprudent," and that he could not for a moment think of suffering him to form an alliance which, after what had taken place especially, he considered was every way so unworthy of him.

"Unworthy of him! How the cruel and haughty words grated upon my ears; and how base and sordid must be the mind that could conceive them! More keenly than ever did I feel my debasement, and the grief and indignation of my amiable parents exceeded all bounds. And yet, notwithstanding all, they endeavoured to tranquillise me. How futile was the task! What could impart consolation to a heart afflicted like mine? It would have been a mercy to me could I have laid myself down and died.

" Oh, Sir Martin! how little did I ever for a moment suspect that you could have acted in such a monstrous, such an inhuman manner! And perhaps he was about to lead another to the altar! Nay, he might already be united! The bare idea of this tortured me more than all, and almost drove me to madness.

" I was once more confined to my bed, and my life was pronounced, by my medical attendants, to be in danger. It was wonderful how my poor parents could support the fatigue and anxiety, both of mind and body, they had to undergo, and to think that I should afterwards make them so ungrateful a return! Oh, what mercy dare I hope for, or expect to receive, after all my guilty conduct?

" My beloved parents! are you still living? Oh, no; it is impossible that you could have survived the base perfidy of your daughter, on whom you lavished every fond indulgence. God grant that he may have taken you to his bosom, and that we may never meet again; for how dare I, wretch that I am, even contemplate encountering your eyes, now that my soul is stained with blood! Yes; the horrible crime of infanticide now weighs upon the conscience of your once innocent daughter.

" Dreadful thought! How it racks and scorches my brain! My hand trembles, and again am I compelled to pause in the melancholy task I have imposed upon myself.

* * * * * * * *

" Once more I take up the pen, although it is with a trembling hand and a faltering heart; for how dreadful are the facts I have now to relate! and in the gloom of this dreary dungeon how frightful are the images that are conjured up before my disordered fancy! But it is a task that I have imposed upon myself, with the hope that this confession may at some future period meet the eyes of one of my own sex, and be a salutary warning to her to shun those paths of vice which have plunged me into irretrievable misery and shame. The thought is a wild one, I admit; but still I cannot banish it.

" Two months elapsed, and by the sedulous attention of my parents, the excellent advice they gave to me, and the consolation they took such pains to impart, I was once more restored to comparative health; but a heavy melancholy, almost as fearful as my most frenzied moments, settled upon my heart, and from which nothing whatever could arouse me.

" With the hope of affording my mind some relief, my parents persuaded me to leave the house sometimes, and inhale the salubrity of the air; but they always accompanied me, and I took especial care to avoid all those places where I was likely to encounter any of my former acquaintances; for I could not meet them without the blush of shame and remorse, so keenly did I feel my own degradation.

" The places I most delighted to ramble among were those I had been in the habit of frequenting in the society of my seducer, particularly the fatal spot where I had met with the accident which had first introduced us to each other; and many were the tears I shed when I recalled the dismal circumstances to my memory, and bitterly did I reproach the hard destiny which had attended me.

" Most willingly would I have concealed my shame and misery in the seclusion of a convent, where I might endeavour to seek forgiveness of my Maker and prepare myself for eternity; for the world was now hateful to me, and I considered that I had no business in it, after the manner in which I had fallen. But my parents would not listen to such a proposition, and still exerted themselves to the utmost to inspire me with fortitude and hope.

" Oh, would to Heaven that they had suffered me to follow the bent of my inclinations, then should I at least have been spared the perpetration of the dreadful crime which now presses so heavily upon my conscience.

" My child daily improved in appearance, and more striking became her likeness to her guilty father. But I could not gaze upon her with the tender feelings of a mother—nay, there were moments when the contemplation of her innocent features inspired me with the most uncontrollable horror. Surely it must have been caused by a presentiment of what I was destined to commit. I was never so happy as when she was out of my sight, and she was almost constantly confided to the care of Ulrica, who was as much attached to her as if she was her own infant.

"It was about this period that I was sitting one evening alone in my chamber, and brooding over my numerous sorrows, when I was suddenly aroused by hearing a gentle tap at the door, and desiring whoever it was to walk in, Ulrica entered the room, with impatience in the expression of her countenance and general demeanour.

"'Oh, ma'amselle !' she ejaculated hastily, when she had closed the door, 'I have seen him !'

"'Seen him !' I exclaimed, looking at her with astonishment, and my heart throbbing with anxiety; 'who—who do you mean ?'

"'Sir Martin de Lancy,' answered the imprudent woman ; 'not an hour since, I met him. He is concealed in this neighbourhood. He has returned to render you justice, and ——'

"I could hear no more, but uttering a scream of agony, I fainted, and Ulrica then saw the imprudence of which she had been guilty, in communicating to me the important and unexpected intelligence so abruptly, and became seriously alarmed for the consequences; but she exerted herself to the utmost to recover me, and at last she succeeded.

"'Oh, Ulrica,' I exclaimed, 'how painfully interesting is the information you have imparted to me ! But tell me, is it true ?'

"'It is indeed, madam,' she answered ; 'you cannot suppose that I would tell you an untruth ; but pray compose yourself, and I will tell you all about it.'

"I clasped my hands together, and sunk on my knees.

"'My God !' I exclaimed, 'hast thou, then, heard my prayers, and has he indeed repented, and returned hither to render me all the atonement in his power? Oh, Sir Martin ! how bitterly must you reproach yourself for the misery you have caused me ! But keep me not suspense, Ulrica; tell me everything. Where did you meet Sir Martin ? —What did he say to you?—How looked he, and——'

"I could not finish the sentence, my agitation was so great, and I paused for breath, and looked with the most intense anxiety in the countenance of Ulrica.

"'Ah, madam,' she observed, 'Sir Martin looked so sad and melancholy, and trembled so violently when he asked after you and the infant, that I am certain his heart is stung with remorse for the suffering he has caused you, and that he is anxious to make some atonement for his past errors.'

"'Heaven send that he may,' I cried, whilst my bosom heaved with the most convulsive emotion. 'But where is he staying?—Why did he not answer my letters ?—Why did he not come at once to the chateau, if his intentions are honest and honourable? Oh, tell me all, Ulrica; you can be able to form no idea of the maddening state of my feelings, or you would not keep me in this dreadful state of anxiety and suspense.'

"'Pardon me, madame,' returned Ulrica, 'but I am indeed most anxious to make you acquainted with all I know; but I wish you, for your own sake, to tranquillise your feelings, and to hope for the best ; for I am certain, I feel confident, that you will not be disappointed. Where Sir Martin is at present staying I know not ; but he said he had been waiting near the chateau, watching, with the hope of either seeing you or me, for the last two days. And, oh, madam, had you heard him appeal to me, and the anguish he evinced at the suffering you had endured, you ——'

"'Yes, yes,' I interrupted, breathlessly and impatiently; 'but quick, tell me all—tell me everything. Oh, God ! so near to me, and yet not to seek an interview with her on whom he has inflicted so dreadful an injury ! Ulrica, you torture me.'

"'Heaven forbid !' replied Ulrica. 'No one can be more anxious than myself to see you comforted, madame ; but it would occupy too much time to repeat to you all Sir Martin said to me, and this letter which he requested me to deliver to you will most probably explain everything.'

"'A letter !' I exclaimed, 'a letter ! and from him whom I had never expected to behold or to hear from again ! Oh, give it me !'

"I snatched the letter eagerly from Ulrica's hand, and as my eyes fell upon the superscription, in the well-known characters of my seducer, my tears gushed forth unrestrained, and I was so overpowered by my varied emotions that I could scarcely contain myself. Two or three times I made an effort to break the seal, but my hand trembled so excessively that I failed, and I sunk in a chair, and for a few moments was almost suffocated by convulsive sobs. Even at that time a terrible foreboding that there was something dangerous in even perusing the contents of the letter crossed my mind, and I hesitated to do so until I had made my parents acquainted with all the circumstances. There was

something, I could not help thinking, grossly imprudent in keeping it a secret from them, even for an instant; and hastily arising from my chair, I was about to make my way to their apartment, with the letter in my hand, when Ulrica supplicated me to forbear, and at least to peruse the contents of the epistle, and endeavour to regain some composure, before I ventured to appear before them, and to communicate that which must naturally so much excite them.

"I yielded to her request, and breaking the seal, with eyes almost blinded by tears, I read the fatal letter from the arch fiend in human form, who, not satisfied with the disgrace, the sorrow, and ruin he had already inflicted upon me, was determined to complete his atrocity by one of the most monstrous plans that could ever have entered into the mind of man.

"Alas! how skilfully had he concocted this letter to his unfortunate victim! Every word that he had written, as I perused it, took possession of my reason, and bound me still closer to his power. How powerfully and how plausibly did he profess his penitence of the wrongs he had done me, and his anxiety to make me all the atonement in his power, by, at least, uniting his fate with mine. How forcibly did he excuse himself for not answering my letters, and declared that it was entirely owing to the opposition of his father, who wished him to marry another woman, whom he could not love, and whose eternal wrath he was determined to risk, if I would consent to become his bride. But he earnestly implored me to keep the fact of his return to Normandy a secret from my parents, for the present, and stated that he had particular reasons for wishing me to do so, which he would satisfactorily explain to me if I would grant him a private interview at a place he would hereafter name. He concluded by imploring me, if I would not drive him to absolute madness and despair, to write him an answer to this letter, consenting to meet him, and to despatch it by Ulrica the next day, to the same place where she had met him, and where he would be waiting to see her.

"Again I perused this letter, and my heart wavered. The tone it breathed was apparently so sincere, that it took almost immediate possession of me. He could surely never be so great a villain, I thought, as to attempt to deceive me in so cruel a manner. Oh, no; his return to Normandy showed how honest was his repentance; and could I leave that man to despair, who, in spite of all that had happened, I could not help loving with an ardour which almost approached to adoration? Oh, no; I could not. My mind revolted from the bare idea. And yet, to keep my beloved parents in ignorance of his return, and the letter he had sent to me, was equally repugnant to my feelings; and ought to have been enough to have excited my strongest suspicions of the integrity of his motives, and at once have thwarted his diabolical designs.

"But the miscreant knew well the poor, weak, credulous fool he had to deal with, and, no doubt, was fully confident, in his own mind, of his success. And it too soon became complete.

"'He, no doubt, has ample reasons for wishing to keep this a secret from my parents, for the present,' I reflected, 'which he will, as he says, explain to my satisfaction when he sees me. I cannot refuse him. I will see him; and may the Almighty protect me from any danger that may threaten me.'

"I placed the letter in my bosom, and cautioning Ulrica not to mention a word to any one respecting what had happened, but to attend upon me in the morning, I dismissed her, without explaining anything further to her.

"When I was alone, how shall I seek to pourtray the variety of feelings which agitated my breast? The reader must imagine them, for I am incompetent to the task. I threw myself on my knees, and earnestly I supplicated the Supreme to guide me how to act.

"And was Sir Martin, indeed, truly penitent? Did he still love me? And was he sincere in his professions? The thought bewildered me with mingled feelings of doubt and delight.

"Then again I hesitated to comply with his request, and two or three times was almost determined to reveal the whole truth to my father and mother, and to be guided alone by their counsel and advice. Oh, would that I could have formed the resolution to adhere to this; then should I have been rescued from complete destruction. But the fatal love I still bore towards my guilty betrayer prevailed; and I at last was fully resolved to risk everything, and to meet him; for now that I knew he was so near, I could not rest until I had again beheld him.

"I at length, having somewhat tranquillised my feelings, sat down, and commenced writing my answer to the letter of Sir Martin. With glowing pathos, I depicted the sufferings I had for so many months endured, and gently reproaching him for the part he had acted, implored him, for the sake of our innocent child—for my sake—that of my afflicted parents, not to attempt, as he valued his own soul's welfare, to deceive me again; but to render me that atonement which he was bound in justice and honour to do, and by which means it could only be expected that the past might be forgiven and forgotten. I consented, at all hazards, to meet him, if he would appoint the place.

"After I had written this fatal answer, I almost repented of it, and was half inclined to destroy it, and to abandon my design; but again the insidious fiend who was urging me on to my destruction prevailed, and I sealed up the letter, and throwing myself dressed upon my couch, I became completely absorbed in tormenting thought.

"I slept not during the night; and, in the morning, my mind was, if possible, in a greater state of agitation than before. How could I meet my parents, I reflected, without revealing those particulars which at present so tortured my mind? And what would they think of my conduct when they should afterwards become acquainted with it? Was this a proper return for the affectionate indulgence they had bestowed upon me? Oh, no; I could not but acknowledge to myself that it was very different. I should have no secrets from them, and especially upon a subject on which their happiness, as well as my own, depended. Again was I half disposed to make them acquainted with everything, and to be guided entirely by their advice; but the earnest entreaties of Sir Martin in his letter, conquered all my objections, and I determined finally to proceed according to his request. Fatal decision! It sealed at once my fate.

"Ulrica soon afterwards made her appearance, and to her, then, knowing that I could confide in her, I communicated the substance of Sir Martin's letter; and she, poor, deluded woman! like myself, could see no cause of suspecting the real motives of my heartless and unprincipled seducer, and commended me for the resolution I had come to to see him, anticipating that he would explain everything to my satisfaction, and render me that justice which was my due.

"Placing the utmost reliance on Ulrica's integrity (as she had been with my parents from my birth), I gave her the letter I had written, for her perusal, and she not only approved of it, but expressed the warmest anticipations of the result.

"Alas, alas! I was held in a complete state of infatuation; my reason must have been demented, or I could never for a moment have given encouragement to such hopes; I must at once have seen through the snare which the villain, Sir Martin, had laid further to entrap me.

"Fearing to encounter the looks and the observations of my parents, I pleaded indisposition, so that I might keep myself confined to my own chamber, and indulge, without interruption or inquiry, in the multitudinous train of thoughts which crowded upon my brain, and (heaven pardon me!) never did I more successfully act the hypocrite that I did upon that occasion.

"My poor mother, of course anxious to attend upon me, and fearful that some serious illness had befallen me, immediately visited me; but so well I acted my part, that she was completely deceived, and, after passing a short time in conversation, left me to myself.

"God knows how I could so well assume the mask as to deceive her entirely; how I could behold her, and hear her affectionate, solicitous inquiries without betraying myself, and at once revealing all that had taken place, I know not, but so it was; but when she had retired, I burst into tears, bitter tears of remorse, and I reproached myself for the deception I had practised upon her, the consummate hypocrisy to which I had descended.

"Most anxiously did I await the return of Ulrica, and placing myself near the window, the minutes appeared like hours until I should behold her again.

"At intervals my heart failed me; I shuddered at the idea of the part of duplicity I was enacting, and I was half resolved to seek the presence of my parents, and to divulge to them all that had taken place, and be guided alone as they should advise; but the evil power that had gained possession of my senses and my reasoning faculties, withheld me, and precipitated me on towards my fate.

"I looked in the face of my child; it was the first time that I had done so with any degree of satisfaction. She no longer appeared to me, as she had before unnaturally done, an abortion. Her father was about to place her beyond the reach of scandal, I imagined. My heart was relieved of an insupportable burthen, and I was stimulated to proceed in the prosecution of my present fatal determinations.

"Ulrica at length returned. How eagerly I met her! She had seen Sir Martin at the appointed place, and he seemed delighted on reading the answer I had written to him. No doubt he was—at the triumph of his diabolical plans. He must have seen at once that he had his poor deluded victim completely in his meshes, and that it would be impossible for me, since I was so far entangled, to escape from them.

"Having desired Ulrica to follow him to the chateau, at which, it seemed, he was staying, he hastily wrote me an answer to my epistle, which I perused with avidity. It was couched in the most glowing and persuasive language, and in every way too fatally calculated to take possession of my senses. Again he repeated his vows of unalterable affection and commiseration for the sufferings I had undergone during the time we had been separated, renewed his professions of making me his wife, if I would consent to become his, and requested me most earnestly, if I would not drive him entirely to despair, to grant him a private interview on the following evening, at the place he mentioned, when he would explain everything, and the plans for the future which he had in contemplation should be clearly laid before me; after which, although it might be at the cost of his own happiness, he would not attempt to bias my inclinations.

' "The consummate villain!   He knew too well how to accomplish his nefarious designs. He was thoroughly acquainted with my weak points, and therefore was his triumph certain.   He had also greatly prepossessed himself in the favour of Ulrica, who, while she innocently thought she was forwarding my interests, became the ready and unconscious instrument in his hands to work my destruction.   I have every reason to believe that the letter which had been forwarded by my father to Sir Hildebrand had been intercepted by him, and for purposes which will shortly be explained.

"But yet, so strong was my affection for him, an affection which certainly merited a far different return, that I forgot all the past; I continued blind and deluded, when the anxiety which he expressed to keep his return a secret from my parents ought to have aroused my suspicions; and I placed every confidence in his sincerity, and prided myself on the prospect of my speedy restoration to happiness and an honourable position in society.   The miscreant!   At that very time he contemplated the complete destruction of myself and my innocent offspring!

"Oh, memory!—oh, remorse! what excruciating torture are ye now inflicting upon me!

" I threw myself on my knees, and in the sincerity of my heart I returned thanks to the Almighty for the happy turn which had taken place in my prospects, and supplicated His guidance and protection.   I listened with pleasure to the congratulations of Ulrica, and received with avidity the prognostications she uttered, which she did in full sincerity and simplicity of heart.   Poor woman! she had, I know, the deepest affection towards me, and would have shuddered at the bare idea of being a party to anything which was at all calculated to bring the least pain or misery upon me.   I loved her even better than ever for the confidence she expressed in the integrity of Sir Martin, and made her repeat again and again the conversation that had passed between them at their interview.

" The description, the very vivid description, which she gave of the observations and demeanour of my seducer, made a firm and fatal impression upon me, and forwarded his inhuman plans.   She agreed with me, that Sir Martin, no doubt, had cogent reasons for not at once making his appearance at the chateau of my parents, and which he could not sufficiently explain in a letter, and she urged me, with all the eloquence at her command, to comply with his request, and to grant him the interview he sought.   Unfortunately, my inclinations were too much in accordance with her own.   The tempter had well played his cards, and I was entrapped.

" After having, in some measure, collected my thoughts, I sat down, and wrote an hasty answer to the note of Sir Martin, consenting to meet him, at the appointed place, on the following evening, which I committed to the care of Ulrica, and she departed immediately to convey it to him; but she had no sooner gone than I half repented of the course I had taken, and would have been glad to have recalled her, but it was too late.

" The part of deception I was acting towards my parents I could not, spite of all my efforts, reconcile to my feelings, and I was several times half inclined to seek their presence, and make them acquainted with the whole facts.   But still, a certain feeling— an irresistible feeling which I find it utterly impossible to explain—prevented me; and thus I was left entirely at the will and mercy of my betrayer.

"Oh! dreadful infatuation!   But for that I might still have been at liberty, and in- nocent of the hideous crime which now presses upon my conscience.

"Again I awaited with impatience the return of Ulrica, that I might hear how Sir Martin received my answer, and I was not long kept in suspense.   She came back, bring- ing with her another note from my seducer, in which he briefly, but fervently, expressed his gratitude to me for my compliance to his wishes, and protested that at the interview which I had granted him he would fully convince me of the honour of his intentions, and satisfactorily explain everything which at present might appear suspicious against him.

" I kissed the deceptive letter a thousand times, and for the first time for many months imagined myself comparatively happy.   Poor, wretched, deluded being! I was at that very time upon the verge of destruction, from which no earthly power was destined to rescue me.

" I passed several hours in company with Ulrica, during which she flattered the sanguine hopes I had unfortunately conjured up in my own mind, and placing every con- fidence in her sincerity and fidelity, I contemplated the future with calmness and feelings almost approaching to happiness.

" Yet several times throughout the day my determination wavered, and I was often, when my parents entered my chamber, and inquired so anxiously and affectionately after my health, upon the point of divulging everything to them, and to abandon my intention of meeting Sir Martin, unless I had their sanction for so doing.

" It was a wonder that my parents did not notice the agitation of my manner, and that their suspicions were not excited accordingly ; but they did not, or, if they did, no doubt attributed it to the indisposition which I had feigned. I felt greatly relieved when they quitted me, and left me to the indulgence of my own thoughts, and the conversation of my confidant, Ulrica.

"I made her repeat again and again the observations which Sir Martin had made to her, and was never tired of listening to them, while the longer I dwelt upon them, the greater confidence and hope they inspired me with. I thought that there was sincerity in all that he had remarked, and I thanked Heaven for the prospect there appeared to be of my character being redeemed, and that my little innocent child would be saved from the obloquy which, through the indiscretion of her mother (if I may apply so mild a term to it), would otherwise, in all probability, have attached itself to her name. Oh, what would be the delight of my parents, I imagined, when they were made acquainted with the penitence of Sir Martin, and that their darling daughter would be restored to an honourable position in society. Alas ! I was every moment forwarding the evil designs of my betrayer, and involving myself in that maze of horror and guilt from which nothing could again extricate me.

" Ulrica remained with me until a late hour, and when she quitted me for the night, she left me in a dream of blissful anticipation, and anxious and impatient for the time to arrive when I should behold Sir Martin.

" It was some time after her departure I retired to rest, so busy were my thoughts, and when sleep shed its balmy influence over me, the most delightful visions were presented to my imagination, and I arose in the morning, buoyant with hope, and altogether in better spirits than I had been since my separation from Sir Martin.

" I entered the breakfast-room with a tranquil and even joyous demeanour, and my father and mother were delighted at the change, and were led to hope that I had at last conquered the excessive grief and melancholy which my disappointment had caused me. They did all they could to encourage and strengthen me in these imaginary feelings ; and in seeing them happy, I endeavoured to be so myself.

" But could I be sincerely happy ? Oh, no ; fearful misgivings, notwithstanding all my efforts, would at times come over me, and I could not help reproaching myself for the ignorance of the truth in which I was keeping them.

" I evaded any allusion to the name of Sir Martin as much as possible, and my parents quickly perceiving that the subject caused me pain, avoided it cautiously, and tried to divert my thoughts by conversing on other topics.

" The day was one of the utmost anxiety to me, and I complained of fatigue at an early hour in the evening, as an excuse for retiring to my chamber, so that I might prepare myself for hastening to the place of assignation.

" The time which Sir Martin had appointed for the interview was nine o'clock, and I only awaited to hear that all was quiet, and that there was no fear of my encountering my parents, to take my departure.

" Again, as the critical moment approached, I hesitated, and was half disposed to abandon my intention ; but my evil genius prevailed, and urged me on to my miserable and deplorable fate.

" Having once more supplicated the protection, and invoked a blessing upon the heads of my parents, I felt inspired with fresh confidence ; and, hearing no one moving in the chateau, I put on my bonnet and cloak, and prepared to take my departure on my important and fatal errand.

" Almost immediately afterwards, Ulrica entered my room, and informed me that my parents had retired for the night, so that I might leave the chateau without any fear of discovery, and that she would be waiting to admit me secretly on my return.

" A deadly faintness came over me at this moment, and I once more hesitated, and leant on the arm of Ulrica for support. Oh, would that the virtuous impulse had gained further power over me, then should I have been saved from the perpetration of the most fearful of crimes, and the most miserable of fates that ever fell to the lot of an unhappy being.

"But Ulrica aroused me, and encouraged me with hope, and I formed the fatal resolution, and followed her silently and cautiously down the stairs, where she lavished upon me her best wishes, and watched me when I quitted the chateau until my form was hidden from her view in the darkness.

"I proceeded on my way with trembling footsteps, and frequently I was compelled to pause, so powerful were the mingled emotions which took possession of and agitated my breast.

"In spite of all my efforts to resist the feeling, I could not but consider the step I had taken, at such an hour, and alone, to meet my seducer, as most imprudent and dangerous; and two or three times I was prompted to return, but my anxiety to behold Sir Martin again, and to hear his explanation, surmounted all other objections, and once more, with renewed courage and confidence, I pursued my way.

"The place of appointment was a secluded spot, where we had often before met, and where our vows of love and constancy had first been plighted to each other, and many and painful were the reminiscences it recalled to my mind. Surely, Sir Martin, after all his protestations, could not there again attempt to deceive me? Oh, no; I could not imagine that such heartless villany could find a place within the bosom of any human being.

"I quickened my pace, and at last, with a palpitating heart, I came in sight of the well remembered spot. And now again I paused, and looked around me. There was no one to be seen, and a trembling sensation of doubt and apprehension came over me. I could not help shuddering at the bold and hazardous step I had taken, and such a foreboding of some approaching evil came over me, that I was half inclined to turn round, and retreat as quickly as I had approached the place of assignation. It was the voice of my good genius that then whispered to me, and fortunate should I have been had I listened to it; but it was not to be.

"While I was still hesitating, the form of a man emerged from the woodland glade before me, and, as the broad moonbeams fell upon it, I knew it in a moment, and uttered a cry of mingled joy and alarm; but was transfixed to the spot like a statue.

"It was Sir Martin; and with rapid steps he hastened towards me, and the next instant he held me fainting in his treacherous embrace.

"Oh, fatal moment! Better, far better, would it have been for me, and those belonging to me, had I died before it could have arrived.

"When I recovered, and found myself pressed to the bosom of that man whom I imagined had deserted me for ever, my emotions were far too powerful for utterance. I can convey but a faint idea of the scene that fellowed between us. But too well did Sir Martin play his part. He saw that he had me completely at his mercy, and he took every advantage of it. He made the most solemn asseverations of fidelity, drew a vivid picture of what he had suffered during the time we had been separated, and when he heard of my accouchment, and declared that he would have taken the readiest means to answer my letters, had he not been prevented by his father. He declared that he had now, at the risk of Sir Hildebrand's everlasting displeasure, hastened to Normandy, with the determination of making me his bride, if I would consent to the same; but that the marriage, for very particular reason, must be conducted secretly; and urged upon me to give my consent to become his bride without acquainting my parents with it, or even of his return, until after its solemnization.

"I confess that I shrank from the first idea of this with repugnance and suspicion; but so earnest were his professions, and so ardent did he plead, that he completely conquered all my scruples, and won from me my consent to all his plans. The idea of becoming his wife, and the joy it would afford my parents, quite superseded every other thought, and I easily became the villain's victim. Oh, God! could I but have formed the slightest conception of the diabolical scheme he meditated, how should I have shrunk with horror! —with what feelings of disgust and hatred should I have turned from him, and have avoided the dreadful fate which was in store for me! Disappointment and despair might have broken my heart; but I should have been spared the awful crime that now presses so heavily on my conscience.

"Gracious Heaven! why didst thou not banish the mist from mine eyes, and show me the miscreant in his true character? I had sinned; but it was through his deceptive artifices, and surely I merited not so severe a punishment as to be plunged still deeper into crime! It would have been a mercy to me had I died before I could behold my betray e again. Then I might have hoped for pardon in eternity; but now I am shut out from every hope. There is nothing before me but the blackest despair.

"Our interview lasted for about an hour, and, suffice it to say, that before we separated, I yielded to all his plans, and wept my pardon for what had already taken place, upon his bosom. I promised to meet him on the following evening with my child, and accompanied by Ulrica, and to elope with him to England, on arriving in which place, he solemnly vowed that he would make me his bride, after which the disclosure might be made to his father and my parents, and he had no doubt that everything would be amicably arranged.

"Surely I must have been mad, or he could never so easily have deceived and persuaded me. Had I really possessed that affection towards my parents which I endeavoured to imagine I did, I could never have consented to abandon them, leaving myself entirely at the will and pleasure of that man who had already so cruelly deceived me. This very proposition, for which he could give no satisfactory reason, and his objection to make me his wife before we left Normandy, ought to have excited my strongest suspicion, and defeated his plans; but I was urged on by a blind infatuation, and there was no warning voice to rescue me from my impending deplorable fate.

"I become tedious; and why should I dwell upon a subject at which my heart revolts in horror, shame, and remorse?

"Again and again we embraced, and when the moment came for us to separate, it was not without the most painful reluctance that I did so. I could willingly, at that time, have resigned myself entirely to him, such was the confidence that I placed in the sincerity of his intentions.

"Sir Martin accompanied me to within a short distance of my home, and there once more repeating his protestations, and again exacting from me a promise to meet him on the following evening, when he would have all in readiness to receive me, we parted, and I entered the chateau, Ulrica having been waiting most anxiously to admit me. She attended me eagerly to my chamber, and when I had gained it, the emotions which I had endeavoured so long to restrain, found vent, and throwing myself on her bosom, sobs and tears, for a time, completely choked my utterance.

"Ulrica exerted herself to the utmost to tranquillise my feelings, and at length she succeeded far better than she might have expected. I revealed to her all that had taken place between me and Sir Martin at our interview, and solicited her serious advice upon the subject. She hesitated for a few minutes, and reflected, but at last she congratulated me on the result of the meeting, and the prospect of my speedy happiness, and expressed her entire confidence in the honour of Sir Martin's intentions, and her willingness to accompany me on my journey.

"The simple-hearted woman, like myself, was quite deluded by the professions and promises which Sir Martin had made, and thus innocently became the instrument and abettor of his nefarious plans, when, like myself, the very idea of acting in so clandestine a manner, and abandoning my parents, ought to have excited her suspicions, and induced her to warn me against his designs.

"She remained with me for some time, and we arranged all our plans for the following evening, and she promised to have everything in readiness, so that we might depart from the chateau without exciting any suspicion, or the fear of detection. She endeavoured to persuade me that my parents would readily pardon me the steps I was about to take, when they were made acquainted with my lawful marriage, and so strongly combatted all my scruples, that I became tranquillised, and wavered not in my resolution. I thought not of the distance that would separate us, and the possibility that I might never behold them again, for Sir Martin had promised me that, as soon as we were married, and he had arranged matters with his father, he would restore me to them, and, if it met with my approbation, we should fix our future residence in my native country.

"This promise I received with all my usual credulity, and it dissipated the doubt and hesitation I might otherwise have experienced. I never for a moment reflected upon the improbability of those promises being fulfilled, and of the outrageous idea of taking me so far away before fulfilling the compact.

"I had resolved to leave a letter behind me for my parents, explaining all that had happened, and imploring their forgiveness, and with this thought I endeavoured to console myself at the prospect of my speedy separation from them, and to look forward with the hope that all would yet terminate happily.

"When Ulrica left me, I could not think of retiring to rest, so busy were my thoughts, and so numerous and conflicting were the emotions which racked my mind.   But when I I gazed upon the innocent countenance of my infant, who slumbered calmly in her little cot, and thought that all chance of future obloquy being attached to her character was about to be removed, my heart expanded with hope, and I anticipated the time when I was to meet Sir Martin, and to depart with him, with impatience.   Oh, Heaven! that I should have been so deluded; that Providence should not have enlightened my benighted mind, and have afforded me some presentiment of the danger which was now impending over me.

"While my mind was somewhat tranquil, I sat down and wrote the letter which I intended to leave for my parents on my departure.   How I found resolution to do so I know not; but I wrote as my wild anticipations of the future, and my confidence in the honour and truth of my betrayer dictated, and Heaven surely will pardon me for the deed.

"This occupied me for some time, and many and agonising were the fears which I shed over it; I offered up my earnest supplications to the Almighty to guide me how to act, and then I perused the letter I had written to my parents, and at last satisfied myself with its contents, and retired to bed, and I was so worn out with fatigue, both of body and mind, that it was not long ere I fell asleep.   But painful and alarming dreams harassed my imagination, and rendered my repose far from refreshing.

"The following morning I was, if possible, more miserable than ever, and my resolution faltered, and half induced me to relinquish my intentions.   Oh, that the voice of reason and of virtue had prevailed, then might now have been comparatively happy; at least, my conscience would not have been burdened with the dreadful crime of murder.

"Horrible truth!   How my heart shrinks appalled at the recollection of it.   Fiends appear to be hissing and murmuring in my ears.   The dreadful idea of eternity maddens my brain.   I see the innocent looks of my poor child as they appeared to me when I perpetrated the hideous deed.   Again I hear that awful plash, as the water of the well received her tender body; I behold the demoniacal looks of triumph of my inhuman betrayer, at the moment when he saw the accomplishment of his diabolical designs, and that he had me completely in his power.   Oh, horror! horror! what a hardened wretch I must be, or my heart would surely burst beneath this weight of guilt.   My brain is bewildered; my eyes grow dim; my hand trembles, and a death-like faintness comes over me.   Oh, would that it were, indeed, death—and yet I am so ill-prepared to die."

*   *   *   *   *   *   *   *   *

Here another pause occurred in the manuscript, but Ethelbert was so deeply interested in it, that he immediately took it up again, and read on as follows :—

"Once more I resume my painful task, with the hope that this, my confession, may fall into the hands of those to whom it may furnish a wholesome warning, and that my persecutor, even though I should perish (and I cannot expect that he will ever suffer me to quit this ancient edifice alive), may meet with that punishment which is so justly his due.

"In the morning, Ulrica entered my chamber at an early hour, and evinced no surprise at the agitation I betrayed, although she endeavoured to console me, and to encourage me with hope.   I showed her the letter I intended to leave behind me for my parents, and she entirely approved of the contents, and expressed the most sanguine anticipations of their being reconciled to the course I was about to take, and that the time would not be long ere we should meet again.   How she could entertain such an idea I have since been unable to form the least conception; but that she expressed no more than her ideas prompted I have every reason to believe.   In fact, she was as much blinded and infatuated as myself.

"She did not altogether fail in her exertions to tranquillise my feelings, and to lead me to hope that all would end well, and that happier times were in store for me; but it was some time ere I could muster fortitude sufficient to meet my parents, knowing that I was so soon about to leave them, and that something might happen, so that I might never behold them again.

"It was with a trembling step that I entered the room where they were seated, awaiting my appearance at the morning meal.   It was impossible that they could help noticing my emotion, and they eagerly questioned me as to the cause; but I pleaded indisposition, and they were satisfied with my answer, and of course could have no suspicion of the guilty thoughts which were at that moment passing in my mind.   Had they done so, how

bitterly would they have reproached me. But they would have rescued me from entire ruin, and I should now have been innocent of the crime of murder.

"It was a day of the severest trial to me, and Heaven only knows how I supported it; how my heart could have been so stubborn as not to fail me. I was most anxious to retire from their presence, that I might in private give free indulgence to my thoughts; but my parents would not permit me, and I could form no reasonable excuse for so doing until the evening; and then, it is marvellous that, knowing how soon I was about to leave them—that before the sun arose on the following morning I should be many miles away from them, and might never more behold them, I did not betray myself; but I did not; and, hastening to my chamber, found great relief when I was alone.

"I was quickly joined by Ulrica, who had made every preparation for the journey, and tried her hardest to comfort and encourage me, as the time approached for our departure. But, notwithstanding all her arguments, for some time my resolution failed me, and I was several times upon the point of abandoning my intentions, and, hastening to my parents, make them acquainted with the whole of the facts, and, on my knees, to implore their forgiveness for having, for an instant, dared to contemplate deserting them in so cruel and clandestine a manner. But the tempter had unfortunately obtained too strong a hold on my affections; and so specious did the promises he had made appear to me to be, that

I could not doubt his truth and sincerity.   He surely, I reflected, could not be the heart-less, the diabolical miscreant to deceive me, and but a short time would elapse ere I should be restored to them as his lawful wife, and nothing could then occur to mar our future happiness.   I imagined that the letter I had written would explain everything to their satisfaction, and they would pardon me for the course I had taken, and which was prompted by the purest motives.

"Fallacious ideas!   How could they, for an instant, enter my mind?

"Darkness at length veiled the earth, and the hour was near approaching at which I was to meet my seducer; and Ulrica, who was perfectly composed and collected, prepared me for my departure.   Again my heart misgave me, and I was once more half persuaded to abandon my designs, and to send Ulrica to the place of appointment to inform Sir Martin of my thoughts; but she aroused me from these gloomy but praiseworthy thoughts, and again inspired me with confidence.   I knelt down, and supplicated the protection of the Supreme; then, with many scalding tears, and imploring blessings upon their heads, I placed the letter on my dressing-case, where it could not fail to meet the eyes of my parents, and prepared myself to take my departure.

"My poor unconscious babe was sleeping soundly, and Ulrica had carefully wrapped it in a mantle, to shield it from the night air, which blew keenly.   I pressed a fervent kiss upon its innocent cheek, and then, almost unconscious of what I did, suffered Ulrica to take my arm, and lead me forth from my chamber, she having previously ascertained that my parents had retired to rest.   As I passed their room door, my emotions nearly over-powered me, and I was compelled to pause; and Ulrica became alarmed lest we should be discovered, and urged me most earnestly, by signs, to proceed.   I thought my heart would have bursted, but, scarcely knowing what I did, I at last suffered her to lead me away, and cautiously descending the stairs, we quitted the chateau, and I found myself in the open air, and proceeding some distance from the place before I was completely aroused to a state of consciousness.   But when I was so, I sadly repented of the step I had taken, and it was almost as much as Ulrica could do to dissuade me from returning. At length, however, I regained courage, and committing myself to the care of Providence, I proceeded on my way to the fatal place of appointment.

"A quarter of an hour brought us to within a short distance of it, and when we had broken from amidst a cluster of trees, I beheld a vehicle waiting at a short distance.   The next instant I was clasped in the arms of Sir Martin, and, overcome by the tumult of feelings which rushed into my bosom, my senses left me.

"When I recovered, I found myself seated in the carriage, which was proceeding at a rapid rate, and supported in the arms of Sir Martin.   Ulrica was seated on the other side of me, with my child, which was still sleeping, in her arms.   To describe the scene which followed between us would be a fruitless task.   But Sir Martin endeavoured to reassure me, by caresses, and lavished upon the infant the utmost apparent affection.   He suc-ceeded but too well in deceiving me, by his solemn protestations, and declared that we should no sooner arrive in England than he would make me his wife.   The miscreant! And all the time he was contemplating the most dreadful of crimes that could possibly enter the human breast

"As we proceeded further and further on our journey, and the distance from my parents became greater, a stronger sense of the ingratitude and cruelty with which I had acted towards them impressed itself upon me, and Sir Martin found it a most difficult task to tranquillise my feelings in the least.   What dreadful anguish must they expe-rience when they should discover my elopement; and I feared that the letter I had left behind for them would fail to quiet their apprehensions, notwithstanding the promises which Sir Martin had held out to me; nor could I entirely banish the doubts and mis-givings which beset my own mind.

"We continued to travel for about two hours, Sir Martin informing me that he was making his way to the nearest sea-port, there to embark for England, when, in consequence of its getting late, and my feeling so much fatigued, we put up at an inn for the night.   It was a night of misery and anxiety, and I slept but little, at in-tervals repenting of my flight, and forming all manner of fearful conjectures, from which Ulrica, who slept in the same chamber with me, tried, but in vain, to arouse me.

"We resumed our journey at an early hour on the following morning, and my anguish of mind was not the least abated; in fact, notwithstanding all the arguments of Sir Mar-tin, it rather increased.   Perhaps, ere this, I reflected, my parents had become aware of my flight, and I pictured to myself their distraction, and the reproaches they would heap upon my head for the ingratitude, the base ingratitude with which I had acted towards them. They could never place any confidence in the promises of Sir Martin, after the manner in which he had before acted towards me, and the anguish he had caused me. And surely I had myself been most weak and imprudent in having yielded to his persuasions, especially when the promises he had held out were so doubtful. Again I appealed to him, and solemnly adjured him not to deceive me, but to tell me at once whether or not his intentions were honourable. The base hypocrite more fervently and with greater apparent earnestness protested his sincerity, and gently upbraided me for entertaining such doubts and suspicions, declaring that as soon as we arrived in England our union should take place, even though by marrying me he should incur the everlasting wrath of his father. The unbounded affection he seemed to lavish on my infant all served to deceive me the more, and to inspire me with fresh confidence; and, by degrees, I became more tranquil than could have been expected, and, committing myself to the care of Providence, I proceeded the remainder of the journey without complaining. Towards the afternoon, we arrived at the destined port, where we found a vessel ready to depart almost immediately to England, and Sir Martin having made the necessary arrangements, we went on board, and, in the course of a couple of hours, she weighed anchor, and we were borne along with a favouring gale, far from my native land.

"So well had Sir Martin succeeded, by dint of eloquent argument and plausible promises, in convincing me of the honour of his intentions, that I was completely deceived, and apparently tranquil. I mentally invoked the protection of Heaven for my beloved parents, and trusted that the time was not far distant when we should meet again, no more to part, until death should separate us, and when they could greet me with pleasure, on being restored to the same honourable position in society it was my former pride to occupy.

"Ulrica encouraged me in these hopes, for she was as regularly deluded as myself by the specious conduct and professions of the practised villain, and many were the glowing anticipations she formed of the future joy which would attend me, and the consolation it would afford my father and mother to find me united to the father of my child, every word of whose assertions she placed the utmost confidence in. Although Ulrica was at that time upwards of forty, she had experienced little or nothing of the world, and no wonder, therefore, that she was so easily led astray. She had in early life herself been disappointed in love; but still that had not deadened her feelings, or induced her to view all mankind with a jaundiced eye; nor did it render her envious of the happiness of the more fortunate of her own sex. She was, as I have before stated, devotedly attached to me and my parents, and would have suffered anything rather than have knowingly become an accessory to anything that might be the cause of misery to us. How, then, would she have revolted from the part she was now playing, could she have foreseen the horrors of which it would be productive.

"Sir Martin, no doubt, with the penetration of the accomplished libertine, had well read her character—ascertained all her weak points—perceived the influence she possessed over me; and thus made her a ready instrument in his hands for the accomplishment of his infernal arts.

"But, notwithstanding all the power which the arguments of Sir Martin gained over me, and the unbounded affection which he evinced towards me and my child, there were times during the voyage, and in the midst of all his protestations, when the most gloomy misgivings would take possession of my mind, and which I found it almost utterly impossible for me to shake off; and when I could not but entertain some suspicion of the honour of his intentions, and reproach myself for the ready compliance I had yielded to his solicitations, and delivered myself over entirely to his power, without previously apprising and consulting with my parents. There were times, I say, when, in my more reasonable moments, I was unable to disguise from myself the unreasonableness of Sir Martin wishing to conceal his plans from my father and mother, and inducing me to leave them in so clandestine and unnatural a manner. Why, if his intentions were honest, should he have hesitated to meet them, and convince them of the same, by at once making me his wife, previously to conveying me to England?

"These were suspicious and difficult questions to answer; but to an accomplished hypocrite like Sir Martin they were trifling; and he combated them skilfully and successfully. I was at length quite satisfied, and yielded myself entirely to his will.

" Had I possessed the most ordinary penetration, or had not my brain been quite bewildered and stupified, I might have read in his looks of exultation the treacherous part he was acting towards me ; but Fate had ordained it otherwise, and I was still led blindly on to destruction.

" The voyage was a pleasant one, and I felt invigorated by the salubrity of the sea-breeze. At length the white cliffs of England appeared in sight, and we landed in safety at Dover. Here a heavy melancholy again came over my spirits, but Sir Martin soon succeeded in banishing it, and in filling my weak and pliant mind with the most blissful anticipations.

" It was night when we landed, and we accordingly put up at the principal inn, where, being all fatigued, after partaking of some refreshment, we retired to rest. Alas ! another night of sin was added to the weight which already pressed so heavily on my conscience. My cruel and heartless seducer once more triumphed over my weakness and misplaced affection, at the same time that he contemplated a crime which surely could only have entered into the conception of a fiend in human form.

" The next morning we resumed our journey, he telling me that for the present—for a few days only, until he had seen his father, and endeavoured to reconcile him to the step he had taken, and to gain his permission to introduce me to him—it would be necessary for him to take me to an ancient residence, situated on his estate, which had only occasionally been inhabited for several years. However, he trusted that I would submit to the temporary inconvenience for the love which he flattered himself I bore him, and assuring me that if his father remained obdurate, nothing whatever should induce him to hesitate in making me his bride.

" I paused, and reflected deeply. I confess that the idea at first appeared extravagant and unreasonable to me, and I urged him, if his intentions were indeed honourable, to remove my doubts at once, by giving me a legal claim upon him, suggesting that a reconciliation might then most probably be effected with his father, when he found that the deed was done past recall. But he triumphed in this as he had too successfully done over all my other objections, and I yielded myself entirely to his will and discretion.

" As we proceeded on our journey, Sir Martin lavished upon me and my offspring endearments of a still more tender nature than they had previously been, and he drew the most glowing pictures of the future happiness that was in store for us. And I believed him, and was happy in the delusion!

" The journey appeared to me an endless one, especially when night arrived, and I was informed by Sir Martin that we could not possibly arrive at the place of our destination until the following day had far advanced.

" We again put up at an inn for the night; but, notwithstanding my fatigue, I slept but little, thinking of my parents, and what the future might be that was in store for me. At times I blamed myself for the course I had taken, and then again I placed every reliance in the integrity of Sir Martin, and endeavoured to make my mind happy and contented.

" I inquired of him the name of the place where we were going; but he evaded it, by informing me it was an ancient tower, and not of very prepossessing appearance, through its having been left to partial neglect ; but as our stay there would, as he had before observed, only be temporary, he trusted that I would for the present put up with the inconvenience.

" I was satisfied, and put no further questions to him upon the subject.

" We travelled by easy stages, Sir Martin diverting the gloom of my thoughts by the most lively conversation, and alternating his affectionate attentions between me and our infant.

" The scenery we had been travelling among had hitherto been romantic and diversified ; but, as the shades of evening began to fall, the aspect of the country was completely changed, and all was wild, gloomy, and desolate. I felt my spirits chilled, and Sir Martin, although he tried his utmost, could not arouse me from their painful state of depression.

" At length the moon arose, and then the dark outlines of an ancient building, placed upon a lofty eminence, for the first time met my observation. I eagerly inquired of Sir Martin its name, and he informed me that it was called the Tower of Bransdorf, and that it was the place of our destination. I felt an involuntary shuddering come over me, and that impression became still stronger the nearer we approached towards it, and I had a better view of its black, frowning, and ivy-mantled walls. But Sir Martin again exerted himself to do away with my prejudices, and with success. He assured me that no harm could possibly come to me there, as he should be almost constantly with me, and the tower belonged to his father, and with that he stifled my objections; and having arrived at the hill, on the summit of which the ancient building stood, we alighted from the vehicle, and began to ascend it.

" All was silent around. Sir Martin led me to a low gothic porch in the south wing, and rung a bell, whose hollow sound reverberated in dismal echoes through the ancient pile. In a few moments the door was opened by a shrivelled old man, who carried a lamp in his hand. He fixed a curious and scrutinising glance upon me and Ulrica ; but beholding Sir Martin, be bowed obsequiously, and led the way up a spiral staircase to a suite of spacious apartments, very well furnished, and which seemed to have been prepared for our reception.

" Sir Martin conducted me to a seat, and then, having spoken a few words to the man in an under tone, he withdrew, and we were left to ourselves.

" I inquired of Sir Martin whether there were many domestics in the tower, and he replied that there was only the old man and his wife, who were in his confidence, and that I might depend upon receiving every attention from them, during the time that I remained there.

" I questioned him narrowly as to the reason of the tower being so neglected ; but he evaded the interrogatory as well as he could, and as I thought it was a subject of no particular importance, I did not press him upon it. Alas! I little thought that the villain had completely entrapped me, and had brought me there for such an hideous purpose."

CHAPTER XXVI.

THE SEQUEL OF THE CONFESSION.—THE INFANTICIDE.

" I was anxious to inspect the gloomy building to which I had been conveyed ; but Sir Martin dissuaded me from it, as, he assured me, I should find nothing in it to gratify my curiosity, as most of the other rooms had been suffered to fall into decay. He also said that it would be advisable, until he had made arrangements with his father, that I should keep myself confined to my own apartments, lest I should be seen by any one, and our wishes be obstructed ; and he assured me that I might make myself quite comfortable, as, whenever he was unavoidably absent from the tower, Ulrica would be in attendance upon me.

" In this manner three days passed away, and nothing particular occurred to disturb me, only my anxiety about my parents, and the solicitude I felt for Sir Martin to fulfil the promise he had so solemnly made to me. He redoubled his affectionate attentions towards me, and it was impossible that I could doubt him ; and thus was I plunged headlong into the gulph he had prepared for me. Daily, hourly, did I become more deeply involved in his guilty snares, from which I could not extricate myself. But surely he must have been a monster of the deepest dye to have carried his deception and cruelty to the extent which he did.

" On the fourth day he told me that, in order to expedite our wishes, and that he might at once place me in a proper position of society by making me his wife, and restoring me to my parents, it was necessary that he should see his father without delay ; and for that purpose he proposed at once repairing to him—he, at that time, as he said, residing at one of his estates situated at some distance from the tower.

" My heart sank within me at the thoughts of a separation from him ; but I saw the necessity of it, and he consoled me by assuring me that it should not be for long, and inspiring me with the hope that his father would yield to his importunities, and that when he returned, it would be to lead me at once to the altar.

" When he was gone, I felt a void in my heart which nothing could fill up, and painful doubts and apprehensions incessantly tormented me. Ulrica did all she could to cheer my spirits, and to buoy me up with hopeful expectations ; but nothing could have the effect of setting my mind entirely at rest. I thought of the misery and anxiety my poor parents must be enduring ; the bitter reproaches they were probably heaping upon my head for the cruelty and ingratitude with which I had behaved towards them, and in spite of the efforts which I made to be happy and contented, I was truly wretched.

"I had never seen the old porter but once since the night on which I was brought to the tower, and his wife never; and all was so quiet within the building, that it was quite evident we were its only inhabitants, and the gloomy mystery which reigned about it inspired me with a feeling of dread. And yet, I had a great curiosity to examine its chambers; but Ulrica reminded me of the injunctions of Sir Martin, and I abandoned the thought.

"Sir Martin was away for two days, and the time appeared to me a perfect age, so powerful was the suspense I naturally experienced. Sometimes I imagined that Sir Martin had repented of his promise, and had again deserted me; but the idea was so preposterous that I soon discarded it, and reproached myself for having encouraged it for a moment. But still I had my doubts (and they had gained the most powerful ascendancy over me) of the success of Sir Martin in moving his father to relent, and I could not but feel the deepest regret at the thought, that, if the former kept his word, and persisted in making me his wife, it must be at the risk of his eternal displeasure, and, perhaps, the ruin of all his future prospects. I felt my pride mortified, and could not restrain my tears, notwithstanding Ulrica tried all she could to persuade me that my fears would turn out to be fallacious.

"At length, on the second evening, Sir Martin returned, and I hastened to meet him, my heart palpitating with anxiety and expectation.

"He embraced me affectionately; but I could immediately see, by the melancholy expression of his countenance, that he had bad news to impart to me, and I guessed too well the purport. His father remained inexorable, and his journey had therefore been unsuccessful.

"Impatiently I questioned him; but he merely replied with a sigh; and desiring Ulrica to retire from the room, he led me to a seat, and remained for a few moments gazing at me in silence, until, unable to endure my suspense any longer, I interrupted him.

"'Oh, Martin!' I ejaculated, 'for Heaven's sake do not keep me in this dreadful state of agony; but let me know the worst at once. Your father remains inflexible; he has refused to sanction your nuptials with the poor, fallen Almira de Montreville, the heartless deserter of her home and too fond parents, and I am abandoned to despair and misery! Oh, I am terribly, but justly punished!'

"'Nay, my beloved Almira,' returned the perfidious hypocrite, throwing his arms around me, 'you reproach yourself too severely, and do me an injustice besides, in forming such hasty conclusions. It is true I have been unable to prevail upon my father to give his consent to our nuptials; but you remember the solemn promise I have made to you, and you surely cannot believe me to be so consummate a villain as to break my word.'

"'Oh, no, no, dear Martin; forgive me!' I cried, returning his salute with all the ardour of my soul. 'I remember all that you have so solemnly vowed; and you will be faithful to your vows, even at every risk—you will make me your wife, will you not?'

"'Yes, yes, Almira,' he replied. 'But pray calm your feelings, and listen patiently to me.'

"'But when shall be the happy time? Oh! you cannot wonder at my insupportable anxiety to know when I shall again be permitted to throw myself at the feet of my beloved parents as your lawful bride, and to supplicate their forgiveness for the bitter anguish I have caused them!'

"'In a few days, Almira,' he said, 'I will perform my promise.'

"'In a few days!' I repeated, with a look of disappointment, and my heart throbbing violently with the intensity of my feelings; 'oh! why not now? Why delay, when my happiness, my very life, depends on it?'

"'It cannot be, Almira,' he answered.

"'Cannot be! Oh, Martin! why this tardiness? Surely you are not about to deceive me?'

"'Then it appears, Almira, in spite of all my oft-repeated protestations of love, you still doubt me?'

"'No, no; you cannot wonder at my impatience and anxiety, separated as I am from my parents, and ignorant as they are of my fate.'

"'I tell you again,' he remarked, 'that in a few days, a week at farthest, I will, notwithstanding the disapprobation of my father, make you my wife; but it is impossible for me to complete my arrangements before. Let that assurance satisfy you, and banish these foolish and unfounded apprehensions.'

"'I will try to be calm, dear Martin,' I replied, 'and to await the happy time; but, oh; tell me what transpired at the interview with your father?'

"'I have much to say,' observed Sir Martin; 'but I am faint and exhausted with my journey, and need some refreshment.'

"'Ulrica has, I know, prepared the evening repast,' said I; 'I will summon her, and desire her to bring it in.'

"I did so, and Ulrica was about to depart, in obedience to my orders, when Sir Martin called her back.

"'And hark ye, Ulrica,' he said; 'bring in wine. It is seldom that I indulge in it; but my spirits are depressed to-night, and it may serve to revive me.'

"Ulrica departed to execute her orders, and Sir Martin, having fixed an earnest glance upon me for a second or two, turned his gaze towards the little cot in which my poor child was calmly sleeping. I could not help noticing a peculiar expression that passed over his countenance as he did so, and an involuntary shuddering passed through my frame. My God! what must have been my feelings of disgust and horror had I known the fiendish thoughts which at that moment were passing in his mind!

"My heart sickens at the recollection of that dreadful night, and my brain once more maddens, as the remembrance of the hideous transactions which took place rush upon it. Oh, why did the monster not adminster poison to me, and thus have ridden himself of all his fears, rather than have made me the guilty, blood-stained wretch I now am!

"How shall I complete my painful task, and relate the awful events of that fatal night! My hand trembles, and can scarcely guide the pen; but still, I have imposed upon myself the solemn duty of unburthening my conscience, in the hope that the world, at some period, may be made acquainted with the whole of the revolting facts, and, though my heart should burst in the effort, I will persevere.

"For several moments, Sir Martin could not remove his eyes from the features of my sleeping babe, and at length a heavy sigh escaped his bosom.

"Surprised and alarmed, I flew towards him, and eagerly inquired what it was that agitated him so violently. He turned upon me a look that was perfectly ghastly; but before he could return any answer to my eager inquiries, Ulrica and the old woman entered with the provisions, which having placed upon the table, they immediately retired.

"Sir Martin eagerly swallowed a glass of wine, and prevailed upon me to take one; then he once more turned his eyes towards the sleeping child, and his countenance was, if possible, more painfully expressive than before.

"'Now, Martin, dear Martin,' I anxiously exclaimed, 'tell me what is the cause of the peculiar emotion you evince, and why do you gaze so earnestly upon our infant?'

"Again he fixed upon me a look which I can never forget, and which should have excited my suspicions and filled my mind with horror, as he answered,—

"'Almira, were it not for the existence of this child, there would be no obstacle whatever to our marriage; my father would give his consent.'

"God forgive me! but such was the effect that the insidious miscreant's words had upon me, that, for a moment, I followed the direction of his eyes, and gazed on the unconscious and innocent babe with emotions of hatred. But I quickly recovered myself, and grasping Sir Martin's arm, in a tremulous voice, I demanded,—

"'For Heaven's sake, what do you mean, Martin?'

"'Almira,' he answered, 'were not my words sufficiently explicit?'

"'Good God!' I ejaculated, 'you surely cannot regret the existence of this innocent pledge of our mutual affection?'

"'Almira,' he returned, 'this is no time for trifling. Comprehend me properly. I say again that this child is the only obstacle to our union with the consent of my father. Would it not, then, have been better, both for itself and for you and me, had it never seen the light of day?'

"Deluded wretch that I was; instead of turning from the monster with terror and loathing, as I should have done, I felt disposed to acknowledge the truth of his observations; and he, seeing the advantage he had obtained, followed it up with all the eloquence and sophistry of which, unfortunately, he was so accomplished a master; and I was lost, lost entirely; my doom was sealed, and that of my child; the measure of my crimes was shortly to be filled, and I fated to become a monster, at whose memory future ages must shudder.

" I cast one glance at the beauteous features of my innocent babe, at which Sir Martin was still gazing intently, and with looks of jealousy. In its sleep it smiled—an angel cherub's smile, which should have aroused all the mother's feelings of adoration in my bosom; but oh, how dreadfully opposite were the passions it excited; had it at that moment have been its last gasp, monster as I am to have to acknowledge it, it would have afforded me more satisfaction. My destroyer plainly read my thoughts in the expression of my countenance, and no doubt he exulted with all the malice of the fiend of darkness over his devoted victims. Again he filled my glass, and, in the bewilderment of my thoughts, scarcely knowing what I did, I quaffed off its contents, little suspecting the stupifying and maddening drug he had taken the opportunity of mixing with it, for the purpose of effecting his infernal purpose.

" He turned at length from the contemplation of the poor babe, and seated himself again by my side, throwing his arms around my waist, and imprinting ardent kisses upon my lips, which pretended endearments I received with every demonstration of delight, and returned them with equal fervour, and far more sincerity.

" 'Oh, Almira,' said the crafty and heartless hypocrite, 'how many pangs would it have saved us, had this poor child never have been born. Then would my father, I am certain, gladly have received you as his daughter, for the voice of scandal would have been hushed, and I might have led you triumphantly to the altar, surrounded by the smiles of my parent and of yours. But now, even though I make you my bride, which I am resolved, in spite of everything, to do, our happiness will be greatly diminished by the knowledge that by so doing we must incur the displeasure of at least one that should be so dear to us.'

" 'Martin,' I suddenly exclaimed, while a torrent of ideas crowded upon my brain, 'are you speaking the truth?'

" 'By all my hopes hereafter, I am,' he answered; 'and even now, did not this poor innocent obstacle exist, my father would not only receive you with pleasure and affection, but is prepared, from the manner in which I have represented you to him, to accompany us as speedily as convenient to the altar, your revered parents being present, and there to bestow upon you my hand, accompanied with his blessing. Oh, Almira, think how dreadful it is, viewing the question in anything but a pecuniary point of view, to bear the weight of a parent's curse—to be excluded from their smiles of affection, and estranged from all their fond endearments; and then say whether—unnatural even though it may appear to be—we have not just reason to regret that it has pleased the Supreme ruler of events to curse us with what, under other circumstances, would be a blessing?'

" The specious hypocrite knew well how to play his part, and, having chosen the arguments which were best calculated to gain an influence over my wandering and distracted reason, again he triumphed. He must have observed the looks of hatred which I directed towards my child, for now, when I come to reflect more maturely upon the dreadful events of that night, I can recollect the expression of malignant triumph that passed over his countenance. The fiend saw that his purpose was secure of success, and, no doubt, he inwardly laughed with the exultation of a demon.

" Again he forced upon me the maddening drink, rendered still more maddening by the deleterious and poisonous drug he had, unknown to me, and when my eyes did not observe his actions, so completely absorbed was I in the tumult of my thoughts, instilled into it, and my senses began to wander. I looked again upon my child, and, in the delirium of the thoughts which the miscreant had implanted in the most diabolically subtle manner in my breast, I wished it dead! I felt convinced that Sir Martin had spoken the truth; that it was the only obstacle to our complete happiness; and the picture he had drawn of the felicity that would attend us—the difficulties which would have been avoided, had it never seen the light of Heaven, were so strongly impressed upon my benighted mind, that I became too ready a tool in his hands to work his monstrous designs, and my own destruction. Why did he not, as he had us both in his power, at once sacrifice us? Why not take our lives, and thus end his pecuniary fears? But, no; he had not the hardihood to become a direct assassin; but, in the black, demoniacal feeling of his polluted mind, had determined that the hideous crime of murder should rest upon the soul of his unfortunate victim.

" But will Heaven not mark his guilt with equal retribution to that which it has visited

upon me ?   Is he not equally responsible for the frightful crime which I, in madness—
madness wrought by him—committed?   Oh, yes; I feel assured it will; and the curse
which I now, in my gloomy dungeon, invoke upon his head, will pursue him to the grave.
May lightnings blast him—wither all his hopes, and, rendering his days one lingering
life of misery and horror, consign him to the tomb at last with all the dread of a terrible
eternity pressing upon his guilty soul!

"'Oh, Martin, dearest Martin,' at length I said, returning the monster's caresses with
equal fervour, 'and have you, indeed, drawn a correct picture of what would have occurred, had our child never been born?   Would your father really have consented to
your becoming my husband!   And would he have pardoned the weakness of which I
have been guilty, had there been no living evidence of my indiscretion?'

"'Had there been no living evidence, my beloved Almira, I repeat that he said he
would,' answered Sir Martin; 'and even now, as the world is not acquainted with it,
were it removed, he would receive us with open arms.'

"I looked earnestly in his face for a moment or two, and stedfastly he met my glance he could see the workings of my mind, and no doubt flattered himself at the time with the success of his diabolical designs.

"'And may not that obstacle, dear Martin,' I gasped forth—but surely it was the demon who had taken possession of me that spoke—'could not that obstacle be removed?'

He grasped my hand vehemently as I spoke, and fixed his eyes upon me as though he would penetrate into my very soul, as he said, in a low hoarse voice,—

"'Yes, yes, Almira; it can be removed, if we can only muster the resolution and the wisdom to do so.'

"'Ah, I understand you,' I returned; 'the poor babe might be placed with some honest individual, who, for a liberal reward, would bring it up with tenderness, and in ignorance of its origin. That is what you mean, dear Martin, is it not?'

"The countenance of the villain loured, and for a minute or two he remained silent. He was evidently disappointed, but he exerted himself to the utmost to conceal his real feelings, and at length said,—

"'Why, my sweet Almira, that would be all very well, and, perhaps, the best method we could adopt to forward our plans, could we find a person to whom we could communicate our wishes, and upon whose fidelity we could depend; but, unfortunately, it is a difficult task to do so; and at any time, while the child existed, the same danger as at present would exist, and the whole truth might be exposed to the world, when we least expected, and the disgrace and obloquy would fall heavier upon us than at the present moment.'

"'Oh, tell me, dearest Martin, how can we accomplish our happiness without incurring the displeasure of your father, or the world's opprobrium?'

"'I have told you; only by the removal, the safe removal, of the obstacle—its removal in such a way as it can never appear again to obstruct us, or to bring misery and disgrace upon our heads.'

"'I do not understand you, Martin; and strange thoughts, complicated, unfathomable ideas, rush to and bewilder my brain. Why do you not become more explicit?'

"'I will, I will, love; but you are nervous; the wine—let me prevail upon you to take one more glass.'

"Distracted, perplexed, maddened with the effects of that which I had already taken, I yielded, and partook of the fatal drink, which completely sapped my senses, and rendered me an easy victim in the monster's hands.

"What afterwards occurred is like a frightful dream to me! Oh, would that it was so in reality. A mist seemed to rest upon my intellect; my powers were all but prostrated. I remember my child awaking; that I took it in my arms, and gazed with hatred in its beauteous, innocent face. The words, 'Were it removed, he would receive us with open arms,' seemed to hiss in my ears; I know not whether they were repeated by my seducer; but I have a perfect recollection of his taking the child from my arms, and clasping it to his bosom, with apparently all the ardour of parental fondness, and immediately afterwards I heard a stifled shriek; he returned the babe to me; its features were distorted; its complexion was livid; it was writhing in strong convulsions. For an instant the feelings of the mother revived within my breast; I screamed for assistance, and pressed my lips in the most distracted manner to the blackened cheeks of my child. I have a strong recollection of Sir Martin's attempting to console me; and, laying hold of my arm, he led me, with the struggling infant at my bosom, from the room, by a private door, which I had never before observed.

"We descended several flights of stairs, and at length arrived in a low vaulted apartment, but the floor of which was boarded over. Sir Martin stooped down, and removed two or three of the boards, and I then found that I was standing on the brink of a deep well, and Sir Martin was by my side. Even now, methinks I behold the fiendish expression of his eyes, as he first fixed them on me, and then pointed to the water beneath my feet. I looked in the countenance of my babe; it was blacker, blacker still; and its little eyes were protruding frightfully from their sockets; it seemed to be in its last struggle. 'Were it removed, he would receive you with open arms!'

"These words acted like magic upon me; I turned my eyes away, and the child was permitted to fall from my arms. I heard a hollow plash as its little form was received by the waters of the well—I heard a demoniacal laugh of mockery and triumph. It rings in mine ears now. My brain whirled round—my limbs tottered—I sunk back—I remembered no more until I awoke to horror and sensibility, and found myself the inmate of the dismal dungeon I now occupy.

"When the stupor which so long steeped my senses had evaporated, I found myself in this gloomy dungeon, reclining upon a wretched mattress, and with no one near me.

"My God! was I then doomed to become a prisoner in that dreadful place, shut up with all the overwhelming horror of my guilty thoughts? And could it be possible that Sir Martin, after all his protestations of love, and the solemn promises he had made me, could thus have incarcerated me? Horror! horror! it is too true!

* * * * * * * * * *

"I have been three days in this horrible dungeon, shut out from every hope, and writhing in the agony of a guilty, blood-stained conscience, during which time I have seen nobody but a savage-looking man, who brought me my coarse provisions, and he refused to answer my questions, when ——"

* * * * * * * * * *

CHAPTER XXVII.

THE RESCUE OF ETHELBERT.—THE DESTRUCTION OF THE RUFFIANS IN THE TOWER OF BRANSDORF.—THE MEETING OF THE LOVERS.

HERE the manuscript abruptly terminated, leaving Ethelbert in a state of mystery as to the subsequent events which had befallen the unfortunate Almira.

The dreadful crime which she had so graphically described, appalled his every sense, and he could almost imagine that he heard the plaintive voice of the murdered innocent, as it was dashed into the well—the well of death—by its wretched and distracted mother; and so strong was that superstitious impression upon his mind, that it was some time before he could divest himself of it.

He was at last interrupted in his melancholy reflections, by again hearing the dismal cry which had before so frequently excited his astonishment and alarm, and which evidently proceeded from the voice of a female, and from a dungeon contiguous to the one in which he was confined. He started hastily to that side of the dungeon, knocked against the wall, and again called upon the mysterious being, and requested her to inform him who she was, and why she was there imprisoned; but, as before, no answer was returned to his inquiries, and he was left in the same state of mystery and suspense as he had previously been.

The man who attended upon him now came to trim his lamp for the night, and he ventured to question him upon the subject, and requested him to inform him whether any unfortunate person, as well as himself, was confined in the tower.

"Oh, you have heard her then, I suppose," said the fellow.

"Her!" repeated Ethelbert; "it is, then, a woman."

"Ay," replied the man; "and nothing, it seems, will stop her infernal screeching."

"Who is the unfortunate being?" eagerly demanded Ethelbert.

"It is not my business to inform you," was the reply.

"Is she confined at the instance of Lord Ruthlyn?" inquired Ethelbert.

"She is not."

With this surly answer he retired, and left Ethelbert, if possible, involved in a greater state of bewilderment than before.

The night passed away in silence; and when, as well as he could guess, the morning came, suddenly he was startled by hearing a strange and confused noise in the tower. He listened attentively, and every instant the sounds became more distinct, and seemed to approach nearer.

The hubbub appeared to proceed from a number of persons, as if engaged in conflict, and several times he was almost certain he heard the voices of men, in noisy and angry altercation. This was succeeded by what appeared to be the battering in of heavy doors, and directly afterwards he could plainly distinguish the clattering of swords, and other significant demonstrations of a contest going on.

The noise grew louder, and seemed to approach nearer and nearer the range of dungeons, in one of which he was confined.

At length the sound of approaching footsteps, and the opening and closing to of several doors was heard, and became more and more distinct, and he was certain that they were approaching nearer towards the dungeon in which he was confined.

" Be they friends or foes," he exclaimed, " they shall at least be made acquainted with the place of my locality."

Then he shouted at the top of his voice, and was gratified in hearing it responded to by a seemingly friendly cry.   His heart bounded in his bosom with the hope of speedy deliverance, and he hallooed and kicked at the door, for the purpose of attracting attention.

" Ethelbert, my son, where are you ?" now cried the well-known voice of his father, and a weight of doubt and anxiety was removed from his bosom, which was almost too much to bear.

" Here ! here ! dear father," he cried ; " I am confined in this dungeon !   Oh, Providence be thanked that has sent you to my deliverance !"

The next moment, while he stood with clasped hands, and his eyes fixed eagerly upon the door, he heard the bolts withdrawn ; a key was applied to the lock, the door flew open, and the following moment his father and several of his retainers entered the dungeon, and overcome with the powerful emotions of his feelings, he rushed with an exclamation of indescribable delight to his arms.

*   *   *   *   *   *   *   *   *

We will pass over the happy scene that ensued between Sir Aldobrand and his son, and having seen the latter rescued from his dreary dungeon, we will seek the lovely Mildred, who was waiting with the most anxious expectation the return of her lover.

Mildred had been gazing from the window, which commanded an uninterrupted view of the Tower of Bransdorf, with a palpitating heart, and her ecstacy was increased when she beheld Sir Aldobrand and Ethelbert approaching.   She hurried into the hall to meet them, and, unable to conceal the emotions which animated her bosom, she suffered Ethelbert to embrace her with all the fervour which the boundless transport of his feeling prompted ; while Sir Aldobrand stood by, and fully participated in their delight.

"Oh, Mildred," at length exclaimed Ethelbert, " and do we indeed meet again ?   Are you really rescued from the power of that heartless man, and enabled to set him at defiance ?   I can scarcely believe the evidence of my senses.   This is a sufficient reward for all the sufferings I have endured in the loathsome dungeon in which I was confined."

" Thank Heaven, Ethelbert," said Mildred, fervently, " that you were not sacrificed to the hatred and vengeance of that guilty man."

Ethelbert could not properly express the gratitude he felt for these observations, which he was convinced were made in all sincerity, and Sir Aldobrand did not offer to interrupt them in their mutual congratulations, for he felt too much overjoyed himself.

It was some time before they could compose their feelings, and then our heroine briefly related all that had happened to her since they had last met, to which Ethelbert listened with mingled feelings of shame and indignation.

" The cowardly miscreant !" he ejaculated, when she had concluded.   " But if he flatters himself that he will escape without punishment, he will find himself much mistaken.   Oh, I will have ample satisfaction for the misery which he has caused us all."

" All in good time, Ethelbert," remarked Sir Aldobrand ; " Lord Ruthlyn, no doubt, when he finds that both you and Mildred have escaped, will be careful not to come in contact with you ; and it is sufficiently satisfactory for us to know that we have completely defeated his diabolical plans.   He can never have the consummate daring to make any future attempt."

" I know not," returned Ethelbert ; " but, after what he has already been guilty of, we have a right to be watchful and wary, and to regard him with suspicion."

" Very true," coincided the baronet ; " but inform us what has happened to you since you have been confined in the tower.   It is a most extraordinary circumstance that Lord Ruthlyn should have chosen that place above all others."

Ethelbert having taken a few minutes to collect his thoughts, complied with the request of Sir Aldobrand, and the reader may very well imagine the astonishment and attention with which he and Mildred listened as Ethelbert proceeded ; but when he related the strange and melancholy cry which he had so frequently heard, and shewed them the manuscript written by Almira, which he had found in his dungeon, their amazement was increased tenfold.

Sir Aldobrand having hastily glanced at the contents of this melancholy and singular document, exclaimed,—

"Good God! is it possible that my wretched brother could have been the atrocious miscreant he is here represented? A murderer! oh, horror! I cannot, dare not, credit the dreadful statement."

"And yet," remarked Ethelbert, "what reason have we to doubt the assertion of the unfortunate writer?"

"She might have been labouring under an aberration of intellect," said Sir Aldobrand, "and certainly some of the statements are so wild and extravagant that it appears scarcely possible they could ever have occurred."

"But there is much reason, notwithstanding, in the whole substance of the fearful narrative," returned Ethelbert, "and I do not see that we have any cause whatever to doubt the truth of what Almira de Montreville states in her confession, especially when we bear in mind the subsequent mysterious conduct and disappearance of my misguided uncle and his lady, after Almira had denounced him from the altar."

"Too true, too true!" said Sir Aldobrand, with a sigh. "I fear there is too much reason to credit the awful tale. Oh, my wretched brother! who could have imagined that you could ever have sinned so greatly! May Heaven have mercy on your soul!"

The baronet paced the apartment for some minutes in a state of the greatest agitation, and Ethelbert was at a loss to find arguments which might afford him the least consolation.

"To think that the name of De Lancy should be stained with human blood!" he said, after a pause, "and that the blood of an innocent child! Oh, God! surely he must have been mad, or the fiend of darkness could never have gained such powerful and fatal ascendancy over him. Alas! what fresh horrors shall we hear of the old Tower of Bransdorf! The manuscript, too, breaks off so abruptly that it leaves us in a state of doubt and perplexity as to what afterwards happened to the unfortunate Almira, and how she contrived to escape from the old tower, and afterwards to appear in the chapel on the memorable day of Sir Martin's union."

"No," remarked Ethelbert; "it is indeed most strange, and I am completely at a loss to fathom it. Did you ever hear whether the parents of Almira were living?"

"No," answered the baronet; "I had no opportunity of doing so, for, until I saw this manuscript, I was not acquainted with the early part of Almira's history, for my brother resisted all my inquiries, and would not divulge anything."

"And do you really think that Almira died of poison at the altar, after invoking the horrible curse upon Sir Martin's head?" asked Ethelbert.

"Oh, there could be no doubt of that," said Sir Aldobrand; "but I am completely at a loss to account for the mysterious disappearance of the body."

"It appears, then," said Mildred, who had been deeply reflecting on all she had heard, "that this singular being who has so often crossed my path, and who was the instrument in the hands of Lord Ruthlyn to decoy me from the castle, is no other than the Ulrica mentioned in the manuscript."

"There can be little doubt of it," remarked Sir Aldobrand; "and if she could be secured, she might be prevailed upon to unravel everything, and set at once our doubts at rest. We must adopt some plan to get her in our power. But it appears evident, from what you have stated, Ethelbert, that there must be, or has been, some unhappy female confined in the tower, and I wonder that you did not mention the circumstance before we came away, so that a search might have been made."

"Oh, you need not feel surprised, my dear father," replied Ethelbert, "that, in my joy at seeing you, and the delightful anticipation of so soon again beholding Mildred, I should forget everything else. But it may not yet be too late to release the sufferer, if she be indeed confined in one of the dungeons of the tower, which I have every reason to believe she is; and, indeed, I am most anxious to ascertain that fact, and to discover who she is."

"No time must be lost in making the necessary search," remarked Sir Aldobrand, "or she may perish for want. She surely must be confined there at the instance of Lord Ruthlyn."

"The fellow who attended upon me strongly denied that she was," said Ethelbert; "but refused to inform me who she was, or by whose commands she was detained a prisoner."

"We have now the means of satisfying ourselves," observed the baronet, "and the

sooner we set about the task the better.   The day is not far advanced, and after we have
rested ourselves for awhile, we had better at once repair to the tower.   Mildred can
amuse herself by perusing the manuscript while we are gone.   I know not how it is, but
something seems to tell me that we are about to make an important discovery, in which
my sweet Mildred may not be wholly uninterested."

"Oh, why should you think so, my dear sir?" said Mildred, eagerly.   "What discovery is it likely there will be made which can be of any particular importance to me?"

"I scarcely know how to answer you, or to account for my own conjectures," returned
Sir Aldobrand; "but still I cannot divest my mind of the singular impression.   You
must recollect, Mildred, how closely connected your history is with the Tower of
Bransdorf."

Mildred sighed as she recalled to her memory the manner in which she was discovered
there by old Sampson Hewley, under such strange and awful circumstances, and an unaccountable feeling took possession of her senses, and she could not help encouraging
similar thoughts to those which the baronet had acknowledged; but why she should do
so she could not imagine.

She would have been glad to accompany Sir Aldobrand and Ethelbert to the tower, for
she still felt the most anxious curiosity to inspect it, particularly those apartments where
she had been found when an infant, and she requested Sir Aldobrand to allow her to do
so; but he objected to it, and she was therefore compelled to yield to his decision.

After they had partaken of some refreshment, they departed on their expedition, and
Mildred was left to herself.

When she was alone, she gave free vent to the emotions which agitated her bosom, and
poured forth her unbounded gratitude to Heaven for the preservation of Ethelbert, whom
she felt that she loved with greater ardour than ever, and fervently hoped that the time
would come, when, the mystery connected with her origin being satisfactorily unravelled,
Sir Aldobrand would no longer refuse to sanction their nuptial vows.   She was certain
that on this result alone her future and complete happiness entirely depended, and that if
she was not destined to become the wife of Ethelbert, no other man could ever possess
her heart.

How deeply did she sympathise in the misery which Ethelbert must have suffered
while confined in the tower, uncertain of the fate which awaited him, or that which had
befallen her.   She was confident that it could only have been equalled by her own, and
she was greatly shocked at the consummate villany of Lord Ruthlyn, who, she feared,
would not yet abandon his designs, but would seek some future opportunity of causing
them trouble.

At length she sat down, having somewhat composed her thoughts, and more carefully
perused the manuscript which had fallen into the hands of Ethelbert in so singular a
manner.   She could not but deeply commiserate the misfortunes of the deluded Almira
de Montreville, and deprecate the cruelty and villany of Sir Martin; but she shuddered
as she did so, and a sensation of the most extraordinary kind took possession of her
bosom, which she was at a perfect loss to comprehend.

Having concluded the manuscript, in order to while away the time during the absence
of Sir Aldobrand and his son, she sauntered to the picture gallery, and fixing herself before the portrait of Sir Martin, gazed at it with deeper interest than ever.

Was it possible that that man, whose noble and handsome features were there so ably
delineated, could ever have been guilty of the fearful crimes which were attributed to
him?   Could he have been the destroyer of female innocence?   the murderer of his own
innocent offspring?   She could scarcely bring her mind to believe it, and yet there was
too powerful evidence of its being true.   She was unable to repress a sigh of regret as
these thoughts occurred to her; and notwithstanding all that had come to her knowledge
respecting Sir Martin de Lancy, she could not avoid contemplating his portrait with a
feeling approaching to reverence.

It was some time ere she could remove her eyes from it, and then, having devoted only
cursory attention to the other portraits, she returned to her apartment, and awaited the
return of Sir Aldobrand and Ethelbert with no small degree of impatience.

In the meantime, the baronet and his son made their way to the tower, filled with expectation, and anxious to penetrate the mystery connected with the building.   If the unfortunate woman had been confined there at the time Sir Aldobrand made the attempt
upon the tower, it is quite certain that they would find her there now; for she could

have had no opportunity of effecting her escape, as it was left in possession of the baronet's adherents ; and they therefore entertained the strongest hope that they should be able to rescue an unfortunate fellow being from misery and oppression.

The man who had attended upon Ethelbert during his incarceration was among the prisoners, and, on arriving at the tower, they made their way to the room in which he was confined, in the hope that by holding out to him a promise of mercy, they sheuld be enabled to elicit from him the information they wanted.

They found him, however, stern and inflexible, and he rejected all their offers of clemency with determined obstinacy, and refused to answer any questions they put to him in a satisfactory manner. He was a hardened scoundrel, and set their threats at defiance.

" This obstinacy can do you no good, but will only serve to aggravate the punishment that will be inflicted on you for the crimes you have committed," said Sir Aldobrand; " whereas, if you were to become candid, and explain all you know, you might even receive a free pardon."

" You talk to me in vain, Sir Aldobrand de Lancy," answered the ruffian. " I know the consequences of the offences I have committed, and do not shrink from them. Do as you please with me. I care not. But you shall elicit nothing from me, and I know you will not be able to do so from any of my colleagues."

" You had better bethink yourself," said Ethelbert.

·' I need none of your advice," returned the fellow, scornfully ; " my mind is made up."

" In what part of the tower is this unfortunate woman confined ?" demanded the baronet.

" Nowhere now," answered the man, with a malicious grin.

" Nowhere !" repeated Sir Aldobrand, with a look of incredulity.

" Not in the tower," added the fellow. " She has been removed hours ago."

" By whom, and how ?"

" I do not choose to satisfy you."

" He only mocks us," remarked Ethelbert. " How is it possible that any one could have been removed from the tower without the knowledge of the men we left in charge of it ?"

" Ha, ha, ha !" laughed the hardened villain ; " you little know the persons you have to deal with."

" It is false. I will not believe you," said Sir Aldobrand.

" Then, if you cannot believe me, why do you waste your time in interrogating me ? However, you are masters of the tower, and can therefore soon satisfy yourselves."

" Will nothing induce you to be more explicit ?"

" Nothing that you can offer."

" You will repent this obstinacy."

" Indeed I shall not."

" And do you still persist in asserting that this woman was not the prisoner of Lord Ruthlyn de Bohun," demanded Ethelbert.

" I do."

" At whose instance, then, was she confined ?" asked Sir Aldobrand.

" That you may find out in the best manner you can," replied the fellow, doggedly.

" Do you know her name ?"

" I do."

" What is it ?"

" What is the use of putting these questions to me ? Have I not before told you that I will not disclose anything ? You may do with me as you like ; I will never reveal that which I have been paid to keep a secret."

Sir Aldobrand and Ethelbert saw plainly that it was only a waste of time to put further questions to him, and not believing his assertion as to the removal of the prisoner, they commenced their search in the dungeons beneath the tower, and immediately made their way to that adjoining the one in which Ethelbert had been confined, and from whence he had imagined the dismal cry to proceed.

The door was standing open ; but the dungeon was completely empty, although it was quite certain, from its appearance, that it had recently been occupied. All that it contained was an old, broken stool and a wretched, dirty mattrass, stretched upon the damp ground. There were also the remains of some coarse provisions, and a stone pitcher containing water.

" This is doubtless the place where the unfortunate woman was confined," said Ethelbert, "and the ruffian appears to have spoken the truth. But how is it possible she can have been removed, and by whom? for I heard her only a short time before your attack upon the tower."

"It must have been done while that attack was being made," said Sir Aldobrand; "but let us examine further, for after all she may be confined in some other part of the tower."

They were about to leave the dungeon, when, happening to cast his eyes towards the ground, Sir Aldobrand beheld a small scrap of paper, which had some writing on it. He picked it up, and found that it was the portion of a letter. But no sooner did he behold the characters, than he started, and turned very pale.

"It is my brother's handwriting!" he exclaimed. "Oh, well do I remember it!"

The only words which he could make out were the following:—

"It is useless to appeal to me, Editha; my purpose is fixed, and ——"

"Ah!" exclaimed the baronet, "a strange thought flashes across my brain. Could the unhappy being who was confined here be the deeply-injured wife of my guilty brother, the Lady Editha?"

"It is not improbable," remarked Ethelbert, "for it is not likely that this letter would have been in the possession of any other person. The mystery increases, and this state of doubt and suspense becomes almost insupportable."

"Oh, should the unfortunate Lady Editha be still in existence," ejaculated Sir Aldobrand, "what would I not give to discover her! But I feel almost satisfied that it was her whom we saw in the chapel of the castle, and who dropped the miniature of Sir Martin which I now have in my possession. Altogether the mystery is perfectly inexplicable."

"It is," coincided Ethelbert.

"How unfortunate it is that we did not search these dungeons before we quitted the tower," said the baronet. "In all probability we should then have discovered the prisoner."

"Yes," said Ethelbert. "It is a pity that I did not think to inform you of what I had heard; but in the confusion of the moment it is not surprising that I should forget it. Come, we do but delay, and after all we may find the unknown prisoner in some other part of the tower."

They left the dungeon, and examined all the rest; but they were entirely vacated, and did not appear as though they had been occupied for many years.

They then entered the room in which the ruffians who had conveyed Ethelbert there had been accustomed to assemble. They found a quantity of arms there, and other articles, which left no doubt on their minds as to the real character of the fellows. They were evidently robbers, and Ethelbert and his father were astonished that they should have had the daring to have taken up their residence in the tower, so near the castle, and should hitherto have escaped detection.

Having strictly examined all the lower apartments, they proceeded to the rooms above, but with no better success; and it was now evident the man had spoken the truth, and that the woman had, by some means or other, which they could not imagine, been removed from the tower.

"This is thoroughly provoking," said Sir Aldobrand; "for, after the discovery of the fragment of my guilty brother's letter in the dungeon, my curiosity is more than ever excited."

As the baronet thus spoke, he approached one of the windows, and looked out. A sudden exclamation from him attracted the attention of Ethelbert, and he advanced towards him, and inquired the cause. Sir Aldobrand pointed towards the court-yard of the tower, and Ethelbert then beheld the form of a woman standing in the centre, and apparently surveying the building with a scrutinising eye.

"It is Ulrica," he exclaimed; "she must have been bold, indeed, to venture here, and when she must be aware of what has taken place. Let us be quick, and we may then secure her."

They left the room, and hastened down the stairs. They were not a second in arriving in the court, but when they got there, she was gone.

Disappointed and vexed, they stood for a moment or two, undecided how to act, but at length they quitted the court-yard, and gained the summit of the hill. They looked down, and beheld Ulrica standing at the foot. She looked up towards them, waved her hand menacingly, and laughed aloud in defiance of them.

"Quick! quick!" cried Sir Aldobrand, "she cannot escape us now."

But no sooner did they commence descending the hill, than Ulrica turned round, and fled with a precipitation which was truly astonishing, and before they had reached the bottom, she had gained a considerable distance, and, dashing through an opening in a high banked hedge, they lost sight of her in an instant.

"The woman has fairly outstripped us," said the baronet; "but she must be secured at some future time, if possible; much depends on her."

"True," remarked Ethelbert; "there can be no doubt that she is deeply implicated in all the evils that have attended us. The worst of it is that we do not know where she conceals herself, or we might take her by surprise. The enmity she seems to bear towards our family is easily accounted for, from her having been the confidential attendant and friend of the unfortunate Almira de Montreville."

They returned to the castle very much disappointed at the ill success which had attended them, and found Mildred anxiously awaiting them. She eagerly inquired whether tthey had met with anything to throw a light upon the mystery, and was as much disappointed as themselves when they informed her. The fragment of the letter, however, which Sir Aldobrand had picked up in the dungeon, interested her, and she was inclined to be of the same opinion as her benefactor and Ethelbert, namely, that the hapless prisoner who had been confined in the dungeon was no other than the long lost Lady Editha herself.

These facts afforded them much subject for conversation, especially the appearance of Ulrica ; and Mildred was clearly of opinion that, until she could be secured, or won over by kindness to confide in them, they would not be completely safe from danger. Sir Aldobrand and Ethelbert, however, endeavoured to quiet her apprehensions, which they considered were groundless, and, after a time, they succeeded.

CHAPTER XXVII.

THE RAGE OF LORD RUTHLYN.—HIS DETERMINATION.—MORE MYSTERY.—THE WARN-
ING.—THE FURTHER FULFILMENT OF THE CURSE.

ALL that night, so memorable for its stirring events, the mind of Mildred was too deeply engrossed by the variety of conflicting thoughts and reflections which they naturally gave rise to, and the consequences which it was not at all unlikely would follow, that she almost sought her pillow in vain. The dark and impenetrable mysteries connected with the old tower, and the fearful details she had perused in the manuscript of the unfortunate Almira, deeply interested her, at the same time they greatly perplexed her, and she would fain have brought her mind to disbelieve that Sir Martin de Lancy could be capable of the villanous acts attributed to him. For the reason of his close alliance to those who were so dear to her, namely, Sir Aldobrand and Ethelbert, she would gladly have scouted the idea ; and also from that extraordinary feeling to which allusion has been frequently made, and which invariably came over her whenever her thoughts were directed to Sir Martin's singular and melancholy history.

Most deeply was her sympathy excited, both for Almira de Montreville and the Lady Editha, but more especially the latter, who, from all the accounts she had heard of her, was a most amiable woman, and had never done anything to merit the untoward fate which had attended her.

The conduct of Sir Martin in this instance, so soon after their marriage, and when no one had a right to imagine but that he loved his new-made bride with all the ardour he had ever professed, was most unaccountable, and the more our heroine endeavoured to arrive at any reasonable conclusion, the more deeply involved did her brain become in the maze of fruitless conjecture. Most assuredly he was the only aggressor, and in no shape whatever could the Lady Editha have been at all to blame. But was the hapless lady still in existence? Recent events half persuaded her that she was, and that it was her whom they had seen in the chapel of the castle, and who was the wretched prisoner whose melancholy wailings Ethelbert had heard, and who had disappeared in so singular a manner from the tower, and this idea appeared to be all but confirmed by the fragment of the letter in the handwriting of his brother, which Sir Aldobrand had found in the dungeon.

From these ambiguous and impenetrable subjects the thoughts of Mildred turned to Ethelbert. Never could she be sufficiently grateful to Heaven for his deliverance from the power of the villain, Lord Ruthlyn, who, she felt satisfied, to gratify his feelings of hatred and revenge, would not have hesitated ultimately to have sacrificed his life. She felt the passion he had inspired her with hourly increase in strength, and she was thoroughly convinced that he returned it with equal fervour ; but her gratification was greatly diminished by the certainty that Sir Aldobrand would never sanction their addresses, while the torturing mystery connected with her origin remained unravelled, and unless it was satisfactorily shown that she was not the offspring of shame, or that her proper station in life was equal to his. And what hope had she any reason to encourage that this would ever be accomplished ? None.

These thoughts greatly agitated Mildred's bosom, and she could not help fearing that there was much misery yet in store for her and Ethelbert, and that it would have been much better for them both had they never met.

At last, all being silent in the castle, and with the hope of being enabled to snatch an hour or two's repose, Mildred did retire to bed, but it was not until the hour of midnight ad long since flown that she sunk into a kind of half conscious dose.

From this she was aroused by plainly hearing the light and stealthy sound of footsteps in the chamber. Startled and alarmed, she sprang up in the bed, and looking timidly around, she was satisfied that she beheld the form of a woman, attired in white, hastily, but cautiously retreating from the room by the door, which she remembered in an instant she had forgot to fasten before she retired to rest. In a moment the form was gone, and Mildred could not hear the least sound of its retiring footsteps on the stairs.

Terror, for a second or two, completely paralysed all her faculties, and she could neither move or utter the least cry of alarm; but at length, wound up to an insupportable pitch of wonder and curiosity, she sprang from the bed, and darted towards the door, and looked beyond, but all was buried in darkness, and no object met her gaze.

She stood for an instant or two transfixed with terror, and her mind was bewildered and distracted as if she had been under the influence of a dream. Her first impulse, however, was to arouse Annie, who slept in an adjoining room, and for that purpose she opened the door, which was not fastened, and entered the chamber.

Annie being suddenly aroused from sleep, and beholding our heroine standing by the bedside, did not at first recognise her; she was, therefore, naturally considerably alarmed, but when she did discover who it was, she exclaimed,—

"Gracious me, my dear young lady, what is the matter? How pale and frightened you look. What has alarmed you, and what brings you here from your chamber at this hour?"

Mildred, for a few moments, was unable to return any answer, but at length she said, in a tremulous tone,—

"Annie, some person has been in my room, not many minutes ago; they aroused me from my slumbers, and I beheld them retreating from it."

Annie looked at her with perfect amazement, as she ejaculated,—

"Some one has been in your chamber, miss! Oh, it is impossible; you must have been dreaming, indeed you must."

"No, Annie," returned Mildred, impatiently; "I am confident I saw the form as plainly as I behold you now. It was that of a female, and clad in white; but in an instant she was gone, and I did not hear the sound of her retiring footsteps on the stairs."

Annie was now more alarmed than ever, but still she could not persuade herself but that our heroine must have been deceived, and she observed,—

"How is it possible that any one could enter your chamber, miss, when there is only one means of ingress?"

"I forgot to fasten the door before I retired to rest," answered Mildred; "and, therefore, it is easily accounted for."

"That certainly was imprudent of you, my dear young lady," returned Annie; "but still, depend upon it, your imagination has only been worked upon by a dream. Who is there in the castle who would have been so bold as to intrude themselves in your chamber?"

"It was no one connected with the castle, I am satisfied; and, from the slight glimpse I was enabled to obtain of the form, I strongly suspect it is the same that has appeared to me more than once or twice before, under similar circumstances. Alas! I fear that danger again threatens me from some secret power."

"Heaven forbid, miss; but this is certainly a strange and alarming adventure. Would that it was morning, that Sir Aldobrand and his son might be apprized of it, and institute immediate inquiries into it."

Annie had now arisen, and attended Mildred into her chamber. Here, having secured the door, and listened attentively to catch any sound that might be stirring in the castle, but all remaining silent, they seated themselves by the window, and, deeply engaged in conversation, anxiously awaited the arrival of the morning, that the circumstance might be communicated to Sir Aldobrand and Ethelbert.

Mildred was so positive, that Annie was now convinced that she had not been mistaken, and she became lost in wonder and alarm.

"But do you not think, miss," she said, after a pause, "that, after all, it might have been one of the female domestics, who might have mistaken your chamber for her own?"

"Oh, no; I'm sure it was the same form that I beheld before," replied our heroine; "once, when a child, standing at the foot of my bed; and on two or three subsequent occasions. Who the mysterious being can be, and why she thus haunts me in so singular a manner, I am at a loss to conjecture."

" It is most extraordinary. But it does not seem that it is with any evil designs, or she might have taken the opportunity of putting her intentions into execution when she discovered you asleep. And by what possible means could she have gained access to the castle ?"

" I am totally at a loss what to think," replied Mildred. The mystery seems to be impenetrable; and it appears as though I were doomed to be kept in a continual state of alarm and suspense."

" I hope sincerely, miss, that everything will shortly be elucidated to your satisfaction. All is now perfectly quiet in the castle, and it is not at all likely that anything will again occur to disturb or alarm you. See, too, the day is just beginning to dawn; but it will yet be some hours before Sir Aldobrand and his son are stirring."

Mildred returned no answer to this, but with eager eyes she watched the grey mists as they gradually evaporated in the east, and gave place to the first crimson blush of day. It afforded her mind some little relief; but still, when she ruminated upon the singular adventures of the night, it was impossible that she could be entirely happy and contented.

Black and frowning amidst the first blush of sunlight, the ancient Tower of Bransdorf met her gaze, and when she reflected upon the many strange and dark transactions which had been perpetrated within the walls of that gloomy building, and the many extraordinary mysteries connected with it, and which in all probability might never be unravelled, she could not help shuddering with a sensation of awe and horror.

Time passed on, and the sun at length burst forth in full splendour, and imparted additional beauty to the scenery around. Mildred did feel her spirits somewhat revive beneath its genial influence, and the terrors of the night were in some degree diminished.

In order that she might endeavour further to recruit her spirits, she proposed to Annie that they should take a walk for awhile in the extensive grounds attached to the castle, until Sir Aldobrand and Ethelbert should have arisen, and as Annie, of course, had no objection to offer, they quitted the apartment, and quietly descending the stairs, they emerged from the castle, and commenced their ramble, Annie doing her utmost, by cheerful conversation, to divert the mind of Mildred from the oppressive and bewildering thoughts which distracted it; and in which praiseworthy effort she was not altogether unsuccessful.

They had rambled about the grounds in this manner for some time, when the sound of footsteps from behind startled them, and, looking round, the astonishment and alarm of them both we need not attempt to depicture when they beheld the tall and gaunt figure of Ulrica approaching them.

They uttered a simultaneous cry of astonishment and alarm; but Ulrica, with a menacing gesture, enjoined them to silence, and then rapidly approaching, she stood before them.

She turned her gaze immediately from the terrified Annie, and fixed it full upon our heroine, who, as the recollection of her former treachery, by which she had been placed in the power of Lord Ruthlyn, rushed upon her memory, was completely petrified with fear, and was unable to give utterance to a syllable. She could only stare at her aghast, and await the result of the unexpected and fearful meeting.

Ulrica, for a moment or two, never altered her attitude, but at last, when she advanced even nearer to Mildred, and grasped her wrist with her long, bony fingers, she could not repress a scream.

" Silence, girl !" fiercely commanded Ulrica, whose eyes flashed with the wildness of madness. " Silence! or you will deeply repent it. Ulrica is not the being to be trifled with, or disobeyed. This moment I could gratify the feelings of hatred I bear towards thee ; but it is not my purpose at present. Events, important events, must operate in due course, and, therefore, for a time thou art spared."

" Fearful woman," demanded Mildred, in a tremulous voice, and eyeing her with increased consternation, while Annie was rivetted to the spot, and could not attempt to fly from the place or to call for assistance. " Fearful woman," repeated our heroine, " why do you thus seek to persecute and intimidate me ?"

" Hast thou never heard of Almira's curse ?" said Ulrica, with a malicious look. " Oh, it was a rare accompaniment to the marriage rites of the deceiver—the murderer; and it is working now, most bravely is it working; and tears of blood shall it extort yet from all the hatred race of De Lancy !"

"And why am I selected as a victim to this cruelty ?" asked Mildred. "What harm have I ever done to you or mortal being ?"

"What harm !" shouted Ulrica. "Girl, girl, thou knowest not the cause there is to loathe thee. But no matter; it is coming—the time will soon be here. Remember the curse—Almira's curse; it will descend with awful and destructive force on all connected with the detested family of De Lancy."

With these words the singular woman spurned the terrified girl away from her, and, dashing along an avenue which led to the gates of the grounds, disappeared from the view, in what way neither Mildred nor Annie were in a condition to notice.

It was some minutes before they could either of them move or speak, but at last Mildred ejaculated,—

"Good God! what fresh dangers are in store for me ? And why should this strange being thus pursue me ? For what reason should I be included in the dreadful curse of the unfortunate Almira ? This torturing mystery is insupportable."

"She is certainly a most singular and fearful woman," remarked Annie; "but surely she must be mad. How she gained access to these grounds, and at the very time when we were walking in them, I am at a loss to imagine. But come, miss, let us re-enter the castle, where we shall, at least, be secure from danger."

"Even that is doubtful, after all that has taken place," replied our heroine. "There will evidently be no safety for any of us until Ulrica is secured."

"What a different character she appears to be to what she is represented in the manuscript of Almira de Montreville," said Annie.

"She is indeed."

"But do you not think, miss, that it was her whom you imagine you saw in your chamber last night?"

"Oh, no, I am certain it was not her," answered Mildred. "But let us away from this place; there may be danger while we remain here."

Annie took her arm, and after having looked around them to see that no one was lurking near, they entered the castle, and once more retired to the apartment they had quitted, as Sir Aldobrand and Ethelbert were not yet stirring. Here Mildred threw herself on a seat, and for a short time was completely absorbed in the thoughts which these singular and alarming adventures had naturally engendered.

She felt as keenly for the danger to which her revered benefactor and Ethelbert were exposed, by the malicious threats of Ulrica, as for herself, and fervently she prayed that the Almighty would avert any calamity that might be impending o'er their heads. Every word that Ulrica had uttered was strongly impressed upon her memory; but as regarded herself her observations were totally inexplicable. Was it because she was supported by the benevolence of Sir Aldobrand, that she should be included in the terrible curse that had been invoked upon his family ? But why should such weight be attached to that malediction ? The Supreme would surely not suffer the consequences of another's crimes to descend upon the innocent.

"No, no," she ejaculated, "I will not believe it. Sir Aldobrand is good, amiable, and just. He never inflicted wilful injury upon any of his fellow creatures. Ethelbert has ever followed in his honourable course, and Providence will never permit them to suffer for the crimes of their wretched and misguided relative."

"You speak correctly, miss," said Annie, "and I'm glad to hear you take this view of the painful and annoying subject. I trust that the good Sir Aldobrand will be able effectually to set at defiance all the evil machinations of his enemies, for I'm certain that he ought not to have one in the world."

At length they heard the inmates of the castle stirring, and Mildred immediately sought the presence of Sir Aldobrand and Ethelbert, anxious to make them acquainted with what had happened.

They both noticed the paleness and anxiety of her looks immediately on her entrance into the apartment in which they were awaiting her, and eagerly they inquired the cause.

With what amazement they listened to the account she gave! and when she had concluded, Sir Aldobrand exclaimed,—

"By Heaven, this mystery upon mystery is enough to tire the patience of any one, especially when we know ourselves to be so totally undeserving of such annoyance. If our enemies can thus gain access to us whenever they please, and at all hours, in spite of every precaution to prevent them, we cannot consider ourselves safe for a moment. That you met with Ulrica in the manner you describe, my dear Mildred, of course is certain; but in respect to the form which you suppose you saw in your chamber, I am inclined to think you were mistaken."

"Indeed, my dear sir," returned our heroine, "I was not. And when it is remembered that I accidentally forgot to secure the door of my apartment, and that it is not the first time I have been subject to such visitations, I humbly presume that there is nothing at all improbable in what I state."

"I am perfectly astounded," observed the baronet. "The depth of the plot which our enemies have concocted against us is far too great for my penetration. It certainly does not appear, Mildred, that this individual, whoever it may be, intends you any personal violence, or she could, it seems, have effected it ere now."

"And why should this woman, Ulrica, pursue Mildred with such enmity?" said Ethelbert.

"I cannot conceive," answered his father, "unless it is that she is under my protection."

"And there has been sufficient proof that she is connected with Lord Ruthlyn," added Ethelbert.

"True."

"Every means must be adopted to discover the secret retreat of Ulrica, so that she may be secured, and made to render an account of herself and her motives," suggested Ethelbert.

"Yes," coincided Sir Aldobrand; "but I am afraid we shall find that no easy task. Could we but obtain an interview with her, and prevail upon her with kindness, she might be induced to disclose all she knows."

"Her hatred for our family, I apprehend, is too deep rooted to be easily eradicated," remarked Ethelbert. "It is astonishing how she can thus contrive to elude us."

They were interrupted in the midst of the conversation by the entrance of a servant, who informed his master that Allan, one of the men who had been left at the tower in charge of the prisoners, was below, and requested to be allowed to speak to him.

Sir Aldobrand desired that he should be shown up, and Allan directly afterwards entered the apartment, with a faltering step, and an expression of countenance which showed that he had something disagreeable to communicate, and moreover that he did not much fancy the task which had devolved upon him.

"How now, Allan!" demanded Sir Aldobrand; "what brings you here? Why have you left the tower?"

Allan attempted to stammer out a reply; but he could not, and the baronet became impatient.

"Why do you not answer me?" he demanded. "Has anything serious happened? What of the prisoners?"

"Alas! Sir Aldobrand.—Oh, dear me!" stuttered forth the poor, simple fellow, and he looked as if he was just upon the point of receiving sentence of death for some atrocious crime.

"Have you gone mad?" said Ethelbert.

"Oh, no—yes—no—yes, please your honour."

"What of the prisoners at the tower, I again demand?" said the baronet hastily.

"Oh, very bad indeed, Sir Aldobrand," replied the man; "but I hope you'll forgive me, for indeed it was not my fault—that is ——"

"Will you be explicit, sirrah!" interrupted his master. "Are the men left in your charge secure?"

"No—yes—no; that is—oh, dear me!"

"No?"

"No, your honour, they are not very secure," answered Allan, mustering a little more courage.

"What do you mean? How is that?" impatiently inquired Sir Aldobrand.

"Because they are gone, Sir Aldobrand."

"Gone!"

"Ye—es, your honour."

"Escaped!"

"Ye—es, your honour."

"Confusion!" exclaimed the baronet. "This is a most unfortunate job. Our bitterest enemies again let loose upon us. You blundering rascal, what excuse have you to offer for this gross neglect of your duty ?"

"Oh, pardon me, sir!" returned the poor fellow, sinking on his knees; "indeed it was not altogether our fault."

"*Our* fault! then you have all been to blame ?"

"Yes, sir—no, sir—that is ——"

"You had better not tire our patience, Allan," said Ethelbert; "but at once, and in a few words, explain all about it. How was it you and your companions suffered the wretches to escape ?"

"I ask pardon, your honour, but please you we did not suffer them to escape ; they went without our leave."

"The man has certainly lost his senses," remarked Ethelbert.

"The poor fellow is only flurried," said Mildred. "My good man, collect yourself, and explain the whole unfortunate circumstance as briefly as possible."

"Thank you, my dear young lady," said Allan gratefully, "I will. I'm sure I'm as sorry as if ——"

"No matter," interrupted Sir Aldobrand; "go on."

"Well, your honour, you know you ordered me and Gregory to sit up with that arrant rascal who so obstinately refused to answer the questions which your honour put to him, and so we did."

"Well, well!"

"Oh, dear! I am so sorry that ——"

"Go on, go on, and do not fear."

"Oh, thank you, sir. Well, all went on right enough, till about twelve o'clock, when it was so very dull in that old tower that I suppose it had an effect upon Gregory, for he fell asleep."

"A very pretty fellow to be set to keep watch over anything, truly," observed Ethelbert.

"Well, and what did you do ?" asked Sir Aldobrand, scarcely able to repress a smile at the man's simplicity.

"Why, your honour," answered Allan, "I tried all I could to wake him; but I could not, and, by degrees, I felt so drowsy myself, that I could not keep my eyes open for the very life of me, and ——"

"And so you fell asleep also ?"

"Yes, your honour."

"And what then ?"

"Why—why, your honour, how long I had slept I don't know; but when I opened my eyes again, I found Gregory still sleeping soundly, and the prisoner gone."

"Proceed, proceed."

"I roused Gregory, in a state of great alarm, and we both made for the door ; but the villain had been too deep for us, for we then found that he had helped himself to the bunch of keys which Gregory had about him, and after letting himself out, locked us in."

"You arrant simpletons !"

"Oh, Sir Aldobrand, pray forgive us ; we did not do it wilfully ; we could not help it."

"Go on with your story. Your prisoner escaped ?"

"Yes, your honour."

"What became of the others ?"

"Escaped also."

"I suppose he kindly let them out ?"

"No doubt of it, your honour ; for when we alarmed our companions, and got out of the room in which he had fastened us, we found that every one of them had gone also, and none of our comrades were aware of it."

"Well, you've made a pretty job of this," said Sir Aldobrand, in a tone of vexation; "now answer me. Had you and your companion taken anything to drink before you fell asleep ?"

Allan hesitated and trembled.

"Tell the truth," said his master.

"Oh, yes, sir," replied Allan, "I am telling the truth ; indeed I am. Well, then, all that I and Gregory had, I declare, was a little drop which the prisoner gave us of his beverage, and ——"

" Which the prisoner gave you ?"

"Yes, your honour ; but it was a very little drop, and he seemed in such a good humour, that we could not refuse him."

"Ah !" said Sir Aldobrand, "I see plainly enough how it is ; the ruffian had mixed some narcotic with the drink he gave these foolish fellows, and has played his game amazingly well. But it is very vexatious to think that they have escaped, when so much depended upon the disclosures which some of them might have been persuaded to make."

"It is indeed," coincided Ethelbert, "and every vigilance must be used to retake them."

"There must," said the baronet. "What time was it that you and your silly companion discovered that the villains had fled ?"

"It was just at break of day, your honour," replied Allan.

"And you say that it was about midnight when the influence of sleep came over you ?"

"It was, Sir Aldobrand."

"Then the wretches have had many hours to themselves to make good their flight."

"It is quite evident they have," observed Ethelbert. "They have well succeeded in their designs, and pursuit would be quite useless."

"I sent some of our men in different directions, with the hope of re-taking the fugitives, as soon as we discovered the escape of the scoundrels," said Allan.

"And of course they have been unsuccessful," remarked Ethelbert.

"I do not know, sir," replied Allan, "for they had not returned when I left the tower to bring the unfortunate intelligence. Oh, dear! I cannot express to your honours the sorrow I feel at what has taken place."

"There, get you gone," said Sir Aldobrand, "and learn to be more cautious in future."

"Oh, yes, I will," said the grateful Allan. "Thank your honours for your gracious clemency."

With that the poor fellow bowed himself obsequiously out of the room, very glad to think that he had escaped so easily.

"This is a bad job," observed Sir Aldobrand, when the man was gone ; "for there is no knowing to what further danger or annoyance we may be subjected through it."

"Very true," remarked Ethelbert ; "and although it is perfectly clear how the fellows contrived their plot, I think it is advisable that we should go down to the tower immediately, in order that we may further investigate the matter."

With this suggestion Sir Aldobrand agreed, and after having partaken of their morning repast, and endeavoured to diminish the excitement of Mildred, caused by the events which had within the last few hours occurred to her, they took their departure.

But, in spite of all they had said, Mildred's spirits were very much depressed, and the escape of the ruffians from the tower served to increase her apprehensions for their future safety ; and, moreover, she regretted it in consequence of the chance there might have been of their making such disclosures as would have unravelled many of the mysteries in which they were all so deeply interested.

In the meantime Sir Aldobrand and his son pursued their way to the tower, conversing on the events which had occurred to Mildred, and bitterly regretting the escape of the ruffians, from whom they had so much cause to dread future evil.

They were not long in arriving at the foot of the hill, on the summit of which the tower was erected, and looking up, they both uttered an exclamation of astonishment and anxiety, when they beheld, standing immediately before the principal entrance to the tower, and looking down upon them, the extraordinary woman of whom they had been conversing, Ulrica.

"By Heaven !" exclaimed Sir Aldobrand, "this woman's actions are unaccountable. No sooner does she enter our thoughts than she appears before us, and at all times and in all places. She seems to mock us, and to set us at defiance completely. But quick, Ethelbert, she surely cannot escape us now."

They darted up the hill ; but Ulrica offered to move not, until they were near the top, when, laughing derisively, she waved her hand to them with an air of defiance, and darting round an angle of the building, with most astonishing rapidity, was lost to their sight in an instant.

They were on the spot where she had been standing immediately after her, and rushed round that part of the tower where she had disappeared ; but they could see nothing of her.

"This is most extraordinay," said the baronet, in a tone of disappointment and vexation.

"She must either have sunk into the earth or got into the tower by some means," said

Ethelbert; "let us enter immediately, and probably we may encounter her, and gain the explanation we have long been so anxious to obtain."

They entered the tower by a private door, and proceeded at once to examine every room, both above and below, and having questioned the men minutely respecting the escape of the ruffians, without being able to make any further discovery, they returned home.

CHAPTER XXVIII.

THE DESTRUCTION OF THE OLD TOWER.—THE SEIZURE OF MILDRED—HER RESCUE, AND DEFEAT OF HER ENEMIES.—A DISCOVERY.—THE MYSTERY UNRAVELLED.

THE escape of the robbers caused Sir Aldobrand and Ethelbert no little uneasiness, and while they used every prompt and necessary precaution to guard against their guilty machinations, they made every search after them, and also to discover the retreat of their cowardly and guilty employer, Lord Ruthlyn.

Mildred was never permitted to walk out alone, for the baronet and his son had very little doubt that Lord Ruthlyn, who was not the man easily to abandon his designs, would make another attempt to get her in his power, and if he should again succeed, they could not but apprehend the worst consequences, urged on as he would be by the desperate character of his base and lawless passion, and, moreover, guided by feelings of revenge against them.

Additional persons were placed in the tower, and every other precaution taken to prevent its again becoming the retreat of their enemies; and every means were taken to discover Ulrica's place of concealment, but all to no purpose, for, notwithstanding the bold and mysterious manner in which that singular woman frequently made her appearance before them, she always contrived to elude them, and to set discovery at defiance.

They often reflected upon the female form they had, upon more than one occasion, seen in the chapel of the castle, and which Sir Aldobrand so strongly suspected to be his long lost sister-in-law, the unfortunate and much injured Lady Editha, and were most anxious to behold her again, and to find out the place where she was secreted ; but at present there seemed not the least probability of their being able to do so, and this kept the baronet and his son in a state of considerable suspense. They had little doubt that the female prisoner who had been confined in the tower at the same time as Ethelbert, was the same unfortunate being who had so strongly excited their sympathy and curiosity, and, if so, they feared that she might have fallen a victim to the cruel persecution and vengeance of her enemies, and, if such was the case, the mystery connected with her would never be unravelled, and they would be left in the same painful state of doubt and suspense. But, if it was indeed Lady Editha whom they had seen, Sir Aldobrand could not but continue to wonder that she did not make herself known to him, and seek that protection which she must be aware he would be so willing to afford her.

Thus several weeks wore away, without anything more particular or worthy of being recorded in these pages taking place ; and the excitement consequent upon the important and alarming events which had taken place became in some measure abated ; but their enemies were secretly at work to effect their nefarious ends, and had already concocted a diabolical plot, by which they hoped to accomplish all their wishes.

It was night, and although the hour was an early one, Mildred had already retired to her chamber, leaving Ethelbert and his father conversing in one of the rooms below. But Mildred felt no inclination to seek her pillow, but seating herself by the window, she gazed listlessly out upon the scenery beyond, and reflected deeply upon the many stirring and singular events of her past life, and wondered whether the secret of her birth would ever be unravelled. She cast her eyes towards the tower, which was dimly revealed to her view by the faint light of the moon, and all the fearful circumstances under which she had been there found, and the many impenetrable mysteries connected with that ancient place, rushed most vividly to her memory. Tears started to her eyes when she thought upon the probable fate of those parents whom she had never known, and a melancholy presentiment all at once crossed her mind that something of a most painful nature was about to happen ; though why she should think so she could not imagine ; still she found it impossible to get rid of the impression.

While she was still wrapped in these meditations, she was suddenly aroused by observing a red glare of light illumining the sky in the direction of the tower, and almost immediately afterwards clouds of sparks and a large volume of flame ascended from that ancient building, which rendered it evident that a dreadful conflagration had taken place. The flames spread with fearful rapidity, and the whole building was soon one mass of raging fire, which threatened its speedy and total destruction.

Mildred did not remain long to gaze on the destructive scene, but flew down stairs to apprize Ethelbert and the baronet ; but they were already aware of the circumstance, which caused the utmost excitement and consternation, and were gathering the servants together, in order to go to the scene of conflagration, to render what assistance they could, and to assist the persons who had been left in the tower to escape.

"Remain in your room, Mildred," said Sir Aldobrand, "till our return, and do not offer to move from it, for there is no knowing what danger may threaten ; for I strongly suspect that this is some deep-laid plot of our enemies, for other purposes than the mere destruction of the tower."

Mildred promised to follow this advice, and Sir Aldobrand, Ethelbert, and all the male servants who could be spared from the castle, immediately departed to the scene of the fire.

The whole of the tower seemed now to be enveloped in flames, the reflection from which illumined the heavens for miles around, and rendered every object as clearly distinct as broad day. The inhabitants rushed from every quarter to the scene of destruction, so that Sir Aldobrand and his son found no want of assistance, and nothing could surpass the excitement which prevailed; though many in their hearts were not sorry to behold the destruction of that old building, which they had ever regarded with feelings of horror and superstition.

So rapidly did the raging element spread, that it defied every effort to subdue it ; the men who had inhabited it fortunately escaped, and in little more than half an hour the Black Tower of Bransdorf was little more than a pile of smouldering ruins.

Sir Aldobrand gazed upon the scene of destruction with astonishment and awe, and he then eagerly inquired of the men in what manner they supposed the fire had originated ; but they all declared their utter inability to form the slightest conjecture, but at the same time vehemently protested that it had not been through any carelessness of their own.

" Then," said the baronet, " it must have been the work of some base incendiary."

" But how could any one have contrived to accomplish such a deed without being detected ?" said Ethelbert. " To me it appears almost impossible. Are you sure that no stranger was admitted, or could have gained secret access to the tower ?" he added, addressing himself to the men.

" Oh, quite sure, your honour," replied one of the men ; " we were careful to keep too strict a look out to suffer that."

" It is most strange," remarked Sir Aldobrand, " and must be strictly investigated."

They now moved away from the scene of the conflagration, and returned towards the castle, greatly excited by what had so unexpectedly taken place.

Sir Aldobrand and his son had not proceeded far, when they were suddenly startled by hearing the loud shrieks of a female towards the right of the road they were traversing, but apparently at no great distance off.

" Ah !" exclaimed Sir Aldobrand, " some unfortunate person needs our aid ; follow me, my friends, for, if we delay a minute, we may be too late."

They hurried in the direction from which the sounds had proceeded, and again the most piercing shrieks saluted their ears. In a few minutes, after winding around a lofty mound, they saw, by the light of the moon, a female struggling violently in the grasp of several ruffians, while a woman, in whose tall and masculine mien they immediately recognised Ulrica, stood by, apparently giving directions ; but the indignation and astonishment of Ethelbert and his father may readily be imagined when they recognised in their helpless victim their own loved Mildred.

Not long had Sir Aldobrand and Ethelbert quitted the castle, when Mildred was startled by hearing the sounds of several footsteps ascending the stairs towards her room, and, before she had time to inquire into the cause, the door was burst open, and Lord Ruthlyn and several other men stood before her. She screamed, but immediately found herself seized by the villains, and was speedily forced away from the castle by a private way, and without what servants were left at the castle having an opportunity to offer any resistance. When they had reached the open air, she beheld Ulrica standing at a short distance, and exulting in the success of the diabolical plot which she had herself concocted.

" Hold, villains !" shouted Ethelbert and his father in a breath ; " release your innocent victim, or dearly shall you pay for your brutality and daring."

Lord Ruthlyn and his infamous associates, seeing the superiority of the numbers that were rushing towards them, did release the terrified girl, who sank senseless on the earth ; and, uttering curses on the defeat of their designs, would have fled from the spot, but, before they could do so, were surrounded, and had no alternative left but to defend themselves in the best manner they could.

" Ah, miscreant," cried the enraged Ethelbert, when he confronted Lord Ruthlyn, " have we then at last met ? Now, by all my hopes, will I punish you for the many crimes of which you have been guilty, or perish in the attempt."

" Vain boaster !" returned Ruthlyn, scornfully ; " I defy and dare you to the combat."

The struggle immediately commenced, with much fury on both sides, and the ruffians fought desperately, but were soon compelled to yield to superior numbers. Two of them were slain, and the rest laid down their arms, and submitted to be made prisoners.

In the meantime the combat between Ethelbert and Lord Ruthlyn was continued with great obstinacy, and being both excellent swordsmen, it was for awhile extremely doubtful which would be the conqueror. But at length Ruthlyn, in aiming a stroke at the head of his antagonist, staggered and fell forward, and in doing so received the point of Ethelbert's sword in his heart, and, with a loud groan, sunk a corpse at his feet.

While this was going on, Ulrica fought with the same desperate determination as if she had been a man, and it was not until she had been disarmed, and received a severe wound, that she could be secured.

Mildred recovered to find herself enfolded to the bosom of her benefactor, and Ethelbert quite safe, while her bitter enemy, Lord Ruthlyn de Bohun, was stretched a ghastly corpse upon the earth.

The prisoners, together with the wounded Ulrica, were removed to the castle, where also the corse of the earl was taken; and when they arrived there, how fervently did our heroine return her thanks to Providence for the providential manner in which she had again been rescued, and that she was in no further danger of annoyance or persecution from her most bitter enemies.

Every attention was paid to Ulrica, for much depended on her recovery; but the doctor stated that the wound was of that dangerous character that there were very little hopes of her recovery.

Ulrica, when she was apprised of her danger, treated it with the utmost indifference.

"I am defeated," she said, "and I care not any longer to live. Sir Aldobrand de Lancy, it is I who have been the author of all this mischief, and I do not hesitate now to avow it. The injuries inflicted on my former mistress by your brother first goaded me on to be revenged against your family, and changed my nature altogether."

"Unhappy woman," said the baronet, "why should you seek to visit with your vengeance those who never injured you? But does the unfortunate Almira de Montreville still live?"

"She does," replied Ulrica; "she is an inmate of a convent in France, and will never trouble you again. Her death at the altar on the occasion of your guilty brother's union with Lady Editha was only feigned, in order to strike greater terror into the breast of her seducer and the murderer of her child, and of all present. It was by my means that she was removed from the coffin, and conveyed to a place of security, where we afterwards worked our plots together. We had the satisfaction of seeing the misery which the curse of Almira had created between Sir Martin and his wife, and we determined to do all in our power to augment it. After secluding himself and his wife for some time in the tower, as you are aware, they both suddenly disappeared, and you never could ascertain where they had gone to; but we tracked their steps. They could not escape our watchful eyes. For some time they resided in a most secluded and solitary part of Scotland, where Lady Editha gave birth to a child. The treatment she received from her husband was brutal, and it was a wonder she did not sink under it. And yet he could assign no motive for his conduct. Probably he viewed her with feelings of fear and jealousy, thinking that, after the exposure of Almira, she could not look upon him with any other sentiments than those of disgust and horror. At length, however, she could endure such treatment no longer, and fled, taking her infant with her, and accompanied by a female servant. She made her way towards this neighbourhood, intending to claim your protection; but she was overtaken by Sir Martin on the way, and by him forced into the old tower, where it was his intention to confine her for the rest of her days. He also determined to deprive her of her infant, and in the struggle which ensued between the distracted mother and her husband, the unfortunate servant, who interposed in the behalf of her mistress, received a wound, of which she immediately died. Lady Editha fainted, and in that condition was conveyed by Sir Martin to a dungeon, where, locking her in, he left her to her fate. He then removed the corpse of the murdered woman, and, filled with terror lest his crime should be discovered, he immediately hastened from the tower, leaving his innocent offspring behind him."

"Great God!" exclaimed Mildred, when Ulrica came to this part of her confession, "my mother—my unfortunate mother!" She could say no more; but immediately fainted in the arms of Sir Aldobrand.

"Tell me, I beseech you, Ulrica," said Sir Aldobrand, "is this poor girl indeed my niece?"

"She is," answered Ulrica.

"Gracious Providence!" exclaimed Ethelbert and his father in a breath; "can it be? But the Lady Editha—say, does she live?"

Ulrica shook her head. "I am afraid not," she answered; "but listen. After the child had been removed by old Hewley and his son, I and Almira, who made the tower our principal retreat, and with all whose secret passages we were thoroughly acquainted, hastened to the dungeon in which Lady Editha was confined, and found her still in a state of insensibility. When she recovered, her astonishment and alarm on beholding Almira and me may readily be imagined. She, however, implored our mercy, and asked for her husband and her child. We satisfied her on the first point; but told her that the infant had been removed, but where we know not. She wrung her hands in despair, and for some time was quite inconsolable. We supplied her with provisions, and then told her that she must now consider herself our prisoner. In vain she supplicated; we turned a deaf ear to her, and left her to her own reflections."

"Oh, how could you act with such cruelty to one who had never offended you?" ejaculated Sir Aldobrand.

"She was the wife of the villain Sir Martin," replied Ulrica, "and that was enough to make us hate her."

"And what became of my wretched, guilty brother?"

"He perished by the hand of Almira, who soon found out the place of his concealment."

"Unhappy, misguided man!" cried Sir Aldobrand, with much emotion; "may Heaven have mercy on your soul!"

Mildred at this moment recovered, and, with tearful eyes, looked affectionately in his face. Sir Aldobrand pressed her to his bosom, and kissed her forehead, and Ethelbert knelt at her feet, with feelings of delight too powerful for utterance.

"My beloved niece," said the baronet, "for such you indeed are, how can I ever be sufficiently grateful to Providence for placing you under my protection, and enabling me to shield you from that fate with which you were threatened!"

"But my dear mother," ejaculated Mildred; "tell me, does she live, and shall I ever behold her?"

"You have seen her," answered Ulrica.

"I have seen her?"

"Yes."

"Oh, when?—where?"

"In the castle chapel, on more than one occasion."

"Gracious Heaven!" exclaimed our heroine, clasping her hands. "Oh, my mother! had I but known you how would I have strove to meet your fond embrace."

"Hear me out," said Ulrica; "for I have still much to say, and I am getting weak. We kept Lady Editha confined for some time in the tower, and she at last became reconciled, in some measure, to her fate, especially as we told her that her child still existed, but that its life depended upon her behaviour, and that should she attempt to escape, it would be immediately sacrificed. She took a solemn oath never to make any such attempt, and we then allowed her many privileges that we had not done before. We even went so far as to allow her to visit the castle in disguise, and placed her in the secret room, from whence she disappeared from you; but finding that too strict a watch was being made for her, we were compelled to prohibit this indulgence, and once more confine her in the tower. It was her whom Ethelbert heard when he was a prisoner in that ancient building. Soon after this, notwithstanding I endeavoured to dissuade her from it, Almira quitted England, and entered a convent, where she at present remains."

"But for God's sake banish this terrible suspense," said Mildred, "and tell me whether my parents still live."

"Your father, as I have before stated, has been dead some years, and your mother, no doubt, has likewise this night perished in the flames in her dungeon."

Mildred uttered a cry of horror, and once more became insensible.

"Tell me, guilty woman," said Sir Aldobrand, "can this really be true? You could not—surely you could not be so monstrous as to consign your unfortunate prisoner to such a horrible fate."

"Why, I am not certain that she has fallen a victim," said Ulrica, "and I now sincerely hope that she has not, for I have already enough on my conscience, and I feel that my life is fast going. The dungeon in which Lady Editha was confined was far underground, and probably may have escaped the flames. If so, it may not yet be too late to save her."

"Ah, God grant that such may be the case!" cried Sir Aldobrand. "Then, there is not a moment to be lost. Come, Ethelbert, let us take with us all necessary aid, and instantly proceed to an examination of the ruins. It is not unlikely that the unfortunate Lady Editha may yet be restored to us."

Sir Aldobrand now rang the bell, and having committed the insensible Mildred to the care of her female attendants, and the necessary assistance being procured, they were soon once more on their way, with beating and impatient hearts, to the ruins.

On their arrival there, they found that the fire was quite extinguished, so that they could venture into the ruins without any danger; and when they had, with no inconsiderable labour, cleared away some of the rubbish, they were gratified to find that the lower or underground portions of the building had not suffered very materially from the ravages of the flames. The steps leading to the dungeons were left almost entire, and they descended them with safety, and made their way to the range of vaults, until their progress was arrested before the door of one of them, by hearing a low, moaning sound from within.

"Thank Heaven!" cried Sir Aldobrand, "our hopes are crowned with success! She is saved!"

They immediately forced the door, and entering the dungeon, found the unfortunate Lady Editha crouching in one corner. No sooner did she behold them, than uttering a mingled cry of joy and astonishment, she fainted.

Sir Aldobrand raised the form of his unfortunate sister-in-law, and conveying her into the open air, applied some necessary restoratives which they had taken care to bring with them; she soon recovered, and opening her eyes, she looked around in astonishment.

"Dear Lady Editha," said the baronet, "be not alarmed; you are with friends. Do you not know me? I am your brother-in-law, come to restore you to liberty and happiness."

"Sir Aldobrand!" gasped forth the Lady Editha. "Can I believe the evidences of my eyes?—my ears? Am I then not left to perish in that frightful prison? But where is Ulrica? She can tell me of my child, from whom I have so long been cruelly separated."

"Be calm, Editha. Ulrica is secure, and has confessed everything. Your child, your beauteous daughter Mildred, still lives, and has been for many years under my protection."

"All merciful Heaven," ejaculated Lady Editha, clasping her hands vehemently together, "thou hast indeed been kind to me, notwithstanding all the many years of bitter suffering it has been my unfortunate lot to undergo. Oh, how shall I be able to support such a sudden and unexpected tide of happiness? And you, my brother-in-law, what a heavy debt of gratitude do I owe you for having preserved my treasure, whom I had never expected to behold again? Oh, take me to my child at once, and let me press her to my heart with a mother's most warm affection."

Lady Editha then sunk on her knees, and most eloquently did she pour forth her gratitude to the Supreme. By the assistance of Sir Aldobrand and his son she was able to walk slowly, and one of the servants had been despatched with all haste to the castle, in order to prepare Mildred for the joyful event.

What language could do justice to the meeting of the mother and daughter? We cannot attempt the task, for we are convinced that we should fail in giving anything like a faint picture of it. Late as was the time of night, it was some time ere they could make up their minds to separate, and then Lady Editha and her daughter both retired to one chamber, where they again and again embraced, and returned their thanks to the Almighty for their restoration to each other.   *   *   *   *   *

Ulrica died three days after she had received the wound, and was decently buried, notwithstanding all her numerous faults, by Sir Aldobrand.

Ethelbert sought the hand of Mildred with the joyous permission of Lady Editha and Sir Aldobrand, and nothing could equal the blissful harmony in which the young nobleman and his beauteous wife ever lived, and they were the admired of all who knew them.

Sir Aldobrand and Lady Editha lived for many years afterwards, to see a numerous family of grandchildren around them, and, in the bliss of the present, they learned to forget all the sorrows of the past.

THE END.